CHRISTIE RIDGWAY

THE LOVE SHACK

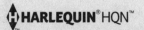

HARLEQUIN® HQN™

Recycling programs
for this product may
not exist in your area.

ISBN-13: 978-0-373-77715-0

THE LOVE SHACK

Printed in U.S.A.

www.Harlequin.com

Dear Reader,

Summer is winding down at Crescent Cove but the magic is still alive and well at Beach House No. 9. Songs about surfing carry through the air, the scents of coconut sunscreen and salty ocean mingle on the breeze. Walk barefoot through the sand and lift your face to the warmth beaming down...another romance is ready to bloom.

Skye Alexander isn't looking for love, however, even when the man she's been corresponding with for months moves into No. 9. Gage Lowell's only here for some brief R&R before returning to photograph danger zones overseas—so there's no sense in getting dreamy over ever-afters. Gage came to the cove eager to get to know his pen pal in person, but pretty Skye might be messing with his impending plans. He never stays in one place for long, but when he leaves Beach House No. 9, might he be leaving his heart behind? I hope you'll enjoy watching these two people come to terms with their feelings and their futures.

How much pleasure I've had sharing with you a summer of love in this enchanting place. I hope you carry with you all its tears and laughter, all its sexiness and fun, for a very long while.

Here comes the sun!

Christie Ridgway

To my mom, for all those summers filled with books.

THE LOVE SHACK

Beautiful dreamer, out on the sea,
Mermaids are chanting the wild lorelei;
Over the streamlet vapors are borne,
Waiting to fade at the bright coming morn.
Beautiful dreamer, beam on my heart,
E'en as the morn on the streamlet and sea;
Then will all clouds of sorrow depart,
Beautiful dreamer, awake unto me!
Beautiful dreamer, awake unto me!
　—Stanza 2, "Beautiful Dreamer" by Stephen Foster

CHAPTER ONE

For the past decade, Gage Lowell had lived on risk the way other people sucked down caffeine. It had been his morning fix, his noonday pick-me-up, his after-dinner beverage with dessert. So the anticipation building in his belly as he approached beautiful but tranquil Crescent Cove didn't make much sense.

It was no Durand Line, that porous border between Afghanistan and Pakistan where he'd braved danger that ran the gamut from Taliban bullets to half-wild bulls. The natives were certain to be less suspicious than the Syrian rebels he'd photographed the spring before. And though the house he'd rented was situated on the sand, just steps away from the Pacific Ocean, not for a second did he suppose this vacation would end like the one he'd taken some years ago—with Gage running for his life and high ground, holding his cameras overhead.

Of course, that tsunami had come out of the blue.

But he really couldn't see how this holiday would hold any such surprise.

Still, expectation continued to hum through his veins. "Stop here," he said to his twin as the car turned onto the narrow road that led off the coastal highway. They'd come straight from the airport. "I'll hoof it to the property management office for the keys. You drive my stuff to Beach House No. 9 and I'll meet you there."

Griffin frowned over at him. "What, I'm your bellboy now?" Though the sarcasm was typical brother bullshit, there was something in his expression that tickled Gage's spine.

"What aren't you telling me?" he asked.

His twin braked the car but didn't answer. Up ahead were the first of the fifty or so eclectic cottages that made up the beachside community where the Lowell family had spent every summer until he'd turned fifteen. The dwellings' designs were a little bit funky and a lot colorful, nestled in lush vegetation—palm trees, hibiscus bushes and various other flowering plants—that had originally been planted so that the two-mile-long curve of sand could serve as a variety of backdrops during the silent movie era: deserted island, cannibal-infested jungle, ancient Egypt.

It had been paradise for Gage, Griffin and the rest of their posse of kids who'd run wild every June through September.

Rolling down his window, Gage breathed deeply of the salt-and-sun-laden air and dismissed his disquiet. He had a few weeks to rest and recharge before his next assignment overseas, and Crescent Cove was the best place in the world for that. "It's still got that ol' magic, doesn't it?" he murmured, reaching for the door handle.

"Wait," Griffin said. "Maybe I should go with you to collect the keys."

Uh-oh. Uneasiness kicked up again. "What's going on?"

"Look. About Skye—"

"Don't say any more," Gage said, already irritated. The older by eleven minutes, Griffin often acted as if he were the much-wiser sibling. "I know her as well as you. Better than you."

"You haven't seen her since we were kids. You might be, uh, I don't know, surprised by how she looks."

"I don't care how she looks," Gage said, aware he sounded a little angry. What? His brother thought he had some shallow set of standards when it came to female companions? Okay, he supposed it could be true when it came to a certain kind of female companion, but that didn't apply here.

"I'm not interested in her appearance." Gage pressed his shoulder against the passenger door and pushed it open. "She's not a woman to me."

His brother might have mumbled, "Oh, hell," but Gage was already on his way toward the footpath that would lead him straight to Skye Alexander.

He knew exactly where the property management office was, just as he knew all the cove's other landmarks from his childhood explorations. Then, Skye's father had been in charge, always dressed in his trademark khakis, wilted denim shirt and bush hat. Skye and her sister could often be found in his office, playing with paper dolls or with their shell collections, leaving Mrs. Alexander free to stay engrossed in her easel and paints.

Skye held her dad's job now. Gage knew this, because they'd fallen into an accidental correspondence nearly a year ago. When planning his R & R a few months back, he'd thought of her and the cove and made a snap decision to rent the beach house where he'd spent those idyllic summers. To surprise his pen pal, he'd reserved it under a fictitious name.

He couldn't wait for her reaction when she saw him. His palms itched, and for a moment he regretted leaving his cameras packed in the car. His hands seemed too empty without them, though he hadn't felt much like taking photos lately, which worried him a little.

A lot.

Maybe Beach House No. 9 would be the antidote to that, too.

Ahead was the simple clapboard structure that was the one-room management office. He slowed his approach, taking in the small yard enclosed by a white picket fence that was brightened by bougainvillea vines of varied colors: fuchsia, white, coral and red. The front door stood open, and a woman's voice floated over the threshold, the notes snatched away by the cool breeze before he could make out the words.

He stepped over the low gate instead of chancing squeaky hinges that might give him away. Then he strolled up the path until he came to a stop on the small, stamp-sized doorstep. The midmorning sun was bright, the interior of the office dark in comparison. Feet planted on the concrete, Gage peered into the dim interior.

A woman was half-turned away from him, a phone pressed to her ear. "Sure, I can email you a scanned copy of Edith's letter to Max. Yes, they are my great-great-grandparents. Sure. Fine." She paused to listen.

For the life of him, Gage couldn't figure out what Griffin's warning was all about. Yeah, his recollection of Skye stalled on her at about eleven years old, but this grown-up version didn't clash with his memory. She'd had that long, coffee-dark hair as a little girl. The woman before him was average height, he'd say, and looked slender, though she was wearing a pair of baggy jeans and a long-sleeved sweatshirt that could have been her father's.

The phone conversation seemed to be winding down,

and Gage felt another surge of eagerness. He couldn't remember the color of her eyes or the shape of her nose, but any moment now she'd turn his way and he'd have a face to put with those letters that had become so vital to him during his hellish two-week ordeal in the middle of nowhere.

"I'm thrilled you'll be featuring the cove in an upcoming edition of the paper. Thank you. If I can answer any more questions, Ali, don't hesitate to call." She clicked off the phone, but still didn't glance toward the door.

Gage felt a smile tugging at the corners of his mouth. He didn't move or say anything for another long moment, while the ocean breeze played with the hem of his jeans and the tail of his thin white shirt. It was stupid, maybe, but he felt as if he was poised on the brink of something and he wondered, weirdly, if he should have brought flowers.

Then, rejecting the odd thought, he lifted his foot to enter Skye's domain. The movement must have alerted her to his presence. She whirled to face him.

And screamed bloody murder.

September 15
Dear Gage,
Salutations from a childhood friend! Your missive to your twin reached me at Crescent Cove's property management office. Thought you should know Griffin's not expected at Beach House No. 9 until April. Loved the picture on the front of the postcard—one of yours? Over the years, I've noticed your photo credit lines in magazines and newspapers and remember the camera you car-

*ried every summer, strapped to your chest like a
second heart.
Hope this finds you in good health, Skye Alexander*

*Skye,
Thanks for the info re: Griff. Are you still playing
tea party at your dad's desk in the Crescent Cove
office? Because I can see you there in my memory.
What summers we had! When it's blistering hot
here, I take off to the cove in my imagination and
lie on the wet sand, letting the cool Pacific wash
over my skin. When the temperature turns freezing,
I remember our tribe of Cove kids playing beach
soccer under a burning sun. Do shore crabs still
make you squeal?
Gage*

Skye Alexander's friend and neighbor Polly Weber
leaned close and whispered in her ear, "You didn't tell
me Gage Lowell was gorgeous."

"You've become friends with Griffin. Since they're
twins, it should come as no surprise." Skye didn't even
glance at the man seated at the head of their table on the
open-air deck. Besides Gage, Polly and Skye, there were
five more people attending the welcome dinner at Captain Crow's, the restaurant/bar located at the northern
end of the cove. Griffin and his fiancée, the twins' sister, Tess, and her husband, and an elderly family friend
were gathered close to the man of honor. Skye had chosen a seat as far from him as possible.

She was counting on distance to calm her heart—it
had been beating with an erratic wildness since she'd

looked up that morning and found a dark figure looming in her office doorway.

He was telling the story now, speaking up so that Rex Monroe, the nearly deaf nonagenarian who lived full-time at the cove, could hear him. "My ears are still ringing from her scream," Gage said. "I meant to surprise her, not send her into a full-blown panic."

"She's been jumpy for months," Rex said, shaking his head. "Nervous like a rabbit since March."

"Really?" There was a new alertness in the younger man's voice, and Skye sensed he was studying her over the plates and glasses.

She pretended an avid interest in the surface of her white wine and ignored the embarrassed heat crawling toward her cheeks. Good thing she was wearing a cotton turtleneck with her boy-styled black trousers.

"Since the spring, you say?" Gage spoke again to Rex.

Before the elderly man could reveal anything more, Skye felt compelled to offer a rationale. "It's the off-season quiet that gets to me, what with the tiny number of full-time residents." And if she didn't find a way to control her persistent anxiety, she doubted she'd survive this year's transition from summer's bustle to autumn hush. "That's all."

She glanced up to judge how Gage took the explanation.

Mistake. Their eyes met. His turquoise-blue gaze shot another electric jolt to her heart. Its beat went crazy again, thudding heavy and uneven against her ribs.

"Fenton Hardy," she heard herself say, her mouth so dry her tongue clicked against its roof.

"Yes, what was that about?" Jane Pearson, Griffin's fiancée, asked. "When Skye told us that was the name of No. 9's upcoming tenant, I recognized the literary allusion, but your brother knew right away that meant it was you."

Skye tore her eyes from Gage and pinned Griffin with a stare. "You did?"

The man shrugged. "It was our secret identity name when we were kids. Fenton is the father in the Hardy Boys books. I figured Gage had a reason to be mysterious."

"I told you, I wanted to surprise Skye…I was planning on surprising everyone, actually, but I didn't realize she'd talk to you about who'd rented the place."

"We were going over wedding details when it came out," Jane said, and she grinned, clearly thrilled about her upcoming marriage to Griffin. "How handy that you'll be the one we inconvenience when we say 'I do' on No. 9's deck at the end of the month."

Gage shook his head. "I've only known you a few hours, Jane, but it's clear you can do better than ol' Griff. I'd suggest myself—"

"I'm sticking with the twin whose globe-trotting days are over," Jane said, emphatic.

"Gage would make a terrible husband," a new voice put in. It was Tess Quincy, the older sister of Griffin and Gage. "He's restless and selfish and likely doesn't wash his clothes often enough."

"Gee, thanks, Tessie," Gage replied, and lifted his arm, pretending to sniff at the sleeve of his shirt. "Love you, too."

"I'm just saying." His sister's eyes went suspiciously bright. "Think about it. Think about if you made some poor woman fall in love with you and then you fell off the face of the earth for over two weeks."

An awkward silence descended, as Gage had been MIA for just that amount of time, troubling family and friends until he'd resurfaced a few days ago.

"You know communication is spotty where I was, Tessie," he said, a new tension in his voice.

"Well, Griffin was very concerned. His twin sense was tingling."

"He's always been a worrywart." Gage's smile looked forced. "I'm here, aren't I? Safe and sound."

Skye couldn't keep her mouth shut. She'd had the same sense that something was wrong when she'd gone too long between letters from him. Her apprehension hadn't eased until Griffin let her know that Gage had checked in by phone—though she'd never in a million years expected him to show up at the cove. "But you're late. Fenton Hardy was scheduled to arrive at the first of the month."

This time it was Gage who didn't seem to want to look at her. "Travel plans changed. Now, can someone tell me more about this upcoming wedding? I'm still having a hard time buying that anyone wants a lifetime with my brother."

The atmosphere lightened considerably after that. Food was consumed. Liquor flowed.

At Skye's side, Polly released a pensive sigh.

She glanced over at the other woman. "Okay, Pol?"

"Oh, I'm good," she said, straightening in her seat. A burst of laughter from the head of the table drew their attention in that direction. "Like I said," Polly reiterated, her gaze resting on Gage, "really, really gorgeous."

Skye allowed herself a moment to study him. "Yeah." She took in his rumpled black hair and tanned complexion. His cheekbones were chiseled, his jaw firm and beneath two dark slashes of brow were his incredible eyes. His beard was heavy enough that he had noticeable after-five stubble that only served to draw attention to his mobile mouth and white grin.

"No wonder you broke up with Dalton," Polly said.

Startled, Skye jerked her head toward her friend. "I didn't break up with Dalton because of Gage." She didn't want to think about why she'd broken up with Dalton. Crossing one leg tightly over the other, she rubbed at her upper arms with her palms.

A husky male laugh drew her attention back to the head of the table where Gage was now engaged in flirtatious banter with their waitress, Tina. As Skye watched, the server toyed with the name tag pinned to her blouse, drawing attention to cleavage she could swear hadn't been on display when she'd ordered her swordfish and steamed vegetables. Clearly Tina had made a wardrobe adjustment for the man of honor's benefit.

"See?" she told Polly. "That's the kind of woman Gage finds appealing."

Her friend glanced over. "What kind of woman is that?"

Skye made a vague gesture with her hand. *The kind who can bear to show some skin.*

"You're twelve times more beautiful than that hussy."

"I wasn't fishing for compliments," Skye said, grimacing.

"I'm not giving any," Polly said. "Just the facts, ma'am. But if you want an opinion, I suggest you ditch the boy-wear and play with makeup again. I know you have pretty clothes in your closet. I remember when lipstick and mascara still mattered to you."

Skye did, too, but now peace of mind mattered more.

Though it was true that baggy sweatshirts and medicated lip balm hadn't exactly brought that about. Head down, she ran her fingertip around and around the edge of her water glass.

"Want to dance?" came a voice, close to her ear.

Skye's head popped up, her eyes widening at Gage's hovering form. He wanted to dance? He wanted to dance with *her?* It was then she noticed that the sun had set, leaving the sky a fading orange. The tiki torches plunged in the sand at the corners of the deck were flaming now, and the atmosphere at Captain Crow's was starting to pump. Customers were two-deep at the bar. People were moving about the small parquet dance area to Bob Marley's "Three Little Birds." Griffin and Jane were out there, wrapped in each other's arms. Tess was dragging her husband, David, in their direction, though he was laughing and protesting at the same time.

"Dance?" Gage said again.

He'd probably been sitting too long, Skye thought. He'd always been on the go as a kid and there was good reason his sister labeled him "restless." She knew for a fact that he only slept six hours a night—one of the personal details he'd shared in his letters.

An amused glint entered Gage's blue eyes as she continued to hesitate. "Am I speaking the wrong language?"

"You're asking the wrong girl," Skye said. "Polly will do it."

"What?" Polly looked up from the phone cradled in her palms, her thumbs poised over the touch screen. "He didn't ask me."

"You like to dance."

"I'm texting with Teague." She shook her head. "He's having an emotional emergency."

Skye glanced up at Gage again. "Teague White. Remember him? He spent summers here, too."

He blinked. "Tea— No! Tee-Wee White?"

"Not so tee-wee anymore," Polly muttered, her thumbs tapping away. "More like big fat idiot."

Not fat, Skye mouthed to Gage.

He laughed, then bent to grip her elbow and tug her to her feet in one quick move. "Let's dance, Skye."

Freezing, she stared at the large, masculine hand circling her cotton-knit-covered arm. Her common sense warred with her fight-or-flight response. *Don't bolt,* she told herself. *Or punch him.* Either option would only bring up embarrassing questions.

"You okay?"

"S-sure." As sure as someone could be who'd broken up with her boyfriend because she'd developed an aversion to being touched.

Before she could think of how to get away from the situation without sacrificing dignity or courtesy, he was towing her toward the other couples moving to the music. One song ended and another began, ukulele notes and the sweet voice of IZ Kamakawiwo'ole singing "White Sandy Beach of Hawai'i" floating through the air like feathers.

Gage released her arm, and, sensing this was her moment, Skye took a big step back. But he grabbed for her hand, reeling her close.

Scattering her thoughts. Honing her senses.

They focused on him, his large, lean frame, and on the nuances of his skin against hers. His fingers were long, his palm hard and calloused, the rough skin scratching the tender hollow at the center of her hand. She didn't think she was breathing as his other palm settled at her waist, just the lightest of touches over the material.

It wasn't a close hold, it was almost impersonal, she knew that, but her blood was shooting through her veins like a comet. Anxiety, she thought, as the heat sizzled her nerve endings. It stole her oxygen along with the words that would get her off the dance floor. Mute, she looked up at him.

Gage returned her gaze, his expression enigmatic but his amazing eyes bright with... Skye didn't know what. He gave her hand a small squeeze. It felt...reassuring.

Maybe. She was so messed up, she'd been so messed up for months that her brain was unable to interpret normal signals. Behind her eyes came the hot prick of tears. Another flush rose up her neck as she imagined the humiliation of bursting into sobs. *Keep it together,* she thought, desperate not to look the fool in front of this beautiful man.

He blew out a little sigh as he moved them to the slow beat of the song. His body didn't brush hers, yet she couldn't help being aware of the breadth of his chest and the lean strength of his arms and legs. "Dinner was excellent," he said. "Nothing better than a heaping serving of beach fries along with sixteen ounces of aged beef."

Skye redirected her gaze to the safer vicinity of his heavy shoulder and told herself to try to relax. "You missed American food."

"I've been dreaming of rare steak for months."

"No." She shook her head. "You don't like your meat bloody."

"Oh, God, did I confess that to you?" he said, his tone aghast.

"You did." She felt a little smile break through her tension.

"What'll it take for you to keep that to yourself?" he

demanded. "In most circles it's considered unmanly to like meat well-done."

She smiled again. "You're plenty manly." Without thinking, she glanced up.

He was grinning, his expression amused, but as their gazes held, his smile died away.

Skye felt another surge of that breathless, uncomfortable anxiety, and a rush of goose bumps shivered across her skin.

The song ended. Gage dropped his hands. The loss of contact didn't calm her jangling nerves and they continued to stand on the dance floor, staring at each other.

A long moment passed, and then Gage shook his head with a wry laugh. "I suppose it's past time to regret that you know so many of my secrets."

Skye didn't answer either way, though she understood his concern. To her mind, it was imperative he stay ignorant of hers.

CHAPTER TWO

GAGE GOT A GOOD NIGHT's sleep, despite or perhaps because of the jet lag brought on by seventy-nine hundred miles of travel. Upon waking to a sun-bright room, he leaned over and clicked off the bedside lamp. It was his new habit to sleep with a light on like a three-year-old, but he wasn't going to try weaning himself for a while.

After dressing in cargo pants and a T-shirt that was probably older than his own thirty-one years, he rummaged through the groceries he'd stashed in the kitchen. Finding an apple, he polished it against his thigh and then took it with him as he stepped through the sliding glass door that led from the living room onto the deck facing the ocean.

No. 9 was the best beach house in the cove. At least he'd always thought so. They'd come here for a decade of summers, and it didn't appear as if much—or anything—about it had changed. Dark brown shingles covered the two-story structure, and the trim around the doors and windows was still painted a bluish-green. It was situated at the southern end of the cove, cozied up to a bluff that pushed into the ocean. The trails snaking up the cliff's rocky side told Gage that daredevils likely still used it as a jumping-off place, just as he and Griffin had when they were kids.

The ocean called to him, so he crossed the deck and

jogged down the steps leading to the sand. The stuff under his bare feet was the consistency of cornmeal, and he continued through it until the grains were wet and moisture sucked at his soles. Then, with his apple held in the grip of his teeth, he bent to roll his pant legs above the ankle.

Even prepared as he was, he cursed as the first rush of water reached his naked toes. *Shit!* It was cold, at least initially, even during high summer in Southern California. Another small wave folded over his feet and he flinched, just like one of the out-of-state tourists who came to California with only images of *Baywatch* reruns or old Gidget movies in mind. Hollywood magic hid the goose bumps, so they were startled by their first experience with Pacific temperatures.

As his toes went numb, Gage continued strolling up the deserted beach, sloshing through the shallow outreach of the surf, breathing in the fresh, wet-smelling air as he munched on his Granny Smith. He had no particular purpose in mind, no intent beyond enjoying the sun on the top of his head and his shoulders, the endless sound of the waves, the precious sense of freedom. There'd been times he'd doubted whether he'd get the chance to experience them again.

Though it was early enough that he had to share the sand with no one other than seagulls and sandpipers, when he reached the midpoint of the cove, he found himself strolling toward a cottage painted a mossy-green with blush-colored trim. Like Beach House No. 9, it was larger than the others in the enclave and had a small side yard. There, he saw a figure on her knees tending a flower bed—Skye, in long pants, long sleeves and a battered, narrow-brimmed canvas fishing hat. Gage realized she'd been his destination all along.

Not as surprised as he might be, he continued forward, then started whistling in order to alert her to his presence. No point in scaring the bejesus out of her a second time. Still, he saw her stiffen as he cast a shadow over her small patch of grass.

"It's ironic that our song is about a beach that belongs to an altogether different state," he observed.

"We have a song?" She glanced up, shielding her face with the shelf of her hand.

In the shade created by the gesture, he couldn't make out much about her heavily lashed eyes. But he'd noted their color last night—deepwater green, with a band of amber circling the pupil—while they'd danced. He whistled a few more bars of "White Sandy Beach of Hawai'i."

She shrugged, and her overlarge sweatshirt slid off her shoulder to reveal a pale pink bra strap. "The cove has plenty of experience acting as a stand-in."

"I remember." His gaze fixed on that hint of bare flesh, though he didn't know why the delicate slope of skin-over-bone so fascinated him. "Silent movies were filmed here."

Her hand fell and she went back to weeding, her head bent so he could no longer see her pretty face. She had classic-beauty bones, wide-spaced eyes, a delicate nose and a soft yet serious mouth. A long tail of hair streamed down her back, the sun finding random gold and red threads in the dark mass. "If you're interested, we now have a room dedicated to Sunrise Pictures with lots of memorabilia on display," she said.

"Yeah?"

"It's connected to the art gallery beside Captain

Crow's. You can take a look anytime, but you'll have to get the key from me or from Maureen, who manages the gallery. We keep the door locked since the trouble we had there last month."

Gage frowned. "Trouble? What kind of trouble?"

"We caught someone vandalizing the place."

He dropped to her level, resting on his haunches. "Jesus, Skye. Are you all right? What happened?"

"A small group of us—Teague, and two of the women who were staying at No. 9—surprised an intruder when we decided on an impromptu tour. One of them got a bump on the head when he pushed past us."

"Did you get a good look at whoever it was?"

"No. We called the police, but the man was dressed in dark clothes and wore a ski mask—like he'd been at a casting call for thief of the week."

Gage took a seat on the grass, rubbing his stubbled cheek with his palm. "What do the police think? It seems just…damn disturbing that anything dangerous would happen here."

She sent him a quick, unfathomable glance. "My sentiments exactly. The police have no idea about…about anything."

"Huh." He directed his gaze down the beach. No. 9 was a fifteen-minute walk from here; he could sprint it in half that. "You need something, you know where I am."

She shrugged. "Thanks, but I'm used to handling things on my own. Keeping the cove going is all on me, now that Mom and Dad have moved permanently to Provence. And I wrote you that my sister, Starr, is living in San Francisco."

"I remember her from when we were kids," Gage mused. "Starr. Starr and Skye. Such unusual names."

"Unusual spellings, too," Skye said, shaking her head. "It was Dad's idea to add the extra *r* and the unnecessary *e*. He thought they looked weightier that way."

Gage laughed. "Your dad was always a character. But Starr goes by Meg now, right? You told me that."

"Mmm," Skye said by way of agreement. "And she's married, after a whirlwind romance with her Caleb. They met at the cove in May, spent a few days together here, then decided to seal the deal. Love liberated her impulsive side, I guess."

"Good for her. Good for them."

A moment of silence passed. "Speaking of family, is yours well?"

"Sure." Especially as he'd kept each and every member unaware of his latest misadventure. "You saw my brother and sister last night, of course. And my parents will be here for Griffin's wedding."

She gave him another sidelong peek. "You're okay with that?"

"With Griff getting a ball and chain?" At her quick frown, he smiled and hastened to amend himself. "I'm kidding…and I really do like Jane. When you wrote me about her, you told me I would."

"She's good for your brother, and vice versa. Did I tell you she worked with Ian Stone for several years?"

He rolled his eyes. "Not Ian Stone, the author of those sappy and maudlin bestsellers you like so much?"

"Nobody should have to defend their choice of reading material," she said, and even in profile, he could see her scowl. "A person likes what she likes."

"And Skye Alexander goes for that oozily overromantic stuff."

She turned her head to narrow her eyes at him. "Maybe

it's the endings that appeal—you know, when the hero dies from some painful lingering illness or an equally painful but accidental act of God."

Gage laughed again. "Okay, okay. I don't want you wishing one of those sorrowful-ever-after outcomes on me. I can't afford to take bad luck with me on my next assignment."

She reapplied herself to the flowers and weeds, wielding a spade. "Griffin says he's done with war reporting."

"I've got to go back," Gage said quickly. Too quickly, he decided, because she cast him a puzzled glance.

"Sure," she said.

"I accepted a new assignment." And he had something to prove, too. Those bastards hadn't taken anything from him. He wouldn't let them.

"Sure," she said again.

Realizing he'd curled his hands into fists, he took a moment to relax his fingers, breathing deep as he gazed around the cove where he'd come to recharge. There was a mini cottage next door, so small it was almost a dollhouse, and as he watched, the front door opened. A pretty blonde stepped out and, spotting him, waved before disappearing around a corner.

He waved back. "Who is your friend again? Polly…?"

"Polly Weber."

"Cute."

Suddenly Skye had pivoted on her knees and was pointing her spade at his throat like a stiletto. "Don't even think about it."

"Think about what?"

"Polly's a kindergarten teacher. She just moved to the cove and, besides me and Rex, will likely be the only one living here come fall."

"So?"

"So if you break her heart, she'll leave the cove. That's just what my sister did. She ran away and didn't come back for ten long years. I don't want that for Polly. I like my friend living nearby."

"What makes you think that I—"

"Three words." She paused, then continued gravely, "The Gage Gorge."

Jesus Christ. A dull heat crept from the back of his neck to his face. "I wrote you about that?"

"Your twin told me about that."

"Which is the slower death, strangulation or drowning?"

"I have no idea," she said, her tone cool.

She should have no idea about the Gage Gorge, either. "For the record, Griffin coined that phrase, not me."

Her silence said more than actual words.

"Look, any guy would do the same. After months of crappy meals and crappy booze, it's natural to want to consume mass quantities of my favorite foods and beverages." And he never wanted to see another juice box or packaged cheese and crackers for the rest of his life.

When she didn't say anything, he plucked at his T-shirt. "I've lost weight!" He'd worried about dysentery when the water they'd given him had arrived in a rusty watering can and from some unknown source. He'd tried sticking with the mango juice, but the thick stuff had eventually made him sicker than the thought of parasites in his H2O.

"By all means," she said, still in that chilly voice, "indulge in your desires. It's really none of my business—as long as your...your *feasting* doesn't extend to my friends and neighbors."

Okay, she was just being snotty now. Feasting, she'd said, as if he were bellying up to a banquet. But they both knew she was referring to something other than nutrients. "It's not a crime to want to get laid."

"But when you're on a 'Gage Gorge' your goal is to get laid as often as possible."

He opened his mouth to argue, then shut it with a snap. After a few long breaths, he tried again. "I think my brother thought he was, uh, enhancing my reputation with that kind of talk."

She sent him a skewering look over her shoulder. "You think being a man-ho enhances your reputation?"

"I'm not a man-ho. Jesus, Skye. I'm just a guy who likes sex and when I haven't had a chance to get any for a few months, then I…I want to have some."

She stood and brushed at the dirty knees of her jeans. "And some more and some more and some more."

He got to his feet, too, and glared at her, because he didn't understand why he felt so damn guilty. "Well, excuse me, Sister Josephina Henry."

"Who?"

"The meanest nun I ever met. Told me I was going to hell when I was seven years old. Ugly old bag, with a wart on her chin."

Her expression told him he'd gone too far. He replayed his words, blanched. "Hey, hey, I'm sorry. I didn't mean to imply you have a wart on your chin."

"Just that I'm an ugly old bag."

"No! No, wait, don't go off in a huff."

But she did just that, disappearing into her house and shutting her front door with a decisive snap. He stared after her, trying to figure out where he'd gone wrong.

He was pretty sure it had something to do with sex.

Why she should care about his interest in that, he didn't know. It was Griffin's fault, he thought. No, Skye's. No, both Griffin *and* Skye were to blame, he decided as he started back down the beach, kicking at the soft sand.

Damn both of them.

And him, too, for pissing off the woman who, sometime during the course of their correspondence, had gone from casual pen pal to personal talisman.

THE NEXT MORNING, Gage was once again up early. He set out for another walk, keeping to wet sand and the neutral company of the shorebirds. The tide was low and he headed for a favorite haunt just beyond the restaurant. There, where another bluff met the ocean, was an extensive series of tide pools, some small, some shallow, some twice as big and twice as deep as a bathtub.

Eyes cast down, he picked his way around them, also carefully avoiding the exposed rock faces where sharp-edged barnacles and dark-shelled mussels crowded together like villagers confronting a common enemy. Peering into a cup-sized crevice in the rock, he started when he heard his name, the soles of his leather flip-flops slipping on the wet rock.

Regaining his balance, he looked over. Ponytailed Skye stood nearby, dressed in drawstring linen pants and a matching tunic the color of dry sand. Despite how they'd parted the day before, he couldn't help smiling at her. For two wretched weeks, she'd walked through his imagination, keeping him sane. Seeing her in the flesh was testament to his fortitude. He'd made it back.

Who wouldn't be glad?

The wind came up, swirling escaped pieces of her dark hair and pressing the thin material of her clothes against her skin. For the first time he could make out the contours of her figure: small high breasts, slender waist, the flare of feminine hips. A flash of heat shot down his spine and curled around his balls. His cock reacted in typical horny male fashion and his smile died.

Hell. She didn't want his "feasting" to involve her friends or family, so he figured she didn't want it to involve herself, either. *He* didn't want it to involve Skye and mess up what she already was to him. Childhood friend. Charming correspondent. Survival technique.

So he shut down his baser urges and approached her with slow steps, smiling again. "Hey," he said. "Good morning."

"Good morning to you, too." The strap of a backpack was slung over one shoulder and she let it slip down her arm as she returned her own smile. "I have coffee."

He watched her pull out a silver thermos. "Is that an offer?"

She glanced up as she poured some steaming liquid into the cap. "How about a peace offering?" The smell of the brew wafted his way as she held it out. "I'm sorry about yesterday… I…I haven't been sleeping well."

"Me, neither." He took the small cup from her and brought the coffee to his lips. "Maybe we should start hanging out together in the wee hours of the night."

She was rummaging in her backpack again, and he saw her withdraw an empty plastic container. Then she crossed to a large, high-and-dry flat boulder and sat down, dropping the pack near her hip. Gage followed suit, hoisting himself onto the rock beside her, then passing the cup of coffee in her direction.

After a little hesitation, she took it, and swallowed a small sip before handing it back to him. They shared the beverage and a companionable silence, each of them looking out to sea.

"I picked up your last couple of letters before I returned to the States," he finally said. "I'm sorry you were worried."

She kept her gaze on the horizon line. "I think it was because you wrote you had a new contact who was taking you to a region you hadn't explored before. It sounded dangerous."

He'd probably telegraphed his own unease. His internal debate over trusting the new guy had gone on for several days. He wasn't stupid—journalists in that part of the world ran into all kinds of trouble, from muggings to murder. But the truth was, every footstep made in a war-torn country was a judgment call and the accolades went to those willing to take the most risk. It had seemed an acceptable trade-off at the time.

Gage realized that Skye was looking at him expectantly. "What?"

"I asked how that worked out—your new contact," she said.

He hesitated. The wind whipped past again, propelling a lock of her long hair across his lips. It was silky-soft and smelled like a flowered breeze. Catching it between his fingers, he made to tuck it behind her ear.

She hunched away from him and grabbed the stuff herself, drawing it around her far shoulder. "Your contact?"

Thinking of Jahandar, Gage fought the urge to spit. "He turned out to be not so good." Understatement.

They subsided into silence again.

"How's your friend's widow doing?" Skye asked eventually. "And her son?"

"Okay," he replied, easily following her train of thought. Ten months ago, a colleague, Charlie Butler, had been abducted and held for ransom by the Taliban. His wife, Mara, the mother of a four-year-old, had been forced to navigate the complex maze of negotiation and counternegotiation along with the crisis management team hired by Charlie's newspaper. The foreign correspondent community had done what they could, suggesting people to call and offering support, even as they'd kept the story out of the news. It was safer for the kidnap victim that way. "I'll try to see them while I'm here. They don't live far."

"You could invite them to the cove. Sun and sand can be healing."

Yeah, that's what I'm hoping, Gage mused, then turned his thoughts back to Mara and her son. No doubt they could use a dose of sun and sand. It had come down to Charlie's next of kin—to Mara—to give the go-ahead on an American military raid to rescue her husband. He hadn't survived the attempt. One of his kidnappers had shot him as soldiers stormed the compound where he'd been held.

"I'm glad Griffin has made the choice to stick close to his woman," Gage said abruptly. "If you love somebody enough, you won't chance putting them through that."

"He loves Jane a lot."

"He does," Gage agreed, shaking off his dark thoughts and breathing deep of the clean, open air. "Speaking of love lives, how's yours?"

Skye made a great show of screwing the empty cap back onto her thermos. "Oh, let's not talk about me."

"Why not? Did something go wrong with you and Dagwood?"

Her eyes narrowed at him. "Dalton."

"Dalton, Dagwood." With a vague wave of his hand, he dismissed his mistake. Fact was, Dalton felt like the mistake. He didn't know the guy, but she'd written that he worked in commercial real estate. Probably wore a suit seven days a week and didn't like to get sand or sea-water on his feet.

"We broke up," Skye said.

"Good—wait, what?" Gage turned to face her. "When did this happen?"

"A while back." Now it was her turn to make an off-hand gesture. "He still keeps coming around, but it's over."

"And you didn't tell me?"

She shrugged.

Call him nosy, but he couldn't let it go at that. They'd shared quite a bit of themselves through their letters. "What was the trouble?"

A flush suffused her face. Her wet tongue came out to paint her upper, then her lower, lip. Gage watched the nervous movement, aware he was getting aroused again. Damn. And damn her for the hesitation that had his hackles rising, too.

"Skye?"

"We…uh…" She cleared her throat. "There were some physical problems."

Dumbfounded, he stared at her. He'd expected to hear the guy was married. Or maybe two-timing Skye with some other single woman. But…physical problems? What the hell did that mean?

Without thinking, he slid close and gripped her upper arms to turn her toward him, a sharp urgency driving him. "Did he hurt you? I'll kill him if he hurt you."

She shook her head. "It wasn't him. He didn't hurt me."

Gage frowned, searching her face for the truth. "Okay. Good." Then, driven again, he yanked her close and buried his face in her hair, breathing in more floral sweetness. "You scared the shit out of me for a minute."

It took another of those minutes for him to realize she was stiff in his hold. God, he thought, releasing her to put some distance between them. She probably considered him nuts. He *was* nuts, because he could still feel the imprint of her delicate form against his chest, the soft mounds of her breasts snuggled against his pecs. His cock throbbed and he shoved a hand through his hair, trying to push from his mind how good she'd felt in his arms.

Fuck. He needed to get laid, whether or not it insulted Skye's prudish sensibilities. Not that she'd have any reason to know about who and what he did between the sheets. He could be discreet.

Though he wondered about his erection, because it was still upright and clamoring for immediate action.

Gage shot to his feet. "I should get back. Give Griffin a call." If his brother refused to go babe-trolling with him, maybe Jane had a friend who was up for sexual adventure. Because that was exactly what he needed.

Skye stood, too, her plastic container in hand. "See you later."

"What are you doing today?"

"This and that." Then she crossed the uneven surface at her feet to peer into the nearest tide pool. "First, I'm gathering some sea lettuce."

"Huh?"

"It's a bright green seaweed—looks just like lettuce."

"I know what it is, I just don't know what you want with it."

She sent him a smile. "I'm going to eat it in a salad. Want to come over for dinner tonight and share it with me?"

"Tell me you're not going to serve it with sea cucumber." They were unattractive orange, sluglike creatures, about as long as a man's hand, with a bumpy, leathery skin.

Her gaze went back to the tide pool. "I think I see one or two of those in here, as well."

He made his way over to take his own look. "You don't really eat them."

"I don't really eat them." She leaped over a nearby pool to approach yet another. "Oh, here's an octopus."

Who could resist an eight-armed animal? Gage walked toward her, sliding a little on some slimy surf grass covering the exposed rock.

"Be careful," Skye admonished.

He shot her a grin. "Thanks, Mom." Upon reaching the edge, he squatted for a better view.

Skye mimicked his position. They were shoulder to shoulder. Her arm lifted, and she pointed toward a small underwater cavern below the surface. "See?"

Gage studied nature's temporary goldfish bowl. It took him a moment, but then he saw the creature, its brown-speckled body about the size of his fist. As they watched, one of its tentacles drifted out and explored the rock overhead. It touched a bright green anemone, which immediately drew in its petals. A trio of starfish, one orange, one brown, one rose, clung to another shelf of rock nearby, huddled close to each other. A small sculpin fish wiggled about the sandy bottom on its own mission.

"Beautiful," Gage said, turning his head to give Skye another grin.

Her head turned, too, and she smiled back.

Beautiful, he thought again, gazing into her face, then homing in on that soft, tender mouth. Her smile slid away and it was so serious now. So seriously in need of a kiss.

Gage leaned forward.

Skye scrambled back, stumbling as she rose. He shot up, too, taken aback by her sudden movement. Her left heel caught on a jut of rock, and the right sole of her slip-on canvas shoe slid on a patch of surf grass. Then she was falling, going ass-first into one of the larger, deeper tide pools.

She didn't submerge all the way, but managed to come to a stand, wet from the neck down. They both stared at each other a moment, and then she burst out laughing. "So much for my dignity," she said, apropos of nothing and between bouts of laughter. "I feel like an idiot."

"You look like one, too," Gage confirmed and leaned down, palm outstretched to help her out. After a moment, her wet hand met his and he pulled, her light weight making it nothing to get her back onto land, water streaming from her clothes and puddling at her feet.

"I probably terrified some poor little sea creature," she said, turning around to inspect the still-sloshing surface of the pool.

Gage's gaze got stuck on her backside, the thin linen of her clothing now transparent and plastered to her skin. Oh, God. She had the sweetest—the *sweetest*—of high, firm asses. His favorite kind.

Then she spun back and the fabric was only the frailest of veils here, too. He could see every lovely line of her: the delicate framework of her collarbone, the gentle slope of her breasts with their cold-hardened peaks, the flat plane of her belly between her hip bones, the gentle rise of her sex.

Gage flashed hot all over. He could have used his cock as a hammer.

"We should get you back home," he said, poleaxed by the strength and insistence of his physical reaction. *Want to have her,* his body was demanding. *Got to have her.*

And Gage had this worrisome premonition that no other woman would do.

CHAPTER THREE

SKYE HAD MADE A DATE with Polly for a caffeine boost in the form of an afternoon latte at Captain Crow's. Her friend was already seated at the bar, blowing across the top of her overlarge cup as Skye approached. "How are you?" she asked.

Polly responded with her usual cloudless smile, "Me? I'm good. I'm always good."

Settling herself onto a stool, Skye glanced around. Starting at about four o'clock, the place would fill with people demanding beer and cocktails, but it was relatively quiet now and there was someone new attending the espresso machine.

He turned and started toward her. "What can I get you, Skye?"

She frowned. He was in his mid-twenties, with shaggy dark hair and a skinny build. His face wasn't familiar. "I'm sorry, do I—"

"Oh, you probably don't." He appeared suddenly self-conscious. "I'm Steve. I went to college with Addy... Addison March, who stayed at the cove last month? We met here for drinks one time and she showed me the Sunrise Pictures stuff."

"Oh. Sure." A grad student in film studies, Addy had cataloged the memorabilia in exchange for a first look at the complete collection. "But did we meet then?"

The barista was a little red in the face now. "No, no. I think she pointed you out to me, that's all. Can I make you a latte, as well?"

"Yes, thanks," Skye said, then watched him hurry toward the big machine at the end of the bar.

"Just another of your admirers," Polly murmured.

"What? No! I don't even know that guy." And she didn't want to know him, because he gave off a weird enough vibe to make her stomach knot. Though to be fair, these days all men gave off a weird vibe to her.

"Well, Gage Lowell seemed very attentive yesterday. I saw him with you in your yard."

"You were the one he was paying attention to. He told me he thinks you're cute." And then she'd warned him off with a rabid intensity that made her squirm a little, remembering it.

"I hate that word," Polly said, suddenly looking as if she'd swallowed something sour. "Cute. I think it's preventing me from having a fulfilling love life."

"I thought it was the word *perky* that was to blame. At least that's what you told me last week."

"I've rethought that. I'm a kindergarten teacher. Perky is part of the job description, so I can't wish it away."

The barista was back. He placed Skye's drink in front of her but was called over to attend another customer before he could strike up more conversation. She blew out a relieved breath that disturbed the froth of foam layered over her drink like coastal fog. "We both know your biggest stumbling block to a fulfilling love life is Teague." Though she'd yet to admit to it, her best friend had it bad for a man who considered Polly his best friend, too.

The other woman's scowl made it clear she wouldn't be confessing today, either, even as a telltale flush crawled up her face. "I don't know what you're talking about," she said, then pinned Skye with a stare. "What's yours?"

She blinked. "My biggest stumbling block? Uh…how about that I'm not seeking a fulfilling love life?"

"Well, you're not seeking an unfulfilling one, either," Polly grumbled. "Why is that? You haven't been out with anyone since giving Dalton the boot, and that was months ago."

"He's been calling again," Skye confessed, sidestepping the subject. "What makes a man unable to take no for an answer?"

"Maybe you just haven't found the right man to ask the question. I get that you don't want Dalton in your life. But what if some other guy—say some other guy named Gage Lowell who insisted on having that dance the other night—came on to you and—"

"Gage would never come on to me." That wasn't what had happened this morning at the tide pools, was it? They'd been side by side, gazing into the water. and then they'd been gazing into each other's eyes.

She'd experienced another spurt of that hot, anxious panic that made her skin burn and her heart beat too hard in her chest. Flustered, she'd had the strange idea that he was about to kiss her and something low, somewhere below her belly button, had clenched—more panic, she supposed. And even as she struggled to stay calm and dignified, her nerves had sent her staggering back.

Foolish Skye.

This whole conversation was foolish. "Do we only have men to talk about?" she asked Polly. "I feel as if I'm at a seventh-grade slumber party."

"Did I put your bra in the freezer?" her friend demanded. "Have we divvied up which member of the latest boy band will take which of us to the prom?"

"Ah." Skye smiled, reminiscing. "I always wanted the devilish-looking one. All the rest of the girls went for the blond or the lead that looked like he should be class president."

"What band are we talking about?" Polly asked, lifting her cup for a sip.

Skye did the same. "It doesn't matter. They're all made up of one of each type. And my favorite was always the guy who looked like trouble."

Polly slid her a sly glance. "He might not be in a band, but Gage looks like trouble to me."

"Why do you keep bringing him up? He is the most commitment-averse man I know. He doesn't stay in one place long enough to have two-night stands."

"You don't have to have a *relationship* with him. My God. It's summer. He's here for a few weeks. Have a fling."

A fling with Gage Lowell? Skye felt herself flush, thinking of his tall body, his wide chest, the intense turquoise-blue of his eyes. He'd held her hand, his fingers lean and sure, and now she thought of them working at buttons, undoing clasps, baring skin. That spot below her navel clenched again, just as it had by the tide pools.

"Think about it," Polly continued. "It's been so long since you've had sex."

Gage. Sex. Skye pushed her latte away, not wanting to add caffeine to her already jittering insides and that low-belly clenching. How she wished Polly had not brought it up, not put those images in her head, not made her think about all she couldn't have.

With anyone.

"I'M REALLY HERE," Gage said as he sat on Captain Crow's deck beside his twin, watching the daily 5:00 p.m. ritual. A man in board shorts stood at the base of a ten-foot pole poked in the sand. He blew a long blast on a football-sized conch shell. Then it was the raising of the flag—a blue rectangle of cloth printed with the internationally recognized shape of a martini glass.

Lifting his beer, Gage toasted the fluttering scrap of fabric. "To cocktail hour." Then he clacked his bottle against Griffin's. "Dogs bark but the caravan moves on."

Griffin ignored that bit of Arabic wisdom and narrowed his gaze at his brother. "You don't have a camera."

"As usual, your powers of observation are staggering. No wonder you won that big hairy prize for your reporting."

"Why don't you have a camera?" his brother persisted, paying no attention to the teasing.

Gage shrugged. He couldn't explain to himself his disinterest in having near what for years had been an extension of his own body.

"Something's wrong," Griffin said flatly. "Damn it, I knew something was wrong. I've known it for weeks."

Gage took a slow swallow of beer. "Where's your evidence? I'm here, I'm whole—"

"You're without a camera—"

"I don't have one with me all the time."

"Yes, you do, unless you're having sex. And that's only because you told me it inhibits naked women. They worry they might become the subject of your camera's eye."

"And I don't want to waste my time with inhibited women, that's true. Life's too short." He took another swig of his beer, enjoying the warm air, the cool breeze off the ocean, the happy, drinking people around them.

Griffin stayed silent, but Gage could feel his considering stare. "And why are you just sitting there—no drumming fingers, no fidgety knees?" his twin finally asked. "I've never seen you sit this still your whole life."

"Maybe I've learned some patience." Cramped quarters and no way out of them could affect a man. When his brother made a scoffing sound, he pointed his bottle at him. "You've changed, too. Good God, you're engaged."

Griffin narrowed his eyes. "You're avoiding my questions."

"Ask one that makes some sense."

"Why Crescent Cove?"

Gage blinked. He hadn't seen that coming. "You're getting married here at the end of the month."

"You didn't know that when you booked No. 9 as Fenton Hardy."

"Does it really matter?" The notion had been seeded by Griffin, he supposed, when his brother had told him he'd decided to take three months at the cove to write his war memoir. But Gage had to admit that there'd been something else—some*one* else cementing the deal.

Even before his two weeks in hell, he'd had this itch to visit Skye-with-the-unnecessary-*e*. He smiled, thinking about her.

Across the table from him, Griffin groaned. "All right, who is she?"

"Who is who?"

"You're thinking about some girl. You're thinking about boning some girl."

Gage frowned. "Don't say it like that."

"That's how *you* always say it."

"You want me to talk that way about you making love with your Jane?"

His brother hooted. "You're calling it 'making love' now?" His two fingers put little scare quotes around the term. "And by the way, if you insult Jane in any way, shape or form, I'll kick your ass. And then she'll do it all over again, only harder. And with sexier shoes."

"Whoa," Gage said, tilting his head. "You've really fallen for her."

Griffin's expression softened. "Best thing that ever happened to me. I was…messed up when I got back. She helped me find my balance again. She *is* the balance."

Gage nodded. Griffin's yearlong experience embedded with the troops in Afghanistan had been harrowing, he'd known that.

His brother hesitated, took another long swig of beer, hesitated again. "I've been seeing a counselor."

"Finally," Gage said, faking relief without missing a beat. "Good to know you're getting some professional assistance for that little premature ejaculation problem you've always had."

Griffin's grin broke quick, felt sweet. "For PTSD, smart-ass."

Gage merely nodded, careful not to offer judgment or advice. "Helping?"

"Yeah." Then he grinned again. "Though regular sex isn't bad for the cure, either."

"Which reminds me," Gage said, frowning. "Did you have to tell Skye about the Gage Gorge? Jesus!"

His brother laughed. "I don't remember relating that odd little quirk of yours."

"It's not a quirk. It's a…it's a…" He glared across the table. "You like sex, too."

"Yeah, and committed sex is the best there is," his twin said, smug.

"Oh, come on." It was Gage's turn to scoff.

"Think about it. You get to know her magic switches and it's a sure thing time after time after time."

"Sounds boring."

"Oh, it can be a fast bump or a slow ride and everything in between. I set up these little challenges for myself. Forty-five minutes of just kissing, say, or using only my index finger to get her off. My ultimate goal is to take her there by hot whispers and above-the-waist touches only."

"Now, that just sounds like work, bro." Though he shifted in his chair, finally restless.

"Not when you're doing it with someone you really care about. It's the one-night stands that sound like work after that."

Without Gage's permission, images formed in his mind—not of Griff and Jane, thank God—but of dark hair and green-and-amber eyes, delicate breasts and a spectacular booty. Then he saw himself closing in for that kiss and the way Skye had leaped away from him— as if he were toxic.

As if she was spooked.

"There were some physical problems."

She'd said that, and he'd gone all caveman, ready to bust Dagwood's chops if he'd hurt her—which she'd denied. So why had she said it?

He turned to his brother, in sudden critical need of an answer. "What's it mean when a woman claims she and a man had some 'physical problems'?"

And this time it was Griffin who couldn't—or wouldn't— reply. And Gage who felt in his gut that something was very, very wrong.

THE SUN WAS LOW IN THE SKY when Skye stepped outside
her cottage to the miniature lemon tree planted in a pot
near the side of her house. Fresh citrus slices would keep
moist the piece of salmon she was planning to grill on
a cedar plank. She wrapped her fingers around one of
the ripe fruits, then yelped when a man suddenly came
around the corner.

"Dalton!" She clutched the lemon in both hands at
chest level, over the startled beat of her heart. "What are
you doing here?"

He was handsome, well built if not tall, smooth-
looking in a summer-weight suit, white shirt and gold-
and-brown diamond-patterned tie that mirrored the dark
honey of his hair and eyes. "A man can't visit the beach
on a summer evening?"

She lifted an eyebrow.

His smile was white. A little rueful. "A man can't
visit the woman who unceremoniously dumped him on
a summer evening?"

"I didn't—"

Now he raised a brow.

Skye pressed her lips together, wishing she could honestly deny it. Still, their relationship had been more of the
casual dating kind, as opposed to steady and heading for
something more. At least to her mind. It was only after
she'd said she wouldn't see him any longer that he'd appeared so seriously interested.

He put a foot on the pathway to her front door, even as
she pressed her shoulders against its pink-painted wood
surface. "Aren't you going to invite me in?" he asked.

She'd not willingly allowed any man into her place in
months. "I'm just getting ready to fix dinner," she said.

He waited as if he thought she'd extend an invitation,

then shrugged. "I'll take you out. We can go to that place in Laguna—"

"Dalton, we've been through this."

"But it doesn't make any sense!" Frustration puckered his forehead. "We were going along just fine, seeing each other a couple of times a week. We were even talking about catching some spring season training games in Arizona."

Dalton took his Dodgers baseball very seriously.

"I know. And I'm sorry that it seemed so…abrupt. You're a very nice man—"

"Then how come you gave me the big heave-ho?"

Apparently Dalton had run across little rejection in his life. He didn't take it very gracefully, that was certain. Though to be fair, her goodbye had come without warning.

"I don't know what else to say—"

"Maybe it's time to stop talking," Dalton said, striding up the pathway toward her. "Maybe it's time I reminded you of a few things."

Skye froze, even as an unnatural fear rose like bile in her throat. *Dalton won't hurt me,* she told herself. *Dalton would never hurt me.* But he was still coming toward her, the light of sexual intent in his gaze. Even the briefest contact would be intolerable.

When he reached for her, she let out a strangled cry. The tang of lemon filled the air and then Dalton was leaping back, cursing at the juice that had streamed onto his slacks and shoes.

Looking down, Skye realized she'd throttled the innocent citrus, the skin and pulp crushed in her fingers.

"What the hell, Skye?" Giving her a fulminating look, Dalton stepped forward again.

"Is there a problem?" a new male voice asked.

She whipped her head to the left. Gage was stepping across her side yard, a white sack in hand, dressed in those olive cargo pants he'd had on earlier, and a T-shirt so faded the words on it were undecipherable. "I... Please," she said.

Please, what? She didn't know; she didn't know anything beyond how glad she was for the interruption. Her stomach was queasy again, her brain dizzy from lack of oxygen.

"Gage Lowell," he said to the other man, one of his big feet coming between her and Dalton. It made her ex step back, though he took the outstretched hand.

"Dalton Bradley." He grimaced, like maybe Gage's grip was a little too strong.

But Gage's smile was easy as he looked back at Skye. "I hope I'm not late." At her blank stare, he added, "For dinner?" Then he swung the white bag at eye level. "I brought dessert."

"Oh. Um..."

Gage snaked a long arm around her to turn the knob and open the door. She took an automatic step back and he followed her in, causing her to move farther along the entryway. "Nice to meet you," he said to Dalton, and then shut the door on his surprised expression.

Next, Gage turned, and his gaze ran over Skye, surveying her face, her hands that were filled with the pulverized lemon, her bare feet, their toes curled into the hardwood floor. "Relax, honey."

When she just stood there, he rattled the bag again. She blinked. "Breathe, Skye. Breathe, honey."

And she found she could. Even with a large, masculine presence standing so close. In her house.

"Do you have any wine?"

"You like wine?" she asked, dubious. "Aren't you more a beer type of guy?"

"I like both." He shrugged. "But the wine's for you. You look as if you need a little something to settle you down."

She couldn't argue with that, so she led him farther into her home. Once they got to the kitchen, as she disposed of the lemon and washed her hands, he stowed his bag in the freezer. Then he rummaged around for glasses and found the three-quarters-full bottle of chilled sauvignon blanc in her refrigerator. Directing her to sit at one of the two stools pulled up to the breakfast bar, he placed a glass in front of her.

The one he held in his hand was clinked against the rim of hers. "If you deal in camels, ensure that your doorways are high."

That shook her out of her bemused stupor. Blinking, she tilted her head. "What?"

"It's an old Afghan proverb."

"But what does it mean?"

"How the hell do I know?" He grinned, then nudged her wine closer to her hand. "Maybe something about making sure an ex stays out of your life."

"I didn't ask him to stay in it," Skye protested.

"The lemon was a good touch. He didn't look pleased about having a trip to the dry cleaner's in his future."

"He's harmless." Except that the confrontation had left her sick and shaking, because of the exaggerated fear she'd experienced for the past few months. Maybe she should have found some way to explain it to Dalton, but her violent dislike of a male touch humiliated her. Shamed her. Made her feel less than a woman.

"So, are we really having sea lettuce salad for dinner?"

She opened her mouth, about to tell Gage she'd been joking about the invitation at the tide pool. But why not let him stay? At least if Dalton took it in his mind to return again this evening, Gage would be available as bodyguard. "I have salmon steaks, too," she said, "but we'll need another lemon."

The aftereffects of the unpleasant encounter with Dalton lasted through dinner. Gage didn't seem to mind her quiet mood, however. Instead, he kept his distance and moved efficiently about her kitchen, doing his half of the work to throw together the meal.

Afterward, he ushered her into the living room and took one corner of the couch while she took the other. Another glass of wine was in each of their hands. "What did he want?" he asked, his voice casual.

"Can we not talk about him?"

"He's got you twitchy."

She didn't want to tell him every male had her twitchy. "I don't understand why he seems to want me so much more now that I broke it off."

"He thinks you're playing hard to get."

"Whoa." Irritation burned off the residual of the day's disquiet. "Then I'm actually starting to dislike him. He should know me better than that. I'm not into games."

"I'll bet he is. That's why he leaped to that conclusion."

"Well." Skye flounced on her cushion. "Now I don't even feel a little bit bad for breaking up with him."

Gage grinned. "That's my girl."

My girl. She felt herself flush, and then she found herself supremely aware that she was inside her house—door closed, drapes drawn—with the very thing she'd been avoiding all these months. A man, confident, big, oozing testosterone without any effort. Her heartbeat spiked high and that low-belly place clenched.

A strange expression flickered across Gage's face; then he slowly reached for the remote control sitting on the table at his elbow. "Want to watch some TV?"

She swallowed. "As long as it's not baseball," she said.

He found a documentary about the Mayan civilization. Maybe it was the narrator's deep, soothing voice. Maybe it was the fact that her sleep had been disturbed for months. But she found her lashes heavier than bags of sand and even as she told herself she could never drift off with a strange male in the house…she did.

She roused to a hand on her shoulder. Batting at it, she frowned, still mostly asleep. "Go away, Polly."

A masculine chuckle tried to thread its way into her consciousness. "I'll try not to be insulted by that."

"Good," she murmured, and turned her cheek in order to get more comfortable.

"You're going to get a crick in your neck if I let you sleep here all night."

Her fuzzy mind started to grow more alert. "You're not Polly," she said, still not opening her eyes.

"Not unless she's been hiding her dick."

Her lashes popped open and she glowered—albeit sleepily—at Gage. "That's crude."

"My middle name." He had slid down the couch to where she was half-slumped against the arm.

She struggled to sit up and gather her wits. "I wouldn't think you'd admit to that."

"I don't play games, either. I don't try to conceal who I am. You know that from my letters."

This close, she could smell his scent. It was clean yet

mysterious, with a spicy, foreign note. "I feel sure there are some hidden pockets to your soul."

"That's exactly where I keep the crude."

She couldn't help smiling at him. "You think you're funny."

"Hey, I've spent a lot of time alone. If I can't make myself laugh, I'm in trouble."

Skye frowned. That had never occurred to her...that when he was out on assignment in wild and dangerous places he didn't always have a support group around him. "Don't you get lonely?"

Gage seemed to ponder that a moment. "I think I will."

He *will?* What did that mean? She opened her mouth to ask, but he beat her to the next question. "Ice cream?" he asked. "That's what I put in the freezer. Or should I let myself out so you can go to bed?"

She didn't want him to leave just yet, she realized. "Ice cream."

He exited to the kitchen, then returned to the living room with a bowl of her favorite flavor. "Rocky road, right? Man, you got my taste buds screaming for relief when you wrote me about your new favorite shop in Newport."

"This is from Icy Delights?" Eager, she stretched for the bowl.

Dropping down beside her, he held it out of reach. "You need to run your dishwasher. Only one clean bowl was left, so we have to share." Scooping up a spoonful, he held it to her mouth.

She opened, took it in, making sure to run her tongue over the utensil to lap up every bit of the delicious treat. "Mmm." Her eyes closed in ecstatic appreciation.

Gage made a low sound. She looked at him, and the

heated blue of his eyes staring at her over the bowl was enough to turn the frozen dessert into sugary soup. Skye felt her blood take on the high temperature as it zipped through her system, smoking nerve endings along the way.

He was so big, she thought. Long limbs, wide shoulders, large feet and hands. Under the tanned skin of his arms, she could see the flex of muscle and the pull of tendons. There was a dive watch strapped on one wrist, and the complex piece of technology only served to make her more aware of the primal masculinity of him.

Her breath stalled in her lungs.

That around-men anxiety was back with a vengeance. She should be used to the panic by now, she thought. Except with Gage it was somehow different. Now the fear made her skin flush and feel too tight on her bones. The sizzle in her system, the breathlessness, the edginess of her mood were a totally separate kind of alarm.

As her heartbeat raced, that place low in her belly tightened. She felt a small rush of moisture between her thighs.

And that's when she realized her response to Gage wasn't her usual apprehension at all. This reaction of her body didn't signal anxiety—it had just been so long since she'd experienced it she hadn't immediately recognized what it truly was.

Desire.

CHAPTER FOUR

STANDING BESIDE THE open door of her car, Skye tossed
her purse onto the passenger seat, lifting her head when
she heard the distinctive crackle of footsteps crossing
crushed seashells. Warned that someone was approaching from behind, she steeled herself to stay calm. No
need to jump out of her skin.

"There you are."

At Gage's voice, though, her heart leaped toward her
throat and then plummeted to her belly. Pressing her
palm there, she pasted on a casual, friendly expression
and half turned toward him, determined to maintain her
dignity. "Oh, hey."

"Thought I could take you to lunch," he said, continuing to stroll forward until he stood nearly toe-to-toe with
her. He wore a pair of battered jeans and a short-sleeved
polo shirt that must have been dyed to exactly match his
eyes. "Payback for last night's dinner."

Her heart bobbed again, a jerky, marionette-like movement. "That's not necessary." Last night's dinner was
something she'd been trying to forget since sending him
on his way after he finished the bowl of ice cream. One
bite had been enough for her.

He tilted his head, studying her face. She could feel
it was flushed, damn it. "Aren't you a little hot in that
sweatshirt?"

Her fingers toyed with the ribbed hem that hit mid-thigh. "I'm perfectly comfortable." All covered up from throat to ankles in the overlarge top and relaxed-fit khakis.

He stood silent a moment, then shrugged. "So… lunch?" As if he read her impending refusal, he sent her a wheedling smile. "Indulge a guy."

Clearly he thought he was irresistible. She swallowed, preparing to deliver an emphatic "no," partly due to feminine principle, mostly due to self-preservation. More time in his company equaled more time suffering the effects of her unwanted and unexpected physical fascination with him. Her mouth opened just as the breeze kicked up and she was muffled by a long swath of her own hair.

Before she could drag it away, his fingers were there, tucking beneath the strands and brushing her hot cheek as he drew the hair behind her ear. The calloused pads lingered on the rim, which went fiery as he absently rubbed the tender curl of flesh.

She felt the touch in a flash of more fire that arrowed down her neck. The erotic burn paralyzed her and she stared up at him, helpless under his enigmatic gaze and deft caress.

"Say yes," he said.

And like a subject to a hypnotist, Skye nodded, then caught herself. "Wait. Whoa. I—"

"You don't wear earrings," Gage said, his forefinger now tracing the lobe of her ear.

Anyone would shiver at that gentle stroke. Anyone would be confused by the new turn of conversation. She blinked. "Not lately…"

"So fragile," he murmured, still playing with her ear, so that his knuckles brushed the sensitive hollow behind it. "And without any jewelry, innocent-looking and… naked."

Oh, God. That word, *naked,* combined with the almost delicate contact of his hand made her dizzy. She hauled in a breath, and his scent invaded her lungs, that same exotic, evocative male scent as the night before. It smelled like some rare, copper-colored spice kept behind a curtain in the last booth of a foreign bazaar.

It made her want to rub her face against his throat.

"I'm hungry," Gage said, still touching her.

Naked. Hungry. She was melting, going liquid inside. So much heat. "Me, too," she heard herself say.

"Lunch, then," he said, his hand dropping. "You mind driving?" He was already moving aside her purse and climbing into the passenger seat.

Her mind caught up to his actions. "No. I… What are you doing?"

"I'm hungry, you're hungry. A meal." His door shut with a decisive click.

Stymied, she slid into the driver's seat. "I was on my way to the mall." It was true, and it was also her last-ditch effort to get rid of him. Men hated shopping.

"Sounds good," Gage said, adjusting his seat to make more room for his long legs. "I need to buy my mom a birthday gift. Maybe I'll find something for the engaged couple."

He glanced over when she continued to stare at him. "What? Won't your trip be more fun with a friend?"

How to answer that? Of course they were friends. They'd been regular correspondents for months, and he'd only be puzzled if she made a big deal about not allowing him along.

And, damn it, she *wanted* to be his friend.

Nothing more…but nothing less, either. She'd loved their letter exchange.

Without another demur, she headed half an hour up the coast to the outdoor promenade of shops in one of the bigger beach towns. The streets in its center were closed to car traffic, but she and Gage still had to keep an eye open for bicyclists, skateboarders and moms pushing Hummer-sized strollers. He didn't say anything as they ambled, his gaze roaming the myriad cafés and restaurants as well as the shops that sold everything any used-to-it-all-and-more Southern Californian could want.

"Culture shock?" she asked.

He turned his gaze from the window of a store that sold nothing but ball caps to look into her face. "I always forget how much…stuff there is available for purchase."

"Is that disapproval I hear?" She tilted her head. "All the 'stuff' offends your sensibilities?"

"I don't have a lot of possessions myself, because I travel so much. I'm like a hermit crab…carry all I need on my back."

"Nothing to weigh you down?"

He shrugged. "It's true I've lived light. I…" His words faded away as his gaze caught on the bare legs of a woman in short shorts and platform sandals. He watched her swaying hips until they disappeared into a high-end lingerie boutique.

"There's something to be said for Western excess," he said, grinning. "Look at all those pretty little nothings."

The stork-legged mannequins in the shop window were dressed in panties cut high and bras cut low.

"Ironic how Western excess results in a definite shortage of T-and-A coverage," she grumbled.

He laughed. "Shall we go inside?"

"No!" she said, mortification washing new heat across her skin. "I'm not going in there with you."

"I'll buy you a present."

"No," she repeated, then quickly stepped into the specialty body and bath products store that had been her destination. Instead of scantily clad mannequins and posters of supermodels in wings, this boutique was decorated with murals of flower fields and lush vineyards. Various lines of organic skin care products were arranged by scent. Skye headed toward the back corner.

"Wait." Gage's head swiveled and he drifted toward a display of products nearer the front. There sat bottles and tubes colored a pale, green-tinged blue. Stacked beside them were hand-hewn blocks of soap the same color. They smelled of freshwater and flower petals. "This," he said, pointing to it. "This is you."

Skye shrugged a shoulder, half uncomfortable, half pleased. "You're right. That's their Melusine line. It's what I use."

He brought a waxy bar to his nose, inhaled. "I like it. It suits you, cool and sweet at the same time."

Another surge of pleasure warmed her, even as her nerves tingled a warning. Should she change her bath products? She didn't like the idea that her personal fragrance was so recognizable. Drawing attention to herself through looks or even scent didn't sit well with her any longer. As she watched, he closed his eyes and drew in another breath of the soap's perfume, clearly enjoying it.

Her nerves tingled again. Maybe it was the kind of detail only Gage would notice, she thought.

Which didn't make her feel any more at ease. Backing away from him, she cleared her throat. "Don't worry about sticking close. Go on out, browse the other shops. I can find you when I'm done picking out the bridal present I'm after for Jane."

If she'd thought the mention of a wedding would send the man on his way, she'd been wrong. He was at her shoulder as she perused a display of orange blossom products packaged in white organza. Hyperaware of him, she selected several items that she'd put together in a gift basket.

"Can I help you?"

They both turned toward a salesgirl, her platinum hair ironed to a shiny fall, her sparkling blue gaze focused on Gage.

His smile spread slowly. "I don't know," he said, not looking away from the young woman, who was dressed in a layered trio of tank tops and a napkin-sized skirt. "Do we need any help, Skye?"

Speaking of scents, she could smell the sex appeal he was beaming toward the pretty blonde. "I'm fine," she said, and turned her back to give the man privacy for his flirtation.

And he did that, flirted, his voice low and warm as he asked the woman's opinion on a birthday gift for his mother. With half an ear, Skye heard her recommend the Melusine products and couldn't miss Gage's quick dismissal of that idea. Next they walked to a row of tester vials and Skye rolled her eyes as the salesgirl insisted on spraying her own skin: wrist, back of hand, crook of elbow, and then held each to Gage's nose for his appreciation.

Her selections were bought and bagged while he was still sniffing at the blonde. He glanced over his shoulder, saw Skye waiting by the door and frowned. "You're ready? I'm sorry."

"Take your time," she said, with a go-ahead gesture.

But he deftly sidestepped the salesgirl as she lifted yet another inch of her bare, fragrant flesh toward his face. "I'll take the plumeria set," he said, reaching for his wallet. "You said you could ship it for me?"

The transaction only took a few more minutes, and then he left behind a clearly disappointed blonde to join Skye at the exit. She started to push at the door, but he took over, swinging it wide with his big hand. "Why didn't you say something?" he grumbled.

"I wanted to give you plenty of time to ask her out," she said.

He narrowed his eyes at her. "Skye…"

"Hey, the Gage Gorge requires—"

"Shut up about that," he said. "That topic's off-limits between you and me."

"It doesn't have to be," she said. "I understand—"

"Off-limits," he repeated, implacable.

Still, she couldn't help being aware of all the pretty women they encountered as they continued to stroll through the streets. More than one female looked at Gage, clearly appreciating his lean good looks and confident gait. A Pilates posse, a small group of women dressed in Lululemon exercise gear and carrying coffees, gave him speculative, sidelong looks. Pairs of office workers in tight suit skirts and sneakers slowed their lunch hour power walks as they passed him by. One nubile young lady, distributing flyers for a new restaurant, made a point of scrawling her number on the piece of paper before handing it to him.

Making the thumb-and-pinky "call me" sign, she grinned as he absently stuffed the sheet into his pocket.

"You're missing a lot of opportunities," Skye chided him. "You shouldn't let my presence stop you."

He shot her a dark look. "Are you trying to annoy me?"

Maybe. Though she was more annoyed at herself at the surge of ugly green jealousy she felt when she thought of him gorging on anyone. "I don't know what's put you in such a mood," she mumbled, trying to cover her own.

"I need lunch," he said, then halted, his gaze fixed on a small café across the street. "And God provides." His tone was nearly reverent. "Fish tacos."

In minutes they were at a tiny table, both with an iced tea and a plate of tacos in front of them. The lightly breaded white fish smelled delicious and tasted even better cocooned in a small warm corn tortilla and garnished with cabbage, grated cheddar cheese, a spoonful of tart white sauce and a squeeze of lime.

He held one taco high. "The young goose is a good swimmer," he said, like a blessing, then ate it in three big bites. An appreciative moan followed.

Smiling, Skye tilted her head at him. "Better now?"

"Almost." Round two went down as quickly as round one.

Her eyes widened as she lifted her first to her mouth. "Until now, I don't think I had an accurate understanding of the depths of your appetite."

He glanced up. "You didn't get a hint last night?"

Skye stilled, remembering the hot look in his eye when he'd fed her ice cream. But surely that had been her imagination—if not projection. Still, her hand twitched, and her taco dropped back to her plate, its contents scattering. Glad for the distraction, she bent her head and busied herself scooping the ingredients back inside the tortilla.

"Maybe we should talk about it," Gage said, his voice low.

Embarrassment burned up her neck toward her face. Did he mean… Did he suspect… Her brain stumbled over uncomfortable thoughts. When he'd left her house the night before, she'd hoped he'd not noticed the effect he had on her.

The way he was still affecting her.

"Skye?"

She still didn't want to look at him. But she did, faking a puzzled expression. "Discuss? There's nothing to discuss."

And to her relief, he let it go. She didn't want to squirm through any conversation he'd want to have about her misplaced interest. In her sloppy clothes and scrubbed face, they both knew she wasn't Gage Gorge material. No need to make them both uncomfortable by spelling it out.

After lunch, they returned to Crescent Cove. Skye pulled into the driveway behind her beach house. The ride back had been silent and, on her side, filled with awkwardness. Gage, however, remained an enigma. For all she knew, he stayed quiet because he was tired, or bored or thinking of that woman whose number he had in his pocket.

"We have to talk about the attraction," he suddenly said.

Startled, Skye whipped her head toward him. "Huh?"

"Don't think I didn't realize." He pinned her with those bright turquoise eyes.

Damn. She supposed the notion of fooling him had

been a pipe dream. An experienced man like Gage would know when a woman was…was drawn to him.

"It was there in the room with us last night, big as life, and I'd like to get past it, Skye. It's not—"

"Don't say anything more!" Clearly it was not a feeling he reciprocated. Who could blame him? She knew what she looked like—colorless and camouflaged in baggy clothes. That's the way she wanted to be, needed to be. Still, the whole situation stung her pride.

Gage cleared his throat. "I'm only trying to say that I—"

"Have really been out of touch for too long. Or your head has been turned by the attention you've received since you got back."

"What?"

She gathered her self-respect around her like a cloak. "Not every woman in the world falls for you, you know."

"Skye—"

"Your ego is overinflated, Gage. I wouldn't be so foolish as to…to want you. There's no way that a woman who looks like this—" she indicated her sweatshirt and wrinkled pants "—would imagine herself with a man like *you*."

And on that undignified note, she dashed from the car.

GAGE TRIED LIGHTENING his expression as he turned toward his sister-in-law-to-be. The scowl he erased was more commonly found on his twin, who had always been the deeper, moodier of the two—at least until Griff had found his Jane. "Wedding stuff going okay?" he asked politely, wrapping his fingers around his beer.

Griffin laughed at him from across the table on Captain Crow's deck. "Yeah, you're so interested in the details."

The couple had arrived at Beach House No. 9 an hour ago to take measurements for…something. Okay, Gage had tuned out the particulars, and only tuned back in when they'd suggested a happy-hour visit to the bar up the beach. His mind had been occupied by other things.

Reaching over, Jane squeezed his hand. "Don't mind him. Wedding stuff's going fine. Tell us about your day. What did you do?"

Gage shrugged. "Went shopping with Skye."

"Oh," Jane said, her forehead creasing. "You're spending time with her, then?"

"Some." Though today's excursion might be the last occasion. Damn woman made him and his ego both feel like asses for his attempt at discussing that little tug running between them. Had he been wrong about the reciprocal sizzle? He thought not, and if so, then he hadn't been wrong to address it.

Skye was his lodestar and his talisman, and he didn't want to compromise those by infusing sex into their friendly, caring relationship.

Except, he reminded himself, feeling another scowl coming on, she didn't seem to care for *him* all that much. Tipping back his head, he took another sip of beer. His gaze landed on a pretty girl sitting alone at a table not far away. Their gazes met, and a small smile curled the corners of her lips.

He liked her light brown hair, lifted from her neck in one of those messy updos.

He liked her V-necked blouse that was low enough to reveal a hint of cleavage.

He liked the fact that she seemed to like him back,

so different from the prickly woman who'd practically stormed from her car after making clear she considered him an arrogant so-and-so.

Why was she his lodestar again?

What he needed, much more than that, was a sex star. Okay, it didn't have to be nearly that stellar. He just needed someone with whom to blunt this horny edge. He acknowledged the pretty lady with a dip of his beer, grinning as her long eyelashes fluttered in a half bashful, half teasing manner.

Griffin groaned. "Get a room, bro."

"Got a room," Gage said, letting his gaze drift back to his brother. "Gotta get a woman now."

"Well, have the decency to wait until Jane and I leave, okay?"

His brother's fiancée had that little pucker between her brows again. "I thought you were, uh, spending time with Skye."

"That was then." Now he wanted to forget the annoying, infuriating, insulting female. *Your ego is over-inflated, Gage.*

Jane's frown deepened. "But, Skye—"

"Look, can we not talk about her?" If he had a chance of getting laid, he had to pretend she didn't exist. The memory of her naked earlobes, her flower-water scent, the way her nose wrinkled when she used that god-awful phrase, *the Gage Gorge,* was attempting to interfere with the satiation of his very normal, natural, nothing-to-feel-ashamed-about needs. "I'm declaring this table, this whole night as a matter of fact, a Skye-free zone."

Griffin and his woman exchanged glances Gage didn't even try to interpret. Instead, he signaled the waitress for another beer and sent over a whatever-she's-having to

Updo. When his twin and Jane finished their drinks and made their goodbyes, he was gratified to see the pretty stranger get to her feet and approach his table.

Yeah. Screw the afternoon. The evening was going to end so much damn better for him.

Several hours later, Gage squinted, trying to bring the hands of his watch into focus. They wouldn't stay still. Lifting his wrist, he addressed the man standing on the other side of the bar. "Does this say it's wiggly time?"

He frowned, because that sounded really idiotic. How much had he had to drink? To clear his head, he sucked in a breath, and a delicate scent he couldn't forget entered his lungs. "Damn woman," he groused. "She can't even leave my air alone."

"What's that?" the bartender asked, stepping closer. "I didn't hear you, friend."

"That's what we were supposed to be," he told the man. "Me 'n' Skye. Friends."

Someone slid onto the stool beside his. His head still bent over his watch crystal, he pitched his voice toward the newcomer. "Are you another pretty woman? 'Cuz there were two...no, three sitting there before you."

"Is that what you're waiting for?" a voice said, low.

"Apparently not," Gage grumbled, "since I've sent three—or was it four?—on their way."

"So many," the person beside him murmured.

The bartender spoke up, a helpful note in his voice. "It was Ladies' Night. He kept opening his wallet."

"And yet I still couldn't cinch the deal," Gage added glumly. With bleary eyes, he stared at the TV screen over the bar. When had Letterman lost so much of his hair? "I must be getting old, too."

"Or maybe more discerning."

The moralistic tone sent Gage's head swinging to the side. His mood, already on morose, slid straight to grim when he saw it was Skye on the next-door stool, wearing another of her circus-tent sweatshirts and a pair of jeans. "What the hell are you doing here? I declared you off-limits."

"I didn't get the memo."

"Blame me, bud," the bartender put in. "I knew you were staying in the cove and I called her when I wasn't sure you were good to drive to your cottage."

"I walked here," Gage said.

"Okay. But I'm not sure you're good to walk to your cottage, either."

"Of course I…" His voice dropped off. To be honest, he couldn't feel his toes.

"Give us a couple of coffees, will you, Tom?" Skye asked. "Black, a little sugar?"

When the mugs were set in front of them, she picked hers up and gave him a sidelong glance. "I'm off-limits?"

"In more ways than one," he muttered, taking his own long swallow of the strong brew. Even if she smelled like damn heaven, he wasn't interested in her in the way he was interested in other women.

"What's that?"

He took another drink of coffee. "Look, I didn't want you around when I…when I…"

"Went on a gorge?"

He narrowed his eyes at her. "We discussed that terminology, didn't we?"

"Sorry—"

"Because it's probably what ruined my evening. I had Updo in the palm of my hand. Halter Top claimed she could tell I was going to get lucky tonight by reading the foam on my beer. Tiffany—"

"Oh, so at least you bothered to find out one of their names."

He frowned at her. "It was engraved on the heart-shaped pendant she wore around her neck."

"What a guy." Skye rolled her eyes. "That's not her name, that's the jeweler it came from."

"As I was saying," Gage continued, "every time I was on the verge of suggesting we retire to No. 9 for some private…conversation, I would hear your goddamn prissy voice in my head."

"I thought it was the margaritas," the bartender said, pausing to top off their mugs. "That's what you blamed it on before."

"Skye can take responsibility for that, too," he said, using the logic of the inebriated. "Because it had to be a woman who decided to screw around with the perfection of tequila, triple sec and lime juice. Flavored margaritas are clearly a female invention."

"What are you talking about?" Skye asked, looking between him and the bartender.

"Mango margaritas were the special tonight," Tom explained. Then he plopped a glass in front of her and poured inside the last icy dregs from a blender. "I don't think they're half-bad, myself."

Gage stared at the orangeish concoction as if it were a snake. He could smell the sticky sweetness from here. Just as pumpkin could take him back to Thanksgiving and peppermint to Christmas, breathing in the mango-redolent air sucked him straight to another time and place. He closed his eyes and felt the grit of dirt on his palms and the sick, uneven thud of his pulse in his ears. His throat closed, rebelling against swallowing, and his belly cringed as he imagined the thick liquid splashing into its aching depths.

"Gage? *Gage!*"

His eyes flew open and he stared, uncomprehending for a moment, into Skye's face. "I imagined you a million times down there," he said absently, "but never could pinpoint your features."

"What? Down where?" Her brows drew low. "What's wrong?"

He shook his head, as if he could shake off the memory like a bad dream. "Never mind." That glass of mango marg still sat there, mocking him, and he slid from the stool. "It's time for me to get out of here."

At his first step, he stumbled a little. "Gage." Skye put out her hand.

He brushed it aside, heading for the exit. "I'm fine."

She dogged his footsteps. "I'll go with you to No. 9."

"Forget it."

"Then you escort me to my place," she suggested.

His feet slowed. Damn. "You walked?"

At her nod, he resigned himself to a few more minutes in her company. By the time they were out of the restaurant and onto the sand, the combination of coffee and chilled air went a long way to sobering him up. He sucked in another long breath and tilted back his head to take in the stars flung against the dark sky. His brain only spun a little.

"You okay?"

"I'd be better if I was with another woman," he said darkly, starting off down the beach.

She sniffed, trudging beside him. Light from the moon made her face seem to glow. "If your heart was really in it, I doubt anything I might have said could change your mind. Or mango margaritas."

He didn't want to go into the whole mango thing. "My *heart* really *isn't* into it. That's not the body part looking for company. You get that, don't you, Skye?"

She lifted both arms. "So find some solo relief. What's the big deal?"

He stared at her.

Her gaze caught on his, skittered away. "What? I think the hairy palms thing is just a myth."

His laughter snorted out. "Still, honey, it's not the same."

One of her shoulders jerked a shrug. "It's all overrated," she said under her breath.

But he heard her. Was that what she'd meant when she said she and Dagwood had physical problems?

"All men aren't selfish in the sack," he said, guessing at the difficulty. "I make certain my partners have as good a time as I do."

"I'm sure," she said, dismissive.

They'd reached her place. She pulled a key from her pocket, reached to insert it into the lock. The mechanism made an audible click, and then she turned toward him, her expression concerned. "Are you sure you don't need my help getting home? It's not far and you appear less, uh, inebriated, but…"

Her mouth was moving, but he didn't absorb any of the words with her insulting *I'm sure* still echoing in his ears. Her unconvinced tone rubbed him wrong, itching at his skin and worming its way under just like her angel scent, her long lashes, her nude earlobes, that unpainted mouth. It was her fault he was alone tonight, and now she was impugning his ability as a lover?

He took an aggressive step forward, forcing her shoulders against the surface of the door to avoid the brush of his body. They stood so close he could feel her hitching breath against his throat. "I swear I'd do right by you, baby. On my honor, I'd make you come twice before entering you."

Her head jolted, thudding against the wood. Eyes wide, she stared up at him. The pale silver of the moonlight couldn't cool the wave of color flagging her cheeks.

On my honor, I'd make you come twice before entering you. Jesus! What had made him speak such a thing out loud? There was horny and then there was clumsy, crude, boorish, and...

...and God, he could see it in his mind. He'd conjured her in his imagination so many times that she slid easily into his bed, under his hands, against his tongue.

"That's never going to happen," she whispered, her eyes almost as big as the monster she probably now considered him to be.

"Of course it's not," he said, stepping back. His bed, his fantasies, his sex life were all—now and forever—Skye-free zones. The other ways he needed her were just too important.

CHAPTER FIVE

POLLY WAS PUTTING SCISSORS to brown paper bag when Teague White breezed through her open front door. He stopped short, taking in the stack of bags, the scraps of paper scattered at her feet, the tagboard pattern and pencil that lay on the coffee table in front of the love seat where she sat. "What's up?" he asked.

My pulse rate. But, accustomed to hiding her physical reaction to him, Polly aimed a casual smile at his shoulder—she had to avoid looking too hard at the beautiful face above it. The stark, masculine bones framed by layers of short hair the same color as his almost-black eyes had the power to rock her world. She cleared her throat to answer his question. "I'm making Australian bush hats."

"Huh," he said. "Brown bags stand up to the harsh conditions?"

She went wooden as he approached, preparing for his usual kiss on the cheek. He hadn't shaved and his whiskers prickled her skin, little needles of sensation that pierced her heart as if it were a pincushion. Pressing her knees together, she kept her gaze averted from him as he lifted the pile of cut pieces on the cushion beside her and took its place.

"Polly?"

Intent on not noticing how close he sat, how she could

feel his body heat reaching across the few inches between them, she'd missed his question. "Uh, what?"

"I asked again about the bush hats, sweetheart."

"Oh." A little laugh burst from her lips. It did *not* sound nervous. After all this time, it was ridiculous to be nervous around Teague. Their years of friendship had inured her to him by now. "They're for my class, as you should be able to guess."

"I'm always surprised at what you kindergarten teachers can do with scissors and paper. Not to mention yarn. I remember the finger-weave belts the kids made last year."

She felt a dimple dig into her cheek as she smiled, gratified he'd remembered. "Those came out pretty well, I admit."

One of his long legs crossed over the other. "You're harshing on my midsummer buzz, though, by prepping for September so soon."

"I hate to break the news. It's no longer midsummer. In three weeks I'll be back in the classroom."

"Then we'd better make the most out of the time we have left."

Polly's scissors paused, midcut. No, there wasn't going to be any "we" about the next weeks. There shouldn't be. There *wouldn't* be.

She'd made that decision after her coffee with Skye. Her best friend's words had slapped her like a palm to the face. *"We both know your biggest stumbling block to a fulfilling love life is Teague."* How had she guessed? It was Skye who also called her "Very Private Polly." If her feelings for Teague were wearing through her usual deep reserve, then she was in trouble.

He reached over now, tugging on the end of her ponytail. "You okay?"

"I'm good. I'm always good."

"Then let's make you gooder and finalize our August calendar. We'll make it one to remember."

"Gooder?"

He grinned. "Hey, I'm just a dumb firefighter."

She glanced away from that flash of white teeth. He wasn't dumb. It was her, who had never managed to shut him out of her life. For four and a half years she'd wanted him, wanted him to see her as more than a friend, and even when their physical relationship never went beyond ponytail tugs and busses on the cheek, she hadn't been able to stifle the yearning in her heart.

Maybe it was because they'd slept together on the first night they'd met, she mused. Just *slept.* They'd both attended a New Year's Eve party at Skye's place, here at the cove. Teague was her childhood friend. Polly had met her in an Asian poetry class in college. The end-of-year celebration had gone on way past midnight and everyone had been invited to crash rather than risk driving home. Accustomed to a much earlier bedtime, Polly had gratefully found her way at 3:00 a.m. to a dark bedroom and an empty pillow.

In the morning, she'd opened her eyes to discover herself sharing a bed with the most handsome man she'd ever seen. Staring into his dark eyes, she'd started in alarm, drawing back so far she'd almost rolled off the mattress. The stranger had rough-whispered, "Easy," and Polly, who was never easy when it came to men, had found herself settling back.

That had always been the strange dichotomy of her reaction to him. He made her pulse jitter at the same time that he calmed her innate wariness. It was a seductive contradiction, and after that morning when together they'd made breakfast for all the other overnighters, they'd become close friends.

But she wanted so much more.

She needed to look for it elsewhere, though, she knew that.

"I'm going to be seeing Tess a lot this month," he said now, his dark eyes going bleak.

Polly needed to look elsewhere because of that desolate expression in Teague's eyes. Because of Tess, the woman he loved.

"Why don't you just avoid her?" Polly asked, acutely aware of how difficult it could be to stay away from the object of one's affection. She was going to do it now, though. Really.

Teague sighed. "I would—do you think I want to torture myself? But there's a lot of events leading up to Griffin and Jane's wedding. I'll be expected to attend, since we've become so close. She'll be there, too, of course, as sister to the groom."

Married sister to the groom. Married sister who was also happy with her husband of almost fifteen years and four kids. According to Teague, there'd been a bump in the couple's connubial bliss earlier in the summer, which was when he'd had a brief reason to hope, but that had smoothed out now.

"I'm never going to get her, am I?" he asked, his voice low.

Polly kept her gaze on her scissors. "No, you're never going to get her." From what she'd been told, it wasn't as if Tess had even led him to believe there was a chance, not really. But he'd seen the beautiful woman on the beach, remembered her from their childhood summers at Crescent Cove and fallen like a stone in the sea. It probably had something to do with the fact that she'd been the famous face of *OM,* a chewing gum touted to "tame a wild mind." More than one adolescent boy had pinned Tess's yoga-pose poster on the inside of his closet door.

Teague bent for the scraps of paper at her feet, gathering them into a ball that he squeezed between his big hands. "So…what do you want to do before school starts?"

Find another focus besides you. It wouldn't be easy, but she figured cold turkey was the only way to go. "I'm pretty busy," she said. "I'm not sure I can commit to anything with you."

She could feel Teague's frown. "All work, no play."

"Hey," she protested. "I'm not dull." Though what else would you call four and a half years of pining after someone who only saw you as a buddy?

"Pol…" He waited until she looked over at him. "What's wrong?"

"I'm good," she said, her automatic reply. "I'm always good."

His dark brows met over his strong, straight nose. "You're Fort Knox, is what you are. Are you hiding something beneath that cheerleader disguise?"

Now it was her turn to frown. "You know I don't like it when you throw that in my face. Yes, I was on the squad. But I also ran track and was secretary of the chess club."

"What moves can the knight make?"

Shoot. Busted.

He laughed at her. "I debunked that myth on our ski trip two years ago, remember? You tried telling me then you were more than pom-poms and herky jumps."

"I think it's weird you even know what a herky jump is," she muttered.

"Sweetheart, I played football. If a cheerleader had a move, all the guys on the team knew exactly what it was. Didn't you figure that out?"

"I avoided dating football players."

He tossed the softball-sized ball of scraps from hand to hand. "Now, this is getting interesting. You're always so reticent about these kinds of details. If you didn't date football players, who *did* you date?"

"Nobody from my high school." Nobody *in* high school. Polly Weber had held secrets then, too. Confident all-American teen on the outside. On the inside, a vulnerable girl looking for validation in disastrous places. So damn needy.

And even if Polly Weber now loved a man who didn't love her back, that didn't make her the same as the insecure, self-destructive child she'd once been.

"…so I could use you," Teague was saying. "It might be beneficial to you, too."

She set her scissors in her lap. "What are you talking about?"

"I'm saying that weddings and all the attending hoopla put people in a romantic mood. Makes 'em want to pair up. You could get some potentials out of it."

"Potential…?"

Teague shook his head. "You haven't been listening. I've been laying out all the good reasons why you should go along with what I asked."

Caught up in her memories, she'd apparently missed a chunk of conversation, because she didn't recall him asking her anything. "Why don't you start over?"

"You're not afraid to date, are you?"

"What are you talking about?" She bristled. "I'm not afraid of anything."

"C'mon," Teague scoffed. "What about heights? Movies with ax murderers? You know you have that thing against clowns."

"Everybody has a thing against clowns."

"True. But my point is, you've been on a man hiatus for…what? How long has it been?"

"I have men in my life."

"They're between five and six years old, Polly. That doesn't count."

"And there's you," she heard herself blurt out.

"But I don't count, either." He waggled his eyebrows. "I'm talking men who want to…" His words died away, and a strange expression overtook his face.

"Men who want to what?"

"To do things to you that I suddenly realize make me extremely uncomfortable to picture in my mind," he finished, frowning.

"Oh." Funny, now Teague couldn't look at *her*. "I'm not averse to that kind of man." It's what she told herself she needed. A new guy. A focus other than Teague.

He was squeezing the ball of scrap paper. "So agreeing to be my plus-one will be perfect for both of us."

"What?"

"Is there cotton wool in your ears? I explained it to you. There're all these wedding things coming up. I need a date."

"Ask somebody else."

"Somebody else might think I'm interested. But you're aware that I'm still hung up on…"

"Tess."

"Yeah. I'm going to be around her all the time. I need you nearby to stop me from looking like an idiot."

The idiot was Polly, her resolve already eroding. *I need you.*

"You can meet some new people, maybe find your Mr. Right."

Attending social events with Teague at her side? How would that help her goal of walking into kindergarten class come September without the wrong man firmly dug into her heart?

"Please, Pol," he said. Then his eyes sharpened, and he lifted his hand to her face, using his thumb to rub at a spot between her brows. "No, never mind."

His hand dropped, but she caught his wrist without thinking. It was hard, strong, and her fingertips could barely meet her thumb. "Teague…"

"I made you frown. I wouldn't ask you to do anything that made you unhappy."

His skin was warm against her palm. She should release him, but it felt so good to even have this small piece of him. Her pulse thudded in her throat and she felt a dizzying lack of air. Shutting him out of her life, she suddenly realized, wasn't going to shovel him out of her heart.

That was going to require a more proactive effort.

And being his plus-one for the next month would give her a chance to track her progress. She could establish a mental grade book like the paper one she kept for her kids, where she marked the date they could tie their shoe-laces and recognize the letters of the alphabet.

She'd work toward not jumping at the sound of his voice.

Not longing for his clean, citrus scent in her lungs.

Getting through one night without an erotic dream of his whiskered cheek against her breasts.

THE PLACE WHERE SKYE felt safest at the cove was not her house—where she'd grown up—but the small property management office that was no more than one room and a door that led to an attached half bath. She'd spent a lot of time in the office during the past few months, surrounded by four walls and the sound of the surf outside. Sometimes she brought her dinner there, as she had tonight, and ate a sandwich and drank a soda while sitting at her desk.

The darkness started to deepen and she lit the bookkeeper's lamp at her elbow, then got up to move around the room, turning on another light sitting on the small table by the leather recliner that had been her father's favorite, then the overhead fixture in the bathroom. The drapes covering the two windows were already drawn. They featured a thick, insulated lining as protection against the sun, and she supposed that from the outside the little building would appear empty.

Uninteresting.

Nothing to see here.

Nobody inside to bother. To terrify.

Skye moved about the room again, surveying different items, touching them, as if they were good luck charms. First there was the movie poster from *The Egyptian,* the last picture made at Sunrise Studios by her great-great-grandparents, Max Sunstrum and Edith Essex. She'd been the actress and he'd been the director-producer of a quiver-full of popular movies that had been filmed at the cove into the late 1920s. Why Max had shut down the studio had been a mystery until last month when film student Addy had found a letter from Edith to her husband. Exhausted by the Hollywood gossip and innuendo, she had requested that they retire from the business. Rumor still persisted, however. Edith had been given a magnificent, maybe priceless piece of jewelry by one of her leading men. It was said to be hidden somewhere at the cove, though no one had caught a glimmer of it in over eighty-five years.

Mounted on the opposite wall from the movie advertisement was one of Skye's mother's plein air paintings— its "on location" style popular with the artists who flocked to the cove. She stood before it now, admiring how her mother had captured the sand, surf and a stretch of the cottages in impressionistic strokes the colors of summer. Way in the distance, at the far end of the beach depicted on the canvas, two children labored over a sand castle. You almost had to squint to see them, but Skye knew the boy was black-haired and sturdy, while the girl was more birdlike, with long brown tresses waving down her back. It was Skye and Gage.

Turning away from her mother's work, she went to the bookshelf where her collection of sand dollars sat in a glass candy jar. "'I'd be rich if I had a penny for every dollar you girls brought home,'" she murmured, repeating her father's favorite phrase. She and her sister had never tired of finding them, believing they were the currency of the merfolk.

It had been a childhood perfect for such fancies, living at the cove. There was the bustle and excitement of summer, energized by the families moving in and out of the cottages, not to mention the day visitors who came to play at the sand and water. In the off-season, the surrounding beach houses most often stood empty, but the minds of Skye and her sister did not. They'd exercised their imaginations no matter how tranquil the cove became.

Which likely only added to the disquiet she'd experience at this summer's end. Her ancestors had made movies, she and her sister had made up a thousand stories and this winter she could see herself conjuring up a bogeyman around every corner.

She'd have to leave to save her sanity. Then the other Alexanders, who loved the cove but had left it behind, would tell her it was time to place their property on the market. Even if they wanted to hold on to it for a few more years, that wouldn't make it easier on Skye, who would be miles away.

If she couldn't live here, it was no longer home.

Sighing, she returned to the chair behind the desk. In a minute or two she'd go back to her cottage, set all the locks, hang the cowbell on the doors designed to warn her of an intruder. Then she'd settle in for another night of fitful sleep. Until then...

She pulled open the right bottom drawer. Behind a stack of files was an old wooden box that had washed up onshore when she was a child. It was of some sort of resilient wood—it hadn't warped from its bath in the salt water—and it used to hold a little girl's treasures: a baby doll the size of her thumb, the shell of a turtle, a book of funny rhymes Rex Monroe had once given her. A packet of letters had been added to the contents.

As she reached for the container, her cell phone chimed. Skye started, cursed her jumpiness, then picked up the device. It was a text message, and the number wasn't familiar to her. When she tapped to open it, a photograph appeared on the screen.

An open ibuprofen bottle, a ginger ale can tipped on its side and a washcloth folded into a compress.

It could only come from one person, the man she hadn't seen since he'd walked her home last night.

She texted back: Ouch.

And Gage responded, Ur talking to me?

Feeling sorry for u.

May not deserve ur pity, but will take it. & I apologize.

Smiling a little, she stared at the cryptic sentiments. After last night, she'd wondered—worried—how their first encounter would go after the incendiary exchange at her front door.

No apology necessary, she typed. Wasn't sure u'd even remember.

She'd hoped he'd forget, actually, because then she wouldn't have to explain her reaction to what he'd said. He'd been teasing her, of course, and hadn't been subtle about it, but his words had poked at her all the same. *On my honor, I'd make you come twice before entering you.*

She was aware she'd gone big-eyed and still, stunned to her marrow.

Gage texted back, U looked as if I'd promised rats to eat ur entrails.

Making a face, she moved her thumbs over the keyboard. Game of Thrones reference?

U betcha, baby.

He'd called her that last night, in a raspy, masculine tone. *"Baby. I swear I'd do right by you, baby."* A shiver worked its way down her back and she stared at the screen, mesmerized by the memory. He'd been teasing and sexually frustrated and none of it was really aimed at her personally, but part of her, somewhere deep beneath the layers of clothes and nerves and nightmares, responded to him on a purely female, physical level. Maybe she should be glad about that, she thought.

But those tears stinging her eyes didn't feel like gladness. They felt like loss. No matter what was stirring deep inside, there was too much ice and fear between it and any man.

She'd never be able to get close to one in that way again.

Her phone pinged again. Skye?

Here.

R u ok?

Sure! The exclamation point was added for emphasis. To cover up any awkwardness he might pick up between them. She wanted him to think she was normal. Like the sanctuary of this little building, the friendship she had with Gage was another thing that made her feel secure. Normal, even.

Her damage had to remain hidden from him.

C u 2morrow? she typed.

C u then.

Her phone went quiet and, letting out a sigh, she slumped back in her chair. If these were her last weeks at the cove, then she wanted to enjoy them as best she could with the pen pal who would be on his way again soon. She'd hide her weakness, her unruly responses and anything else that might reveal too much.

On another sigh, she let her head rest against the seat cushion and wrapped her fingers around her phone. It felt warm to the touch, and she tightened her hold on what seemed like a tangible connection between herself and Gage. Maybe it was dangerous to want to hold even such a small piece of him. After all, she knew he wasn't going to stay. But then she didn't have what it took to follow up on the ache she had for him, anyway.

What if he'd arrived last summer? she wondered.

But he hadn't, and perhaps that was a boon. Perhaps this poignant pain served to underscore how futile it would be to care for a man who would never settle in one place. With one woman.

Maybe she dozed. She must have, because she was suddenly alert, heart galloping in her ears. The phone had fallen from her lax fingers to the desk. Was that what had woken her?

Her breaths were unsteady and loud in the room. Outside the office, the ocean spoke *shh shh shh,* and she struggled to heed its warning. Something was tickling at her primal brain and she carefully moved her head to look about.

All seemed normal, these four walls still her safest haven.

It was just her skittery nerves, she told herself. *Keep it together. Breathe through the anxiety. Don't be such a ridiculous goose.*

It was still summer and she couldn't afford to let the fear get the best of her so soon.

Then a new noise came from outside. It was a scraping sound. Maybe metal against wood? Like someone prying at the locked door.

Someone was trying to get in!

Her brain screeched the words in her head, and her flesh went cold. Rigor mortis seized her muscles as her gaze glued to the entrance. There was no inward sign of tampering, but that noise came again.

Scritch. Scritch. Scritch.

This time, she lurched out of the chair. Her half-paralyzed body moved with clumsy jerks as she Frankenstein'd toward the bathroom. She could lock herself inside there, she thought in urgent panic. There was a hook and an eyebolt—

—that wouldn't stop anyone.

She knew it wouldn't stop *him*.

Frozen again in fear, Skye stood in the middle of the office as horror dried her mouth and seized her lungs. That other night, she'd managed one scream before his hand had been there, fleshy and foul with bitter sweat, and then he'd gagged her with a kitchen towel. Later, she'd realized she could have yelled until she was hoarse and it wouldn't have mattered. It had been off-season and there was no one near enough to hear her over the ceaseless surf.

Scritch. Scritch. Scritch.

The sounds grated against her hypervigilant nerves. Skye's skin twitched and she stared down at her feet. *Move,* she commanded them. *Move!*

Move where? a dull voice in her head countered, resigned to what she'd been dreading all these months. *He'll just find you. He'll just touch you again. He promised he'd finish what he started.*

And then she thought of the last man who had touched

her. It wasn't him, that disgusting bastard with his stinking sweat. It had been Gage, dancing with her at Captain Crow's, making her feel like a normal woman for the first time in a very long while.

Gage. Gage!

She found herself by her desk, unaware of how she'd made it there. Snatching up the phone, she fumbled with the buttons. The screen lit, and then she managed to tap Call. His voice sounded in her ear.

Relief and fear made her head spin. "I'm at the office," she choked out. "I need you."

"What?" he said. "Skye?"

She swallowed, and then revealed everything she'd vowed to keep from him. "I don't feel safe. Help me."

CHAPTER SIX

GAGE SPRINTED UP THE BEACH. His phone was in his pocket, but he didn't pause for a 911 call, though the thought flitted through his mind. Not only was he unsure of the exact emergency, but he knew he could reach Skye way before any patrol car.

All looked quiet ahead of him. Some of the cottages had their roof-mounted canister lamps, trained to spotlight the surf, turned on, but the sand itself was shadowed and empty of people. There was a glow coming from the direction of Captain Crow's at the northern end of the cove, but Skye's office was a quarter mile south…and appeared dark and deserted as he drew closer.

As unease bubbled in his belly, he redoubled his pace while trying to maintain his calm. During his career he'd faced dozens of dire situations and always managed to keep his head. But it felt near to exploding now—his chest, too, as his heart thundered against his ribs.

"Skye!" he shouted as he leaped onto the office step. His knuckles thumped against the door. "Skye? Are you all right?"

Silence. His composure fractured, and he found himself hammering the wood with both fists. "Skye!"

More silence.

He yanked out his phone and started jabbing at the display to dial her number. Was she hurt? Had she left?

A dozen questions whirling through his fragmented mind, he almost missed the crack in the door. A yellow edge of light leaked out. "Gage?" a voice croaked.

He shoved at the wood to make room for himself. Skye gasped, but the sound didn't register over his vital need to assess the situation. Inside the brightly lit room, he blinked, getting his bearings.

Everything appeared fine. He didn't know what he'd expected. Upended furnishings? A threatening stranger? But the room looked cheerful, with everything in its normal place...

Oh, shit.

Everything in its normal place except for Skye, who'd retreated to the far corner. She slid to the floor and curled into a self-protective ball, her knees to her chest, her arms wrapping her shins, her head tucked low. The pose was so disturbing he felt a clutch at his throat.

"What the hell is going on?" he demanded in a harsh voice, then winced as she cringed, her body folding tighter as if she was trying to disappear.

His gaze sped around the room again, still finding nothing alarming. In quick strides, he made it to the bathroom doorway. The closet-sized space was empty of anything other than toilet, sink, soap and towel dispenser.

But ghostly feet were tapping up and down his spine and Skye hadn't moved. Anxiety shook his insides again, but he tried to smooth his expression as he hunkered near her. "Skye?"

She jolted as if in fear, shaking him to the core.

Keep your head, he reminded himself. *Keep her calm.*

"Skye. Honey." This time she didn't twitch a muscle, and it felt like progress. "Was...was someone here?"

He could feel her struggle to find her voice. Finally she spoke, the words low and thready. "I don't know."

Ignoring his yammering pulse, he studied what he could see of her. Sloppy, oversize clothes. Bare feet shoved into a pair of shoelace-less sneakers. Her person didn't seem to have come to any harm, but her body shuddered with a fine tremor.

"Why did you call me?" he asked.

"I want to feel safe."

Okay. "What made you feel unsafe?"

"I thought I heard someone trying to get in." Her head inched up and she peeked at him over her knees, her pupils nearly overtaking the gold band surrounding them. "Did you see anyone?"

He shook his head slowly, as if she were a wild animal that might flee if he moved too fast. "No. But let me go look again." He made to stand and her hand shot out, gave his knee a brief grip, then retracted as if she'd been burned.

"Don't leave. Don't leave me."

"All right." He blew out a silent breath of air and tried to determine what the hell he should do next. Clearly she was frightened, traumatized maybe, and he didn't want to make a misstep. Maybe her friend Polly? But Skye had called him.

Gage kept his voice gentle. "Would you like some tea? I can take you back to your house—"

"No." New tension stiffened her body. Then he saw her shoulders slump. "Maybe. In a minute."

They kept to the corner, she with her spine to the wall, he sheltering her with his bigger body. He could smell her flowers-and-water fragrance and he breathed in the scent, using the long inhale to steady his ragged pulse. She was physically fine, there was no immediate threat, but he still felt on high alert, nerves jangling. It took all his newfound patience not to leap up and pace about the room.

But he'd learned that sometimes the only power he had was that of waiting it out.

Long moments later, her chin lifted. She didn't meet his gaze. "There was no one around? You're sure?"

"I didn't see anyone. I'll check further when you're ready for me to do that."

"I heard scratching. Maybe at the lock or at the door?" The hand she used to push her hair back from her pale face still trembled.

"When you're ready," he reiterated, "I'll look." Though he wanted nothing more than to take her into his arms, he held his position. "Should I call the police?"

"No." Her hair swirled around her shoulders in adamant refusal. "It's okay. I...I guess I'll just have to go home." Placing her palms on the plaster behind her, she drew to a stand.

Gage came to his feet, as well. "Whatever you say."

But it was what she didn't say that became the sticking point. At her nod, he did scrutinize the front door and the lock. Both the wood and the device were old, pitted and scarred by their exposure to the wind and salty air. The rustic look suited the cove, but effectively hid any sign of recent tampering. Then he followed her to her house, another three-quarters of a mile south. She was maddeningly silent during the walk.

And still wordless as she unlocked the door and made to slip inside.

"Skye?" he said, astounded. That was it?

Pausing, she gave him a wan smile. "Sorry for your trouble. Thank you."

Thank you? His temper sparked. She'd scared the shit out of him—she was still scaring the shit out of him—and she expected he'd walk away without a full explanation?

"What kind of fucking friend do you think I am?" he demanded.

She flinched.

Keep your cool. Keep your head. Shoving his fists inside his pockets, he took a deliberate inhale through his nose. Then he tried again, using a gentler tone. "What kind of friend are you, who doesn't offer a pal a beverage?" Without giving her time to demur, again he pushed his way past her and shut the door, closing them both inside.

He glanced over his shoulder as he headed for her kitchen. "I'll take beer if you have it. Or some of that wine you like."

Her footsteps clapped against the hardwood as she followed him toward the room at the center of her house. When he reached the refrigerator, he yanked it open, then threw her another look.

The handle slipped through his suddenly nerveless fingers. *Oh, God.* "Skye? What is it, honey? What's wrong?"

She stood in the kitchen entry, staring inside the tiled interior of the room as if a horror movie played out on a screen he couldn't see. "This is where he tied me up," she said in a colorless voice. "I thought he'd come back tonight. I thought he'd found me at the office."

He leaped for her in a Superman bound—he must have, anyway, because one moment he was ten feet away and the next he was close enough to hear her stuttered breathing. But he wasn't sure she was completely aware of his presence, because her body swayed as she looked past him, to the table and chairs at the far end of the kitchen. "One minute I was looking through some mail, and the next, he had my arms pinned behind my back."

Gage lifted his hands to grasp her shoulders, yet halted before he made contact. *Keep your cool. Keep your head.* "Maybe we should go somewhere else, honey. No. 9? Or leave the cove altogether?"

"Not yet." Her gaze flicked to his. "I'm not leaving the cove yet."

"The living room, then."

"No," she said, and color flagged her pale cheeks. "*No. I grew up in this kitchen. I have a lot more happy memories here than bad ones."

He stepped aside as she walked past him, her stride resolute. "I carved pumpkins on that counter. We had a family dinner every night at that table." She made it to the refrigerator, rummaged around and came out with a couple of beers. "You okay with one of these?"

"I'm not okay!" He wasn't okay with any of this. "Jesus Christ, Skye, what the hell have you been hiding from me?"

He saw her fingers tighten on the long necks of the bottles as her gaze drifted to her feet. "I haven't shared this with anyone—besides the police, that is. I don't want to—"

"What happened?"

Her eyes jumped to his. "I—I was the victim of a home invasion. Five months ago a pair of men broke into the house."

Stunned, Gage just stared. Skye frowned, muttered, "You asked," then made her way to the wooden table, where she dropped the beers with a *clack.* In a jerky movement, she pulled out one of the chairs and took a seat. Her hand trembled a little as she drew one bottle toward her.

Gage sat down across from her and allowed seven seconds of silence to pass by. Then he couldn't stand it any longer. *"What the hell happened?"*

"I don't—"

"What. The. Hell. Happened?"

Her gaze flicked to him, flicked away. "Fine, then," she said, sounding angry.

He liked the fury much better than the fear. "Spit it out, Skye."

"It was late one night. The off-season. I was in here, flipping through mail like I said, when a man grabbed me from behind. There were two, but only one...only one was *him*."

"Someone you recognized?"

"No." She shook her head. "In the glimpse I had of them before I was blindfolded, one wore a ball cap and bandannas over his face. The other, a ski mask. That one, he went through the house, searching drawers and cupboards—presumably looking for stuff to sell. The first man—" She broke off.

Five months ago they'd been regular correspondents. "Why didn't you tell me any of this? You wrote me about a dozen important moments in your life."

She smiled a little. "And a hundred unimportant ones."

But those had brought them close, too. He'd read and reread every detail under a sputtering lightbulb, and the accounts of everything from her first date at fifteen to her current fight with the cable company had made him sure he knew her like he knew his own heart. "You kept this from me," he said.

"What was I supposed to say?" Skye asked, lifting a slender hand. "'Dear Gage, unsettling situation here. A man blindfolded me, gagged me, tied me up. Then he used a knife to slice off my clothes. I was...touched. Threatened sexually. I was sure I was going to be raped.'"

Gage shot to his feet so fast his chair tipped, the back slamming to the floor. Skye jumped, and he cursed himself for betraying his upset. *Keep your head. Keep your cool.* Leaning down, he retrieved the chair. With it returned to its upright position, he sank back down and ran his hands through his hair.

Feeling slightly more in control, he met her gaze. "How bad were you hurt, honey?" he asked in his gentlest voice.

"I was scared out of my mind," she admitted. "He enjoyed that, I think. As he ran a knife over my skin he spent a lot of time talking about what would come next."

Gage could hardly breathe. "What did come next?"

"The searcher returned to the kitchen and hauled my—my molester into the living room. From what I could tell, he was honestly appalled by his partner's actions. They had a low-voiced argument, and then they left. I managed to inch the chair to the landline phone, work a hand free and call 911."

Sweet Jesus. Gage picked up the sweating bottle of beer and rolled it across his forehead. "I assume they didn't catch the men?"

She shook her head. "No fingerprints, no clues left behind."

What remained instead was Skye's lingering fear. "How have you managed after that?"

"I..." She bit her bottom lip. "It's like I said. I have many more good memories than bad. And in the summer…the cottages are full and people are having fun on the beach and it's almost as if it never happened."

Except for when it wasn't like that, he realized…when a strange noise or unbidden memory would reach out to catch her. Catch Gage's girl, the talisman that had kept him sane. The lodestar that had brought him safely home.

He rubbed his temples. "What now?"

"Now?"

"I won't just leave you here."

Some expression he couldn't name crossed her face. "You're going to just leave me here before September ends. We both know that."

"I mean right now. Skye—"

"Don't worry. I get through these little upsets. I'm accustomed to spooking myself." She got to her feet. "Let me see you out."

He stared up at her, disgruntled by the dismissal. "What if I want the beer?"

"You don't want the beer."

What he didn't want was this! Skye, his Skye, having gone through such a thing. *"I was…touched. Threatened sexually. I was sure I would be raped."* His gaze took in the stubborn set of her chin, then ran over her camouflaged figure in the masculine, too-large clothes.

He'd told Griffin she wasn't a woman to him, but now he hurt for her because he understood why she was pretending she wasn't a woman to herself, either. "Oh, honey," he murmured. "I hate what he did to you."

"Me, too."

"Nightmares?" he asked, well acquainted with the monsters the dark held.

"Some." Then she yanked on the hem of her oversize

sweatshirt, her gaze on her shoes. "And you probably realize I…cover up."

"The experience left you cold?"

Her head jerked up, her gaze met his. "Yes. I'm cold, outside and inside. When people—men—look at me I remember the feel of his eyes on me, the scrape of the knife along my skin, the rough touch of his hands. I hear his voice and think of what he promised to do and I feel cold and dirty and ugly. I'm no longer Skye. I'm something—someone I don't even like to see in the mirror."

Rage at the man who'd done this to her bubbled in Gage's belly like black tar. But he kept his voice level and calm. "You're still there. Not one of your warm, womanly pieces have been lost. They're just playing it safe for now."

"Sure." She gave him a disbelieving half smile, then turned to leave the kitchen. "I'm going to be okay. I just need some rest."

What else could he do but trail her to her front door? Still, when he got there, he paused, rage and sympathy and impotence churning in his gut. He'd been beyond powerless for two weeks, and despised every moment of it, but he'd go through that experience again ten times over if he could erase Skye's pain.

"Are you really going to be okay?" he asked.

"For the summer, yes. Not so sure how I'll do once the cove goes quiet again."

He frowned. "Meaning?"

"I may not stay here," she said with a shrug.

Her words rocked him. No Skye at the cove? It was like imagining the summer without sun. The ocean without waves. Seagulls without wings.

"Where would you go?" he asked.

"A nunnery, maybe," she said with another unamused half smile, "as permanent celibacy seems a definite possibility."

Oh, Skye. Staring down at her small, serious face, he could no longer hold himself apart from her. Touching was imperative. Murmuring something that was half apology, half reassurance, he reached out and pulled her to him.

She stiffened, but he held firm. "Let me," he said against her hair. "Let me do this." And when, after another moment, she relaxed against his chest he closed his eyes and breathed out a grateful prayer even as he breathed in her sweet, lovely scent.

It seemed like the most natural thing in the world to draw his lips along her soft hair to the tender skin at her temple. He dropped a baby kiss there, just the slightest press of his mouth to the fluttering pulse that he then felt compelled to taste with his tongue.

Skye quivered at the damp contact and her chin lifted. As they stared into each other's eyes, an urgency rose in him, a breathless insistence not unlike that he'd felt when he'd been running up the sand. Running to her.

And now that he had her…

He lost his head.

Gage's mouth came down on hers. His fingers tightened on her upper arms, but instead of fighting him, her body yielded, going boneless. He reassured her anyway. "This is me," he said against her mouth, then licked the seam of her lips.

They parted, and she quivered in his hold.

He didn't make any quick moves with his tongue. He just toyed with her mouth, painting the soft surfaces, sucking on the plump upper curve, letting her feel the edge of his teeth as he delicately bit the lower one. She was panting, her breath hot against his chin, and when he heard her moan...

He plunged.

She made a sound deep in her throat. With one arm around her waist, he gathered her closer and fed on her mouth. It was crazy, this intense need to have her, to know her flavor so intimately, but it had him in its thrall. She seemed equally absorbed, her lips still open to him, his shirt tangled in the grip of her fingers. When he broke to allow them air, she stayed glued against him, her body heat mingling with his.

Nuzzling her hair, he knew the moment the brief spell broke. A small whimper sounded. Her hands dropped. She stepped out of his arms.

Without a protest, he let her go.

"That shouldn't have happened," she said.

When she meant she hadn't thought it *could* happen. Skye hadn't believed that she could—even for a moment—lose herself and her lingering terror in the pleasure of a man's kiss.

In Gage's kiss.

"That *really* shouldn't have happened." She took another step back, a panicked expression on her face.

Gage, on the other hand, felt calm and centered for the first time since receiving her call, his next steps clear in his mind. He owed Skye in ways she'd never know, and he'd make payment on the debt by convincing her that the sweet fire had been no aberration.

Her sexuality still burned, and he would be the one to prove it to her. Not only because it was obvious an attraction ran between them, but because he knew he had her trust.

He wouldn't break it. Instead, he'd do everything in his power to reassure her she was still a woman. What else were friends for?

SKYE HAD GOTTEN DRESSED before dawn, determined to get started on an idea she'd come up with weeks before. With a cup of coffee downed, she was caffeinated enough to put her muscles into pushing the living room furniture to the center of the floor. Next, she rolled up the hall runner. Following that, she stacked the kitchen chairs atop the table. Old sheets served as tarps to cover the furniture and then she retrieved the tools from the garage: rollers, pan and brushes. She was lugging in cans of lemon-chiffon-colored paint when she heard someone at her front door.

Pulse tripping, Skye froze. Every instinct she had told her who stood on the other side. Those same instincts warred with each other in loud demand: *Pretend you're not home! Welcome him in!*

Part of her was relieved he now knew the truth. She wouldn't have to paper over her odd edginess. He'd understand her jumpy nerves and aversion to being touched.

Except she'd let him touch her last night.

Kiss her.

And she'd managed not to faint in panic.

Another thump sounded on the door. "I hear your brain whirring in there, Skye," Gage called through the wood. "Take a deep breath and let me in."

Still, she hesitated.

"I bear fancy coffee."

Feeling ridiculous, she set down the cans and made her way toward the door. One comfort kiss from him didn't mean he anticipated another. She'd probably been a lousy partner in the whole thing, she thought, turning the knob. Had she even responded? She only remembered *absorbing*—his heat, his strength, his exotic-spice smell.

A blush crawled up her neck as she pulled open the door. Her heart stuttered as she took in the sight of him, breeze-ruffled dark hair, piercing blue-green eyes, faint smile on his lips. His alert gaze gave her an intense study and she suspected he could see every toss and turn, every sleepless minute, every second thought she'd had since bidding him good-night.

She shouldn't have called him from the office.

She shouldn't have shared her secret.

She shouldn't have let him kiss her.

"Stop thinking so much," he advised, stepping over the threshold. He placed a cardboard cup in her hand.

"Thank you," she said, sniffing at the rich scent of fresh grounds. "How far did you have to go for this?"

"Captain Crow's."

Her eyes rounded. "They don't open until eleven."

"Unless you're me, and you strike up a conversation with the prep cook who starts work at seven."

"Ah."

"Get your mind out of the gutter," he said, uncurling his forefinger from around his own cup to point it at her. "His name is George and he has a wife and three kids."

"My mind's not in the gutter!" Well, not since she woke from a twenty-minute midnight doze during which she'd imagined herself stretched out on her bed, Gage standing at its foot, slowly stripping off his clothes.

He grinned at her, then reached into his front pocket to pull free a slim camera. Still juggling his coffee, he managed to bring the viewfinder to his eye and snap a shot. "I'll call it 'Guilty as Charged.'"

"That's an invasion of privacy," she said, frowning at him.

"I think that blush indicates that you've been mentally invading mine."

"Gage!"

He laughed. "Relax. Nobody will see the photo but the two of us."

"I don't want *you* looking at me," she grumbled.

Ignoring her, he took a slow perusal of the living room. "What's going on?"

She swallowed a mouthful of coffee. "I've been planning on repainting some rooms, rearranging the furniture in others. Sort of..."

"Reclaiming your territory?"

"Yes," she said, grateful that no more explanation was necessary. He understood her so well. "Yes, exactly."

"You should have written to me when it happened," he said, his voice low. "I would have done something, anything—"

"Gage, you were thousands of miles away."

"I know, but—" He blew out a frustrated breath. "But I can do something now. Let me help. Let me help you paint. I'm the best furniture mover you'll ever meet."

She sent him a skeptical glance. "Don't you have better things to do?"

"Actually, no. You'd be doing me a favor. I get tired of my own company pretty quickly these days."

It was her turn to study him. "That's a surprise. As you've pointed out before, your job means you spend a lot of time alone."

He lifted a shoulder. "Too much time, it seems. Give me a paint roller, Skye, I'm begging you."

What could she do when her pen pal put it like that?

And the fact was, his assistance helped her in more ways than one. Not only was he tall, skilled with tools and willing to do whatever asked, but being around him leached the awkwardness she'd been feeling over the kiss, even though they started work in separate rooms. She took the kitchen and he the living room.

They expected to meet in the hallway.

But before that, she caught him taking more pictures. "What are you doing?" she said, craning to look at him from her place on a stepladder.

"Just practicing. I haven't held a camera in weeks."

Weird. Because she remembered him never being without one since he was nine or ten. "Why not?"

He shrugged, and snapped again. She thought he'd focused on the back of her hand, speckled with pale yellow paint freckles. "That can't be pretty," she said.

"In the eye of the beholder," he commented as he wandered off.

Half an hour later, she brought him a cold glass of iced tea. He'd opened the front door so that the breeze cleared out some of the paint fumes. Her gaze was drawn to it, and she tried to quell her instant quake of worry. Usually it was double-locked and dead-bolted. At night she hung a cowbell from the knob.

"I'm between you and your nightmares," he murmured, taking the glass she proffered.

As she glanced away from the concerned look in his eyes, her gaze snagged on the camera he'd left on top of the sheet-draped sofa. She cleared her throat. "I never asked—how did professional photography come about?"

He pursed his lips, appearing to think. "I suspect it all begins with Rex Monroe."

"Rex?" He was ninety-something years old, and a

longtime resident of the cove. A Pulitzer Prize–winning war correspondent, he'd complained about the Lowell twins every year they'd summered at Beach House No. 9.

"He was annoyed with me and Griffin one fog-shrouded afternoon. We were wrestling and yelling at each other in his yard. If I remember correctly, he yanked us into his house by the scruff of our necks and told us we needed to better ourselves instead of batter our brother."

Skye laughed. "He has a way with words."

"In his study, he had an old manual typewriter and sitting next to it, a Kodak Brownie camera. It was a classic even then, something he'd had since the 1950s, but he…he let me touch it. Showed me how to use it. Griff was engrossed with putting letters onto paper, but that Brownie…the world looked different to me through its lens."

"Different how?"

"I controlled it." He finished off his tea and set the empty glass on the windowsill. "I could cut away the parts that didn't fit my vision. I could focus on the subjects *I* thought needed to be seen. The appeal of that never left me."

"So in college…"

"I studied political science, not photography. But one spring break I went with a philanthropic group to Mexico with the intention of building a school by day and drinking tequila by night. We were there when the region was shaken by a magnitude-7.9 earthquake. The photos I took were the first that made it out…and they were the beginning of making my reputation."

"And you continued globe-trotting and taking photographs," Skye said. She didn't know why the words made her melancholy. Gage had found his place in the world, just as her place was here at the cove. Or *had* been at the cove.

Okay, melancholy explained.

A crease dug between his eyebrows. "What's wrong, honey?"

She didn't want to say the words. *This all ends here. We'll never again be at this place together.*

Once summer's over, we'll never again be together anywhere.

Still frowning, he approached her slowly. She didn't move; her feet felt weighted to the floor, made as heavy as her heart by the notion that this was the aching end of everything. "Skye," he whispered, and his fingers were just as gentle as his voice when he pushed a wisp of hair off her forehead.

"Don't," she whispered back, feeling as if she were teetering on the edge of the tall bluff at the south end of the cove, with only cold water and jagged rocks to welcome her at the bottom. *Don't push me. I'll never survive the fall.*

Instead of obeying her unspoken words, Gage stepped closer.

She jerked back, her pulse rocketing.

He only smiled. "Sweet Skye. Don't worry, I'm not going to kiss you again." Then he leaned around her to grab a rag draped on the sheet-shrouded wing chair behind her.

"I didn't... I don't—"

His second smile held more mischief. "Unless you ask me to, that is."

Pulse still racing, Skye stared after him as he returned to work, unsure of her reaction to his provocative statement. Was it relief...or disappointment?

CHAPTER SEVEN

TEAGUE WHITE WAS ZONED OUT, staring into his beer, when a voice found its way into his consciousness. "Hey, you okay?"

He looked up, coming back to the present. August evening. Captain Crow's deck. Tables pushed together and a big gathering of friends drinking, laughing, talking, as part of the ongoing dual celebration of Gage Lowell's vacation and his twin Griffin's impending nuptials.

His gaze slid to the questioner. It was the bride-to-be, Jane Pearson, who was seated near him along with her fiancé. Skye, Polly and Gage were gathered at his table, as well. "Sorry," he said. "I'm a little out of it. Didn't get much sleep last night." There'd been no down time during his last twenty-four-hour shift.

Polly studied his face. "Work was tough?"

He grunted, then took up his beer for a swallow.

"I don't know how you do it, Teague," Jane said. "You go from 'tough' hours on the job and slide right into party time."

Griffin leaned back in his chair. "I once did a story on Doctors Without Borders," he said. "The men and women engaged in that kind of work are experts at leaving the dark stuff on a high shelf."

"I suppose you have to separate yourself in some way," Jane murmured.

Teague was saved from examining his psyche by the sound of female laughter at the other end of the conjoined tables. They all looked over to see Tess Quincy pulling her recalcitrant husband up by the elbow. His grumbles only made her laugh harder.

God, she was beautiful, Teague thought.

At thirty-three, she was no longer the long-legged girl he'd admired from afar when they were both kids summering at the cove. And she wasn't the gorgeous nineteen-year-old star of TV commercials who'd become the unexpected darling of the country. He'd had her poster hanging in his bedroom. Her image had been the screen saver on his very first laptop.

When he'd run into her on the sand in front of No. 9 in June, he'd almost thought it was the beach house's purported magic that had conjured her there. For him. He'd fallen fast.

Now, as he watched her husband, David, follow her onto the dance floor, he didn't wish that the two of them hadn't reconciled. Clearly, the man doted on her. Tess radiated happiness. But he couldn't help feeling a little sorry for himself.

"Hey, honey pie," Griffin said to his almost-bride. "It's your song."

"As covered by Teague's first love," Skye put in.

"What?" Curiosity sparked in Polly's big blue eyes. "Do tell."

Teague shifted in his chair and cursed the DJ who'd decided to play The Jewels' cover of Cowboy Junkie's cover of Velvet Underground's "Sweet Jane." "Can we talk about something else?"

"Not while I'm alive," Polly said, flashing him one of her brilliant smiles. Then she turned to Skye, whom he'd known all *his* life—which was clearly much too long. "Spill."

"Now that I consider it," Skye said, tapping her chin with a finger, "it's his second *big* love. The first was the exchange student from Belgium who attended our high school junior year. He moped for months after she returned home to the land of waffles and chocolate. Then—"

"I had other girlfriends," he declared over her, annoyed.

"But no one you really flipped for until Amethyst Lake came into your life."

Polly hooted. "Amethyst Lake? That sounds like an anime character."

"Her real name was Amy Lake," Teague said stiffly. "Amethyst is her stage name. She's the singer for The Jewels."

His best-friend-who-was-a-girl continued to snicker. "When was this?"

"It was...five years ago?" Skye posited. "Right before you two met, Amethyst and her group left on tour, never to return."

"Wow," Gage said admiringly. "It's the stuff of fantasy, dating the hot lead of an all-girl rock band."

"Why didn't anyone ever tell me?" Polly demanded of Skye, then turned to Teague. "Why didn't *you* tell me?"

The back of his neck was burning. "Let's talk about someone else. Surely I'm not the only person with a romance he or she would rather forget."

Gage raised his eyebrows in the direction of his sister-in-law-to-be. "I heard that Jane dated the famous author Ian Stone."

Griffin leaned forward, sending his brother a hard look. "We don't speak of Ian Stone."

"Jeez, okay," he said, hands up. His gaze roamed the table. "Polly, you look like a girl with a torrid history."

Teague nearly snorted. She looked like a girl who won the Girl Scout cookie prize and celebrated by sharing an ice-cream soda with the boy voted most likely to become a Jesuit priest. "Polly's closemouthed about her past, but you gotta assume it's so clean it squeaks."

Skye elbowed her friend. Teague glanced over at the movement, caught her whisper. "Wait, doesn't he know about—"

"Girl dance!" Polly called, her gaze avoiding Teague as she yanked Skye from the table by the hand. The beat of The Weather Girls' "It's Raining Men" was rocking through the speakers. "Jane, you come, too."

And so, before he could completely assimilate the "doesn't he know about," the women were gone, deserting the men for the small parquet floor, where they shook their asses and shimmied their shoulders in ways you only saw in movies like *Dirty Dancing* or when females were partnered with each other. Teague stared. He didn't know Polly had those moves in her.

"I used to think watching that was hot in junior high," Gage commented. "It only gets better as I age."

"Or as you get hornier," his brother said. "Making any progress on the Gorge?"

Gage scowled at his twin. "Like Ian Stone, we won't speak of it."

"Oh, hell," Griffin said, groaning. "That's a bad sign. And I promised Jane I'd warn you again about getting involved with Skye. As in, don't. Is that what's going on?"

Skye? She was his friend, too. Teague looked between the twins.

"It's none of your business," Gage said.

"You don't know—"

"I know much more than you do." Gage tossed back the rest of his beer. "Don't mess with me on this, Griff."

The tense atmosphere was palpable. Teague glanced over his shoulder, compelled to check on the women, and happened to catch the segue from rock beat to the slow groove of blues. The women slowed, too, and a man sitting at a table behind Polly gave her the obvious one-two and rose from his chair.

Teague didn't know what got into him, but he had his hands on her before the other guy could introduce himself. He immediately took her in his arms and side-stepped her away from her would-be partner, even as Polly's clearly surprised face turned up to his. Yeah, he was a little flabbergasted himself.

By how good it felt to hold her like this.

Had they never danced together?

He tried to remember as they swayed to the sultry rhythm of "At Last" by Etta James, and supposed not. They'd hiked together, skied, taken road trips with bicycles. Pal stuff, and often as part of a larger group of friends.

"You're small," he said. He thought of her as athletic and energetic, but under his hands, he could feel her delicate bone structure. Her face was all female, of course, the clean lines of her features dressed up with the blond hair and blue eyes. But he'd never noticed how incredibly…feminine she was. He glanced down the space between their bodies. She wore some kind of filmy, hippy-style top with jeans. Strappy shoes, with a platform that elevated her height by several inches, revealed her slim, slightly tanned bare feet.

She had adorable toes. Every nail was painted blue, yellow or a combination of the two, and each one was different from the other. A silver ring circled the second toe on her left foot, a tiny enameled butterfly poised atop it as if ready for flight.

His gaze traveled back to her face. "You're such a girl." He knew it sounded as if he'd just discovered the fact, which wasn't true. From the first he'd known she was female and hell, he'd been a little proud of himself for having such a close friendship with someone from the opposite sex.

But he'd managed that by rarely thinking about her at the same time as…well, sex.

Now that he'd taken in those painted toes, that butterfly, the absolute America's Sweetheart-ness of her face… *Shit*.

Her sandy eyebrows drew together and she frowned at him, the corners of her pink mouth turning down. "What's this all about?" she asked.

He didn't know. He couldn't explain it. But things just didn't seem the same with her slim fingers in his and his palm molding the curve of her waist. "Uh…"

She sighed. "Is this your chance to get close to Tess?" she whispered.

Who? "Oh, Tess."

Rolling her eyes, Polly shifted so that he had a different view of the dance floor over her shoulder. "Get your fix," she murmured. And there was the beautiful Tess in his line of sight, a smile on her face as she pressed her cheek to her husband's shoulder.

"Better now?" Polly asked.

"Perfect," Teague said, pulling her a little nearer and closing his eyes. "Exactly right." He let himself enjoy her for another long minute.

Then, to prove Griffin was onto something, Teague took a breath and eased Polly and her newly acknowledged femininity away. He imagined himself putting them on the highest mental shelf he had, where all disconcerting and disturbing memories and events belonged.

GAGE LIFTED HIS ARMS overhead and twisted from side to side as he and Skye walked up the beach. They'd decided on a visit to the tide pools, and had just passed Captain Crow's in time to witness the five o'clock conch cell ceremony. Not thirty minutes ago, they'd completed her paint-and-rearrangement project after three days of joint effort.

It was good to be outside, though they were among a throng—formed in large groups or gathered in small clusters—enjoying an afternoon on the sand. In August, as was fitting, summer brought its A game to Crescent Cove. The blue sky was tempura-paint bright and the sun smiled like a benign god from its place within it. The ocean's waves raced each other to kiss the feet of little kids who dragged buckets of wet sand and beach treasure through the foam. The air tasted like a salty treat, and even the breeze was warm, coloring Skye's cheeks pink and her mouth rosy.

She glanced up, as if feeling his regard, and tucked an errant strand of hair back into the tight braid she wore down her back. "You should send me a bill."

"What? Why?"

"I owe you for all the hours you put in," Skye said.

"It's nothing—" he started, then had to grab her elbow and tug her back, saving her from being plowed over by a young man carrying his bikini-clad girl toward the surf. She shrieked, mock-beating at him, and they watched as he strode into the water. When he reached waist-height, he dropped her. A second later, he disappeared into the depths, too, either the victim of a sea monster or a sharp yank on the ankle.

Skye laughed—a little wistful?—and moved forward again.

Gage trailed behind, following her zigzagging movements as she avoided sunbathers, Frisbee tossers and sandcastles under construction. Her feet stuttered a little as she encountered a couple entwined on a blanket, clearly having forgotten their public surroundings.

She gave Gage a quick glance and then sidestepped the lovers' blanket. On his way to do the same, he managed to jiggle the Love God's foot as he passed. The other man's head jerked up and he glared over his shoulder. "Small children," Gage reminded the guy. "Grandmas."

As they continued onward, Skye smiled at him and rocked her thumb toward her chest. "Grateful."

He grinned back. "No problem. But I don't blame him. It's easy to get carried away on a day like today."

"I'll take your word for it." She came to a halt as they reached the first of the tide pools cut into the rock. Bending her knees, she squatted at the edge, moving easily in her usual baggy uniform, this time a pair of carpenter's pants three sizes too big and a long-sleeved T-shirt that could have fit him.

He hunkered beside her, taking in the little world created by the low tide. Sea stars, a scuttling hermit crab, little silver fish he couldn't name. Colorful anemones were doing their thing, waving their tentacles as a way to draw their prey toward their mouths.

"Oops! Watch out!" a voice called from behind them, and they both turned, just in time to avoid a collision with a bowlegged toddler chasing a rubber ball. The red orb landed in the tide pool with a splash, and Gage saved the kidlet from taking the same path by hooking an arm around the little boy's waist.

"Thank you," said a woman, a mere breath behind him. Her hair was the same auburn as the child's and she immediately plucked him from Gage's hold. "Jamie! You need to listen to Mommy," she scolded her son, who was practicing for teenhood by pretending she didn't exist. "Thank you," she repeated, then thanked Skye, too, who retrieved the ball from the water and handed it over.

"Adorable," Gage commented, watching as the young mother headed off, the little guy on her hip.

"Which one?"

He frowned at Skye, but she was back to perusing the tide pool. "I don't look at every woman as possible…date material. I was talking about the boy."

"I guess I didn't suspect you thought much about little kids."

"I've got three nephews and a niece. I like them a lot."

She glanced at him. "But you don't want children of your own."

"I'd be a piss-poor parent, what with all the travel and the nature of the job," Gage said. "What about you?"

With careful footsteps, she picked her way over to the next pool. "I had the best childhood ever, here at the cove. Sure, I wanted to pass that on."

Wanted. Past tense. Gage walked up behind her, giving in to the urge to run his palm along the warm surface of her sleek, long braid. "But not now?"

She crouched low, still looking into the water and not

at him. "Maybe if I could make babies like sea anemones. Some of them just divide in half to reproduce."

"Well, shoot. That takes all the fun out of it."

"If you say so." She ran her fingertips over the surface of the pool, then released a little sigh. "I wish…"

He hunkered beside her again, and made another near-ghostly pass at her braid. She twitched a little but didn't protest. "You wish?" he prompted.

"I'd like to feel normal again," she confessed under her breath. Then her already pink cheeks went red from embarrassment as she flicked him a glance. "Forget I said that, okay?"

"Why? Of course you'd like to feel normal again." He hesitated, wondering if now was the time to bring up a maybe-touchy subject. "Skye…I'd like to help."

"What?" She shot him a second glance.

"I'd like to help you get over your…aversion."

Her color deepened. "I wasn't begging for a volunteer."

"It's an offer. An offer to see if I can help you past this."

"I don't need your pity," she said, shaking her head.

"That's not what I feel for you, Skye." What he did feel was tenderness, consideration and…and an odd, almost vital need. Maybe it was arrogant of him, but he thought he could do something for her. He *needed* to try to do something for her.

"What would you get out of it?" she grumbled.

"I liked kissing you."

Now she stared straight into the tide pool as if it held the mysteries of the universe…or because it was a convenient way to avoid his eyes. "You told me you wouldn't do that again."

"I said it would have to be your idea," he corrected.

"But let's take kissing off the table for now. Just come back with me to No. 9. I have something there you should see."

"Is it porn? I never liked porn."

He laughed. "No, it's not porn. Your opinion of me is very low, by the way. I don't pull out the porn until the third, maybe fourth date."

When she rolled her eyes, he laughed again and then curled his fingers around her elbow to lift her to her feet. "What do you have to lose?"

"My self-respect."

He bent close to her ears. "Or your self-restraint. Give yourself a chance to let go a little, Skye." His fingers went to work on the band at the end of her braid.

"What are you doing?"

He sifted through the strands, releasing them from their tight binding. "Let the wind catch your hair, honey. You look so pretty with it a little wild."

It swirled around her shoulders as they walked to the opposite end of the cove. An awkward silence tried to wedge between them, but Gage wasn't having it. He reached down and took her hand in a firm grip, though was unsurprised when she immediately tried slipping free. "Just relax," he said.

"I can't believe I'm doing this," she muttered.

"There's no 'doing' to worry about," he reassured her. "I told you that. I just want you to look at something I've been working on. It might make a difference."

"Gage—"

"It's worth a try, right? If it goes wrong, then it's just me, good ol' pen pal Gage." *And if it goes right?* a voice whispered in his head. *What then?* How far would he let things go? He didn't know.

By the time they made it to the southern end of the cove, she appeared half relaxed, half resigned. "I won't hold this against you," she said. Then added, "Unless it's porn."

He lifted a brow as he unlocked the sliding door leading into the living room from the deck. "You're sure hung up on that."

"I am not!"

With his fingertips at the small of her back, he ushered her inside. "There's no shame in being visually stimulated." He smiled as she glanced at him over his shoulder. "I'm sorta counting on it, honey."

"It *is* porn."

He laughed, and then grasped her by the shoulders and propelled her into the small room he used as an office. The space was shadowy, drapes over the windows to prevent a glare on the screen of his laptop, which sat on the desk. He pulled out the large office chair before it and pushed Skye onto its wide seat.

Tapping a few keys brought the device to life and brought up the image he wanted to show her. When it appeared, she froze. "It's me," she said.

It was. He'd started with a photo he'd taken of her at twilight, standing on the beach. The sky, the ocean, the sand were all different gradations of gray and Skye was silhouetted against them from behind. He had some mad photo-editing skills, if he did say so himself, and he'd whittled her out of the sloppy clothes so she was a womanly outline. While her head, hands and feet were an opaque black, she appeared to be dressed in a colorful, patchwork quilt catsuit. Except—

"Oh." She'd figured it out, already mousing over one of the small shapes of the "quilt." It bloomed bigger as she hovered on it and there was the photograph of a seagull he'd caught in soaring flight.

Her hand moved and another image went from tiny to large. It was part of one of her letters to him, the "Dear Gage" in her distinctive handwriting, the one that always sent a wash of warmth and anticipation through him when he saw it on a yet-unopened envelope.

Her fingers traced over the mouse pad, opening new images: Captain Crow's martini flag; covers of her favorite books, from Ian Stone to George R. R. Martin; a photo of one of her mother's plein air paintings; a child leashed to a boogie board, emerging from the surf.

"When did you do this?" she demanded. "You've been at my house helping me."

"I don't sleep much." No sense giving the nightmares time to take hold.

"Oh, Gage." She sat back, staring at the latest thumbnail she'd expanded. It was her house, looking cheerful and welcoming with its potted lemon tree and flower-covered trellis.

"All those things are still inside you, Skye," he said gently. "All the things that make you special. That make this place special. No one can take any of them away."

With a quick movement, she popped out of the chair. It swiveled and the seat bumped her forward, but she didn't seem to need the encouragement to step near and give him a hug. It was friendly. Sisterly.

He had no reason to expect more.

But he wanted more. For her.

Disentangling himself, he stepped around Skye and took the chair. "I did another for you." *All for you.*

He called up a second screen, a second image. Skye

again. The twilight, the patchwork catsuit. But the thumbnails were of a different type. More personal. Intimate.

As he hovered over one, glancing back to read her reaction, a realization seized him. This wasn't just for her. It was for him, too.

CHAPTER EIGHT

SKYE STARED AT THIS NEW representation of herself. The other had been dressed in bright colors and she'd been delighted when she expanded the shapes to discover they were really cove flowers, cove people, cove comfort. She hadn't viewed them all yet, but she knew they'd each bring a smile to her face. A grin, actually, because Gage had chosen them for her.

But these, these were not strictly Gage's choice—in the same sense.

Because they were her. All her.

He hovered over one thumbnail, and the photo enlarged. Flesh-toned, a soft-angled curve.

Skye swallowed. "That's my ankle bone."

"Pretty feet," he said.

The next, a slice of the small of her back. She must have been reaching, painting a high spot, probably, because the hem of her shirt was raised. The too-big pants hung low on her hips. And there was the curve of her waist, the scoop just above the dimples of her butt.

That place prickled now. She moved from her spot behind Gage's chair, surprisingly drawn though not one part of her body had brought her pleasure in months. Her breath drew in quick as he snaked an arm about her and tugged her down to his lap.

She would have jumped away, if at the same moment

he hadn't expanded another thumbnail. There was her hand, with the yellow paint freckles, and it looked funny and oddly sweet and reminded her of how well they had worked together. How hard he had worked to make her comfortable with him.

Her fingers stretched toward the mouse pad. He let her control the unveiling then, and she opened new photographs, all of herself. There was the feathery dark fringe of her eyelashes, the slender column of her neck, the defenseless curve of her palm, her fingers half curled over it as if she cradled something precious inside.

She frowned. "When did you take that?" The hand looked so...vulnerable.

"When you had a little catnap yesterday after lunch."

Uneasiness trickled through her. That was the second time she'd fallen asleep when she was alone with him. It shouldn't be possible—but it had been from the very first. Despite the anxiety she'd been suffering from for months, deep inside, below the defenses and the fears, she trusted him.

Of course she trusted him. This was her friend. Her pen pal Gage.

Still, she saw that her fingers shook a little as she hovered over yet another small rectangle. It bloomed, and there was her mouth, tender-looking, half parted. As if in expectation of a kiss.

Skye's chest tightened and heat washed over her skin. Her lips, the real ones, tingled. That low-belly clenching was back. Nerves—no, she knew what it was. She'd acknowledged it days ago.

Desire.

It raced through her blood, making her heart bang

against her ribs like the clapper on a bell sending out tidings of…of gladness.

She was so glad that she wanted to kiss. To kiss Gage.

The air disappeared as she slowly turned her head to look at him. Even in the dim room, his incredible eyes smoldered with a soft heat and he studied her face with an intensity that made her shiver.

Yet he didn't make a move. She was still surrounded by him, his thighs hard beneath her, his chest rising and falling as it took in oxygen she couldn't find. But he remained still as that burning, ardent want made its way through her system.

"Gage…" she whispered. When she licked her lips, his gaze followed the movement. "I…"

He touched her cheek with one fingertip. That tiny point of contact unspooled another ribbon of heat that rippled across her skin. "All for you," he said, his voice quiet. "Whatever you want."

She wanted that kiss.

Shifting on his lap, she moved into better position, sitting sideways across his legs.

He watched her without comment. When her hands gripped the solid heaviness of his shoulders, she felt a twitch beneath her bottom. It stopped her for a moment, the evidence of his arousal reminding her he was flesh and blood. A man.

A voice began whispering in the back of her mind, getting louder with each passing second. *His* voice. The scrape of a cold blade against her even colder skin. A cruel, groping hand on her breast. *"You like that? You'll like what's next even better."*

She trembled, her fingers tightening on the slope of

muscle and bone that was so big, so masculine, so much more powerful—

"Come back, Skye," Gage murmured. "Come back to me."

And like that, she was returned to the moment, back with her pen pal, her friend, the one who could see inside her. Who knew her well enough to remind her of all the fractured pieces that she thought his kiss might just make whole.

Before she lost her nerve, Skye leaned in. His mouth was warm against hers, his lips smooth, the contrast between them and the whiskered grit of the surrounding skin making her insides jitter. She lifted one hand and cupped his lean cheek, angling his face so she could press her lips harder against his.

His mouth opened and her tongue slipped inside.

Her clanging heart redoubled its rhythm even as they both froze. Then he rubbed the edges of his teeth against her tongue. She gasped as he bit down, trapping it inside his mouth. Then he sucked, slow and gentle, the action unhurried, yet so carnal that her breasts swelled, the tips contracting to hard points that stung with the need to be touched.

Instead, Skye touched Gage. She wormed both hands beneath the hem of his T-shirt, her fingertips riding the ridges of his belly muscles. His breath hitched and she lifted her mouth, needing to take in air, too. But she didn't want to stop…not just yet. Her lips brushed over his chin and the tickling whiskers there. Harsh breaths moved his chest against her hands as she palmed his hot skin. When her thumbs brushed over the points of his nipples, he groaned. She swallowed her own groan, shivering, as she ran the flat of her tongue along his jawline.

He tasted tangy, like the air at the cove, and she lapped at it, reveling in the flavor.

His hand shot up, fingers spearing into her hair at the back of her head, then quickly released. His arm dropped to his side, even as she felt a new rigidity in the muscles beneath her palms. She kneaded his pectorals, appreciating the sleek skin, the rough softness of hair, the power that he gave her to play.

"Take this off," she said, withdrawing her hands to pluck at the soft cotton of shirt. "Please?"

"All for you," he murmured again. "Anything you want." One hand reached behind him and he leaned away from the seat back to pull off his shirt. The movement brought his chest closer to hers, and suddenly she needed more. As he threw off the fabric, she stripped her own T-shirt away.

They stared at each other, both of them breathing hard. He'd yet to relax against the seat, and with every inhalation his chest was tantalizingly close to her erect nipples, which were pressing into the lace of her bra. Moving as slow as a starfish inching across rocks, Gage lifted his hands to her waist. His fingers gripped her gently, turned her more completely, so instead of sitting across his lap, she straddled him.

The hot, moist center of her legs pressed into the thick bulge at his crotch. Without even thinking, she rocked against it, rubbing, pleasing herself, assuaging and stoking the ache there at the same time.

Gage's fingers flexed and then one palm brushed up her spine, bumping over the strap of the bra that now maddened her. She wanted it gone. She wanted them skin to skin.

Her fingers unhooked the front clasp herself. She

shrugged the undergarment from her shoulders. Gage fell back against the seat, his gaze fixed on her breasts.

A chill rushed over her bare skin and her lashes drifted low. *He* had looked at her there, she'd felt his lascivious eyes on her even when her own were blindfolded. His ragged fingernails had bitten into the tender side flesh and she'd whimpered behind the gag, hating herself for releasing the sound of fear. The ugly memory continued building in her mind, word upon word, image upon image playing against the back of her closed lids.

"No, Skye," Gage said, his voice sharp. "Open your eyes. Open your eyes and see it's me."

She half lifted her lashes.

Dipping his head, he caught her gaze. "It's me," he said again, and raised his hands, brushing at her nipples with the backs of his knuckles. "My touch."

Skye shuddered, and it was pleasure quivering through her again. Gage slid his palm under one breast, his skin warming hers, lifting the weight of it. Without taking his eyes from hers, he lowered his mouth and kissed her nipple. Then he licked it, laving a circle around the contracting point. She drew in a quick breath as the sweet pleasure speared deep in her belly. Her hands slid to either side of his head, his sleek hair against the sensitive inside of her fingers. He began to suck, drawing her flesh into his hot mouth, and she squirmed, the place between her thighs throbbing.

"Oh, God," she said as he switched to her other breast. His fingers toyed with the wet nipple, rolling and squeezing. Desire dizzied her as he continued to play with her breasts, torturing her nipples with soft licks, spiking her need with the edge of his teeth.

Her hips rocked against his pelvis. His rigid erection fit against her, providing friction—except not enough.

Anxiety rose in her—not the same kind as before, but a fretful sense of frustration. It had to be now, she thought. Right this second she had the chance to recover what had been lost. But satisfaction only hovered, and she was afraid if she didn't find it now, she never would.

A hoarse moan sounded from deep in her throat. Her fingers tightened on his skull, pleading wordlessly for a different touch, a stronger stroke, something…something more. *"Gage."*

He lifted his head from her breast. "Shall we move—"

"No. No. *Please.*"

"Shh," he said, his gaze seeming to take in the situation. "It's all right."

"Please." She wiggled against him, aggravation threatening to splinter the need, just when it had to be honed.

"Here, baby, here." He slid lower in the chair, adjusting their fit. When she moaned again, he slipped a hand beneath the waistband at the back of her pants, then her panties. His hot palm against her bottom jolted her heart, and jolted her forward just that infinitesimal, necessary distance. *Rightthererightthererightthere,* she thought as he took her mouth in an aggressive kiss. His erection pressed upward, his free hand came between them. Over her pants, he ground the heel against the top of her sex.

Pleasure layered over pleasure. She rose on it, like a surfer being taken by a wave. Her arms circled Gage's neck and she thrust her tongue against his as she bore down on his next upward thrust.

Instead of falling down the face of the wave, she flew right off the top of it, her body shaking against Gage as the release shuddered through her. A flush broke over her skin and tears stung as a succession of emotions coursed through her: physical bliss, mental relief, unadulterated joy. Something that had been lost was found.

And then she came to herself, and the reality of what that recovery had cost struck her, hard. She was half naked in Gage's arms, her forehead pressed to his shoulder, one of his hands sweeping up and down her spine. She'd…she'd *led* her pen pal, her friend, into a physical intimacy that might have ruined that other relationship with him that she cherished.

She felt selfish and awkward and horribly embarrassed. "This is terrible," she said, scrambling to get off him. Not daring to look at his face, she swiped up her shirt and quickly yanked it over her head and shoved her hands through the sleeves. Lace caught her eye and she snatched up her bra, stuffing it into the front pocket of her pants.

"Skye," Gage began, his voice gentle.

"No." She backed away from him, addressing the neutral zone of his kneecaps. "You shouldn't… I shouldn't…" *Argh.* "'All for you,' you said. 'Only for you.' Everything's…imbalanced now." Ruined. She'd let her stupid physical problems mess up the best male-female relationship she'd ever had.

"Not imbalanced," Gage said, his voice wry. "Would it help to know you made a liar out of me?"

Her gaze jumped to his.

He straightened in the chair and pushed his fingers through his hair. "You're not the only one who got off, baby. And that hasn't happened to me with my jeans on since I was about fourteen years old. Does that make you feel better?"

Skye shook her head as she continued to back away. It

was time to go, because the only thing that would make her feel better was to find out this was all just one of her bad dreams.

POLLY WAS SEARCHING for her car keys when a rap sounded on her front door. She knew that rap. Sighing, she considered pretending she wasn't home. But that wouldn't work. Teague would have seen her Volkswagen Beetle parked in the driveway behind her cottage.

He knocked again. And like metal filings to a magnet, she found herself drawn to the door. As she pulled it open, he waved a bakery bag in her face. "Your favorite muffins."

"You shouldn't have," she said, breathing in a scent so delicious she automatically stepped back so he could walk inside.

"Pass right by the bakery on my way home from the station."

How considerate of him, she thought, to make the stop even though he was coming off a twenty-four-hour shift that began and ended at 7:00 a.m. "I'm going to get fat," she protested, even as she drew in the mouthwatering aroma of zucchini, cinnamon and walnuts.

"Your body's perfect."

At the deep note in his voice, her gaze flew to his. But he wasn't looking at her. Instead he busied himself placing the bag on the breakfast bar that separated the small living room from the tiny galley kitchen. Polly walked to a cupboard to pull out a couple of plates.

"You brought one for yourself, yes?" she asked.

"I'm not hungry."

"Then I probably shouldn't take the time to eat, either," she said. "I'm on my way to my old classroom. I have to

box up the last of my things in preparation for the move
to the new building."

"Want some help? I don't have to be back at the station until 7:00 a.m. tomorrow."

"No." She softened her voice. "No, I couldn't ask you
to do that on your day off." And yes, though she'd agreed
to be his plus-one for the wedding-related events, she
needed to discourage this casual dropping-by. The plus-
ones were for determining how well the weaning-off was
going…but if there was never any true separation, then
how could she judge?

"I don't mind."

"I do." She bustled around, tying a sweatshirt at her
waist and scooping her purse off the countertop. "Now
if I can only find my keys," she muttered.

Brushing by her, Teague strode into the kitchen. He
popped open the narrow pantry door, rummaged a moment and then his hand emerged, dangling a bristling set
of keys. "Here you go."

She frowned at him. It wasn't the first time he'd retrieved her missing ring. "How do you do that?"

"It's easy. If you get in late, you come home and make
a cup of tea. It was Movie Night with your teacher group
yesterday evening, ergo, you absentmindedly left your
keys on the shelf beside the Celestial Seasonings."

"Ergo," she repeated, admiring, but added, "I don't
always make tea once I get back."

"Only when it's late, like I said. If they go missing
after a session at the gym, look beside the bathroom
sink—you always wash your hands the minute you return from your weight-lifting class. Following a run to
the grocery store, check the refrigerator."

"I'm not sure if I'm more annoyed by my predictability or by my lack of discipline. A smarter woman would have some kind of dish to set them in by the door."

"One of your few imperfections, Pol. Cut yourself a break."

Oh, she'd been far, far from perfect. "Still, I don't see how you can be aware of things I don't know myself."

He shrugged. Then he gave her a two-fingered salute. "Later, Gator."

Gator. His private name for her that had morphed somehow from her protest against him using the inevitable and unimaginative "Pollywog." That he used it now made her look more closely at him. "Wait." There was something about the way he held himself… "Are you hurt?"

He halted halfway to her front door and glanced over his shoulder. "Nah. Just tired."

Polly narrowed her eyes. Teague never talked about his job as a firefighter, unless it was to share a joke he heard at the station or to discuss what he should make when it was his turn for dinner duty. Yet she'd be a ninny not to assume he witnessed violent, disturbing things when he went out on calls. They couldn't all be kittens in trees.

Her instincts told her that today he was having trouble doing that compartmentalizing that Griffin had mentioned the other night. He needed a distraction, and she didn't have it in her to withhold it. They were both public servants, after all.

"You really want to help in my classroom?"

He turned to face her, a smile breaking across his face. "I would be happy to."

And she was happy to have him, she told herself. Using an extra set of hands didn't mean her real plan had changed. Yes, she was still giving up her foolish dreams of him, even if he sat beside her as she drove them to the elementary school that was in the center of the beach town up the highway.

She led him toward her classroom and unlocked the heavy door. "Some of the buildings are pre–World War Two, and while they're being updated I've been assigned to another on the other end of campus."

He took in the stack of boxes she'd already filled. "You've made progress."

"I've been packing a little at a time," she said. "It's mostly the reading area that's left." With a nod, she indicated the far corner, separated from the main room by a floor-to-ceiling peeling plywood facade shaped and painted to look like a whale's yawning mouth. "Though I won't be sad about leaving ol' Jonah behind. I inherited him from the previous teacher, and if you ask me, kids aren't all that excited about going into the bowels of a mammoth mammal to enjoy their books."

Grabbing up a couple of empty cartons, she ducked beneath Jonah's flaking, pearly whites. Teague followed, and they both approached the shelves of books set against the walls. Floor cushions were scattered about for those children brave enough to read inside the whale. Teague took one of the boxes from her. "Is there a method…?"

She waved a hand. "Just how you find them on the shelves would be great. I may reorganize them differently in the new classroom. I'm trying to decide if I want to come up with an enticing theme for the reading niche or just go the simple route. The truth is, I don't have the skills to construct anything on a Jonah scale."

His first handful of books made a soft thud against the cardboard. "What would you choose instead of a whale?"

"A castle, maybe? Something that would ignite their imagination."

"I remember from my visit last year that they've got imagination to spare."

She laughed. The kids had wanted to know if he had a Dalmatian, if he'd ever rescued someone stuck in a toilet—that was from last year's resident bad boy, Barrett—what he dressed as for Halloween since so many kids dressed up like the fireman he was. "Still, I try to infuse excitement into anything that has to do with reading or letters. We even use my old pom-poms. Boys *and* girls."

He stopped. "Huh?"

"Close your mouth, Mr. Macho," she said, grinning at him. "We have arm gestures that represent the alphabet. The kids can't wait to be the class cheerleader of the day—the one up front with the big tufts of plastic streamers."

"I'd like to see that," he said.

"I'll arrange for a demonstration when you come in again on Career Day." When *you come in.* Damn, she thought, replaying the words in her mind. That wasn't separation, now, was it? But she couldn't deny her kindergarteners one of their favorite visitors. Firefighters were the rock stars of the five-year-old set.

Teague removed a full box from the reading area and came back with an empty one. As he scooted past her, his foot knocked over a lidless plastic bin, spilling its colorful contents. "Oops. Sorry," he said.

"No problem." They both knelt, both reached for the same piece of red-and-white fabric. Their fingers tangled.

An electric spark seemed to jump between them. Her gaze lifted to his face and she saw that he was staring at her with a new, dark intensity. It scrambled her pulse, evaporated the air in her lungs and made her want to lean forward. Lean into him.

He shot to his feet, breaking the contact. "Whoa… I…" His hand rubbed his face and he shook his head, as if trying to clear it. "What's that?" he asked.

"I…" He wanted her to explain that combustible reaction? Then she noticed he was looking at the red-and-white item in her hands. "Oh." To cover up her fluster, she jammed it onto her head. "It's part of a costume. Cat in the Hat. I wear it when we read Dr. Seuss."

His brows rose. "You wear the whiskers and the tail, too?"

She stuffed the hat back in the plastic bin. "And the red bow tie, if you must know the truth."

He returned to emptying the shelves of books. "I didn't think you could still surprise me, Polly," he murmured.

What did that mean? Was he referring to what had just happened when they touched, or did he merely mean her penchant for dress-up? "I'm a woman of mystery," she told him.

"What, you've got a Mata Hari costume in there?" he asked, glancing over his shoulder.

When he focused again on the books, she plucked out a pinafore, a mob cap and granny glasses from the costume bin and quickly put them on. "Not Mata Hari—Old Mother Hubbard."

Turning, he burst into laughter. "Really, Pol? You go to all this trouble?"

"And more," she said. From one of the higher shelves, she picked out a binder. "Check out last year's class album. Among other things, I dressed as Raggedy Ann, a friendly pirate and, of course, one of Maurice Sendak's wild things."

Teague looked over her shoulder as she turned the pages. In each she was surrounded by last year's kids, all who would be in first grade next month. She sighed. "I'll miss them."

"They're damn cute," he agreed, then sighed himself.

Turning her head, she scrutinized him through Mother Hubbard's glasses. "What's up?"

"Just thinking. You know I want kids."

He never failed to mention his interest in having a family. "Most men your age aren't as eager as you are."

"Yeah. But I've told you about my childhood—the whole lonely only thing was just that…lonely. I'd love a do-over with my own tribe…rushing off to soccer games or swimming lessons. Squabbles over Scrabble. Campouts in the backyard telling ghost stories."

"You can have all that."

"Gotta find the right woman," he said. "And for a time I thought…Tess had those four adorable kids. It was as if she and her family were made just for me."

Polly swallowed, trying to lubricate her suddenly dry throat. "That was David's family. David and Tess's kids."

"Yeah." He rubbed his hand over his hair.

"And other people's kids don't stay that adorable for long."

He slanted her a look. "Pol, your job is other people's kids. You seem to think they're pretty adorable."

"Mmm." She shut the album and turned away from him to place it in the bottom of an empty box.

"Polly?"

When she didn't answer, he put his hand on her shoulder and spun her to face him. "What is it?" he asked. His fingers took hold of her chin, to tilt her face toward him. "Something's wrong. What aren't you saying?"

You're an idiot! she wanted to yell. *Here I am, a woman who clearly likes kids as much as you do, who has similar interests and priorities.* Had he not felt that sexual jolt when they touched? Did he not see her at all?

Or was she too entrenched in the Polly-the-pal role?

"Pol?"

"It's nothing," she said, backing away from him. Nothing that she seemed able to change. Her hands reached around for the pinafore bow, preparing to untie it...then they dropped to her sides.

Was that where she'd gone wrong? The role-playing? Here she was, hoping to attract a man, and the only time she stepped out of her part as Pal Polly, she dressed up as Old Mother Hubbard.

Maybe it wasn't time to surrender her dream, but time to modify her strategy. Instead of continuing as the comfortable, never-make-waves friend, she would force him to consider her in an entirely different light. In a few days she'd agreed to be his plus-one at an engagement party thrown by Tess.

Polly would go there, dressed to kill and determined that Teague finally see her as a sexy female.

CHAPTER NINE

February 15

Skye,
It seems particularly dark tonight. An interpreter
I've often used lost both legs and an eye this morn-
ing when the car he was traveling in ran over an
explosive device—one of those IEDs you say you've
been reading so much about. I went by his house
to give some money to his family. With him unable
to work, his wife and children will have a hard go
of it. I met them a few months ago and spent an af-
ternoon with his sons helping build a jump for the
skateboard they'd been given by a homebound ma-
rine. Their mother fussed about the sport's danger
to her boys, but her husband and I laughed it off.
"What's the worst that could happen?" we said.
Skinned knees, sprained fingers, they were noth-
ing compared to what we've seen.
   The oldest boy is twelve. When I visited today,
I gave him and his little brother all the chocolate
and gum left from the last package my mother sent.
That's all I had for this now traumatized family: a
fistful of cash and another of foil-wrapped sweets.
The twelve-year-old thanked me politely, though,

then drew me aside. Could I find work for him? he asked. Maybe he could interpret like his father. When I asked if he wasn't afraid to take on such a dangerous job, he told me that skateboarding had given him courage.

I know the feeling well. The adrenaline rush of risk-taking is damn addictive. But that's not why his father had been in that bombed car this morning. He'd merely been trying to support his family.

I'm off to a place I know where they'll pour me some good Russian vodka. They serve it in teacups and I plan to drink several, getting drunk and staying grateful that my choices and decisions don't affect a wife and children.

Gage, who hopes you're now not regretting our correspondence

Dear Gage,
Of course I'm not regretting our letter exchange! I'm so sorry to hear about the interpreter. But remember, although you might not have a wife and kids, you do have family you're close to...and friends! Be careful with yourself for us.

The package with this letter contains treats I hope you like...or will like to share. Please at least chew one square of bubble gum yourself and remember the Crescent Cove Bubble-Offs we used to hold (though I think it was Griffin who was always named Official Chew Champ, right?).

Last, the time difference between us is almost twelve hours, so this morning I lit a candle for you...during your night. Although I'm on the other

side of the world, I hope a little of its glow some-
how reaches you.
Yours, Skye

In her role as the Crescent Cove postmistress, Skye approached the home of Rex Monroe, the ninety-plus-year-old who had lived full-time at the cove for as long as she could remember. She took a path that skirted the rear of the cove bungalows, avoiding the more direct beach route. Rex's place was situated near No. 9, and she didn't want to give Gage a chance to see her.

She didn't want to give herself a chance to see him, either. He'd probably feel obliged to address her embarrassment over the interlude in his office and then she'd feel like an idiot for avoiding him. And *then* they'd be back where they'd started…spending time together during which she experienced quivers of desire that were totally wrong.

Because they were for the totally wrong man.

She wasn't so messed up that she didn't *want* to see herself as a sexual being again, but she wasn't convinced that one topless climax could be deemed a cure. And failing in front of Gage—with Gage—in some well-meaning attempt on his part to usher her through a complete, start-to-finish sex act could utterly ruin her self-esteem as well as the special relationship they'd had these past months.

It was better to keep her distance now, and once he was gone from the cove, they could restart their conversations—via paper and from thousands of safe miles away.

As she came around the side of Rex's bungalow on her way to his front door, she heard familiar voices. Jolting back, she was forced to press her hand against the ocher-colored stucco to retain her balance. Gage was there, sitting with the elderly war reporter on his front porch.

The sound of more distant shouts and whoops had her peering around the corner again. Men were on the south bluff, some of them still climbing the path up the side, others perched at various stopping points. Shaking her head, Skye grimaced. None of the posted warning signs had ever reduced its lure, but she made a mental note to tack up one or two more.

"I haven't seen you up the cliff this visit," she heard Rex say to Gage. "First thing you and your brother did every summer was see if you could jump from a higher point than the year before."

"We did a lot of stupid stuff when we were kids," Gage replied.

"I wouldn't disagree with that. You're lucky I didn't have you hauled off and sent to juvenile hall."

Gage laughed. "Instead, you had that police officer come to the cove and give us his version of 'Scared Straight.'"

The old man harrumphed. "Someone had to look after your mother's interests. That poor woman was at her wits' end, especially with your father only coming to the vacation house on the weekends."

"So you made sure you were a nosy, interfering neighbor."

"Nosy! Interfering!"

"What? Did I hurt your feelings?" Gage's voice was laced with amusement. "I thought you considered nosy and interfering among your very best qualities."

Rex made a noise that sounded suspiciously like a smothered chuckle. "Well, you're much more polite than your twin. What a foul mood he was in when he first came to No. 9."

"I heard about that."

"And he went cliff-jumping, even though you think that's kid stuff now. Jane went, too, once."

"Jane? What the hell? He should be more careful with her."

"I don't know the whole story," Rex said. "But I do know he loves her, though she deserves far better."

"Told her that myself. Said she should choose the handsomer twin."

"As if you'd settle down," Rex scoffed.

"As if I would," Gage replied.

Just another excellent reason for her to keep that distance from him, Skye told herself. Though he said he wasn't the settling-down type, though she *knew* he wasn't the settling-down type, it was better not to give her heart even a chance to wish differently.

"Your next assignment's already set up?"

Gage grunted in answer.

"You don't seem so keen to go," Rex observed.

No? Skye risked another peek around the corner. Gage had his head tipped back against the wall, and his eyes were closed.

Rex nudged him with a leather-clad foot. "Son?"

"I'm keen, I'm keen," Gage replied without moving a muscle. "But give me a break. I'm only a couple of weeks into my R and R. Don't want to think about work right now."

"Hmm," Rex said. "I didn't know you considered your life's work, well…work."

A weighty silence descended. "Nothing's changed,"

Gage finally said, his voice tight with tension. "I love what I do. Can't wait to get back to it."

Frowning, Skye studied the now-hard lines of his face. While she was aware he'd been saddened by the wounding of the interpreter, and before that, the death of his friend Charlie, she'd never sensed the edginess that was infecting today's mood.

Maybe she should invite him over for dinner and—

No. That's exactly what she wouldn't do. When he was safely away from the cove, back doing what he loved in some foreign place that offered him the challenge and the risk that he always seemed to crave, *then* she'd attempt getting him to open up.

"Your brother's not going back to danger."

"He had a hard time of it," Gage said. "I thought about coming to the States when he got behind on the memoir—I knew something was wrong then. He needed a good kick in the butt."

"Jane provided that."

"Yeah. I think she screwed his head on straight."

"There's a little more to it, though," Rex remarked. "Your brother…well, what he suffered has gone by a lot of names over the years. Battle fatigue. Combat stress."

"He told me he's getting counseling for PTSD."

Skye would have felt guilty for eavesdropping, but Griffin had mentioned it to her himself. She'd become close to Gage's twin and his wife-to-be, and they both were quite open about the challenges Griffin had faced upon his return from war.

"What about you, son?" Rex asked.

"What about me?"

"As Griffin finally accepted, you don't have to be

holding a gun to have an acute reaction to difficult, violent, frightening experiences."

"It's different for me. Griff's job was to see it all, feel it all, tell it all. I'm more of an observer."

"He thought that, too—that his reporter's objectivity gave him some sort of immunity. It didn't."

"But he didn't have a camera, like me. It's like armor... it's a layer between me and what I see. It keeps me safe."

"Not safe from everything," Rex murmured.

Another of those heavy silences descended. Then Gage cleared his throat. "No, I've not been safe from everything. But I'm going back, Rex."

"Nobody's stopping you," the elderly man said, his voice mild. "What *is* the next assignment, then?"

"I'll be taking photos for an in-depth piece on ransom farms."

"What the hell are those?"

"The kind of moneymaking venture that comes up anytime, anyplace there's haves, have-nots and a law enforcement body that is either corrupt or overwhelmed by other concerns."

"Kidnapping," Rex said.

"Yes, and on a large scale—for monetary, not political purposes. Dozens of people at a time held for ransom in remote locations. Organized crime groups use abandoned buildings, isolated caves, sometimes underground bunkers."

"Well, damn," Rex said. "No wonder you need the R and R if that's what you're looking forward to. You're sure you don't want to rethink that return?"

"It's a story that's got to be told. It's what I need to do."

Skye moved off then, Gage's inflexible tone yet another warning about the risks of getting too close to him.

Goose bumps pricked her skin as his words played again in her head. *I'm going back, Rex... It's a story that's got to be told. It's what I need to do.*

What she needed was to stay clear of him, no matter how curious his moods or how compelling his allure.

"I'M GETTING MARRIED barefoot," Jane announced idly as she and Skye and Polly wandered through the shoe section of one of the mall's department stores.

Skye shared a startled glance with Polly, then stared at the bride-to-be. Had she misheard? "Uh, barefoot?"

At Jane's matter-of-fact nod, Skye blinked. "But that's...that's just wrong," she finally said. "We all know you're about the shoes."

"Exactly why I'm not wearing any on my wedding day. I was making myself crazy trying to find the exact right pair." She made a face. "It was Griffin's idea, actually, which is when I realized I was making him crazy, too."

"Yet another reason to avoid the love thing," Polly murmured. "A woman shouldn't have to give up her shoes."

"I didn't *have* to," Jane said. "And I merely am giving them up for a few hours. But the love thing put the wedding thing into perspective. Though I'm looking forward to the day, it's the rest of our lives that truly matter."

Polly shrugged. "Me? I'm still taking shoes over love."

Skye raised her brows. "Pol, how has that love avoidance actually worked for you?"

"Let's get to the dress department," the other woman said instead of answering. Her ponytail bounced as she headed for the escalator. "I have a job to do."

A girls' shopping trip had certain hallmarks. The promise to reveal every item tried on. The hysterical outburst behind a locked dressing room door when something that looked fabulous on the hanger turned into a colossal flop when worn by a real body. The begging of the flop-dressed's friends to please, please let them share in the horror.

After laughing so much all three shoppers cried, just a little, it was time for a lunch break. They didn't leave the mall, as Polly and Jane were still on the hunt for outfits to wear to the upcoming engagement party being thrown by Griffin's sister, Tess. They opted for the department store's small café.

While waiting for their salad orders to arrive, Skye's phone buzzed, indicating a text message. She scooped it up without a thought, then froze when she saw who it was from.

He hadn't tried to contact her in the four days that had passed since that…that episode. She looked up, aware her friends were paying attention. "It's Gage."

Jane's gaze sharpened. "He's reached out?"

"What do you mean?" Skye asked.

"He hasn't been returning Griffin's calls. Set his twin sense to jangling again."

Skye's belly clenched. Her instincts had been screaming at her last month when he'd gone silent—but at the time he'd been halfway across the world. Communication could be unreliable, he'd pointed out when he'd arrived at the cove, and she'd been so relieved to see him she'd let it go.

But now he'd gone AWOL again? Of course he was still living at No. 9; she knew that, as she'd seen him visiting with Rex that one afternoon. It did seem suspicious, though, that he'd avoid talking to his twin.

"Aren't you going to see what he says?" Polly asked.

But the distance thing had been working so well!

Her reluctance must have shown on her face, because her friend smiled a little and said gently, "It's just a text."

"Fine," she muttered, feeling foolish as she brought up the message.

Miss u.

Oh. The words pierced her heart. A liquid ache poured into her veins and everything inside her went soft, including her determination to dissociate from him. *He misses me.* Her fingers fumbled trying to type a speedy response. Miss u 2.

We're good?

Skye didn't have it in her to answer anything besides Sure.

His next text made her laugh. Funny man. She figured he was doing it on purpose, amusing her as a detour around the awkwardness he knew she felt. It didn't seem fair, though, that he seemed to have managed that interlude with her in his lap without losing an ounce of assurance. *Men.*

"So, what does it say?" Polly demanded.

"He heard the three of us are together. Wonders if we're girl-dancing again, and if so, would I text him the address so he can come by and watch?"

Polly leaned back so the server could slide her plate in front of her. "No dancing. Tell him we're having a pillow fight in our underwear."

Grinning, she did just that. Several minutes passed,

long enough for her to get started on her plate of greens. When his next text arrived, she immediately opened it.

Sorry took me so long. The paramedics just left.

Alarmed, she typed back, WHAT?

My heart stopped.

Snorting, she shared it with the other two, which gave Jane a great idea that they followed through with once their meal was finished. On the store's home goods floor, they talked a bored salesclerk into taking cell phone photos of them bopping each other with the display pillows. The Lowell brothers were each sent a copy.

"Maybe that will get them talking to each other," Jane said.

Skye continued to stare at her phone, frowning. The photos just snapped brought home the strong contrast between herself and her friends. Both of the other women were dressed in breezy sundresses and cute flats. Sheer lipstick brightened their mouths, and they seemed to sparkle with life. She, on the other hand, looked drab and almost unhappy in her baggy khakis and button-down shirt, fastened at the cuffs and up to the throat.

She *was* unhappy.

"Back to shopping for the perfect dresses," Polly said. "You're sure you don't want something new, Skye?"

Well, of course she *wanted* something new…but could she bring herself to wear it? Glancing back at that gloomy, covered-up image of herself, she bit her lip. She'd once been a young woman who wore pretty outfits and played with her hair and makeup. She wanted to be that woman again.

"I could maybe try a few on," she said cautiously.

Polly grabbed her elbow and hauled her to the elevator as if afraid she might change her mind. "I saw the cutest one for you when I was going through the racks."

The other thing about shopping with friends was that they could bulldoze you into selections you'd never choose for yourself. But behind the louvered dressing room door, Skye couldn't complain about Polly's pick. It was as if the dress had been designed precisely for Skye Alexander of Crescent Cove.

The sleeveless, moss-green bodice was held up by thin straps. It wasn't low-cut, but it did reveal her shoulders and collarbone—and was the exact color of her eyes. The full, knee-length skirt was of a slightly deeper green and printed with life-sized fish swimming through seaweed. A light underlayer of tulle gave it just the tiniest amount of pouf.

"Time to model," Polly said, knocking on the wooden door.

Skye hesitated, but then flipped the lock. Her two friends crowded into the opening, their gazes assessing.

Her skin prickled, goose bumps rising over all the newly revealed flesh. "I don't think I can do this," she said quickly, even though she knew the cut of the dress was quite modest. Still, a sidelong glance at the mirror showed a wealth of skin that she'd kept covered for months. "Maybe it's not me."

Bare arms, bare shoulders, bare throat. "Or it's so much of me," she murmured.

"It'll knock Gage's socks off," Jane said.

It was on the tip of Skye's tongue to say he'd already

seen her more exposed than this. He'd stroked her naked arms, kissed her naked shoulders, rubbed his whiskered cheek against her naked throat.

And if she'd allowed that, she thought, with a sudden sharp pang of longing, surely she could manage the dress. She wanted to appear pretty again! Normal.

Like the repainting of her kitchen and the rearranging of her living room, it would be staking a renewed claim on herself.

"I'm buying it," she said, before she could chicken out.

As they stood in line at the checkout, Jane cleared her throat. "About Gage…"

Skye turned to her, frowning at the other woman's serious tone. "You're really worried about him?"

She nodded. "I trust Griffin's instincts on this," she said, then hesitated. "Maybe you could get him to open up."

"Me? If he won't talk to his twin—"

"The two of you have been so close."

If only you knew how *close,* Skye thought. But that was part of the problem. There was an imbalance in their relationship now. He was the issue-free, hey-anything-to-help half of their pairing.

"Griffin's convinced something happened during Gage's last assignment. Something he hasn't shared with anyone."

Skye's hand tightened on the new dress. *Maybe not so issue-free.* "There was an interpreter he worked with—"

"No. He told us about that. It's bigger, Skye."

Worry continued to niggle at her as she put that together with things he'd said since returning to the cove. His sleepless nights. His desire to escape his own company. The remark he'd made to Rex while sitting beside the older man on his porch. *"I've not been safe from everything."*

Still, what gave her the right to disturb his secrets?

Because they festered when they went unspoken. She knew that better than anyone.

"You'll try talking to him?" Jane asked.

It would mean Skye would have to forget her vow of distance. But she already knew she would, she thought, sighing. Gage was the man who'd run to her rescue, who saw inside her soul, who'd held her in his arms and given her pleasure she'd thought gone forever. Of course she'd do what she could for him.

Because she cared more for her friend than for the safety of her heart.

CHAPTER TEN

TEAGUE SETTLED ON THE SMALL couch in Polly's living room and ran his hand over the new shirt he'd purchased for the engagement party at Tess's place. Then he fussed with the collar and second-guessed the color. It was a pale vanilla shade, and with his luck he'd spill something on it right away. He could hear Polly moving around her bedroom and bathroom as she finished getting ready for the event—he'd been early and she'd answered the door in her robe—and he decided it wouldn't hurt to remind her of her assignment.

"Pol," he called out, "just elbow me if I'm staring at Tess too long, okay? I'm counting on you to prevent me from making a fool of myself."

His best-friend-who-was-a-girl's voice floated through her half-closed bedroom door. "How well do you really know her, Teague?"

"What?"

"Can you tell me her favorite color? Does she like musicals? Where's the one place she wants to visit before she dies?"

Teague stood, too restless for couch cushions. Ever since that dance, holding Polly in his arms and swaying to the melody of "At Last," he'd been unaccountably edgy, a foreign state for a man usually calm and relaxed. "Her favorite color? The red of cherry Lifesavers. Of course she likes musicals, everything from old Nelson Eddy and Jeanette McDonald movies to that latest on Broadway. She wants to see India before she takes her last breath."

A long silence followed. Then Polly said, "Teague, that's me."

He wandered to the window and watched the waves rush onto the beach, their ceaseless rhythm unable to soothe his jittery nerves. "Well, I like your answers."

Another silence. Then Polly stuck her head out the bedroom door. "That makes absolutely no sense."

He glanced around. Her hair was in a shiny golden fall that brushed her shoulders and trailed toward her terry-wrapped breasts. He jerked his head away, refocusing on the surf. "Why do I get the sense you don't approve of Tess?"

"Tess herself is not the issue," Polly said, her voice going fainter as he imagined her returning to the depths of her bedroom, "but I admit I don't like how you're hung up on her. She's married."

"We can't help who we care about," he grumbled.

"To a point, I get that. But I'm not going to let myself get moony over some—I don't know—Hollywood actor or guy I just happened to glimpse in the produce section—"

"What Hollywood actor?" he demanded. "What guy in the produce section? Have you been trolling for men at the grocery store without telling me?"

A frustrated sound came from her direction. "I'm not trolling anywhere. The point is, I don't let myself fall for someone I don't have a chance of knowing or seeing again. Someone I don't have a chance of building a real relationship with. If I did, or you did, you'd just be wasting your time, or…"

Turning his back on the window, he crossed his arms over his chest. "Or...what?"

"Or you'd be doing it out of self-protection. You'd be putting your feelings somewhere, with someone, who was safe. Because deep down you'd know you're not really risking your heart."

In Teague's current mood, the thought was too complicated to unpack. Sighing, he cut to the chase. "You're saying I'm never going to have her."

Polly walked into the living room, in some red number with matching red shoes. Her favorite color. "You're never going to have her."

He spun back to stare out the window. "Shit."

"Teague?" Polly asked, her voice softening. "This is not news to you. What's the actual problem?"

His collar felt as if it were strangling him. He inserted a finger under it, wiggling the cotton fabric to get more room. "This stupid new shirt," he muttered, though his skin felt too tight, as well. Why'd she have to appear so damn appealing?

"You look very handsome in it," Polly remarked. "But I don't think that's what's eating you."

"Tess—"

"It's not her," Polly said over him. "Something else is getting to you. Is it work? You don't ever talk about that."

"There's nothing to say." He'd taught himself long ago to separate his job from his civilian life...and from his civilian friends. The pictures that sometimes stayed in his head didn't need to be passed on to anyone. His father, another firefighter, had told him that from the very first.

Teague heard his best-friend-who-was-a-girl come up behind him. He could smell her, something like roses. Possibly addictive. Incredibly bothersome. From the corner of his eye, he could just make out her golden hair and her sweetheart's profile. Her lips were as red as her dress, and he quickly looked away from them, refocusing his gaze on the surf. Stealing glances of Polly's mouth wasn't easing his weird, twitching nerves any.

Then she touched his bare forearm. The contact zapped him, an electrical shock that sent him jolting away from her.

He stared down at his skin, checking for a burn. Smoke.

"Teague," she said. "*What* is wrong?"

His answer was automatic, even as he continued to inspect his unmarred, but still smarting flesh. "Tess—"

"You don't even know her!" Polly exclaimed. She flapped her arms, clearly impatient. "My God, you don't even know me, and I've been one of your best buds for nearly five years."

He stared, sure he'd never seen her temperamental like this. They were both usually easygoing, their moods a laid-back match. "Of course I know you," he said, keeping his voice calm and reasonable. "You're an open book to me."

She rolled her eyes and tapped one foot. The movement drew his gaze to her toes. This time they were painted a swirl of hot pink and passion red—the colors, he thought in an odd turn of fancy, of a French kiss, if such a thing could be described that way.

"There's so much you've never bothered to find out about me," Polly muttered.

As in what it would be like to thrust his tongue between those perfect lips. Or slide his hand into the bodice of that dress to cradle the warm resiliency of her breast. He cleared his throat, trying to eradicate the errant thoughts, and shoved his hands in his pockets because his goddamn slacks were now starting to tighten. "Cheerleader, track team member, faux secretary of the chess club. Usually the most even-tempered, sunshine-souled person I know."

"Please don't use the word *perky*."

"Kindergarten teachers have to be perky."

"That's what I said," she muttered, her gaze on the floor. "But I'm more than all those things. Sunshine-souled! Please. I have shadows. Dark places."

"Yeah," Teague said, "you're right. I know, for example, that your dad did a number on you and your mom."

Her head jerked up. "What?"

"I put the dribs and drabs you trickle out together. You were thirteen when your parents divorced, the only sibling left at home. Your mom hung on, but not so well. You tried to perky your way through it."

Polly was staring at him, her eyes as blue and wide as the perfect, cloudless sky on this August afternoon. "I never told you that."

"You didn't have to. I've met your mother, remember? Nice lady, but it's clear she leans on you. You do her taxes, Pol. You helped her figure out that snafu with her medical bills."

"I'm good at math."

"You're damn great at giving the impression you're good at everything. Maybe that's why you don't have a guy—it's intimidating to some of them."

"I have guys."

"We've already decided the kindergarten set doesn't count." He tilted his head. "Do you ever see your dad?"

"He's not interested in knowing me, either," she muttered.

Teague frowned, reaching her in two strides. He put a finger under her chin and forced her gaze to his. Those blue, blue eyes. "What did you say?"

"He cut me out of his life. My brothers…they were finished with college, living on their own. He spent time with them. Does now, too. But I was the one at home, witnessing Mom's pain, and when I happened to mention that…" She drew a finger across her throat. "I think being around me made him feel guilty."

"Oh, Pol…" He stroked his thumb along her soft cheek, aching for her. And then, as his gaze fixed on her half-parted, rosy-colored mouth…aching for her. Her perfume tempted him, tantalized, like a come-hither finger. A new tension took over his muscles, hardening him everywhere as he found himself bending toward her lips.

"Polly," he whispered, his voice rough. The moment stretched, endlessly long.

She stayed silent, but he heard the catch of her breath, saw the rise of female flesh press against the dress that he now noticed wrapped her cleavage and appeared to fasten with a single button under her left breast. Heat prickled along the nape of his neck and down his back and he felt Polly quiver beneath his hand.

Her trembling reasserted his common sense. This was Pol, his best pal! Stepping back, he glanced at the watch strapped to his wrist. "Hey, we better get going or else we'll be late. I wouldn't want to disappoint Tess—"

"Disappoint *Tess?*"

Uh-oh. The eyes of his best-friend-who-was-a-girl were sparking blue fire. He'd never considered Polly high-strung, but he just might have to revise his opinion. "Um…"

"Disappoint *Tess?*" she repeated.

"Well…who else?" he asked.

Her mouth pinched together into a little mulish shape that he probably shouldn't point out looked just like a heart, because of the red lipstick. *"Who else?"* She whirled away from him, whirled back. "You are…are… Words can't even describe."

"Well, while you're coming up with some other manner of communication, can we get a move on?" He didn't think it was prudent to be here, alone with Polly, when her temper was high and his nerves and libido were acting up. He was a heartbeat away from saying something stupid like "You're beautiful when you're furious."

She was his buddy, not beautiful.

He was glad he stopped himself from saying that, too, because she was staring at him as if she was trying to remember where she'd left her favorite butcher knife.

His feet shifted on the floor, his instincts going on highest alert. "Look, Pol—"

"No, you look," she said, and then her fingers reached for the little button beneath the bodice of her dress.

He took another hasty step back, but it was too late. Between one breath and another, she'd unfastened the thing, and sure enough, there was nothing else to keep the cherry-red fabric wrapped around her body. She shimmied her shoulders and the fabric dropped, pooling at her feet in a circle. It looked like the petals of a flower, a hibiscus maybe, with Polly's mostly nude body rising from the center.

Polly's mostly nude body.

Oh, God. There it was, her small, strong body covered with nothing but those strappy sandals and a pair of flesh-toned lace panties. Her chest moved up and down, drawing his gaze to her small, palm-sized breasts, the pale pink nipples tight. His belly tightened. His cock went hard.

And it hit him then, that he'd had fantasies of this, of her, in the deepest darkest hours of the night. Fantasies that he'd done his best to forget if they flickered across his consciousness during daylight.

In shock, he took another step back. And then another, and another and another until his shoulder blades slammed against the front door. Mind reeling, he stood paralyzed, still struck dumb. Then he tried for coherence. "Polly…" He made a vague gesture. "This…"

You…you've staggered me, he thought, his mouth too dry to push out the words. *And I don't really understand what's happened.*

"Just go," she said, spinning on her heel. "Just go away."

And he did it, he obeyed her, rushing off without even taking the opportunity to gawk at her fine ass. Because he was convinced he'd make less of a fool of himself at Tess's party than he'd managed to do in Polly's bungalow.

WALKING UP THE FRONT path to his sister's elegant Spanish-style house in the upper-middle-class suburb of Cheviot Hills, Gage found himself wishing desperately that Skye had agreed to come with him. He'd texted her and asked—since yesterday, they were back in contact, if only via phone so far—but she'd been obliged to meet a repairman at one of the cottages and would arrive later.

Feet planted on the front porch, he hesitated. Stalling, he knew, because once inside he'd be stuck. Damn it, why hadn't he waited for Skye? Then he would have had a buffer between himself and what he'd face inside. Like that visit he'd made to the mall, he knew the party would deliver another jolt of culture shock. There'd be a shitload of people he'd be expected to small talk with, and he had a bad feeling that celebration or no, his twin was going to corner him. Maybe he shouldn't have ignored Griff's calls, but in the days and nights during which he'd holed up at No. 9, waiting for Skye to get over her unnecessary awkwardness and return to him, Gage had found himself unable to sleep. It wasn't due to that little lap dance he and his pen pal had enjoyed—he was a guy and not so hung up on perfectly natural bodily responses and perfectly pretty partial nudity. It was some residual aftereffects of his near disaster overseas that were to blame.

His brother would have known something was up if he'd heard Gage's exhausted voice. He still might, even though after the yeah-we're-good-again text exchange with his pen pal, Gage had managed twelve hours of shut-eye. With all the lights on, of course.

An unfamiliar couple came up behind him, and he was forced through the door, drifting in their wake. A household helper—hired for the occasion, Gage assumed—had let them in, so he was able to keep to the periphery of the party, unnoticed. Most of the action appeared to be poolside, and he stood in the shadows of the spacious backyard observing the other guests. Men and women were dressed in summer SoCal casual—that ran the gamut from crinkly cotton worn with shandals—rope-soled, awning-striped canvas footwear—to silk sundresses studded with sequins and glittery beads. A dozen kids were playing in the pool, the smallest at the shallows of the beach entry, while others scooted around the large Baja shelf like stingrays. Above the chatter of the partygoers, he heard "Marco!" and the expected response, "Polo!"

The pool game took him straight back to his own childhood. He'd lived in a place just like this—a family neighborhood that revolved around kids and comfort. It had chafed at him, growing up. It wasn't that he hadn't appreciated his family and the privilege of his comfortable upbringing; it was just that it had felt so between-the-lines to him, and he'd never been good at coloring that way.

His gaze caught on a figure stationed by the children playing in the water. It was his sister's husband, David Quincy. Deadly Dull David. Gage had called him that from the very beginning, and the memory made him feel like a louse. David was an accountant, the head numbers guy for a big talent agency. Sure, he was the type to dot all *i*'s and leave no *t*'s uncrossed, but he'd also made his wife happy for fourteen years, and seeing him smile at his youngest son, Russ, sent a second pang of guilt through Gage. Where the hell had he gotten off criticizing the other man? There was a good, thriving family here.

In a good, thriving place. After what he'd seen over the past decade, he wasn't going to bitch about first-world luxury. Maybe it took third-world experience for him to see it with fresh eyes. All he knew was that the atmosphere didn't hem in his spirit as it had done before.

Probably because once you experienced a real cage, you recognized the difference.

"There you are!"

Gage stiffened at the sound of his brother's voice, already on guard. Then, reminding himself of the reason for the occasion, he turned toward him, hand outstretched. "Hey. Congratulations again. Great day for a party."

His twin's grasp was strong, his gaze sharp. "Thought maybe we'd have to send out a posse to round you up."

"I'm not late."

"Of course you aren't," Jane said, coming up to the men and kissing Gage's cheek.

He took her hand, admiring her crisp, lemon-colored sundress and ribbon-laced shoes. "Every time I look at you, I have this pressing urge to put you away somewhere safe, like a pretty, perfect toy. You know, Griff is going to smudge your dress with his grubby fingers or rip a seam by playing too rough."

Jane laughed, and flashed a look at her groom-to-be. "I sure hope so."

His brother sent her a private smile that caused Gage to avert his eyes. *Yeesh,* he thought, feeling scorched by the heat they were giving off. Maybe Griff was right and there was something special about committed sex.

"Can you two excuse me?" Jane said. "I see someone waving at me."

As she walked away, Griffin followed her with avid eyes. Gage whistled, noting his brother's hyperalert gaze. "You don't have to go guard dog, bro. Not a cloud in the sky, so a lightning strike is out. Runaway buses tend to avoid backyard garden parties."

"I'm not taking any chances," he murmured, still looking after her. "I almost lost her once."

Skye popped into Gage's mind. *"I was...touched. Threatened sexually. I was sure I would be raped."* He pulled out his phone, filled with a sudden desperate need to know she was okay. His thumbs flew. Where r u?

"I wonder if I almost lost you, too," Griffin continued.

"Huh?" Gage responded, distracted by the concern he felt for Skye. He stared at the small screen of his phone, willing it to light up with her answer.

"Did I almost lose you?"

"They let me go," he murmured, this time texting, WHERE R U???

"Sweet Jesus." Griffin breathed it out like a curse. "I knew it. What happened? Who had you?" he asked.

At the same time that Skye texted, Look up.

Gage did, and his breath caught in his chest, a sharp, painful ache.

She stood on the other side of the pool. Twenty or so people surrounded her, but their colors ran together, their figures fading like a watercolor picture left out in the rain. Only Skye and he existed in this new world. Dressed in shades of deep seawater, she seemed to be wading through it, green swirling about her torso, fish swimming past her thighs.

Griffin was saying something, making demands maybe, but Gage felt himself taken out on a tide, drawn toward the dark-haired beauty who called to him like a siren. He hadn't seen her since that day in his office, and though he knew she'd felt embarrassed, he'd thought himself relatively unmarked by the experience.

But…but something was different between them now.

Was it because she looked different? Her glossy hair was loose, waving around her shoulders. Her eyes, surrounded by a wealth of luxuriant lashes, held all the mysteries of the sea, and he needed to get close enough to demand she speak them from the rosy softness of her tender mouth.

It was like walking through a dream, the air soft, sounds muted, his limbs heavy. When he reached her, he kept his arms stiffly at his sides, his fingers curled into fists. If he touched her, she might disappear, like some mythical being you were only allowed to glimpse at the equinox or during an eclipse or when the capricious gods decided to wreak havoc upon your human heart.

A little smile played at the corners of her bewitching lips. "Well?"

He shook his head, trying to shake off the twined feelings of dread and delight that were wrapping his body like seafarer's rope. Mutineers had been punished like that, thick dock line cinched around them from shoulders to ankles before they were cast into the ocean.

Gage felt as if he were going under.

His gaze ran across the fine-pored perfection of her bare throat and shoulders, the length of her slender arms, the sweet hint of knees and then her naked calves and ankles. She held herself still under his regard, and he could tell the effort cost her something.

He didn't feel bad about that, not for an instant, because he suspected he was going to be paying for this moment for the rest of his life.

"I'm—I'm wearing a dress," she finally said.

"You're wearing a dress," he answered in solemn agreement.

She tilted her head. "Perfume even."

A note of it tickled his nose, her fresh scent paired with a darker note of something that smelled female and seductive and worked its way down his spine and around to his cock like a slender, knowing hand. He sucked in a harsh breath, feeling as if the balance of power between him and his vulnerable pen pal had inexorably shifted.

Self-consciousness clouded her eyes. "You don't like it?"

A wry smile tugged at his lips. He probably didn't—

but not only because of how hermit Skye's new, shiny shell affected him. Other men would take a second look at her now—not to mention a third, a fourth—and the idea of that didn't sit well. Something primal inside him wanted her to be his and his alone.

He ruthlessly squashed the thought.

"Gage?"

But he couldn't quash the impulse to express how beautiful she was, not when he could practically see the rising tide of doubt inside her. Reaching out, he ran a fingertip over one delicate shoulder strap. "You look incredible. So incredible I lost my voice for a minute or two."

The rigid set of her shoulders relaxed and a second smile flickered over her mouth. "That's what a woman hopes to hear."

"But you made the changes for yourself, right?" he asked, gazing into her deep ocean-colored eyes. As much as he appreciated the transformation, whether wearing camouflage or sexy clothes Skye would always be a standout in his mind. "It's your own approval that matters first and last, sweetheart."

She studied his face as she seemed to consider the comment, then she nodded. "I did do it for myself." Her palm touched his arm, sliding down until her hand curled around his. "But you'll stick close?"

Of course he should have refused—there was potential danger in this new need he felt around her—but he was beyond refusing her anything. As her fingers tangled with his, it was like more sailor's work, a tether securing them together. He'd always been intrigued by the names of nautical knots: Bowline on a Bight, Icicle Hitch, Rat-Tail Stopper. If there was a name for the tie now binding him to Skye, though, he figured it could only be Big Trouble.

As the afternoon wore on, however, he decided he'd worried for nothing. They wandered about the party together and he found himself actually enjoying it. Between them, they knew most of the people there. He introduced her to some of the Lowell cousins. After that, she tugged him toward a couple standing by the dessert table and introduced them as Layla Parker and Vance Smith, July's occupants of Beach House No. 9. Vance had been a combat medic in the platoon Griffin had been embedded with in Afghanistan, and had been wounded trying to save the life of Layla's father, his commanding officer.

The officer's dying request had brought the pair together and now they were, well, *together.* Layla, it turned out, had baked the very excellent champagne cupcakes that Gage enjoyed while they talked. She also flashed a brand-new engagement ring and chattered to Skye about wedding plans and a new house in avocado country near Vance's family's ranch with such enthusiasm that Gage had to grin at her groom-to-be.

"Lucky you," he told the other man. "Sounds like she really wants to be your wife."

Vance ran an affectionate hand over his fiancée's hair. "It took some persuading—and maybe more than a little Beach House No. 9 magic—but I'm damn glad to say I believe you're right."

Gage was saved from responding to the magic comment when a voice across the pool hailed the other couple. He and Skye moved on, deciding to seek out his nephews. His niece, Rebecca, had apparently left childhood for adolescence like a small-town girl heading for the big city—on speedy transport and with little luggage—but

Duncan and Oliver were the same scamps he remembered from his last visit. Little Russ had been a bump in his mother's belly when Gage had last encountered him, but he was a small, sturdy person now. Looking content and sleepy, he sat in Skye's lap, his chubby cheek pressed to her chest, his baby hair against the bare skin of her throat.

Gage pitched a Wiffle Ball to the bigger boys, calling out encouragement as they drove for the fences with a plastic bat. His sister, Tess, even smiled at him as she came to collect her kids to make sure they ate some dinner. She'd been mad ever since he'd returned stateside, upset about those weeks he'd been incommunicado, but now it appeared she'd let bygones be bygones.

Except her smile died as she brushed past him, Russ in her arms. "I'll kill you if you hurt her," she said between her teeth.

"What? Who?" When of course it was obvious.

Her eyes narrowed, darting from Skye to him.

Instead of playing dumb this time, he held up his hands in surrender. "I have the very best intentions," he said. Meaning it.

They were friends, intimates you could even say, but they'd taken the physical relationship as deep as it would ever go. He'd reminded her of sexual pleasure, shown her she could reach it again, and that's where it ended. As much as he was drawn to her, there wasn't going to be any more flesh-to-flesh contact. There didn't need to be.

That didn't mean he was going to push her away. She was still an effective shield between himself and his nosy brother. Griffin kept sending him looks whenever they encountered each other, looks that Gage pretended not to notice as he asked Skye a question or fetched her another drink.

At one point they were standing with the engaged couple, Jane chatting with Skye, and under the cover of the female conversation Griffin spoke to him in low tones. "You're going to explain yourself," he said. "Before you leave tonight."

"Sorry, not on my own timetable," he said, wearing his most innocent expression. "Told the lady of the cove I'd get her back when she asked. She came with Rex and he left early."

Not long afterward, he caught the lady in question stifling a yawn. Since it was well past dark and he was unwilling to push his luck—he didn't put it past Griffin to lock him in a room with the intention of eliciting a confession—Gage suggested they make their goodbyes and head back to the beach.

That went off without much of a hitch beyond the gleam in Griffin's gaze that promised Gage couldn't get away forever without a confrontation. Well, they'd see about that. Certainly there wasn't going to be any soul-baring this night. As he hustled Skye from the house, he spied Teague sitting by himself in a corner, staring off into space.

"What's wrong with him?" he said, nudging her with an elbow.

She glanced in the direction he indicated. "Oh," she said, sighing. "He has this thing for your sister."

Poor dude. Tess was wholly committed to David and the kids. Yet… "She's right there," Gage pointed out, "and he seems to be oblivious. I'd say something—someone—else is on his mind."

Skye climbed into the passenger side of his car, and he shut the door behind her. When he settled into the driver's side, she looked up from her phone. "I can tell you he was supposed to come with Polly but she refused at the last minute. She texted that it's a long story."

"Ah." He didn't press any more. Let everyone keep their secrets, including him.

The ride back to Crescent Cove was quiet but companionable. Gage relaxed, thinking he'd made it around or over the obstacles he'd dreaded earlier in the day. The party hadn't been so bad; he'd mostly avoided his prying twin, and even the alarming sense of change he'd felt upon seeing Skye had subsided.

Everything was contained and under control.

Without thinking, he drove to No. 9 and parked in the driveway. "Damn," he said, realizing his error and reaching for the ignition again. "I need to get you back to your place."

"Let's just sit here for a minute." She put her hand on his knee.

As heat from her touch rocketed toward his crotch, alarm returned with a vengeance. *Shit.* He wrapped his hands around the steering wheel and gritted his back teeth.

"Gage…" Her voice trailed off, then she cleared her throat as if hesitant about what to say next.

He glanced at her, then hastily looked away. At Tess and David's, the other partygoers and his family had distracted him after the initial wallop of glimpsing her in that dress, but now her changed appearance struck him again. Oxygen caught in his chest as the image of her skin, glowing like a pearl, was burned into his brain.

So much of her was…bare. Though of course he knew the cut of the garment she wore was actually quite modest. It was all a matter of degree…or maybe it was just

Skye. The bravery that it took for her to shed her concealing layers was sexy in itself.

She cleared her throat again, drawing his glance a second time. Now he couldn't look away. He'd been doing a damn good job of shrugging off that afternoon in his office—ignoring the memory of the satiny weight of her breasts in his hands, the thrust of her nipples against his tongue, the curve of her bottom against his hot palm—but in this moment it all came back in surround sound and Technicolor. She'd climaxed in sweet tremors against his cock, detonating his own release. The only thing he'd regretted about the interlude was that she'd moved away from him so fast. He would have cherished the chance to hold her sated self against his body.

He'd die for another go at it, he admitted to himself, and knew that lust was setting fire to those promises he'd made to Tess and to himself. *So what?* said the devil on his shoulder. *You've already proven getting physical with her won't ruin the relationship.* Shifting in his seat, he faced her more fully.

She was an effing beauty. Or she wasn't. Christ, he didn't know what an objective person's viewpoint would be on the subject. There was no way he'd ever be impartial when it came to the lady of the cove. He only knew that she was gorgeous to him, within and without, every side of her: the courageous spirit, the wounded soul, the friend who'd been his lamp in the dark night of his life, the lover he wanted to satisfy again…and again and again.

Perhaps his sudden spiking lust was a tangible thing, because she made a little sound and drew her hand from his knee.

He wanted it back, caution be damned. He wanted her to touch him everywhere.

So he initiated the contact. Moving as slow as if penetrating water, he brought his palm to her face. He cupped her cheek, then drew his fingertips down the side of her throat and across her collarbone.

Her breath hitched. "Gage?" she whispered. "What are you doing?"

"I'm finding you irresistible," he confessed, and nudged a shoulder strap off the slope of bone. It fell like the stem of a wilted flower against her upper arm. He did the same on the opposite side. "I need to look at you again, Skye. Will you let me?"

Instead of answering, she went wide-eyed and very still. Taking that as a yes, he inserted his forefinger at the center of her straight-cut bodice. Anticipation curled in his belly and his skin tightened against his bones as he tugged on the fabric, slowly working it below her breasts.

With a charged sort of bemusement, she stared down at his hand as if his touch enthralled her. She still wasn't moving; there was just the finest trembling beneath her skin. Clearly she wasn't immune to him, either, and in fact he thought she might be entering the same dreamlike state that he'd suffered from earlier that day.

He'd say he took cold-blooded advantage of it, but his blood was running hot, boiling even, burning through his veins and making his pulse jump.

"Skye," he whispered, his tone reverent, as his gentle tugs and pulls resulted in her breasts popping free. It seemed they both held their breath then while they watched her nipples tighten on their own to stiff points.

"I…" She swallowed, as if needing to lubricate her

dry throat. "Funny how short a time it takes to get accustomed to exposing more skin."

It sounded like a little joke, but her expression was flat-out serious. He brushed the back of his knuckles against the jutting tips of her breasts. Her breath hitched as he took one between his fingers with a tender pinch. "It's because you trust me," he said.

"I do." She seemed to be marshaling some thought, even as she stared, fascinated, at the hand that toyed with her breast. "But…but you can trust me, too."

"Mmm." He leaned forward to press his mouth to her temple. Affection and sexual ache had never been a twosome in his mind, but when it came to Skye, he felt both in equal measure.

"Wait," she said, sounding almost fretful as he dropped kisses across her forehead. "You're making me forget. I had something I wanted to talk to you about. Ask you."

He hardened his touch on her nipple and she gasped. "Ask away," he murmured against her ear, then traced the curve of the rim with his tongue.

"Something…" Her word ended on a groan as he bit her lobe.

"Something?" he prompted, smiling against her cheek. God, how he loved her involuntary, shivery reaction to him. Her whole body responded to his touch. He could feel the goose bumps rising, the heat infusing her skin.

Her head turned, her mouth seeking his.

He withheld the kiss, drawing back, teasing out the desire. "You wanted to ask?"

Her hands clutched his biceps. She was clearly dazed. "What?"

"Your question, baby." He was hard and throbbing everywhere, but how sweet it was to have the power to subvert her thought processes. "What do you want to know?"

She blinked a couple of times, her gaze going from bleary to semiclear. "I…I want to know what happened to you," she said, her voice low and still husky with desire. "Because something did. Something bad happened right before you came back."

Gage froze. *Shit*. He wasn't yet home free. Another person was after his secrets tonight. "No, Skye…"

Her mouth went mulish and she brushed his hand away to right her bodice, yanking it upward. The interior of the car seemed to cool by several degrees. "Trust goes in both directions," she said, sounding more determined by the second. "You know you can tell me."

But telling would do no one any favors, not that he would admit to even that. So it came down to redirecting her focus, right here, right now. Perhaps if she hadn't started pressing for answers, he would have marshaled some second thoughts about pursuing more intimacy. Perhaps he would have settled for appeasing the devil on his shoulder with a mere few kisses before letting her go. But now there was only one guaranteed diversion.

To begin, he leaned close again and kissed her.

CHAPTER ELEVEN

GAGE'S MOUTH WAS HOT and his tongue slid into Skye's, stealing her breath and taking her wits right along with it. She'd managed to drag herself out of the sexual spell he'd cast over her for a brief moment, but now he threw her straight overboard again. The fact that he'd avoided her question barely registered.

Her hands clutched at his biceps, trying to stay afloat, but she was sinking fast, her mind going dizzy as prickling heat broke out everywhere—on bare skin and clothed skin, sensitizing private places that swelled and throbbed along with her heavy heartbeat.

Protest was a flickering thought, like the TV's light against the wall in a darkened room. She closed her eyes, ignoring it to ride the rising pleasure. It felt so good to be touched, to have his warm, male presence beside her, both secure and exciting. She'd worried that trying a full-on sex act with him wouldn't work, but everything seemed to be full speed ahead, so why not go with the flow?

His lips crossed her cheek and angled down her throat. Her head fell back and he speared his hand in the back of her hair to hold her in place. He feasted on her skin and she felt her blood rising to the surface to meet his kiss. Her breasts ached, pushing against the bodice of her dress, and she moaned, grabbing blindly for his hand so he could provide some relief with a firm, masculine touch.

He smiled against her skin and let her press his palm to her fabric-covered chest. But he didn't knead her skin or test the fullness. Instead, he merely let his heat transfer through the material, adding kindling to the fire already inside her. "Maybe we should change the venue," he murmured.

Change the venue? The phrase sounded too technical for her brain, reduced as it was to primitive, primal reactions. "I don't know what that means," she said, then whimpered as he moved upward to suck on her earlobe.

His laugh was seductive in its arrogant surety. She should dislike it, she thought, but in the state she was in and because of her tenuous hold on her sexuality, she was grateful that he seemed certain of exactly how to proceed.

He could be the one in charge, she thought. No problem. Please. And then she whispered it, her voice breaking in desperation for something more. "Please, Gage. Please."

He laughed again, soft and indulgent. "Let's go inside."

She fumbled with the handle of the door, but her fingers were clumsy. Gage had it open before she did, and then she realized she'd forgotten she'd toed off her sandals. Leaning over, she reached for them, but Gage was again first. The crushed shells on the driveway crunched as he squatted and took up her shoe, then slipped her foot inside. His fingers brushed her bare skin as he made quick work of the fastening. Then she felt his mouth against her ankle.

She sucked in a startled breath at the hot wetness of the kiss, shuddering with the unexpected delight. He placed a second on her shin, then another on her knee, sending a hum of bliss up her femoral artery and from there to the rest of her body. Placing his palm over that damp third kiss, he spun her on the leather seat so her legs dangled out the opening. Her left shoe was buckled as deftly as the first.

Trembling, she waiting for a second set of kisses, and he didn't disappoint. His mouth brushed her ankle, the sleek skin of her calf, the cap of her knee. Then, sliding the blades of his hands inward, he nudged her knees apart. The hem of her dress, caught at his wrists, rose with the movement, almost to the bottom edge of her panties.

Cool air washed her hot skin. Skye stared, captivated, as he lowered his head and the rasp of his evening beard teased the soft inner skin of her upper leg. Her hand tangled in the silky dark locks of his hair, but she didn't have the strength to push him away. Or the will. She could only quiver as he gave a tiny bite to the vulnerable flesh, moan as he sucked there, hard. The sweet, stinging delight hadn't abated before he left a second love bite on the other inner thigh.

Desire was crashing her nervous system and she was certain she couldn't walk as his hands curled around her waist to draw her to her feet. "I won't be able to stand," she protested.

"I'll help," he promised. "C'mon, honey."

Her body swayed as her weight landed on her feet and he had to slide an arm around her hips to keep her upright and against him. "Told you," she said, leaning into his chest.

He kissed her cheek, her ear, her temple. "You should come with a warning label."

"What?" She frowned up at him.

"'Combustible,'" he said. "I expected you'd be a lot harder to warm up, lady."

"I *am* hard to warm up! I've always been hard to warm up, even before—" She broke off, not wanting to voice the thought. It had no place here, not now. Not tonight.

Not when he was laughing at her again, in that indulgent, arrogant way he had. "It's just me, then, I guess," he said, looking smug.

She was too grateful, too needy, to argue with him at the moment. Lifting to her toes, she fitted her mouth to his and kissed the superior smile from his face. He cupped the back of her head with his palm, and their mouths worked at each other, finding angles and tasting surfaces, until Skye broke away with a gasp.

Clinging to Gage, she sucked in great lungfuls of air. "Oh, God."

"Oh, yeah," he said, his hot breath stirring her hair. "This is going to be so good."

It was going to be everything she'd worried she'd never have, she thought as he led her toward Beach House No. 9. He continued to drop random kisses on her face and hair as they approached the door, as if he couldn't stand not to have his mouth on her. She gripped him in turn, one hand fisted in the shirt at the small of his back.

They climbed the short flight of steps and then he fished for the keys. She leaned into him as he unlocked the door and pushed it open. Their hands entwined, he drew her inside.

Where lights blazed.

Blinking against the harshness, Skye felt as if she'd been slapped awake. Her heartbeat slowed and the simmering desire cooled a little. She glanced over her shoulder, at the dark night. People kept insisting there was magic at Beach House No. 9, but to her it had been outside—in the shadows, where he'd stoked her desire with burning kisses.

"What's wrong?" Gage asked.

"It's...bright."

An odd expression crossed his face and she couldn't decipher it, although there was enough illumination for intricate surgery. "Yeah," he said, then lifted his free hand. He tucked her hair behind her ear, rubbed the pad of his thumb across her lower lip. "Let me dim it down a bit...or would you like to go home? Has it killed the mood?"

The strong lamplight had something going for it—it clearly displayed the rugged good looks of the man still holding her hand. Much of the time when she thought of Gage, what occurred to her first was his voice in the letters he'd sent to her, or his view of the world that she glimpsed through the photographs he took. But now there was no missing the rugged, masculine splendor of him. In a pair of barley-colored, heavy linen pants that he wore with a white, loose-weave shirt, he appeared both elegant and exotic. He might have stepped from an isolated jungle bar where he'd just met with a reclusive warlord. Or perhaps he was bound for a small South American country via single-prop airplane.

There was an aura of relaxed expectation surrounding him, as if he was ever prepared for a rebel uprising or a knife fight with a local thug...but was sure as hell going to enjoy himself until that eventuality actually came to be.

As she continued to study him, his piercing, turquoise eyes narrowed, and he gave her a quizzical glance.

"Honey?" he said, brushing his thumb over her mouth again. Her lips began to throb and her heart thudded painfully against her ribs, its tempo once again speeding up.

Dark or bright, she still wanted him.

He was angled cheekbones and male ego, black-pepper whiskers and searing kisses. She tightened her fingers on the hand holding hers and wrapped the others around his heavy wrist to draw him close, feeling her temperature rise to fever level. "I want you," she said fiercely, because it was true and the opportunity might never come again. "I want this."

His forehead touched hers. "Go outside on the deck for a minute," he said. "I'll pour you some wine, turn down some lights."

Excitement flowing like kerosene into her already burning bloodstream, Skye obeyed. She kept her back to the house as she stood outside, her gaze on the surf. Still, she was aware of lights going off, others dimming. In a few minutes, she felt the wooden planks beneath her feet reverberate with his footsteps.

She shivered in anticipation, quivering harder when his hand cupped the nape of her neck, beneath her hair. He turned her and placed the stem of a wineglass in her hand.

Flickering candlelight caught her gaze. She angled her head toward the house and saw that the living room was dark now, except for the fat pillar candles that sat on the mantel and on the coffee table. She wondered if he'd lit the others that were in the big master bedroom downstairs. There was one on the long bureau, she knew. A second and third on the small tables that flanked the bed.

Where she would lie with Gage, the two of them tonight, naked together. Swallowing hard, she looked back at him. "I—" A sight over his shoulder gave her sudden pause. "Oh, no," she said.

"What?"

"Oh, *no.*" She pressed her palm over her heart, which was thudding for an entirely different reason now. "They're back," she whispered, her body going cold, desire abating. *"They're back."*

Gage glanced behind him. "Who's back? Honey, what—"

"The men," she croaked out. "That man."

"What are you talking about?"

Her finger shook as she pointed at a cottage up the beach. "The Rutherfords are supposed to be gone. They went up the coast for a few days. There's someone in there—you can tell."

"Maybe they decided to postpone their trip."

She shook her head. "I waved at them as they drove off. Mary Rutherford called when they were an hour out and asked me to go in and check that the iron was off. I know I locked up behind me."

Gage had turned fully around to inspect the cottage in question. Lights were on in the windows, and there was movement behind the drawn sheer curtains. "I'll go check it out. You stay here."

She clutched at him. "No! It's dangerous. We should call the police, or…"

"And I will," Gage said gently, "if I think there's a problem. You go inside No. 9 and lock the door. I'll be right back."

Once he left, her stomach roiling with anxiety, Skye paced around the beach house's living room. She turned on the overhead light, and while both the front and sliding deck door were locked, fear kept a stranglehold on her throat. Gage was out there, putting himself at risk. Cold at the thought, she grabbed up the crocheted throw hanging over the couch and wrapped herself in the fabric.

The act of covering up calmed her a little, and she sat on the edge of a seat cushion, rocking back and forth. The sound of the surf was loud in the room, and she tried breathing along with it, but nothing calmed her churning belly or her hyperactive imagination. It spun a dozen scenarios.

Trying to hide from them, Skye pulled the woolen throw over her head. She pressed her forehead to her knees and whispered to herself over and over and over. "It will be all right. It will be all right. It will be all right."

At the rap of knuckles on glass, she jackknifed up, swallowing a shriek. Her brain hiccupped before she recognized Gage, standing on the deck. She scurried to the slider and fumbled with the locking mechanism. "Sorry," she called, her voice anxious. "I'm sorry."

"It's okay, honey," he called through the glass. "Take a breath. Everything's okay."

When the door finally snapped open, she didn't have the muscle power to slide it wide. Gage took over, then stepped inside, bringing the scents of salted air and wet ocean with him.

Her gaze ran over him. "Was it them? Did you call the police?" She darted around him to once again flip the lock. "Did they see you?"

"Skye." He touched her shoulder.

She jerked at the contact, then whirled, her shoulders pressed to the glass. The fight-or-flight response tasted bitter on her tongue, and she stared at him, her bones rattled by tremors.

Gage went still. "Easy, easy. It wasn't anything you're thinking."

"What…" She swallowed, trying to ease her dry mouth. "What…who…exactly was it?"

"Monica Rutherford, and a handful of her teenage friends."

"Monica?" She was seventeen years old, going into her senior year at high school. The girl, her parents and her younger siblings had been spending a month at the beach for the past few years, an escape from the summer heat in the nearby San Gabriel Valley. "Her mom said she was going to be staying with a school friend while they took their short trip."

"Monica and company thought it would be more fun to escape adult supervision by overnighting at the beach house."

Skye let out a shaky breath. "Uh-oh."

"Our young friend Monica has a healthy guilty conscience, however. The minute I arrived and mentioned you expected the house to be empty, she and her buddies couldn't jump into their car fast enough."

"Were they—"

"I didn't see any signs of drugs or alcohol. They promised they were heading straight back to Pasadena."

Skye stumbled to the couch, dropped onto it.

"I made sure the place was locked up tight," Gage added. "That's the end of it. They won't worry you like that again."

Eyes closing, she rested her head against the back cushion, feeling both weary and resigned. "I don't think that's the end of it."

"Sure it is," Gage said. "You have my personal guarantee."

She rolled her head to look at him. "Until the next time something unexpected but perfectly innocuous turns up. Then I'll have another freak-out. Face it. I'm crazy."

"Skye—"

"I'll always be jumping to the wrong conclusions and jumping out of my skin, too. I'm never going to get my life back."

"Sure you will."

She eyed him with pessimism, then held out her quivering hands. "You think so? Look how I'm shaking."

"Take some more deep breaths," he advised. "And let me get you that wine I left in the kitchen. I need a glass myself."

She babbled at his retreating back. "If it's for Dutch courage, don't bother. You won't have to deal with me and my messed-up sexuality any more tonight. I'll go home in a minute."

He glanced over his shoulder, one eyebrow raised.

"I'm too screwed up for you to want to…well, screw. I get it. No one's interested in doing the deed with a certified loon, even someone who engages in things like the Gage Gorge."

He muttered a curse and walked into the kitchen.

She raised her voice. "I'm not going to hold it against you or anything. We'll never mention any of this again."

"Do you talk this much when you're in bed?" he asked, his voice floating through the entry.

"I don't remember being in bed with anyone, ever," she called back. "It's past the shelf date of my short-term memory and it wasn't memorable enough to make it into my long-term banks."

"Good," he said, coming back in with a glass in each hand. His face was perfectly calm. As he passed the light switch, he flipped it off with his elbow, and the room went back to romantic and candlelit. "I like a fresh slate."

"Didn't you hear a thing I said?" she demanded, taking the wine he held out.

He sat on the other end of the couch and stretched his long legs in front of him. "I heard the forbidden phrase 'Gage Gorge,' and for that you will be punished."

Her eyes rounded. "Ha-ha." Then she looked down at her wine, aware once again of her dry throat and an odd, illicit tingling sensation below her belly. "What do you mean...punished?"

He shrugged. "Get your sweet ass into the bedroom, and I'll show you."

Despite herself, she felt her skin flush. He was just joking around, right? "Is this some outlandish practice you learned in your travels?"

"I've been to many foreign places, Skye. Turns out our American Puritan streak means most of us are not very adventurous."

Oh, he was having fun with her now. "But not you," she said, then sipped at her wine while peeking at him through her lashes.

"Who was the first to set sail on the raft we made one summer?"

A grin broke over Skye's face. "I think every mom in the cove was mad at my dad for letting us watch that documentary on the voyage of the Kon-Tiki."

"We could have used a little better quality control, that's for sure," Gage admitted. He lifted the hem of his shirt to expose his flat belly. "I still have the scar from when the raft broke up on the rocks."

Skye slid closer, the dim light making it impossible to see from so far away. "Where?"

As he set down his glass on a side table, he drew the shirt farther upward. Now she was close enough to get a glimpse of the washboard ripple of his belly and the dark disc of a nipple. Still no scar. "Where?" she demanded again.

"Come a little closer," Gage coaxed.

It was as if Satan had changed places with him, his voice was so smoky and dark. Skye's gaze jerked up. His eyes were disguised now, their usual screaming blue two pools of deep shadow. Without touching her, he took her wineglass out of her now-nerveless hand and set it beside his own. Then he lifted his shirt over his head and tossed it away.

"Oh," she breathed. "You don't play fair."

"A little something else I learned along the way." He gestured toward the top of his rib cage. "My old wound is just about right here."

Part of her was desperate to get closer, to succumb to his invitation, but her still-jittery nerves and residual queasiness made her pause. All the teasing, all the big talk in the world didn't mean she could handle the entirety of what came next.

"Do you want to know your punishment, Skye?"

The *p*-word sent another rush of heat flooding through her and sparklers of tingling sensation flowered again. "Wh-what?"

"I'm not going to touch you."

Her gaze slowly lifted to his face.

"You can touch me all you like. But if you want to feel my skin on yours—you'll have to make that happen."

She blinked. "How?"

He smiled Satan's smile, lazy and sure. "Pick up

my hand, put it where you'd like. Bring yourself to my mouth."

Her trembling started again, but this was the good kind, the hot-and-cold kind that made her breasts and the place between her thighs swell. The love bites he'd left on her inner thighs began to throb. Still wrapped in the crocheted throw, Skye realized she was about to incinerate. Panting a little, she fought her way out of the blanket and pushed it to the floor.

Gage hadn't moved a muscle. His gaze was still fixed on her. "Would you touch *me* with your hand, Skye?"

His own were resting on his thighs, lax. Hers were in fists, and she unsprung her fingers one by one, until they were both spread like sea stars in a tide pool. Then she lifted her right arm, using her palm to cup his cheek.

Closing his eyes, he made a low sound of appreciation in the back of his throat. His whiskers prickled the tender cup of her hand, and she teased herself with the sensation, subtly stroking. Her thumb brushed the smooth surface of his lower lip.

Gage dipped his head, caught the pad between his teeth.

Skye gasped and felt herself go wet. His tongue swirled over the tip, circling, circling, and then he sucked, reminding her of the way he'd played with her nipples the other afternoon as she sat on his lap.

They recalled it, too, and stood stiff against the built-in bra cups of the new dress. She squirmed a little, and they shifted against the fabric, a private self-caress.

Gage released her thumb. "Oh, there's another rule," he mentioned, his tone casual.

"What?" Her hand fell from his face, back to her lap.

"No touching yourself, either. I saw that little shimmy."

She felt her face go red. "I wasn't touching myself."

"Hell, yes, you were." He pointed a finger at her. "No wiggles. No secret clenching, either."

Her inner muscles instantly tightened, and she almost moaned at the sweet pleasure of it, even as she felt another rise of heat on her face. How could mortification be such a turn-on? "I don't know what you're talking about," she said, aware how defensive she sounded. "And I don't see how you can...can tell any of that anyhow."

"Because I'm paying attention," he said in his Prince-of-Darkness voice. "I'm paying attention to *you*."

She shuddered, desire rising. Gage was drawing her toward him, his gravitational pull just like that of the moon on the ocean. She drifted closer, until she could see that he was flushed, too, the flickering candlelight showing the heightened color crossing his cheekbones.

Without thinking, she placed her mouth on the patch of warmth, her lips skating across it to find the masculine jut of his elegant nose. She followed that, too, then dropped lower to take a kiss.

He let her, opening so that her tongue could slip inside. She heard herself moan, appreciating the taste of fermented grape, berrylike and earthy at the same time. As she leaned closer, his body heat burned her upper arm.

Wanting more of it, she broke the kiss, then practically crawled over him so she could press her face to the muscled perfection of his chest. She felt him suck in a quick breath, but he held still, allowing her to rub her cheek and mouth against sleek skin and soft hair as if she were a cat.

Her lips encountered his nipple, its center point hardened. She played her tongue over it, lashing it with little flicks, and he groaned. Lifting her head, she took in his heaving chest and his now-fisted hands.

"Who's punishing whom now?" she whispered, thrilled with the husky tease in her voice.

"Witch," he said, but he was smiling. "Give me another kiss."

She did, and though he continued to refrain from touching her with his hands, he still seduced her, his lips moving on hers, his exotic-spice scent rising around them. The kisses caught her like a fish in a net; she was wholly consumed by them, by him. Her hands were on his shoulders, her bottom on his lap, and when her eyes fluttered open to see his fingers wrapped in the fabric of her skirt, it was his restraint that made her the rest-of-the-way sure.

"Take me to bed," she said, licking the line of his jaw. "Punish me there if you have to."

"If I get you to bed, the punishment is finished. Pleasure takes over."

"Oh, God."

He laughed, the devil satisfied with his wickedness. Then he had her up, off the couch. She didn't remember the walk to the bedroom. Inside, it was as she expected, lit by more candles, the wavering light as unsteady as her pulse. The bed looked huge, the covers already turned back. Her eyes were trained on it as she heard him say, "Strip."

Her gaze jumped to his. He grinned at her, the devil gone back to the deep blue sea, perhaps, leaving Gage behind. Her Gage. "Subtle," she said, chiding him.

He lifted his hands. "I'm afraid these might do damage to that pretty little piece of temptation."

But he had to get involved anyway, because Skye

couldn't manage the hidden back zipper herself. After a moment of watching her struggle, he strode over and bent his head to kiss her shoulder as his deft fingers ably managed to draw down the metal tab.

He chased her newly bared skin with his mouth, all the way to the dip at the small of her back. On his knees, he gently pulled the cloth until it fell at her feet. He nuzzled at the dimples above her panty-covered bottom.

Next he insinuated his tongue just beneath the top elastic band of the undergarment and worked its soft wetness from the side of one hip to the other.

"Oh, God," Skye said again, fervent.

Then Gage was standing again, and it was she who was off her feet, her back against the cool sheets, his body coming down beside hers. Elbows bracketing her head, Gage devoted himself to kissing her. Skye sought for purchase in a world gone hot and sweet and topsy-turvy. One hand clutched at the sheets, another gripped the waistband of his linen trousers. Her right leg twined over him, trying to bring him closer.

He pulled back, his face gone serious, and quickly jerked off his pants and boxers. Then there was nothing between his body and her but the candlelight, licking over the hollows and curves. His sex was fully aroused, thick and aggressive, and she took a breath, prepared to push back the panic. But it didn't arrive.

Because Gage was there, his concentrated gaze studying her face, gauging her reaction. *"I'm between you and your nightmares,"* he'd said that day while painting her living room, and she believed now that it was true.

"I'm okay," she said, feeling a little shy about the admission. "I'm okay."

It was Gage's turn to be fervent. "Thank the Lord."
But still, he was careful as he lay down beside her.

She turned into his body, wanting to feel its heat and
masculine intent. Though he didn't rush to the next level.
It was as if they'd started all over again, delicate kisses
to her face, tender strokes of his tongue into her mouth,
the lightest of brushes of his big hands over her breasts.

She arched into him, silently begging for more, and
he gave it, sliding down to lick at her breasts and suck at
her nipples and tickle her belly with soft caresses of his
tongue. He drew the scrap of her panties down her legs
and then he was between her thighs, his elbows widening them, his thumbs exploring the furrow of her sex.

"Oh," Skye said, jerking onto her elbows in sudden
alarm. "Well. Um."

He glanced up. "Yum? My thought exactly."

Her face burned. "Gage," she protested.

"Skye." He sighed a little, his breath brushing across
the wetness that was seeping from her. "If you must, look
at this as part of the punishment."

"What?"

"Or the pleasure," he said, and bent his head.

She fell back to the pillows at the first stroke of his
tongue. Her body seemed to coil, one sharp, quick twist
taking her all the way to the precipice. He laved the
pleated layers of her, opening her flesh so that all the secrets there were uncovered as she panted to stave off the
imminent explosion. His thumbs slid over liquid-glazed
softness, working to reveal her most sensitive point. It
throbbed, exposed to the air and to his eyes, and again
Skye waited for fear or vulnerability to steal her pleasure.

But nothing could do that, not when it was Gage who
was looking on her as if he'd found hidden treasure. His

tongue flattened over her clitoris and she jerked upward, to him, not away from him, and then his lips closed around the pearl of flesh. Suckling.

Sending her straight into screaming pleasure.

But not oblivion. Because it could only be this sweet by not forgetting who it was that treated her with such passionate care.

GAGE GROANED IN PLEASURE as he took Skye over. She was trembling, her body shaking through an orgasm fiery and strong. Sue him, but he felt ten feet tall, and hornier than he'd ever been in his life. He eased up on her sensitive skin, delicately lapping at her flesh before lifting away from her.

One of her hands fell to his shoulder, and he took it in his, kissing her knuckles as he moved to the pillow beside her. She was watching him with half-closed eyes. "Um…"

"Yum," he said again, helpfully.

The outline of her lips had been smudged by his kisses, making her mouth more red. Definitely swollen. The corners turned up and she gave him a reluctant smile. "You are bad."

"I am good," he said, leaning in to kiss her chin, her cheek, the downy arch of her dark eyebrow. "I am very, very good. Admit it."

"I can't deny that, but…" Her expression was too serious.

"It's okay to have fun, Skye. We can play here, honey."

She appeared uncertain. So he teased her with a flurry of baby kisses, pecking them on her face and down her neck until she giggled at the tickling and pushed at his chest. He grabbed her shoulders then, flipping to his back and bringing her over him.

Her body went still, as his cock pressed into her belly. Then her eyes rounded and her muscles tensed. "Do you have condoms? If you don't—"

"I have condoms."

She relaxed. "Okay, then," she said, looking at him expectantly.

When he didn't move, she frowned. "Do you want me to get them?"

"The condoms?"

"Of course, the condoms." She wiggled against him, forcing him to clamp his hands on her butt before they wouldn't need a rubber after all.

"We've got something to do before that," he told her.

"What something?" She squirmed again, and he laid a light slap on one tempting buttock. "Ouch," she protested. "What was that for?"

"For forgetting the promise I made to you."

A line developed between her eyebrows. "What—"

And then he saw she remembered, her eyelids flaring, her whole body heating in his arms. "I can't," she whispered. "You won't."

"You can. I will." She'd come again before he entered her. Two times, just as he'd told her.

He watched her mouth open, and expected more argument, but then she just dipped her head and treated him to a lavish, wet kiss. He groaned, twisting again to take her under him. But she was like an eel, squeezing out from beneath his larger frame to gain advantage.

The bed turned into a sweet battleground then. She was determined to make him break, he decided as she held down his shoulders and extracted more kisses. Probably thought she could get him to cry "Uncle" or at least "condom." But he was determined and she was already turned on again, her breath panting as he flipped her to the mattress and turned his attention to her breasts.

They were so pretty, soft and full, with hard nipples that he pressed against the roof of his mouth just to hear her moan. His palm slid down her belly and over her hip and he knew he was winning when her knee canted to the side, instinctively asking for his touch. Still teasing her breasts, he brought his hand to her swollen, flowered flesh, reveling in the slick heat there. He slid his thumb to her clitoris just as he sucked harder on her tight nipple and she was gone again just like that, her eyes squeezed tightly shut as her hips pulsed.

In the aftermath, her arms and legs were splayed across the mattress in exhausted abandon. Running his gaze over her, he chuckled. "You look like a victim of disaster."

One eye opened. "Disaster? Is that what you call yourself?"

He grinned at her. "I call myself Stunning Sex Man, because I believe I just delivered two spectacular orgasms."

Both of her eyes were staring at him now. "Stunning Sex Man?"

"New superhero. Bounds into bedrooms and dispenses incredible, passionate experiences to beautiful women."

She frowned. He wondered if she might object to the "women" aspect of his job description. Instead, she tapped her chest with a finger. "*I* want a superhero name. What could I be?"

"I don't know… Didn't you meet with a repairman today? You could be Plumber's Helper Girl."

That galvanized her. She sat up, then went on attack, bringing him down to the mattress in a wrestling move that brought her knee a little too close to his jewels. "Hey, hey, hey," he said, grabbing her wrists while laughing so hard he couldn't breathe. "Be careful. You almost emasculated Stunning Sex Man."

"That's what you get. Plumber's Helper Girl. Bleh. I want a sexy name, too."

"Have to prove yourself, babe," he said, still laughing.

"I'll prove myself," she said, then reared over him again to lock her mouth to his.

She kissed the laughter out of him. He tried remembering this was fun, that they were engaging in play time, that he was Stunning Sex Man, but then she lifted her head and he looked into her face. It took his breath, framed as it was by the long, mermaid-wavy length of her hair. That strange feeling he'd had when he first saw her by Tess's pool overcame him again.

The air was hard to move through. It slowed his actions, made everything but his heartbeat sluggish. He cupped her face in wonder and she stared at him, as if alert to this new turn of things.

This serious turn of things.

His blood chugged through his system, his cock screamed at him for immediate release, but it was all slow motion, the way her lashes fluttered, the way her body turned, then spread for him, the way he reached for the condom, rolled it over himself. Candlelight gleamed on her lips, wet from his kiss. He stared at them as he fitted his body to hers.

She made a sound as he breached her. A moan, a plea, it came to him as if through water. His body was shaking with only an inch of himself inside the heated tightness of her. He pushed, rolling his hips to ease his way.

Whispered words echoed through the room, his.

"Relax. Yeah. Just like that. Oh, sweet. Tight. So damn tight."

Then he was in, all the way, and he closed his eyes at the firm hold of her, wrapped around him like a sleek fist. Friction came next, the slide and squeeze, and though he saw only blackness from behind his eyelids, this particular darkness was okay because Skye was with him. Not the imaginary Skye, not Letters Skye, but the flesh-and-blood siren of the cove who clutched his shoulders and made soft, pleading sounds in his ear.

He wouldn't last long, but he gritted his teeth because ending too soon would be the true disaster. His body pumped, he felt the bite of her nails at his shoulder and when he dropped his head to place a sucking kiss at her neck, her telltale quiver freed him from restraint. He picked up the pace, his pulse racing, too, and as she lifted into each of his thrusts, he slid his hand between them, opening her around the thickness of his cock, spreading her folds so he could find the sweet spot.

Touching there, a wet, sure stroke, that set her free.

And he spun into his own climax, pulled along by the tether that was binding them.

CHAPTER TWELVE

Dawn colored the sky an opalescent pinkish-gray, the color of the pearls in the long, flapper-style string that belonged to her great-great-grandmother, the famous silent-era actress Edith Essex. Unlike the jeweled collar, the infamous piece that was the source of scandal and rumor, the pearls' location was known. Her sister had worn them on her wedding day in early June, her face glowing as she promised herself to the man who had restored her faith in love after she'd suffered from a tragic loss. As she prepared to leave on her honeymoon, she'd given them to Skye, saying they'd be hers to wear next.

At the time, when she'd been hiding from a man's glance, not to mention shrinking at the mere thought of a man's touch, she'd suspected they wouldn't see another nuptials until the next generation. But now? She glanced back at Beach House No. 9, where she'd left Gage sleeping, sprawled on the bed like a large piece of beautiful, breathing flotsam washed up onshore.

She'd awakened at first light and, walking along the beach to her house, it appeared she was the only early riser in the cove. Tess had told her once that it was the ironic truth of summer…kids and vacationers were just starting to get accustomed to sleeping late when it was time to return to the early wake-up calls of school or work. It reminded Skye that September was fast approaching, and then most of the cottages would go empty for the off-season.

Gage, too, would be gone, but what he'd helped her rediscover wouldn't. Last night had proven she was a woman again, capable of urges and desires that were strong enough to overcome her memories and fears. As the morning breeze teased at her loose hair and sent shivers down her bare arms and legs, she thought she actually might now be liberated from the sloppy clothes and tight braids that she'd used as a shield between herself and her fears over the past several months.

But that newfound freedom wouldn't stop the seasons. The cove would go quiet and still, just as it was this morning.

She shivered, then purposefully turned her mind from that thought to replay a moment of the night before. Stunning Sex Man! Her lips curved. The arrogance of him! But God, it was so attractive, just as all the incarnations he'd displayed last night had been. The seductive devil, the playful lover, the serious man who'd come inside her body in such slow degrees that she'd felt a hot tear slip down her temple, so needy was she to be completely joined with him.

She'd ached to have him inside her, and when he'd finally filled her, their hearts beating against each other, some bright knowledge had flashed inside her. Something like…like…fate.

Or doom.

Because yes, following right after, like the thunder after a lightning strike, a deep dark knell of warning had reverberated through her.

She might have run from it, from him, in the aftermath of her third orgasm—*three!*—but he'd curled so closely around her after his climax that she'd been unable to slide from the bed. Then she'd dozed off herself, only waking to find he'd let her go.

The way she was letting him go.

She was well aware, now that the night was over and the distractions of burning glances and smoldering kisses had cooled, that she'd failed in her plan to have him open up to her. Instead, of course, he'd opened *her* up.

It wouldn't happen again. There was no need for an unwise, somebody-might-take-it-too-seriously repeat. She'd even abandon her hope of getting him to spill his secrets. It required a closeness she couldn't afford any longer.

Blowing out a long breath, Skye approached her front door. She was mere feet away when Polly emerged from her little cottage. Her eyes went wide at the sight of Skye.

"The walk of shame!"

Heat rose up her neck. "Pol—"

"I've never been so proud of you." The other woman grinned. "You finally got into bed with the man you've been mooning over all these months."

"Mooning? No—"

"Face it, Skye, you used to go shivery in anticipation when the mail was delivered. So…what was the turning point? Did Tess serve aphrodisiacs?"

That reminded Skye that Polly had missed the party. "What happened to you? Why did you turn down Teague?"

"Because men are dopes. Well, Teague's a dope. Maybe your guy is different."

"Gage is not my guy."

Polly tilted her head. "Really? So, he sucks in bed?"

"No." At her friend's knowing glance, she felt herself blushing again. "He's actually Stunning Sex Man."

Polly snorted. "What?"

Skye swallowed her smile. "A superhero. A yet-undiscovered one. I may take up writing comic books just to chronicle his greatness for the world's appreciation."

Her friend grabbed her elbow. "Okay, this calls for a private talk-and-walk. I was going to head for the tide pools, but this gets you any destination you want."

"I'm a little chilled," Skye said, resisting.

Polly dragged her up the beach, her grip merciless. "Your memories will keep us both warm."

So they continued northward, Skye throwing out a few hints here and there, without getting too personal. Polly sighed and moaned when appropriate, and her friend's good humor and clear envy put Skye in a better mood.

"I need Stunning Sex Man sex," Polly said, upon reaching the tide pools.

"You'll have to find your own superhero," Skye said quickly, then sent her friend a quick glance. "Though he's still not my guy."

"I can't think why not. Remember that summer fling I recommended?"

"Because that offer isn't on the table. He was just being a…a friend to me last night."

"We should all have such good friends," Polly muttered.

"Like you and Teague?"

The blonde sent her a glance under lowered brows. "We're not talking about Teague. I've kicked him out of my life."

Skye glanced southward, once again arrested by the quietness of the cove. Yes, autumn was on its way. "Then it will just be you and me," she said. With Polly next door, perhaps she could face it.

Still, it seemed doubtful. While she might have taken back her femininity, she could feel those bogeymen just waiting to pounce. Her heart thumped unpleasantly at the idea of it.

"Just you and me," Polly repeated. "That could work. What's our equivalent of bros over hos?"

Still pensive, Skye shrugged.

Polly snapped her fingers. "I've got it. Friends over men." She extended her fist. "Forever."

Skye gave it a gentle bump with her own. "Friends over men forever," she said, smiling a little. All right. Maybe that prospect could keep her at the cove.

POLLY SAT ON HER SOFA, using a lap desk set over her thighs as she made out name tags for her kindergarteners. The front door was open to let in the warm late-afternoon air. Playful little-kid shrieks rising over the shush of the surf reminded her of school recess. A game of tag, perhaps, or little girls chasing after the object of their affection. And, as if she'd conjured him, the object of hers was suddenly casting a shadow on her living room floor. Teague White stood in the doorway, looking a little uncertain.

And a whole lot delicious.

She lost herself for a minute, just gazing at him. He was so man-handsome—all broad shoulders and lean hips—in a pair of beat-up jeans and a T-shirt advertising a 10K race. They'd run it together, he keeping his pace to hers, despite his longer legs. At the race's end, they'd wandered through the park scooping up freebie yogurts and energy drinks. She'd seen a couple of women sliding speculative glances his way and had once caught him looking back in return. Instead of encouraging him to make conversation, she'd put her hand on his arm, wincing.

The woman had moved on—assuming he was Polly's, as she'd planned. "Tendonitis acting up," she'd guilelessly explained to him, and let him find her a seat and an ice pack. Without a smidgeon of guilt.

Naughty Polly.

Now he braced one hand on the doorjamb. "You haven't returned my calls. You've ignored my texts."

If *ignoring* could be called snatching up her phone every time one came in, then agonizing over the decision to reply or not. She put aside the piece of tagboard on which she'd written "Madison" and moved on to "Noah." "I've been busy. Class lists came out."

His footsteps clapped against the hardwood as he came into the room. She took a quick peek at his face, but if he remembered seeing her standing in that same spot, virtually nude, there was no sign of it. She'd wondered about his plan for handling the situation. He was a straightforward type of guy—and she thought his style would be to attack it head-on. As she wrote "Olivia," she prepared herself to hear him demand, "What the hell was that about?"

She had no idea how to respond if he did. Driven by impulse, she'd thrown off the dress with the vague hope that he'd be overcome by a lust so powerful that it would plow through the barriers between them: their years-long platonic friendship and his avowed devotion to another woman. When instead he'd retreated, wearing an expression of abject horror, Polly had known it was past time to give up on him.

He cleared his throat, and her fingers tightened on her

pen, her mind spinning through all the possible ways she might answer his inevitable question.

"Your..." He hesitated. "Your printing's so perfect."

Astonished, she jerked her chin up. She stared at his face, the lean cheeks, strong jaw and unreadable expression. He was going to ignore the memory of the naked girl in the living room? Unsure whether to be relieved or just further insulted, she shook her head. "Nothing about me is perfect."

He looked perplexed. "So...how's your class shaping up?"

"More boys than girls," she said. "Including a Bradley, a Beau, a Brody and a Bobby."

A quick grin flashed over Teague's face. "Another chance to prove your totally unscientific, entirely anecdotal name theory."

She nodded, solemn. "Yes. I'm sure once again I'll gather ample evidence that B-named boys skew bad on the behavior spectrum."

"Of course, I also know they're often your favorite."

"All girls have a thing for bad boys."

His smile was wry. "Maybe that's where I've gone wrong."

Polly sighed. "Teague—"

"I came by," he said, talking over her, "to tell you about this shower thing coming up for Griffin and Jane."

She was already aware of it. Instead of being women-only, it was a couples party. "I can't make it."

Teague frowned. "Polly, you promised—"

"I'm sorry. I'm busy then."

His brows came together over his dark chocolate eyes. He ran his gaze over her face and she could feel a liar's blush crawling up her neck. It hypersensitized her skin, and for a moment she imagined it was his mouth caus-ing the heat and the prickling sensation. Her longing for his touch mortified her and she set the lap desk aside and stood, needing to disrupt the turn of her emotions.

She glanced at her watch. "Look—"

"I didn't tell you the date and time of the shower," Teague said slowly.

Taking a breath, she squared her shoulders and looked him straight in the eye. "It doesn't matter the date or the time. I won't be able to make it."

"Polly—"

"I'm no longer available." It killed her to say it, but she had to move on. He never saw below the surface of her, nor did he seem the least bit curious about what they might have together if they took the relationship in a dif-ferent direction. "And now I have to go."

"Why?" Teague demanded.

She answered the question she suspected wasn't the one he asked. "I have a date," she said, tapping the face of her watch. "I'm meeting someone at Captain Crow's, and if I don't get going right now I'll be late."

His brows shot up. "You have a date?"

"Don't look so shocked. Some men actually find me attractive."

"It's not that," he said. "It's just…I…I…"

Without waiting for him to stammer out a save, she stomped toward the door and grabbed her purse off the hook on the wall. Then she fished out her keys and ush-ered him out. Finally she locked the door behind them both.

Sparing him no second glance, she headed up the beach.

"Later, Gator," he called out from behind her.

Her feet almost halted, the private nickname chipping off another corner of her heart. Ignoring the pain of it, she continued along the sand.

At Captain Crow's, her date sat waiting at the long counter facing the beach. There was a Dodgers ball cap on the stool beside him, the agreed-upon sign. Pasting on her best smile, she held out her hand. "Ben?" It wasn't lost on her that his name started with a *B*.

Jumping to his feet, he gave her palm a sure grip. He didn't seem bad in any sense of the word. Thirtyish, with sandy hair and hazel eyes, he looked a lot like her teacher friend Maureen, who was his sister and the one who'd organized the setup. He slid the cap off the seat and pulled it out for her. "What would you like to drink?"

Her white wine took only moments to arrive and she clinked the glass against his bottle of Negro Modelo. "To...?" she asked.

"New friendships," Ben said.

She didn't let her smile fall, although it wasn't a sentiment she supported. Friendships, she had. The last thing she wanted to expend energy on was another male pal.

But she discovered she did like Ben. His sister was friendly, easygoing and a pleasure to talk to—and he was just the same.

As he began telling her about his work in IT, her attention wandered. It wasn't that she wasn't interested; it was just that there was a strange feeling feathering over the back of her neck. Taking a quick glance over her shoulder, she targeted the source of her disquiet.

Teague! He was sitting on the other side of the deck, nursing a beer. And staring at her. Her temper kindled. Where did he get off bird-dogging her?

To demonstrate her disdain, she swiveled on her stool,

presenting more of her back to him. Then she gave Ben her full focus. He told a funny story about a coworker who claimed a massive computer conspiracy whenever he forgot his latest password. When he couldn't log in, he thought it a sure sign that the government—or one of his sons' friends; they both had the same nefarious purposes in his mind—had hacked into his accounts.

Laughing, Polly stole another secret glance toward Teague, though she cursed herself for it. A woman had taken the seat beside him. Brunette and voluptuous, she seemed to be carrying on a conversation without much input from Teague. Unlike Ben, Polly highly doubted his contribution to any discussion would be talk about his job—he never offered much about that. Which, she decided with another narrow-eyed glance at Big Boobs, was a good thing. From the occasional social event she'd attended with Teague's coworkers, she'd come to understand that firefighters carried around a virtual get-laid-free card.

Ben was so nice she felt comfortable accepting a second glass of wine. But then, with sunset approaching, they both seemed content to end the outing. "My sister was smart for suggesting we do it like this," he said. "'Not to exceed two hours means no big pressure.'"

That had been Maureen's promise to Polly, and the only reason she'd agreed in the first place. Not that she didn't want to move on from her best-pal/now-biggest-mistake Teague, but blind dates usually sucked. "I had a good time," she told Ben, holding out her hand once more. She didn't let herself look around the deck as they said their farewells and made friendly but noncommittal noises about meeting again.

She liked that even more about Ben and was happy

to give him her cell phone number before he headed to the parking lot and she back to her beach cottage. After unlocking her front door, she decided not to go inside quite yet. There were two vintage metal garden chairs on the miniscule porch, and she sat in one to watch the sun complete its scamper from the sky. The end of day always made her a little melancholy, probably because of those first months after her father had left. As dark settled in, she'd had to accept that another day had passed without her parents' reconciliation.

Another day gone without her father reaching out to his daughter. Ultimately she'd had to accept that he'd divorced her with as much finality as he'd divorced her mother.

Closing her eyes, she let her head rest against the wall of the cottage. It would be all right, she reminded herself now, as she had then. And this time she was old enough not to make stupid blunders in her search to fill the void of a man's absence in her life. In a couple of weeks she'd have rows of little bodies to occupy her during the day and she'd fill her evenings with paperwork and classroom prep.

What did she need a man for when she had enthusiastic hugs from five-year-olds to look forward to? A romantic bouquet was no better than a handful of wilted dandelions grasped in the grubby fist of one of her ubiquitous *B*-boys. This yawning loneliness would be filled soon with parent conferences and after-work hash sessions with her female teacher friends.

"Polly."

She opened her eyes. The sky was silver, all warmth bled from it, and the masculine figure in front of her was a dark silhouette. She didn't need to see a face to know who it was.

"What are you doing here?" *Big Boobs boring?*

"I thought I'd just…check on you. Things seem—"

"Check on me?" She didn't let him finish. "What for? You're not my big brother."

"I know. I just saw you with that guy and I…" Teague's voice trailed off.

"You…what? You wanted to see if I'd bring him back here with me?"

It was too dark to see Teague's expression, but she could feel his rejection of the idea. "God, Pol. No."

"Why not?" Everything she'd been feeling lately— frustration, dashed hopes, jealousy, loneliness—rolled into an ugly, uneven ball of annoyance, thumping around inside her belly. "You don't think I'm attractive enough to get him into my bed?"

"Polly, that's not what I meant at all." He sat on the chair beside hers. Its seat was narrow, his legs were long and one of his knees brushed hers.

She jerked away. "Then what did you mean?"

"I know you. I know you wouldn't just meet some man for the first time and bring him home with you. You're too…I don't know, that's just not what you'd do."

A bitter laugh barked from her throat. "That just shows how wrong you are. You've got some squeaky-clean image of me that's completely off the mark."

He went still. "Is that right?"

"That's right."

There was a long pause. "Is there something you want to tell me?" he finally asked.

There were a dozen. How she sometimes stared at his hands while he ate and imagined him feeding her juicy slices of peach in bed. The illicit thrill she got out of rubbing sunscreen on his back. That she never asked him to reciprocate in case he guessed why his touch raised goose bumps on her flesh.

"Pol?"

She folded her arms over her chest. "Yeah, there's something you should know. There's a good reason I give all those bad boys a second chance…because I was once a very bad girl myself."

It didn't take a genius to understand why she hadn't shared this with him before. While she might have put up a token objection every time he referred to her as "perfect," she'd held the truth close to her chest because she figured he preferred her that way. But now that she knew he didn't prefer her at all—in any romantic sense—she might as well burst his bubble herself.

"How bad could you have been?" he scoffed, though she thought she detected a note of uncertainty in his voice.

"Pretty bad," she said, matter-of-fact. "I lost my virginity to the private tennis coach my mother hired after my father left. He was thirty-five years old."

Teague stiffened. "And you were…?"

"Fifteen. He was hot, newly separated from his wife, and my backhand didn't actually need as much work as some of my other physical skills."

"Jesus." Teague rubbed a palm over his face. "Jesus, Pol."

"The next year, I had an internship at a small accounting firm. I don't know how old Greg was—he refused to tell me—but he was another lonely divorcé."

This time Teague didn't say a word, but she knew

he held his breath, clearly waiting for the denouement. Well, then.

"Senior year in high school, there was this mean girl who made fun of the one friend of mine who refused to go away like all the others I'd pushed off during the divorce. It was a cruel campaign of ridicule that didn't let up even after the mean girl beat my friend for Homecoming Queen. I got her back, though."

"How?" he asked, his voice tight.

"I fucked her daddy," Polly said, matter-of-fact. "Then anonymously emailed her a photo of her smiling papa between the sheets of a stranger's bed."

"Oh, Gator."

The nickname made a high whine start in her ears. She'd probably never hear that word on his lips again. She steeled her spine, and sent him a cool look. "So, what do you think of Perfect Polly now?"

He reached out, found her hand. "I think she was looking for love in all the wrong places."

The compassion in his voice made her stomach jitter. She jumped to her feet, her hand sliding from his as she dashed for her door. Opening it, she allowed herself a single backward glance. "You nailed it. And how funny is that, when you've never nailed me?"

CHAPTER THIRTEEN

June 1

Dear Gage,
Well, my sister has packed her bags and driven off.
I thought she might be persuaded to stay at the cove
and manage the properties with me, but once again
it's a man who sent her on her way. Not at a run
this time...it's a happy, not a tragic reason, thank
goodness. Still, it doesn't change the fact that I'm
the only Alexander left in Southern California and
I'm rethinking my stubborn determination to stay.
Maybe it's time for Crescent Cove to be someone
else's legacy.
Skye, contemplating other horizons

Skye,
Could you trust anyone else to preserve the magic?
No pressure (ha) but I don't think I could. I see my-
self visiting there one future day and taking photos
of you surrounded by your children, the next gen-
eration that will curate the living museum that is
the cove. Shall I come sooner? Maybe my camera
and I can remind you of the extraordinariness of
your heritage.
Gage, alarmed

Dear Gage,
Don't come! I'm aware that might sound unwel-
come, but I believe some things are better served
as memories savored from afar.
Yours, Skye

When Gage woke alone the morning after he'd had Skye in his bed, her state of mind was in no doubt. If she'd been on the pillow beside his, he might have worried, but her absence said everything.

That what they'd done between the sheets had been nothing.

Well, of course it wasn't *nothing*. Good God, not that, but it had changed nothing between them. He'd lusted after her, she'd lusted right back and despite her momentary hiccup after suspecting intruders in one of the cove cottages, they'd had a satisfying adventure between the sheets.

He was glad he'd proved to her that there was fun to be had there. Sure, there were those final moments of… of…somberness, when he'd felt connected to her in a way that went beyond the physical, but certainly that made sense. They'd shared so many thoughts through their letters that it was only natural that the lovema—sex—was on a slightly different-than-usual plane.

Despite his lack of concern over their night together, he wished he'd had a chance to visit with her in person the following day. But he'd had to scramble to make a sequence of meetings set up by his photography agent. The L.A. traffic had been its usual beastly self, swallowing him up and only spitting him out after his dinner meeting ended at 10:00 p.m. Exhausted by all the business, social, and vehicular maneuverings, he'd fallen into bed at No. 9. It was the second best night of sleep he'd had since Jahandar had taken him to that fateful meet in the arid countryside.

Now, though, with a shower, breakfast and a few hours of catching up on world events under his belt, he decided to seek out Skye. They'd exchanged cryptic texts between his appointments the day before, and she'd seemed in good spirits, but he was going to make sure all was well. With his time at the cove dwindling, he refused to be patient about any lingering awkwardness she might feel.

He needed to know that Skye knew she could be with him in the days that remained without *being* with him.

It was nearing midday as he walked up the beach. He figured she might be home for lunch. Maybe he'd grab her by the hand and take her with him to Captain Crow's for a sandwich.

But as he neared her bungalow, he saw that someone else had gotten there ahead of him. A man stood on her porch, obscuring almost all Gage could see of Skye's slender figure. He lengthened his stride, eating up the asphalt of her front walk.

"Skye!"

She peered around the other guy, and that's when he realized there were male hands on her shoulders. *Hands that were not Gage's.*

His feet stuttered to a halt as a caustic green acid seemed to pour into his gut. Had he eaten something rotten for breakfast? But what was rotten, he realized almost instantly, was the idea of another man touching *his* siren of the cove.

Shit. That wasn't good.

"Gage?" She sent him a distracted smile. "Did you need something?"

Her companion—that ex of hers—now turned to look at Gage, his arms dropping back to his sides. "Oh," the man said. "It's you."

Gage ran his gaze over the other man's natty outfit. He apparently had golf on his agenda, unless dressing like an ice-cream man and wearing white tasseled shoes had become the latest fad in the States. "Dagwood," Gage said with a nod.

"Dalton," the ex corrected, not the least amused.

"Whoops." Gage tried to look repentant.

Rolling her eyes, Skye stepped around her visitor. "Did you need something?" she repeated.

It was his first real look at her since he'd fallen asleep spooned around her body. He'd nuzzled the curve of her neck and shoulder, breathing in the scents of Skye and mutual lust as he fell into sleep.

Perhaps she remembered that, too, because a faint flush stained her cheeks. Her hair was unbound again, the lovely dark mass of it no longer contained but allowed to stream down her back. A faint gloss of lipstick shined her soft mouth and she'd shunned the menswear for a formfitting T-shirt and a full skirt of thin cotton layers that skimmed the top of her knees.

Again, it wasn't a particularly revealing getup, except in that it revealed that Skye was feeling more comfortable in her own skin.

Her skin... His mind spun another memory. He remembered the smooth heat of her thighs, the tender flesh between them. His mouth had left love bites there, and he wondered if he'd find his marks still on her if he tossed up those filmy sheets of fabric and bared her for his gaze.

"Gage?" she asked expectantly.

He cleared his throat. He'd had a purpose; it just seemed to have slipped his mind. "I...uh..."

Dalton interrupted. "I only have a few minutes before I have to leave to make my tee time," he told Skye.

"If you've just a few minutes," Gage said, starting forward again, "you'd better get a move on. Traffic's a bitch."

The other man frowned at him. "Thank you, but—"

"No thanks necessary." Gage looked at Skye and jerked his head in the direction of the restaurant up the sand. "You. Me. Lunch."

"Oh, I don't..." Her words trailed off as he reached over and snagged her hand. Her gaze fell to their entwined fingers, her expression arrested.

Gage knew why. It was the Bowline on a Bight, the Icicle Hitch, the Rat-Tail Stopper. The Big Trouble he'd called it two days before. That sense that they were inextricably bound was washing over him again.

It was because they were such good friends, he thought, his fingers tightening on hers.

Pen pals.

Except neither of those relationships explained the absolute sense of...of rightful belonging that overtook him when touching her like this. They lifted their gazes at the same time and he stared into her eyes, their color the deep ocean green where every mystery of the universe dwelled. He couldn't breathe.

"Skye," Dalton said, his voice impatient. "I really need just a little bit more of your time."

Gage needed just a little bit more of Skye—or a lot more, he admitted to himself. Going back to platonic pals wasn't an option any longer, he was beginning to realize. Unless he left the cove early, unless he skipped his twin's wedding and hopped on a plane this very after-noon to take him thousands of miles away, he was going to have more of Skye.

If she'd let him.

Her eyes were saucer-wide and he squeezed her hand again. "Let's go have lunch at Captain Crow's," he said, his voice gruff.

"I…" She glanced at Dalton. "I can't right this min-ute. Wait for me there?"

Leave her alone? With a man who couldn't seem to understand the word *no?* Gage shook his head. "I don't think—"

"It's fine," she assured him. "I'm fine."

He gazed on her another long moment, gauging for himself.

"All right," he finally conceded. "But don't think you can escape me." With effort, he tacked on a small smile to lighten the warning.

Her flush deepened. "I'm not sure escape was ever an option," she murmured. Then she withdrew her hand from his. "I'll be there soon."

Dalton sent him a pointed look of triumph, which Gage ignored, despite another deluge of the evil acidy stuff flooding his system. *Your victory is just temporary, dude,* he thought, then shoved away the notion that what-ever concessions he won from Skye himself wouldn't be long-lasting, either.

But his discomfort didn't ease up, even when he was shown to a free umbrella-topped table on the restaurant's crowded deck. The day was so beautiful it almost hurt to look at it—the sky azure, the foam of the toppling waves a brilliant white, the sand sparkling from the mica that caught the sunlight. Squinting against the glare, he drummed his fingers on the varnished wood, impatient for Skye to join him. Impatient to get the cards on the table.

His order of iced tea was set in front of him, and he brought the sweating glass to his forehead, hoping it would cool him down a little. His nerves jangled and his libido was hopping about like a jumping bean. He'd never felt so damn unsettled when it came to a woman. *Jesus.*

What would happen if she didn't say yes?

What the hell had she done to him? he suddenly wondered, resentful. A continued liaison was never part of the plan. He'd considered going to bed with her in terms of…of a sort of good turn, their night together her sexual Rx, and instead he was the one who now felt a little sick.

With jealousy. With want.

With need.

Women!

He scowled at the one walking by his table, then realized it was Skye's BFF, Polly, who hesitated as she passed. "Are you all right?" she asked, giving him a wary look.

He grunted, and shoved at the chair opposite him with his foot. "Would you like to sit down?"

"I'm not sure," Polly said, a glint of humor in her eyes. "You look a little dangerous."

"I need a distraction."

She made a play at glancing around. "The day isn't gorgeous enough for you?"

"Maybe this place is too gorgeous," he said. "It's making me soft." Stupid.

"Oh, yeah, that's right. You're the guy who always needs a challenge," Polly said, slipping into the free seat. "Are you bored here?"

Not for one minute. Though he supposed an indefinite dose of Crescent Cove might get monotonous. If it was a permanent home like Tess and David's Cheviot Hills, he'd probably go nuts in a month…though the ocean was ever-changing, no sunset was the same, and the horizon hinted at endless possibilities.

"I've got obligations overseas," he said.

"And you can always get your cove fix through letters," Polly suggested brightly. "I assume you'll keep corresponding with Skye."

"Well, of course—" He halted. She might not reply. If he screwed this up and left things on bad terms with her, then he'd have lost that lodestar that had kept him sane. That he might need to keep him sane again. Shit.

Maybe he better keep his hands off her in the future after all.

He was staring, unseeing, at his iced tea when he heard the clearing of a female throat. His head lifted, and there she was. A breeze came up. It played with the layers of fabric at her knees and caught at her hair, dragging it over her face. She clamped her hands to her thighs to keep her skirt in place. Gage jumped to his feet and tended to her hair himself, pulling it back with both hands to tuck the glossy mass behind her ears. Then he cupped her face in his palms, gazing at the delicate beauty of her.

His body went on high alert, his muscles tightening. Instinct urged him to put himself between her and the gusty breeze, and the too-bright sun, and any other element that might endanger her. Doubts and second thoughts evaporated. He wanted to wrap himself around her; be both her fortress and her sanctuary, and then, when he was gone, the lover she never, ever forgot.

"I'll leave you two alone."

Startled at the intrusion, he glanced over to see Polly rising from her seat. "Yeah," he said, already dismissing her from his mind. "Thanks for the company."

Without even waiting for the other woman to move off, he was staring at Skye again, the pull of her like an undertow, but he didn't give a shit about survival.

He touched his forehead to hers, and felt her tremble in his hold. "You know, we seem to generate some powerful juju between us," he told her.

She nodded, trembled again.

He laid it on the line. "Forget about lunch. Come back to my bed. Stay there until it's time for me to go."

SKYE WAS TUGGED AWAY from Gage, just as his words started to sink in. *Come back to my bed. Stay there until it's time for me to go.* Polly had her by the arm, and it appeared she had no intention of letting go.

"I'll bring her back shortly," her blonde friend said to Gage, in her cheery, kindergarten-teacher voice. "You just sit tight."

Gage opened his mouth as if to protest, then shut it. He must see the same implacability on Polly's face that Skye did. Though a pair of sunglasses covered her eyes, her friend's expression was set and her jaw was firm.

"I just need a few minutes of girl talk." Polly continued towing her in the direction of the bar. Upon reaching it, she practically lifted Skye onto one of the stools. For a small woman, she had wiry strength that came from a career of wrangling little kids. "Thank me," she said.

"For what?" Skye glanced back at Gage to see that he'd resettled into his seat and was staring out at the ocean. "What the heck was that about?"

Come back to my bed. Stay there until it's time for me to go.

"I'm giving you a chance to think this through without being under the influence of Stunning Sex Man."

"You heard what he said?" *Come back to my bed. Stay there until it's time for me to go.*

"I was standing right beside you, not that I expect either of you noticed with all the pheromones buzzing around you like electrons circling atoms."

"'Powerful juju,'" Skye murmured.

Polly called out to the guy behind the bar. "Hey, Steve, could we get a couple of lattes?"

It was that same young man who'd served them that afternoon a couple of weeks before, the one who was the film friend of Addy's. It didn't take him long to concoct a couple of caffeine-and-milk beverages, and he smiled at Skye as he slid her oversize cup in front of her. "Nice to see you again," he said. "You don't get in here much in the afternoons, I guess. That's when my shifts are usually scheduled."

"No." She gave him a polite smile. "I've been pretty busy this summer."

"Searching for the famous jeweled collar?" he asked, picking up a bar towel and sliding it across the surface. "Has it come to light?"

"No." He was looking at her so expectantly she felt compelled to say a little more. "But Addy found a letter from my great-great-grandmother to my great-great-grandfather that seems to at least confirm its existence. As a matter of fact, a local reporter is writing a feature about it for the Sunday Lifestyles section of the newspaper. It's supposed to come out later this month."

His hand paused in its wax-on, wax-off movement. "I'll look forward to that."

Skye lifted her cup to her lips. "This weekend's paper or the next."

"And I'll look forward to talking to you more about it, too." He smiled. "I've scored some evening shifts so maybe we'll run into each other more often."

Something about that smile of his set Skye's nerves jumping. "Uh, sure," she said, and was relieved when a waitress came up to him with drink orders. She leaned close to Polly. "Does he give you the creeps, or is it just me?"

Her friend shoved her sunglasses to the top of her head as if to get a better look at the barista. Skye drew back, concerned by the shadows under her friend's eyes. "Polly, what's wrong?"

The blonde flicked her a glance. "I'm good. I'm always good."

Skye frowned. "I'm not letting you get away with your usual pat answer."

"It's nothing you need to know about."

"Are you kidding? You just meddled in my life. I think it's only fair that I get to be nosy about yours."

Polly glanced at her again, then heaved a sigh. "Fine. Maybe it will be instructive to you." Leaning down, she blew across the surface of her drink. Then she straightened without taking a sip. "I told Teague my secrets. You know, about…about my wild teenage rebellion."

Skye was careful to let nothing show on her face. "I was surprised you hadn't before. You've been so close to him."

The other woman shrugged. "Maybe I was afraid to

shatter his illusions. He always thought I could do no wrong."

Skye placed her hand on her friend's arm. "Pol, you were a kid acting out in kid fashion. You didn't do wrong, you just did…"

"Stupid. Hurtful."

"Because *you* were hurting. You know that, right?"

Polly smiled, but it didn't make her appear any less tired. "The double major in psychology and education knows that." She touched her chest with her fingertips. "But in here there's a piece that's not so sure."

"What did Teague say?"

"I didn't give him much of a chance to say anything."

"Still," Skye said loyally, "he *is* a dope."

"Told you."

They were silent a minute. Then Skye picked up her latte. "Out of curiosity, how did you think I might find your situation with Teague-the-dope instructive?"

"Heck, I don't know." Polly glanced over her shoulder in the direction of Gage. "Maybe it's safer to keep your secrets?"

Wasn't it too late for that? Skye wondered. He knew about the home invasion, he knew about the problems it had caused for her…but he didn't know everything. She stole her own peek at him. He appeared relaxed in his chair, but she could see his fingertips drumming on the tabletop.

He didn't know how close she was to falling for him.

If he did, she suspected he wouldn't have made that tempting, delicious demand. *Come back to my bed. Stay there until it's time for me to go.*

"So…are you?" Polly asked.

Skye turned her head to look at her friend. "Am I what?"

"Going back to his bed."

"It would just be temporary. He's leaving the cove after the wedding."

"Which is exactly why you should think twice, or thrice, or...what's four times?"

Skye shrugged. "Twice twice? And wasn't it you who was encouraging me to have a summer fling? You seemed a hearty proponent of temporary sexual gratification not all that long ago."

Pursing her lips, Polly seemed to mull over the idea. Then she blinked, straightening on her stool. "Hear that?"

"Are the voices in your head starting up again?"

"Ha-ha." Polly pointed toward a speaker hanging over the bar. "It's a sign. A warning. Bananarama's 'Cruel Summer.'"

The barista paused in his stroll down the bar. "We've been playing summer songs all day. You don't like this one?" Before they could answer, he reached toward a computer sitting beneath the shelves holding the call liquors. Quick keystrokes, and the music changed.

Justin Timberlake singing how this couldn't be mere "Summer Love."

That was the warning, Skye thought, chilled.

And then a hot, heavy hand clamped down on her shoulder. "Time's up," a voice growled in her ear.

Her breath went short as desire shot through her, a dizzying cocktail of heat and giddy excitement. The place between her thighs clenched. Slowly, so slowly, she turned her head to look at Gage. His eyes were piercing blue in his tanned face. He hadn't shaved that morning, and she knew the whiskers would be rough on her skin. He'd leave a chafed trail behind—around her mouth, down her neck, on the pale slopes of her breasts and the delicate skin of her thighs. She'd probably revel in it.

His hand squeezed her shoulder. "Well?"

Another summer moment popped into her mind. Her mother had signed her up for a weeklong sleepaway camp, and before leaving Skye had felt this same mix of sickness, sadness and incipient excitement. Hadn't she made it back from that experience safely?

Skye slid off her stool. Gage stepped back and she shot a look at Polly. Her friend wiggled her fingers, then shrugged, a "What can you do?"

Nothing, Skye thought, placing her hand in Gage's. As his fingers closed over hers, desire surged again, along with an almost melancholy feeling of inevitability. *"Don't think you can escape me,"* he'd said.

She'd always known she couldn't.

The only question was whether she could escape losing her heart.

CHAPTER FOURTEEN

THAT NIGHT, POLLY DIDN'T know what prompted her to nudge aside her front curtains. But some instinct had her crossing the living room floor, the flannel of her men's-style pajamas flapping around her ankles. From Skye's place next door, a floodlight was trained on the surf. It lit up the sand, too, giving it a glaze of silver. At the edge of its ghostly cast, closer to Polly's house than to her friend's, she saw a man sitting on the beach, his back to her.

Teague.

She dropped the curtain and retreated from the window. What the heck he was doing out there this late—it was close to midnight—was not her problem to ponder. Usually she'd be in bed herself by now, but insomnia had decided to move into the tiny cottage with her.

Biting her lip, she looked toward the front door. Should she…? *No.* The four walls were too small for her, Teague and sleeplessness. Good sense precluded her from going out to him. Telling him her bad girl secrets had only served to make her feel more vulnerable and insecure. In this state, who knew what other dangerous information—*I love you, I've loved you for years*—she might unwillingly reveal?

So instead she retreated to the bedroom and shivered as she slipped between the cool sheets. It was the only good-sized room in the house, large enough for her wrought-iron queen-sized bed with its very high mattress as well as the tall lingerie chest in the corner. The matching bureau had to be stored in the closet, but she still had access to all her things.

When she'd moved in at the end of last month, Teague had installed a hanging jewelry rack on the interior side of the door.

What a pal.

In return, she was leaving him alone in the cold night.

Shoving the thought away, she closed her eyes and tried picturing her upcoming students—the Olivias, the Beaus, the Bobbys.

But what popped onto the screen of her mind was that image of Teague sitting on the beach, dressed only in a T-shirt and jeans. Another shiver went through her, as she thought of how chilled he must be by now.

Or not. Maybe he'd already headed for home. Maybe he was driving back to his place that was twenty minutes away, the car heater blasting, leaving her to lie here, needlessly worrying about him.

Frowning at his rudeness, she threw back the covers and hurried into the living room without pausing for her slippers. She gripped the corner of the curtain, then jerked it back with a flourish, like a magician about to reveal that the rabbit had disappeared.

The bunny was still out there.

Damn his big ears. She stomped to the front door, worked the locks, then yanked it open. "Shoo" was on the tip of her tongue. But strange noises floated above the sound of the surf. Musical notes?

Curious despite herself, she hurried across the chilled sand toward her former best buddy. Getting her first frontal glimpse of him, she came to an abrupt halt, her heels digging in the damp grains. It was Teague, all right, sitting cross-legged, a bottle of something wrapped in a brown bag propped in front of him. He cradled a ukulele to his chest.

Polly stared. "Since when do you play an instrument?"

He squinted up at her, as if her face were too bright. "Wha?"

Sinking to her knees, she sniffed at the brown-bagged bottle. Booze. "You're drunk," she said, surprised. He was always very careful about the amounts he imbibed.

He plucked at the instrument's strings. "Pozzible," he said, slurring the word.

"Why?"

"Can' talk." He made a tipsy, big-armed gesture that she realized was him miming zipping his lips, then locking them and throwing away the key. "M'father'z advice. Don' talk 'bout it."

Polly decided not to try to decipher his mood. As she'd been saying for weeks, she was moving on from him… except she couldn't move on until she got him off her beach. "Let's go," she said, grabbing for his wrist.

His skin was corpse-cold, his arm a deadweight. "Came here," he said, a big lump of unmoving, drunk man. "Didn' mean to." His head turned slowly, as if taking in his surroundings for the first time. "But…"

"You're here," she said, impatient. "But inside here will be more comfortable than outside here." Putting more effort into it, she tugged on his arm as she got to her feet.

He rose like a sleepwalker and stumbled after her. She kept her hand on him, worried that if she let go he might wander in the wrong direction. The ukulele's neck was gripped in his fist as she towed him up her steps and into her living room. She breathed a sigh of relief as she shut the door behind them. Step one to getting him out of her house and out of her hair was getting him into her house and sobering him up.

"So, when did you take up the uke?" she asked, glancing down at it. "And why?"

"Hobby. For stress." He blinked at her. "Where's m'booze? Helps, too."

Stress? He was one of the most laid-back men she knew. She pushed him toward the breakfast bar. "No more alcohol for you. I'm going to fix you some soup and a sandwich."

"Thank you, Pol," he answered in that earnest way of drunk people as he struggled to maneuver himself onto a stool. The ukulele fell to the floor with a clatter and he ignored it. "Owe you…owe you…"

His stare caught on a bowl of fruit. "Owe you an apple."

He owed her an explanation, but she wasn't going to press for one. Instead, she heated up a can of soup and slapped together some bread, meat and cheese. She poured him a glass of milk and even draped the throw blanket from the couch over his shoulders as if he were a small boy.

The thought sent a swift and unexpected shaft of pain through her heart. She could imagine it too easily, a little guy with Teague's dark hair and eyes, his easy charm and even temperament. It was stupid of her, she knew, but tears stung the corners of her eyes. She'd never wanted riches or fame, just simple things like a teaching career, a family. A husband whom she could believe in.

Teague.

But that was a dream not to be, she reminded herself, and turned her back on him to wash up the sauce pan and then make half a pot of coffee. She didn't look at him again until she placed a mug of dark brew beside the drained milk glass.

He was staring at his empty soup bowl and looking more miserable than she'd ever seen him. Even when Tess had dashed his hopes almost as soon as he'd had them, he'd never appeared so grim.

The milk-pourer in her wanted to ask what was wrong, but the woman who needed to get over an unrequited romance wouldn't let that happen. She couldn't allow her emotions to get further engaged.

Then he reached for the uke, which she'd retrieved from the floor and set on the stool beside him. He placed the fingers of his left hand on the neck and strummed with his right thumb. It sounded terrible.

A hobby to help with the stress.

He strummed another jarring chord. Polly winced. "That's really awful, you know."

His head came up and she could see that the food and nonalcoholic drinks had gone a long way to sobering him up. "Yeah." Grimacing, he set the instrument aside again.

A tense silence welled up between them. Should she insist he leave now? Was he safe to drive? Because it wasn't safe to have him here, where he only fueled more dreams, where he only made her feel things she'd vowed would remain unspoken.

"I suppose you want to know..." he started.

"I don't want to know anything!" She whirled around and grabbed up the dishrag, blindly scrubbing at the clean countertop.

Another moment passed. Then she heard the stool's legs scrape against the floor. "Okay. Yeah. That's best."

When she didn't hear further movement, Polly peeked over her shoulder. Standing, he stared down at the class roster she'd left out, with the one-inch-by-one-inch photos of her students affixed beside each name. His finger traced a single line, over and over.

"What is it?" Polly heard herself ask. "What's wrong?" Too late, she wished she'd shoved the dishrag in her mouth.

Teague looked over, his face set in tired lines. "I…" Then he shook his head. "No. I'll be on my way. Sorry I disturbed you."

His expression disturbed her now. Drunk she could dismiss him, but exhausted and upset was a different matter altogether. "What won't you say?" she demanded, as she recalled him on the beach, telling her his father's advice. *Don't talk.*

"Had a few bad shifts, that's all."

Those shifts he never spoke of. The job he didn't discuss beyond raunchy jokes and firehouse recipes. Teague's father had been a firefighter, too. Had his instructions been to hold all the stress of the position inside? To never speak of it? Sympathy swamped her.

"Tell me," she said, tossing the cloth into the sink and coming closer. It rattled her more than a little to see easygoing but always-in-control Teague in a mood. "What's wrong?"

He collapsed back onto the stool and lowered his head to one hand. He massaged his temples with thumb and fingers. "The past couple of weeks we've had some disturbing calls. I just need a little time to…process."

To put the experiences up on that high shelf he had,

Polly thought with sudden insight. But wouldn't there come a time when there was no more room for another? Didn't he have to sort them out and clear some away in order to cope with the next batch?

"Care to share with me?" she said, putting her hand on his shoulder.

Not looking up, he shook his head. "It's better to keep things…pretty here. I don't need to bring disturbing stuff into this house or into your mind."

"Because your father protected your mother that way." Despite that—or because of it?—Polly knew the woman had ultimately left her husband and son.

Teague shrugged. "Most firefighters hold things back from their wives, their girls, their friends."

"I'm made of strong stuff. You know that." She put a teasing note into her voice. "I didn't pass out when I heard you attempt the ukulele."

He shook his head, still stubborn. Still miserable.

She couldn't stand it. "One word," Polly coaxed. "Just one simple word."

Silence descended again. Then he suddenly opened his mouth. "Shoes," he said, as if some unseen force had yanked it from him.

Instead of speaking, she merely firmed her hand on his shoulder.

"It's been a fucking week of shoes," he said, his voice low and rough.

"Shoes—"

Before she could finish, he grabbed her close, burying his head at the curve of her shoulder and throat. It was a tight hold, as if he were going down in vast waters and she were the single life preserver.

Without even thinking about it, her arms came around

him in a secure embrace. "Tell me," she murmured, pressing her cheek to his dark hair. "Tell me about the shoes."

Another long silence passed, and then he started speaking again, his voice still low. "A kid will get hit by a car—knocked right out of her shoes. You…you get to a scene and find the injured girl in the bushes, but a pair of pink, glittery sneakers left behind on the crosswalk."

She rubbed his back, soothing.

"Or there'll be a rollover accident, a minivan and its contents tossed everywhere. People screaming. Children crying. And then there's the baby, contented as a cow, hanging upside down from the straps of a car seat, chewing on the rubber sole of his daddy's work boot." He hauled in a breath. "Then last night… Oh, God, Gator. Last night."

She swallowed, trying to calm her unsteady pulse. "What happened last night?"

His hands clutched at her, as if assuring himself she was real. "House fire. Moving fast. One of the family's sons was missing. We couldn't find him."

The agony he'd clearly felt then pierced her ribs and headed straight for her heart. She wanted to back away, to break free of him and put her hands over her ears, but self-protection had stopped being an option. "What—" She had to pause and lubricate her throat. "What happened?"

"It was a big place. Three stories. We were searching room by room and I tripped over a pair of shoes, crashing into and breaking through some louvered closet doors, scattering the ski equipment inside. At the very back of the space was the kid, curled in a ball, his arms over his head. I might have missed him if I hadn't fallen and disrupted all the gear he'd taken refuge behind. I might have pulled open the doors to check but still not seen him."

Relief made her knees weak. "Lucky for him about those shoes," she murmured.

"They were his brand-new basketball high-tops. When I told him what happened, he thought his mom would be mad because he wasn't supposed to leave them out." Then Teague looked up, his gaze intense and staring straight into hers. "His name is Brett. One of your *B*-boys, Pol. And being bad was what saved him. When I thought of that…"

"When you thought of that…?" she prompted, whispering.

"I don't know." He shrugged. "I just had to come to you."

A hot sting of tears burned her eyes. To hide them, she let her lids close, and so she didn't see Teague's lips coming nearer; she only felt them brush her lashes, trace down her cheek.

It was a gentle, comforting caress. As platonic as every other they'd shared. Then his lips found hers, and she tasted the salt of her tears on their smooth, warm surface. Without thought, she opened her mouth to taste them with her tongue.

She heard and felt Teague's sharp, indrawn breath. Heated embarrassment flushed through her, and she attempted retreat. But his hands tightened on her.

His lips pressed harder. It became a real kiss.

Polly's head spun. It was what she'd always wanted, a dream she'd stopped waiting for. Their tongues touched, tangled, and she felt need flush over her from head to toe. Between her thighs, she went wet.

One of his hands speared the hair at the back of her

head. His touch was masculine, masterful, keeping her in place so that he could take control of her mouth. She shivered in hot delight, thrilled by his hard hold.

His palm covered her shoulder, following the slope of it atop the flannel until his thumb brushed the outside of her breast. He stilled for a moment, and then his hand slowly moved to cup her, his palm seeming to test the slight weight. Polly's nipple tightened to a painful bead and she clutched at Teague's shoulders to keep upright.

He broke the kiss and she saw that his color was up, a flush across his cheekbones. His hands went to the buttons of her boxy top, and she couldn't breathe as he unfastened them with skillful fingers.

A good man to have in an emergency, she thought, her head muzzy from lack of oxygen. But then he brushed the flannel sides away from her naked chest, and air refilled her lungs on a gasp. Teague just looked at her, his gaze avid, his own breath harsh as he stared.

She shivered, and he covered both breasts with his hot palms. Polly moaned as her nipples poked his flesh. Still staring, as if he was fascinated by the look of his big hands on her naked torso, he leaned toward her, licking at the hollow of her throat.

Polly jerked into the wet contact, and he made a soothing noise as he drew his mouth lower, moving one hand around her ribs and to her back. He pressed there, urging her inches closer, and then his mouth was on her breast.

She gasped again, closing her eyes as he sucked on the nipple, light but insistent. Her thighs clenched, and she felt another rush of wetness.

Her hands plunged into his hair. It had never been like this for her before. She felt hot all over, slippery inside, yearning everywhere from the roots of her hair to the tender skin between her toes. Every part of her wanted contact with him, but she was afraid to speak that aloud in case he woke to the fact that he was in the throes of passion with his platonic friend.

Teague released her flesh and looked up. "Polly," he murmured. "Polly—"

She muffled him with her own kiss, desperate, and desperately worried that if he said her name one more time he'd realize that yes, it was Polly, Polly Pal who was in his arms. Her tongue slid into his mouth, and his hands clamped on her hips, then slipped beneath the waistband of her flannel pants to cup her bottom.

He groaned, the sound a sweet buzz of desire against her tongue. His fingers kneaded the soft flesh that he held and she felt another dizzying rush of heat engulf her. She'd wanted him before; his smiles, his charm, his male competence had called to her from the very beginning— not every man could make expert omelets!—but this was something else altogether. There was no way she'd anticipated the effect of his hands on her in sexual urgency.

And there was no sense in trying to apply the brakes now.

After all, she doubted she could ever go back to being his friend, she thought, so she might as well give it all as his lover. Shrugging, she allowed the flannel top to drop. Then, still kissing him, she shoved her thumbs into the elastic waistband of her pants and yanked them down, letting them fall to her ankles.

She was completely naked to him.

He jerked his head away from hers, breaking the kiss. She heard the slow suck of his breath as his gaze took in her nude form. Trembling, she didn't hide from the perusal, knowing she was not voluptuous and not tall and definitely not Tess.

But she was his for the taking.

And as if she'd said it aloud, he did.

One moment she was standing before him; the next they were in a race down the hall. In her dim bedroom, he took her by the shoulders and propelled her backward until her hips hit the end of the high mattress and she fell onto the bed.

She stared up at him, breathing hard, and felt another shimmer of delight work through her as he reached behind his neck with one hand to toss away his T-shirt. He toed off his shoes and shoved down his jeans and boxers and there he was—there *it* was—the aggressive jut of male flesh that said he wanted to be here.

Her stomach jittered in anticipation and she scooted up toward the pillows, but he caught her ankles and hauled her back. The height of the bed was such that if he stepped forward—

Then he did. Pushing her thighs wide apart, he moved into the space. The thick head of his penis brushed the inside of her thigh, and she jerked, the heat of it like a brand. He circled one hand around her thigh, keeping her open for him, and then grasped the thick stalk of his sex.

He directed it toward her pleated flesh, but instead of thrusting, he nudged her layers apart with short strokes and gentle prods. Her body flowered easily for him, making it clear she was more than ready for him. But he continued toying, playing, tapping at her clitoris and then sliding wetly down to her entrance to tease her with the promise of penetration.

Her fingers clutched at the bedclothes, and she arched her hips, trying to entice him into her heat. The hand encircling her thigh controlled her, though, and she made a needy sound low in her throat.

Teague's gaze lifted from the place where they weren't quite joined, to her face. His eyes were glittering, his skin seemed to be stretched tightly against his cheekbones. She'd never seen him look so harsh, his handsomeness almost brutal with desire. Another wave of sexual longing ran through her and she shuddered against the cool sheets. "Please," she said. "Please don't make me wait another minute."

Her skin was throbbing everywhere, her inner muscles were rhythmically clenching with her body's need to be filled, her clitoris was so sensitive that when he gave it another delicate tap, she lurched, driven a giant step closer to orgasm.

"I won't," he said, and his hand pushed her thigh even wider.

Exposing her. Exposing everything.

He stared down, seemingly mesmerized, and then he penetrated, a slow, thick parting of her flesh. Moaning, Polly closed her eyes at the exquisite sensation. She was so ready for him that there was only the tiniest, sweetest pinch of discomfort as he continued inside. *Oh, yes.* He was hot and smooth and—

He wasn't wearing a condom.

Her lashes flew up and she opened her mouth to warn him, but then he rooted deep, and she gasped at the goodness of it. He held himself motionless inside her, and she could feel her muscles clenching around him, her body trying to incite movement. She moaned with impatience.

"Shh," he murmured, and caressed her hip. "Let yourself get used to me."

Pleasure was breaking in little waves across her body.

Condom, she thought sluggishly, her mind trying to bring the word to her mouth. She was on the Pill so she wouldn't get pregnant, but—

"God, Pol." Teague suddenly jolted, his body almost leaving hers so she had to clamp her knees against his flanks to keep him close. "No, no. Listen, I'm not wearing protection."

His urgent voice cleared her own mind a little.

"Do we really need it?" she asked. "Because…because I'm thinking not."

He stilled, staring at her face. "Polly…"

She met his gaze. "I'm thinking not," she repeated. Teague was well aware she was on birth control. Just last month, on their way to a weekend of wine-tasting with friends, she'd had to ask him to turn around to retrieve her forgotten little packet of pills. As for STDs, they were close enough to know that wasn't an issue, either.

"Are you sure?" he asked, his voice hoarse.

"Yes." They might not have a future, but they had so much trust between them she knew they could do this without barriers.

At that thought, her inner muscles squeezed him. He groaned and then began to move, thrusting into her with deep intent. She wiggled and he tightened his hold on her hips, keeping her still as he continued to pump inside. Desire threatened to swamp her again, as the feeling of being at his mercy was delicious, all she'd ever wanted. She gave herself up to it, sinking into the mattress and opening her mind and body to his forceful thrusts.

Then he started pulling her into each one, and a wave of heat broke over her skin. She moaned, her eyes closing at the inexplicable goodness of this man's touch. Nothing had ever been like this for her. It was possible she might just be a female body to him, a way to work out the stress he'd been feeling, but she had no regrets with orgasm just inches away. Aware it was ready to pounce on her, she half opened her eyes.

To find Teague gazing down at her. His fingers were hot brands on her hips as their eyes met and he plunged into her again. Oh, he was well aware this was her, Polly thought, panicking a little. But his next thrust shattered her concern. It was so good she lifted into it despite his firm hold, writhing while he held himself deep.

As he pulled back, she cried out, but then he was driving deep again. Her body gathered around him, gathered in on itself, her muscles tense everywhere, and then Teague slid one thumb to her clitoris, circling once, twice, until bliss shot free and she fractured, joyful sensation raining down like hot, happy tears.

Groaning, Teague thrust once more before he came in great shudders of his big body.

Lying boneless on the bed, Polly kept her eyes closed as he withdrew and climbed onto the mattress. He pulled her up to him so that he was propped on the pillows and she was against his shoulder. His big palm gently stroked her shoulder.

Okay, Polly thought, bracing herself. Here came the regrets. Here came the moment when he would make excuses, throw on his pants, leave and perhaps never be heard from again.

"Well, Gator," he said softly. "What now?"

He wasn't leaving. He wasn't making excuses. Instead, he was putting the ball in her court.

Polly's heart raced. She could lay it on the line. Tell her final secrets. Confess her love and see where that might lead. Her mouth opened. And words came out in the bright, chirpy voice she used for selling indoor recess on rainy days. "You ever hear of friends with benefits?"

It was all she'd never wanted.

IN HIS SISTER'S BACKYARD, Gage sat on the edge of a large cement planter, partly screened by the fronds of a thriving queen palm. He tipped back his bottle of beer and took a long swallow, then let his gaze roam about. Just a week after the engagement party, his sister was in gonzo hostess mode again, throwing a shower for the bridal couple. This crowd appeared to be a smaller subset of the other, but again there was a table piled high with presents.

He kept his gaze on the gifts when his twin came to lean beside him. "Where the hell are you going to put all the loot?" he asked Griffin. "I thought you said Jane's place is tiny, and she's already got you crowded in there."

"We're on the hunt for new digs. Have a line on something not far from the cove, as a matter of fact."

Gage didn't respond, but he heartily approved of the idea. If his bro and Jane settled near Skye, he wouldn't think twice about insisting they keep an eye on her once he was gone. Without turning his head, he sought her out now himself, and smiled when he caught sight of her laughing with Tess. Her hair was caught up in an artful bun-looking thing, with wavy pieces left to lie against the back of her neck and along one cheek. There was something about the carefree style that made him want to pull out the pins and then take her to bed.

He'd been doing a lot of that since she'd put her hand in his on the deck at Captain Crow's a few days before. Skye continued to be an enthusiastic partner between the sheets, her fears, it seemed, mostly forgotten. Satisfaction made his smile deepen.

She didn't question his avoidance of complete darkness, but since she'd been beside him, he'd managed to make do with only the bathroom light burning through the half-opened door. He'd found sleep easier, too, and had better rest when he did nod off.

Living in the moment with Skye, at the cove, was turning out to be the best damn idea of a decade. Nothing was going to mess that up, not if he could help it.

Griffin cleared his throat. "You know, we never finished that conversation we started at the engagement party."

"What conversation?" Gage asked absently. He was counting the buttons on Skye's little mermaid-green sundress. They ran from neckline to knee and were the shape of tiny starfish. Likely a bitch to unfasten. Was there a hidden zipper or something?

"The one where you come clean about your last assignment and why the hell you went MIA."

His mind jerked to attention. *Shit.* Instead of letting his brother see his alarm, Gage took another long sip of his beer. Then he set it on the ledge beside him and crossed his arms over his chest. "I don't know what you're talking about."

"I hate to break it to you," Griffin said, "but your body language is a dead giveaway."

Gage cursed his brother's skills of observation. Damn reporters. "Let's talk about something else. This is supposed to be a happy time…and all about you and Jane."

"Jane and I are great. And we *are* happy. But it's you who has me worried."

"Look," Gage said, wincing at the defensive edge to his voice. "I didn't bug you when you were holed up in No. 9, acting weird as shit. Skye wrote me about the parties. Rex said you were cliff-jumping again—the higher the better."

"I admit I had—have—issues. I'm working on them."

"Let me work on mine in my own way, all right?" And his way was the Skye-way, soaking up summer and the scent of her skin at every opportunity.

His brother's sigh sounded like acquiescence.

Gage risked a glance at him. His twin was staring, and their eyes met. People often asked him if it was creepy, to see his own face on another man, but when he looked at his brother he only saw their dissimilarities. Griffin "presented" in a different manner, he thought. While he'd been born only a few minutes earlier, he had the gravitas of the older brother. Gage had been the one to disregard consequences.

That thought gave him a guilty start and he redirected his attention, stealing another glance at Skye. Was he acting irresponsibly there? But the smile on her face and the relative wealth of skin she felt comfortable showing now said no. This afternoon, he'd been a fingernail away from convincing her to put on a bathing suit and go out with him for a swim.

"What are you looking at?" Griffin said, sounding suspicious.

"Nothing." He grabbed up his bottle of beer. "I'm just recalling I have a best-man duty to fulfill. What are we going to do about a bachelor party? I could throw a classic, you know, martinis, poker and trash talk at No. 9. Or could you fit in a quick guys' getaway to Vegas?"

Damn, he thought, instantly regretting the suggestion. Las Vegas would mean leaving Skye. Their final goodbye was coming soon enough.

"Nah," his brother answered. "When Dad gets here,

why don't we just take him and David out for drinks one night? They can tell us both about the joys of married life."

Gage groaned. "What, bamboo sticks under the fingernails too tame for you?"

"Don't let Mom hear you disparage marriage."

"I don't disparage. I think marriage is just great for Mom and Dad. And for Tess and David. There's people all over the world who make it work."

"Including, now, me and Jane."

"Yeah." He studied his brother, noting the ease of his body and the faint, satisfied smile he wore. "It's really what you want."

"It's really what I want. *She's* really what I want."

"That's sappy enough to make me want to hurl right into this planter," Gage said, "but I admit liking you looking so contented. I guess Jane will have to be the sacrifice for your happiness."

Griffin shook his head. "Dumb-ass."

"But you say it with such affection." Their eyes met again and a dozen unspoken messages passed between them, all condensable to one single idea: *I'll always have your back.*

"So," Gage finally said, "Dad, David and drinks. We'll find a good night for it."

"Hope you're not too disappointed about skipping strippers and titty bars."

He waved that away. "Not disappointed at all."

Going suddenly still, Griffin narrowed his gaze at him. "You're getting regular sex."

"What?"

"Gage Gorge sex just makes you restless. Antsy, like you've eaten too many candy bars." His brother pointed a finger at him. "You're calm. Serene, I'd even say, which means you're getting the real thing now, the libido-sating kind of sex."

"My libido is not the least bit sated," he scoffed. "Jesus. You writers have overactive imaginations."

"I can tell what I can tell," Griffin said.

"You can tell shit. For your information, I'm calm because…because I like the cove. It's a good place to rest. I'm in recharge mode." He took another draw on his beer and studiously avoided looking toward the last place he'd seen Skye.

Then a flicker of color drew his eye, and his gaze shot to the fluttering hem of a blue-green skirt. Skye's skirt. He couldn't help staring at her legs, then her slender hips, then her—

"Shit," Griffin muttered.

With a casual turn of his head, Gage looked to his brother, one eyebrow raised.

"Don't give me that." Griffin huffed out a sigh. "You're with Skye, aren't you?"

Gage didn't consider it a true secret. He wasn't ashamed to be with her, that was for sure. "If you weren't so damn protective of her, I would have mentioned it sooner."

"You're together," Griffin said, as if requiring exact clarification. "Together together."

Impatient with the questioning, Gage glared at his twin. "Yes."

"And you've thought this through?"

It wouldn't be good form to deck the groom-to-be. "You want the truth? I'm doing my best not to think at all. How's that? Some of us aren't fucking navel-gazers, okay?" He'd had two weeks of no company but his own and what he could conjure up in his mind, and that was enough inward exploration to last a lifetime.

When his brother just stared at him, Gage forced himself to lower his voice and relax his rigid spine. "It was a…a long, grueling stretch, that last assignment."

Griffin nodded. "Some of them are like that."

"Yeah, some are worse than others." Gage took in a deep breath of fresh air. "So before I get back to the usual frustration, stress and bad food, I'm chilling at the cove, enjoying myself with a woman I really like. We have an…affection for each other, Skye and I. We know each other very well."

"Through your letters."

"Yeah. So it just seemed natural to take the relationship to this place." Completely natural, which was why he didn't have to overexamine it.

"What happens when you go?"

Gage shrugged. "I go. She knows that. But until then, it's sunshine and sea breezes and…"

"Your little love shack on the sand," Griffin said.

It made him grin. No. 9 had the power to make the past recede and fill the present—fill him—with contentment.

"You're looking a little happy there yourself," his brother observed.

Why deny it? Especially when he saw the siren of the cove heading in his direction. He aimed his grin at her. She wore earrings that were long strings of beach glass in alternating colors that matched her dress and her eyes.

Now that the cat was out of the bag, he didn't hesitate to slide off his perch and grab her hand to pull her close to him. "Hey," he said softly, drawing her freshwater scent into his lungs. "How you doing?"

Her green eyes slid to his brother.

Gage squeezed her fingers. "Don't pay attention to that ugly dude," he told her.

A smile played at the corners of her mouth. "Ugly," she scolded.

Griffin patted her shoulder. "Should I catalog all this guy's vices for you, Skye?"

"No need," she said, and she reached up to touch his twin's hand as if he were the one who needed comfort. "Stand down, friend."

Without comment, Gage plucked his brother's fingers from her bare shoulder. "Having fun?" he asked, lowering his voice, his eyes only for her. Lifting his free hand, he let the back of his knuckles trace her cheek.

Griffin made a sound, then walked away. Skye's gaze flicked in his direction. "Uh-oh. Your twin does not approve."

"Forget about my twin." His fingers stroked her throat. She shivered, and he saw her gaze focus on his mouth. A surge of satisfaction warmed his blood. "You want to be kissed?"

"Not here," she said quickly, glancing around.

"Oh." His smile was knowing. "You want *that* kind of kiss."

The blush that spread across her pretty face did him in. He slid both arms around her and drew her to him, spreading his legs so she was nestled close to his chest and they were half-hidden by the fortuitous palm fronds. Angling his head, he found her mouth with his, stroking in with hot demand. She seemed to have a second's thought of pulling away, but then she melted against him, her fingernails curling into his chest like a kitten's.

"Dangerous," he murmured, breaking the kiss, though he found himself bussing her forehead, her cheeks, her nose. It was impossible to get enough of her, he thought, then frowned. There would come a day when he'd board a plane and what he'd had already would have to be sufficient.

"Let's go back to the cove right now," he said, feeling a pressing need to get them there, to the place where he'd banished the future. He and Skye could lie in bed, engage in some more blissing-out on the present.

"Okay, but— Oh, I almost forgot. I ran into someone you know. You need to say hello to her first."

"Her?" Jesus, she hadn't encountered some woman he'd previously hooked up with, had she? "Wait…"

She started tugging him out of their semiconcealment. "I invited her to come to the cove day after tomorrow."

Now he let himself be moved, because he sincerely doubted she'd ask some former bed partner of his to their special place. "If you're referring to my aunt Joanna, I already talked to her and please, let's tell her we won't be around then after all. She'll bring the peanut brittle she considers her specialty, and I can't risk going halfway across the world with broken teeth."

Damn Aunt Joanna, for making him think of his looming departure.

"Wipe that vicious frown off your face. It's not your aunt Joanna. It's Mara Butler. Griffin knew her Charlie, too, went to visit her last week, and she's here tonight. She says she'd love to talk to you."

Mara Butler. Charlie.

Charlie Butler. His war correspondent friend who'd been kidnapped. Killed.

Gage slowed his footsteps. "She's definitely coming to the beach? Day after tomorrow?"

"Mmm-hmm. With her little boy, Charlie's son, Anthony."

Damn. His friend's widow was going to visit the cove. And, Gage thought, his chest filling with a painful, prescient regret, most likely bringing unpleasant reminders of his recent past with her.

CHAPTER FIFTEEN

As HE APPROACHED THE CRESCENT COVE beach at near dusk, Teague thought he should be sitting on top of the world. It was a given, right, because "friends with benefits" was right up there with "March Madness" and "nachos with extra jalapeños" in the Real Man's Lexicon of Favorite Phrases. Instead, he felt as if something were sitting on top of *him*. This lousy mood had to go, however. Polly had almost kicked him out of her life a few days before, and he figured he'd really tick off his best pal if he showed up at tonight's beach bonfire as surly as a singed bear.

He didn't want to chance losing her, with a desperation that he found a bit surprising. But hell, she'd always meant a lot to him.

Maybe his mood was a belated hangover kicking in. Two evenings ago his booze of choice had been whiskey and he should have suffered from brain pain on waking. But after he'd left Polly's bed—thought processes reeling from all that had happened and what she'd proposed—he'd swallowed pain reliever tablets and a quart of water before falling onto his own mattress. In the morning he'd opened his eyes, feeling better than he had any right to.

But now there was a grinding sense of something gone wrong churning in his belly, and he tried ignoring it by tightening his grip on the big spray of roses in his left hand. Having been called into work for a half-shift meant he'd been unable to attend the bridal shower or reach out immediately to Polly. It was time to rectify that. Hoping what he wore on his face looked like a smile and not rigor mortis, he used his other to knock on Polly's front door.

She opened it, her big blues rounding in surprise. "What are you doing here?"

"I got a text from Skye. About the bonfire?"

"Oh."

Polly looked flustered. And guilty. "Did you not want me to come?" he asked, his stomach chewing on the thought.

"Of course not. No." She waved a hand. "We're all always happy to see you."

The bite of a thorn reminded Teague he'd brought flowers—and that his fingers were suddenly strangling them. "Here," he said, thrusting them at her. "These are for you."

Polly automatically reached for the bouquet, but she looked at them as if they were stinkweed instead of her favorite romantic red roses. "You shouldn't have."

"I wanted to."

She glanced up at his face. "No, I mean you really shouldn't have. Did anyone see you bringing me flowers? People will talk."

He tried shrugging off the tight claws of his ill temper. Polly never annoyed him. They'd gotten along so well until recently...until those two confusing occasions, the first when she'd dropped her dress, the second when she'd made some angry but cryptic remark about him not nailing her. Christ, he'd taken care of that, hadn't he?

He rubbed at his aching forehead. "I bring you stuff all the time."

"Muffins. That kind of pen I like. Not…"

"Fine," he ground out. "Now I'm hoping Skye won't be p.o.'d that I brought her the ingredients for s'mores. Do you think that sends a wrong message, too?"

"If so, it will be Gage who delivers the news to you," Polly said, heading for the kitchen. "Probably on the end of his fist."

That diverted him for a moment. "What?"

Her place was so small that Teague could watch her put the roses in water from the doorway. She fussed with them, then threw him a look over her shoulder. "I warned her, but she wouldn't listen."

He frowned. "You're telling me they're involved now? Physically?"

"Mmm," Polly said, still arranging and rearranging the flowers. She was wearing white denim jeans that were rolled at the ankles and an oversize sweatshirt that…that was his, he realized. His well-worn fleece from the firefighter academy, originally engine-red, now washed to a soft strawberry.

It gave him the oddest satisfaction to see her in it, even though it covered up the incredible body he'd explored the other night. She was built like a gymnast, light but strong, and he'd marveled at her shape and texture, enjoying them with his hands and his mouth, even as one part of his mind couldn't believe he was in bed with his best-friend-who-was-a-girl.

How had it begun? There'd been her sympathetic tears, his affectionate kiss, and then, *pow,* it was mouth on mouth, hands on skin, full freaking penetration.

He'd not taken her tenderly, he thought, replaying the event in his mind. It wasn't the first time he'd thought of it, but it was the first time he did a mental rerun when she was so near. Heat shot toward his groin. What would she do if he strode over to the sink and picked her up, then carried her caveman-style to the bedroom and the high mattress that was perfectly positioned for him to—

He blinked, aware she was staring at him.

"Uh, what?" he asked, hoping she didn't notice that he was more than halfway to aroused.

Polly tucked her golden hair behind her ears in a nervous gesture that wasn't normal for her. "I said, Skye claims she and Gage are having a summer fling."

It took Teague a moment to remember who exactly Skye and Gage were. "Summer fling," he murmured. It was another happy phrase from the Lexicon. Could he and Polly be heading for one of those?

But she was looking at him with a hint of unease in her gaze, and he thought he better not take anything for granted. Especially, as he kept recalling, because he'd gone he-man on her in bed instead of taking the friendly, fond-and-gentle route. Shit. Had he been too rough? The stressful week had shaken him, and then when he'd started talking about it…well, it had bared something in him.

He'd been raw in every sense of the word.

"We should get out there," Polly said, gesturing to the beach. "Especially if you're the s'mores supplier."

Teague followed her lead. Next door to Polly's tiny place was Skye's much more substantial home. On the sand a few feet from her front door, a metal fire pit was already stoked and blazing. A dozen people were assembled around it in the almost dark, some standing, some in collapsible chairs. He greeted and was greeted in return, then obligingly took up the task of getting the music going via iPod and stereo dock. The music player's owner had already created a playlist, and before long over the crackle of burning wood and the quiet rush of waves he could hear "Endless Summer" by Aaron Lewis followed by Katy Perry's "California Gurls."

The summer cheer of the songs lifted his mood. He grabbed a can of beer from the ice chest on the porch, then grabbed a second, the light kind that Polly preferred, and looked around for her.

Firelight caught in her bright hair and warmed her features as she sat in one of the gathered chairs. Her beauty didn't scream *look at me*, but it was arresting all the same. During years of friendship, through late nights at parties and on early morning ski runs, somehow he'd managed to filter her looks and sexual appeal from their relationship.

Until the other night.

He caught her looking at him, and held up the light beer, an unspoken offer.

She quickly shook her head and dove into conversation with the woman sitting in the chair beside hers. Skye sat on her other side, and Teague wondered if Polly had chosen that spot on purpose, flanking herself with girlfriends in order to avoid him.

He remembered her worry that someone had seen him bring her flowers. *"People will talk."*

Annoyed all over again with the concern, he stalked toward her. Her eyes flashed to him and she jumped to her feet, taking a fast walk in the opposite direction. *Shit.* He'd really blown it the other night, apparently. All that filtering he'd managed over the past four and a half years had been to the very good purpose of not letting sex screw up the closest relationship he had with another person. Now that they'd gone there, she could hardly meet his eyes.

Double shit.

"You're looking very ferocious," a voice said at his elbow.

He glanced down at Skye, another female friend of his. He'd known her longer than Polly, but somehow the cheerleader blonde was the one he called when he was in the mood for a bike ride. She was the woman he let pick out his new shirts and tsk over the ragged ones he refused to throw away.

"Maybe I'm worried about you and Gage," he said, glancing over her head to find the tall man laughing with his twin. "Are you sure you know what you're doing?"

"Don't you go Polly on me, too," Skye said. "For two days she's been dark looks and deep frowns."

His fault? Teague wondered. "You don't suppose something else might be bothering her?"

Skye shrugged. "She's doing her 'I'm good. I'm always good' thing again. There's a reason I call her Very Private Polly. It's hard to know what's going on inside her head."

Teague's shoulders tensed. He could guess all too well what was spinning beneath that bright blond hair: second thoughts about taking their relationship to the physical level. Damn it! Glancing around, he tried to make Polly out in the darkness. Light from the fire flickered over faces, but none were hers.

Gage joined them and Teague talked with the couple without absorbing anything that was said. Instead, he kept a sharp eye out for the absent Polly, his mood only dipping lower as he listened to the songs drifting across the sand.

There was a Fountains of Wayne tune about a girl who couldn't be found. It sounded breezy and beachy until you really listened and realized beneath its happy beat, the guy was bemoaning the girl who'd got away. Then it was "The Warmth of the Sun." The Beach Boys sound could go sad in a heartbeat, their harmonies carrying a distinct, melancholy edge. The next song in the shuffle was Green Day's "When September Ends," and Teague felt another clutch of concern. That month had yet to arrive, and already he felt as if he was mourning.

His friendship with Polly?

Shit.

Tossing his empty can in a waiting recycle bin, he decided to track her down. Another woman snagged his wrist as he moved past the bonfire. "Have a s'more," she said, pressing a napkin and treat in his hand.

He looked down at her. "Tess," he said. "I didn't see you before."

"We haven't been here long. I came bearing wire coat hangers." She smiled at him. "How are you? We haven't had a chance to talk lately."

Bemused, Teague just stared at her. Sure, she was still pretty astonishing to look at. But she didn't do a thing to his pulse rate any longer. What had Polly said?

You'd be putting your feelings somewhere, with someone, who was safe. Because deep down you'd know you're not really risking your heart.

Tess tilted her head. "Well?"

"I…" His gaze drifted over her. On the other side of the fire, he finally spotted Polly. Her gaze was on his, but the instant she saw him catch her staring, she turned and walked into the darkness beyond the circle of their party. "I've got to go." Teague handed the graham cracker concoction back to his brief—and pretty foolish, he now realized—summer crush. Then he strode after the woman at the forefront of his mind.

At her door, he caught up with Polly. She must have been a million miles away, because she gasped when he touched her back.

"Don't scare me." She turned to face him, her hand flying up to her throat.

His eyes narrowed, taking in her expression revealed by the glow of the porch light. *Don't scare me.* "Pol," he said, grasping her by both shoulders. "Did I...did I do that the other night? Did I scare you? Make you uncomfortable?"

"Of course not," she said, but her gaze skittered away.

He tightened his grasp on her. "No lying between friends. I'm sorry if telling you about the shoes—"

"You don't need to apologize for that. I don't need to be protected. I was happy that you were able to share something that bothered you."

"I don't like you thinking I'm a whiner."

She frowned at him. "You weren't whining. I've heard you whine. That was when your team didn't make it to the Super Bowl."

"Funny." He couldn't dredge up a smile, though, because he knew things still weren't right between them. "Polly, the sex..."

Her feet moved and she stepped away from his hands. "Do we have to talk about that?"

"God. I knew it." He let his eyes close for a moment. "I shouldn't have let that happen. I'm sorry—"

"Please quit apologizing."

"But I regret—"

Her fingers fisted in the collar of his shirt. "If you say you regret being with me like that I'll scream."

"If you scream, someone will hear. People will talk."

It's what she'd said about the flowers, right? "I'd say it's you who—"

Her mouth crushed his. She was a short thing, but she'd gone on tiptoe so their lips were grinding together, and lust shot like a meteor through his body. Teague rocked back on his heels, but she came right with him, her body pressed against his.

He staggered back, off-balanced by her slight weight and the absolute searing power of the kiss. His head angled and he slid his tongue into her mouth, the erotic combination of beer and Polly hitting his taste buds. He clutched at her hips, scooping her closer against him.

It was like that other night all over again. Zero to sixty in a single heartbeat.

Needing air, he lifted his head, staring at her blue eyes and damp mouth. "God, Polly. We should…we should talk."

She turned, leading the way through her front door as if she wanted that, too, but the instant it was shut behind them she was kissing him again, one leg winding around his hip so their lower bodies were flush. "I don't want to talk," she said against his mouth.

Her fingers were already attacking the buttons on his shirt. Teague knew he should stop the headlong flight. But that meteor was still blazing across his personal sky, and his reaction to her still so astounded him—this was Polly!—that his logical thoughts were flung away with his shirt.

She slid her palms up his chest and he jolted into her touch, then shoved his own hands beneath the firefighter sweatshirt. Her torso was sleek and hot against him and he shuddered, so aroused that his cock was throbbing behind his pants.

Turn her, take her, his instincts clamored. He could push her against the door and have his way with her, driving into her giving heat within seconds. But he'd been on Mindless Rut the other night, and she deserved better. His friend deserved that tenderness he'd neglected before.

Grabbing one of her wandering hands, he towed her down the hallway to her dark bedroom. There was that big bed, primly made up now, and he tore at the covers to get to the cool white sheets.

Slow, he reminded himself. Slow. His hands shook as he cupped her face. "Beautiful Polly," he whispered.

She fumbled with the button of his jeans, and he had to capture her eager fingers. "What?" she asked, pouting a little. "Why?"

He drew the sweatshirt up. "Because we're slowing this down. I'm making sure you get some benefit out of the whole 'friends with' deal."

A look crossed her face that he couldn't decipher. Then she went on pants attack again and they started grappling with each other, which turned into groping each other, which turned into another set of frantic kisses and hurried hands, and then they were naked and rolling around on the sheets. He found himself laughing, his hand holding her wrists above her head as he subdued her beneath his bigger body. "You behave," he told her.

"Told you I was a bad girl," she said, mischief in her voice.

That they could be teasing like this, even while exploring this new and unfamiliar turn to their friendship, slayed him. The night she found him on the sand, the words he'd shared with her had uncovered pieces of him he rarely showed anyone. But this was rare, too, this absolute intimacy that was both urgent and intriguing.

He bent to kiss her neck, inhaling the scent that he'd savored for four-plus years on a purely pal basis. "God, I'm going to lick you all over."

No one ever accused Teague of not following through. Despite Polly's breathless pleas and her sexy, squirming body, he held out against stroking into her until he'd stroked her everywhere with the flat of his tongue and the caress of his lips. It was some of his best effort—but she deserved it and more, his best friend.

Her luscious taste was still in his mouth as he rose over her. She was panting in the aftermath of orgasm. He brushed her hair away from her face. "I went bareback before," he said.

"I know," she whispered. Her mouth was reddened from his kisses.

"I wasn't worried, because—"

"I remember," she said.

Of course she did. They both were aware she took birth control pills, that both of them were clean. Nevertheless… "I have a condom in my wallet."

"I have condoms in the bathroom," she countered.

He looked into her face. Very Private Polly, Skye had called her. But not with him. "Since we've shared so much…"

"It seems right that we do this without anything between us."

The permission he'd been waiting for. Slowly, because it felt so good that he needed time to absorb the pleasure, he sank into the giving heat of her. She moaned, the flush renewing on her face.

His big hands slid beneath her hips to tilt her into his unhurried thrusts. A shiver worked through her body. "Teague," she moaned.

He drove in again, and dropped his head to kiss and suck one of her reddened nipples. She jerked up, and he felt the telltale tightening in his balls. When he bit down on the hardened tip, she jerked again, crying out, a sound of cresting pleasure.

His movements were steady and sure then, rhythmic and demanding, and she lifted into each one. He groaned, low in his throat, knowing he had just seconds before cataclysm. Hoping to take her with him, he slid his hand between them.

She stiffened, her pelvis lifting into his as his thumb brushed the engorged nub of flesh. Her next cry took him over and he spilled into her as her contracting muscles closed around him.

In the aftermath, he lay on his back and gathered her close again. Replete and feeling damn good about the universe, he was astonished and then alarmed when something hot and wet dropped onto his shoulder.

Polly was leaking tears.

Oh, shit. "What's wrong?" He went on one elbow to look at her. "Did I hurt you?"

She shook her head.

Panic drained all the satisfaction from his body. "Polly." *Oh, God.* "This whole friends-with-benefits thing is such a bad idea. What can I do? How can I fix it?"

"It's not your fault, it's mine." She held the back of her hand against her nose. "I—I've been lying. I'm not really your friend."

"What?"

"I shouldn't have let this happen again. But I saw you with Tess, and I felt stupid and jealous and I really, really want to be angry with you for being in love with her, though I know that isn't fair."

"What?" he said again, thinking of that last brief encounter with the former woman of his dreams. Her presence had barely registered, he'd been so concerned about Polly.

"You've been making me nuts," she said. "There's all your big talk about wanting kids, wanting a family, but then you go and fall for someone who's already taken."

"The fact is—"

"You shouldn't love her," Polly said, her voice fierce. "You only love her because it means you risk nothing. Teague, you're never going to have her."

"Sure, but what does that have to do with this? With us?"

She rose from the bed and dashed for a robe. Then she threw his jeans and boxers at him. "You have to go."

The expression on her face was so serious, he did as she asked. Her hands on his back, she practically pushed him down the hall to her front door. But he drew the line at leaving before he had his shirt on—swooped to grab it—and before he had a clear explanation. "You're serious? We're not friends?"

"No. We're not friends." She closed her eyes. "That's over."

God, how it hurt. "Gator, I don't understand—"

"Because I've loved you for years, all right? I've been *in love* with you for years, but you've never really seen me, or you would have seen the truth."

Stunned, he stared at her. "Polly—"

"Go," she said. "Just go and stay away."

And because a feather would have knocked him over, he did.

SKYE LOCKED THE DOOR of the room that held the Sunrise Studios archive and headed back to the beach, Mara Butler beside her. The other woman sighed a little. "I love that story of your great-great-grandparents. He sacrificed his career, his passion for her."

"Did he consider it a sacrifice? While we have the letter that makes clear she was the one who wanted to get out of the silent-film business, we only have her side of the story. She thought he would have wanted to make movies forever, but obviously he wanted to make Edith happy more."

Mara breathed out another sigh, then tented her hand over her eyes and gazed down the stretch of sand. "I hope Anthony's okay."

"I'm sure he's fine. Tess is looking out for him and he has her little boys to play with. Duncan and Oliver will make sure he's having fun."

"You're right." Mara slanted her a smile. "I have a tendency to hold on to him pretty tight."

"Nobody would blame you for that." Skye studied the other woman's profile as they strolled in the direction of Beach House No. 9, where the Lowell-Quincy clan was gathered to discuss wedding logistics and entertain Anthony and Mara Butler. Her reporter husband had been held for ransom and then killed when the American military went in to rescue him. Charlie Butler had left behind Anthony, who was now five, and the fragile-looking Mara, who'd had the soul-squeezing responsibility of okaying the failed attempt at releasing her husband from his captors.

She hunched her shoulders and shoved her fingers in the pockets of her shorts and glanced at Skye again. "People blame me for other things."

Her heart thudded hard against her ribs. "Surely not..."

There was heartbreak in Mara's blue eyes. "Not every

country leaves it up to the loved ones, you know. But that's the U.S. rule, so it's the next of kin who make the decision and bear the guilt if it doesn't go right. Charlie's parents will never forgive me."

"Oh, Mara," Skye said. "That's terrible."

The other woman shrugged. "I understand their pain. Some days I have a hard time forgiving myself. But…but we had to try. For Anthony."

"Of course you did." Skye patted the woman's shoulder and could feel her thin, birdlike bones. "I'm just so terribly sorry."

Mara dashed a hand over her cheek. "No, that would be me for bringing all that up on this beautiful day at this beautiful spot." She smiled at Skye. "It's quite a legacy. You can't be sad in a place like this."

"I think you can be sad anywhere," Skye replied, "but today we can do our best to enjoy ourselves." That had been the whole intent of inviting Mara to the cove, to get her mind off her troubles. "Which I think calls for walking with our bare feet in the water, don't you?"

Grinning now, the other woman slipped out of her sandals. Skye followed suit. Then they trotted to the surf line, both inhaling sharp breaths as the cold water rushed over their toes and ankles.

Skye looked at Mara. "As my dad always says, 're-freshing.'"

"Is 'downright cold' not allowed?"

"I've been trained not to say it," Skye admitted as they continued splashing through shallow water on their way back to No. 9. "We don't want to discourage the visitors who keep the cove busy all summer long." With a nod, she indicated the crowd of day tourists and cottage guests.

But it would be so different, so deserted as fall took

over. Skye could sense the change in seasons coming already. The air smelled different as summer drew to a close, the slightly bitter scent of drying grasses adding to the sweet aroma of sunshine.

"What's it like during the off-season?" Mara asked, as if reading Skye's mind. "What do you do?"

"I keep busy, with maintenance and upkeep projects that I can't accomplish during the peak months. In the tradition of my father, I do what I can myself. I'm great with cleaning products as well as a paint roller and brush, though I don't tackle plumbing or electrical beyond the very, very basics."

"I'm thinking of taking a home repair course myself," Mara said. "Even though Charlie was gone a lot of our marriage, he'd tackle the honey-do list when he came home. It must be great to be even minimally capable."

"Yeah," Skye murmured. Until her monster-in-the-closet fears made that capability moot. For the hundredth time she wondered if she could make it through the desolate months ahead. There'd be Gage's letters to look forward to, she reminded herself, though that thought didn't cheer her much.

"Anthony!" Mara's fingers suddenly closed around Skye's arm. "That's Anthony's scream!" she said, then lurched down the sand at a run.

Skye caught up with her just as the other woman skidded to a halt, a sheepish expression on her face. "It's okay," Mara said. "I believe those are shrieks of joy."

Up ahead, Gage and Griffin were in the water, supervising their nephews, Duncan and Oliver, as well as Anthony. The other little boys were five and seven, and accomplished shallow ocean-goers. Anthony looked more tentative and wore a pair of neon water wings on his skinny upper arms, but had a grin on his face even as he squealed every time he was splashed by a low, foam-topped wave.

Duncan was encouraging the younger boy to get on a small canvas raft with him and Oliver. When Anthony glanced up at Gage, the man smiled and bent over to help him onto the apparatus. Then the twin brothers waded into the surf, one to launch the raft on the small waves, the other to catch it at the sand before starting the fun all over again.

Skye knew she was staring, fascinated, at the half-naked man who had been all hers for the past several nights. In a pair of low-slung board shorts, he was tanned and strong, his arm and back muscles rippling as he maneuvered the raft through the water.

Come back to my bed. Stay there until it's time for me to go.

He was her lover. Her summer fling. A shiver rolled across her skin as she thought of the long nights and the sleepy mornings. Sometimes she wondered if she should hold back a little, just for self-preservation's sake, but then he'd stop whatever he was doing and look at her in that alert way of his—as if he sensed her retreating and disapproved. She'd flush hot and her breasts would tingle and that low-belly clenching would happen, which she absolutely recognized was arousal now, and thoughts of preservation seemed a case of too little, too late.

He'd get a glint in his eye, curve his finger at her and then she'd be close enough to breathe his body heat, her gaze fixated on his mouth.

It would curve, an all-male, all-macho smile. *You want a kiss.*

Never a question, because she *always* wanted his kiss.

Mara was talking, and Skye had to force her gaze off that wet, tanned man flesh in order to absorb her words.

Something about Griffin appearing pretty relaxed for a man about to get married.

"Even Jane doesn't seem rattled," she said.

"You're right. Maybe because it's going to be at No. 9, where they met," Skye said.

"I heard it was your idea to have the ceremony on the deck."

"It seemed natural." Skye glanced over to the beach house in question, and pictured how it would look on the day of the wedding. White tulle wrapped around the railings, flowers and candles everywhere, barefoot Jane walking down the aisle demarcated with sand toward her devoted groom. She sighed.

Mara grinned at her. "Do I hear wedding envy?"

"No, no." She stopped before she protested too much. "I admit to enjoying the romance of it, though."

"Jane told me about their whirlwind courtship. I'm so glad Griffin's given up the war reporting. I never asked Charlie to do that...."

"Do you wish you had?" Skye asked.

The other woman shrugged. "I married him knowing what his life was like, the kind of work he was driven to do. Would it have been fair to insist he change? Now I wonder. Your great-great-grandmother asked her husband to give up his passion—perhaps I should have asked Charlie to do that, as well."

Skye didn't know how to answer. Yes, Max Sunstrom, her great-great-grandfather, had given up the movie business, but that was probably because his passion for his wife was greater than his passion for creating silent-era classics like *Sweet Safari* and *The Egyptian*.

Like Mara, though, Skye thought she'd refrain from

asking or expecting a man to walk away from what he loved for who he loved.

"Are things serious with you and Gage?" Mara asked.

Skye glanced over. "How do you know there's a me and Gage?"

"Felt it in the air," Mara said, then laughed. "Oh, and Jane happened to mention it."

Relieved that she wasn't so obvious with her feelings, Skye's gaze slid to him again. He was striding through the surf, one of his nephews riding atop his shoulders. They looked enough alike to be father and son. For a moment—just a tiny moment—she let herself imagine it. A life at the cove with Gage. Dark-haired children playing pirates and mermaids on the beach. Boys poking at clumps of rotting kelp with sticks, girls bringing back handfuls of treasures to put in jars that held collections of shells or beach glass.

Gage smiling at her over their glossy heads. *You want a kiss.*

With an abrupt pivot, Skye turned her back on the image. "Let's go find Jane and Tess," she said to Mara. "We can sip cold drinks on the deck and watch the action from under an umbrella."

But she'd find some other action to watch, Skye promised herself. She'd keep her gaze off Gage and her mind off a future that wasn't to be.

They were trudging through the soft sand on the approach to No. 9 when wet arms suddenly grabbed her from behind. Startled, she squealed, but didn't struggle as she understood instantly who it was. His hair was wet, too, and the sopping strands made her shirt damp as he nuzzled her neck. "Got you."

She pretended to bat at the forearms banded under her breasts. "You're getting me all wet!"

He snorted, then moved his mouth to her ear. "Come with me to your place and I'll take care of that," he whispered.

Her eyes closed at the sweet, dark promise in the words. "We have a friend visiting," she said primly. Mara had gone ahead of them and was now mounting the steps to No. 9's deck.

Gage turned Skye in his arms. "How's she doing? I appreciate you showing her around."

"I'm happy to—I like her a lot. But I think she's having a hard go of it."

"Yeah." All the playfulness seemed siphoned from his mood, and his gaze shifted away from Skye's face to look off into the distance. "I'd hoped a little Crescent Cove enchantment might help."

Lifting her arms, she linked them around his neck. "Are you all right?"

He shook his head. "Seeing little Anthony made me think of things. It made me think of Charlie and it made me think about…about what could have been."

What could have been. And what couldn't be, Skye thought, her mind returning to that little fantasy she'd cast with Gage and dark-haired children that looked just like him. As if he sensed her mood lowering, too, he pulled her close and pressed her head to his chest.

And his beating heart indeed made her more hopeful—as if the mere fact that he was alive promised all things were possible. Her gaze shifted to where she'd last seen Mara. Even with the other woman's example right in front of her, Skye couldn't help imagining a future that would never be.

CHAPTER SIXTEEN

AFTER MARA AND ANTHONY left the cove, and all of Gage's relations returned to their respective homes, Skye made dinner for him at her house. They'd been spending their evenings at No. 9, but tonight she was considering sending him back by himself and sleeping at her home…alone.

Yes, she'd experienced that spurt of optimism, but good sense counseled it wasn't smart to get too accustomed to company.

Gage prowled the kitchen while she cleaned up after the meal. He poured her more wine and grabbed a new beer from her fridge for himself. "Close the door from which the wind blows and relax," he said, tapping the lip of his bottle against the rim of her glass.

"If I thought you knew, I'd ask you what that means," she told him, wishing he'd at least heed the admonition to loosen up. He was more restless than she'd ever seen him and his constant movement put her on edge, too.

Or maybe that was because she was contemplating her lone bed, with no one in it to share the nightmare hours.

He was flipping through the catchall basket that sat on the counter where she dumped grocery receipts, pizza coupons and other offhand items that a tidier woman would relegate to the trash can on a more regular basis. She was considering wondering aloud if his actions weren't an invasion of privacy when he went still.

Frowning, she craned her neck to get a look at what had garnered his sudden interest. She hoped to God she hadn't left about any scraps on which she'd doodled ridiculous junior-high-style sentiments like *Skye + Gage 4 Ever.*

"How well do you know him?" he said.

"Who?"

"Dagwood." Gage flipped the rectangle of paper in his hand toward her. It was a photo taken at a semiformal event sponsored by a business association. She'd been Dalton's date and they'd been snapped by the professional who'd taken everyone's picture on their way inside.

"You know what his name really is," she said, frowning a little. "I don't know why you pretend you don't."

"Because he looks like a Dagwood," Gage said. "How well do you know him?"

Drying her hands on a dish towel, she gave him a wary glance. "I'm not sure what you're getting at."

"Could he have been the guy who tied you up?"

Shocked by the question, Skye stared at him. "No!"

"Think, honey, don't just react. Could it have been him or maybe some pervy buddy of his?"

"No." Agitated, she ran her hands through her hair, then tucked them in the pockets of her shorts. "I don't know why you'd suggest such a thing."

"Because I'd like to solve the mystery."

"You think I wouldn't? But the police believe it's a random event. There weren't any similar crimes in the area before, haven't been any since, and the men walked out of the house with just the cash from my wallet—which wasn't much. So there's no incentive for them even to return."

Unless the creepy one, *him,* came back to fulfill the sexual threat he'd promised.

Just like that, memory attacked. She could feel the awful prick of the knife across her chest. How her naked flesh felt only more vulnerable surrounded by shredded clothes. The blindfold's pressure on her eyes. A stranger's hoarse, disgusting voice. *I'll come back one day and finish what I started.*

The contents of her stomach revolted, and she felt herself go clammy. "Oh, God," she muttered, then rushed for the bathroom.

Gage was on her heels. She slammed the door in his face and took great gulps of air, trying to calm the pitching and tossing seas in her belly.

"Honey, are you all right?" His concern came through the paneled wood.

"I'm fine." Her fingers clutched the porcelain rim of the sink as the sense of certain upchuck slowly faded.

"What can I do?"

She splashed cold water on her face, took a few more deep breaths, then pulled on the knob to face him. "You could not bring up that night again, okay?" Her palm pressed to her belly as if it could contain another bout of panic. The afternoon with Mara had definitely unsettled her, she decided.

"It wasn't Dalton," she told Gage. "It wasn't anyone I know. I'm sure of it."

"Okay, okay." He grimaced. "I'm a little off today. Sorry."

The afternoon with Mara—and thinking of Charlie—had unsettled Gage, too. "All right."

He rubbed his knuckles against the top of her head,

a fond noogie that made him even more forgivable. "C'mon, let's go outside for some fresh air."

On the porch of her house sat two wide-bottomed, thick-cushioned chairs. He took one, but when she tried to take the other, he snagged her arm and pulled her into his lap. His strength surrounded her, and she let herself relax against him for a moment, his warmth and the rhythmic sound of the surf dispelling the last of her queasiness.

Still sleeping alone tonight, she reminded herself.

"Are you going to see him again?" Gage said in her ear.

She turned her head so they were nose to nose, astonished that he'd ask. "You mean Dalton?"

"When I'm gone, are you going to start dating him again?"

It wasn't any of Gage's business. As he said, he was leaving. But she was too tired to point out either of those things and settled back on his shoulder. "No."

He sifted his fingers through her hair. "So…what did he want the other day when he was over?"

"To make clear I understood he was dumping me."

Gage's movements stilled. "I thought you'd already broken up with him."

She shrugged. "He conveniently forgot that part, I guess."

"What a Dagwood," Gage said, his tone disgusted.

Skye laughed.

They sat together in silence, the whispering hiss of water on sand the only sound besides some faint music floating down the beach from Captain Crow's. The stars were bright in the dark velvet of the sky and she could make out the haze of the Milky Way. It drifted across the constellations like a bridal veil.

When Gage left, they'd never share another night like this, she thought, not even under separate skies. As she'd learned, when it was night here, it was day in that other part of the world.

If she asked, would he light a morning candle for her?

"Gage." Thinking of his return to that dangerous part of the world raised another concern. "Mara told me about the precautions and protocols the foreign press adhere to when they're overseas. You do that, right? Make sure you're as safe as you can be?"

She felt him stiffen a moment; then he scooted lower in the cushions, his arm across her waist to hold her more securely. "Those precautions and protocols didn't save Charlie, did they?" he said.

"No, but you *do* leave notice of where you'll be going and when you expect to return, right?"

"Exactly what Charlie did."

"Gage—"

"Let's not talk about it anymore, okay?" Shifting her so she was sideways on his thighs, he leaned close. "Isn't this better?" he said against her mouth.

It was, even as she knew he'd set out to distract her. The kiss consumed her with heat and greedy need, and all niggling worries and maudlin thoughts fled. She threaded her fingers in his hair and opened her mouth to the aggressive thrust of his tongue. He slid his hand beneath her shirt at the small of her back, and the slight roughness of his palm brought out goose bumps that climbed her spine and then spread up the nape of her neck and over her scalp.

He groaned and found the back clasp of her bra, unhooking it with ease, then sliding his hand around her ribs to cup the weight of her breast. His mouth trailed over her cheek to her ear as he toyed with her nipple, pinching at the ruching flesh until she squirmed on his lap. He was thick beneath her bottom, hard and eager.

"Let's go to bed," he whispered, his warm breath tickling the whorls of her ear. He nipped the rim and she shuddered.

"Gage…" He was muddling her mind. There was that promise she'd made to herself, remember? She had to… she had to…

The specifics evaporated as he urged her to her feet, then kissed her again, her upturned face cupped in his hands. His forehead pressed hers. "I want you naked."

She wanted that, too, and hauled in a deep breath to tell him so. But oxygen brought clarity. Hadn't she decided to sleep alone tonight? "Maybe it—"

Her protest was cut off by another luscious, delicious, demanding kiss. Without thinking, she had her hands on his skin beneath his T-shirt, her palms absorbing the heat and play of muscles along his spine. A grunt sounded from deep in his throat, and her response was instinctive: she tilted her hips to press against the bulge of his arousal.

His hand palmed her bottom, keeping her close, making her squirm. He broke this kiss. "God, Skye—"

A wolf whistle pierced the darkness. A passel of kids jostled each other on the beach, wading in the shallows at the surf line. "Get a room," one yelled.

Skye buried her face in his chest, half-embarrassed, half-amused.

"Shit," Gage said. "Let's get inside." Without waiting for her answer, he tugged her through the doorway.

In the entry, though, she resisted farther forward movement, her head and her hormones going to war again: *Don't get used to this! But he's a limited-time offer!*

Gage glanced at her over his shoulder, his expression puzzled.

"I think I should sleep alone," she blurted out.

Still holding her hand, he turned to study her face. "All right," he said after a long moment. "If that's what you really want."

It wasn't what she really wanted! It was never what she really wanted! "I... No, never mind." She stepped forward and wrapped her arms around his waist and butted her head against his shoulder. "It's been a long day."

His sigh blew against her hair. "Yeah. Yeah, it has." He rubbed a comforting hand down her back.

Skye leaned into him, drawing his exotic-spice scent deep into her lungs. Closing her eyes, she reveled in the moment of closeness and warmth. Weeks ago she hadn't wanted a man to look at her, but this particular one had slipped through her barricades and earned her trust. Why would she put him at arm's length?

He tucked his fingers beneath her chin, bringing her gaze back to his. "Would you rather we both go back to No. 9? Spend the night there?"

Skye hesitated.

His hand took another soothing pass down her spine. "We haven't been to bed here. Is that what's bothering you? Me and you in this particular house?"

It was today that continued to bother her, Skye knew. It was the time she'd spent with Mara. As much as she liked and empathized with the other woman, those afternoon hours had reminded her of the danger looming in Gage's future. He'd be on his way to more risk soon, while every moment she spent with him risked her heart.

Insist on sleeping by yourself, her common sense whispered again. *Make a move. Start putting distance between you.*

"It's not the house," Skye told him, and she massaged her right temple where an ice pick was suddenly trying to gouge through her skull to get to her brain.

He made a soft, sympathetic noise. "You have a headache." His fingers closed around her wrist and drew her hand away. "I can fix that," he said, then started towing her, his touch gentle.

To her surprise, he turned into the bathroom that had two doors, one that opened into the hall and the other into her bedroom. It was a large space, tiled in old-fashioned white and pale yellow, and included two pedestal sinks, as well as a walk-in shower with nozzles on opposite walls.

"Wha—" she started.

"Shh," he said, disappearing for a moment to turn on a bedroom lamp. When he reappeared, he flipped off the overhead so that the only light was what spilled from the other room. She found the dimness soothing and, bemused, allowed him to press her down onto the closed lid of the commode.

He reached inside the tiled enclosure and flipped on both fixtures. Water pattered down like rain from the circular showerheads. Then he crossed to her and knelt to tug the sandals from her feet.

"I can do that," she protested, but he hushed her again.

"Let Dr. Lowell do his work," he said.

In moments she was naked and so was he, and they were under the soft, warm spray. "Close your eyes," Gage whispered, tilting back her head to drench it thoroughly. Next she smelled her shampoo, and he had his hands on her again, his fingers massaging her scalp, creating light suds.

The headache was barely a whimper now, and seemed to wash down the drain when he drew her back under the water to rinse her hair. "Good," she said, feeling lethargic now that the pain had abated.

"Good," he confirmed, kissing her lightly. Then he went to work with soap and cloth, washing her with slow, hypnotic strokes. No flesh went untended; he started at her forehead and ended at her feet, always unhurried, always with deliberate movements that were caring but not sexual in nature.

The attention loosened her joints and liquefied her muscles until she had to lean against him to stay upright. His chuckle was soft in her ear, and she kissed his bare shoulder as he shuffled her back under the spray. "I think I could fold you into a Jell-O mold about now."

"Mmm," she said, feeling like a spoiled lap cat.

"Better?" he asked.

"So much better," she said. "Today…"

"Today?"

"It hit me hard. Mara's pain—"

"I know," he said, and held her against him, with the water raining down and his heartbeat a comfort in her ear. He was semiaroused, but he didn't seem impatient to stoke her fire. "Let's go to sleep, Skye."

She blinked up at him, her lashes sticky with wetness. "Sleep?"

His smile was fond. "Just sleep. We have all the time in the world for the other."

But they didn't! They didn't have time! Skye was loath to be the one to point that out, however, and said nothing as he wrapped a towel around his waist then dried her off with more tenderness.

In the bedroom, he reversed the process with the

lights, turning on the one in the bathroom, then flipping the switch on the lamp so that the room was near dark. "Nightgown?" he asked, and she nodded, crossing to the bureau herself.

The sleeveless, thin cotton garment floated over her damp body and when she crawled between the cool sheets, she shivered. Gage gathered her close, his nakedness already warm, and she burrowed her back to his front and let herself drift away, floating on an ocean of sweet forgetfulness.

Later, she woke, instantly aware of Gage's heavy arm across her waist and a need to use the facilities. She slipped free of his hold, took care of business, then flipped off the bathroom light. Tiptoeing across her floor, she heard him make a little sound.

Dreaming, she thought, with a smile.

Then another sound came from his throat. More guttural. Urgent.

"Gotta get out of the dark," he suddenly muttered. "The dark is gonna kill me."

"Gage," Skye said, alarmed at the rough rasp of his voice. He sounded as if he'd been screaming for a week straight. She hurried to his side of the bed, sat on the edge.

"I can't read the letters in the dark." His groan sounded as if it was tortured out of him.

Skye's stomach tightened. "Hey." Her fingertips brushed his shoulder.

He sat bolt upright. Even in the shadowed room, she could see his eyes were open, though he moved his head about as if he was blind.

"Gage." Her palm cupped his whiskered cheek.

At her touch, he jerked, then reached out to grasp her

upper arms. His fingers curled, digging tight. "Give me light, you fuckers," he yelled in that ruined voice. His eyes were on her face, but unseeing. *"Give me goddamn light!"*

Shocked, she could only stare at him.

Then he shook her, hard enough to rattle her teeth. She bit her tongue, the sharp pain causing her to cry out. Only then did Gage freeze. He blinked several times, clearly orienting himself to the real time and place.

"Oh, God," he said. "Skye." He released his hold on her and lurched across the mattress toward the bedside lamp on the other side. Fumbling to turn it on, he almost knocked it to the floor.

When light flooded the room he inhaled deeply, over and over, as if the yellow glow were oxygen. His back was to her, and she could see the shudders that racked his large body.

Something was definitely wrong. Something big. The issue that his twin had been sensing? "Gage—"

"The lights were off. I can't have all the lights off."

"Why?" she asked, keeping her voice soft.

He waved a hand, the movement jerky. "A little phobia." His voice sounded breathless.

Without another word, she got off the bed and padded into the bathroom. She brought back a glass of cold water, handing it over as she stood in the lamplight.

He drank it down in thirsty gulps. "More?" she asked, taking the empty cup from him.

Shaking his head, he glanced up at her and went rigid. "Oh, God," he whispered. "Oh, baby." His hand shook as it reached toward her upper arm.

She looked down, saw the ring of incipient bruises above her biceps. There was a matching band on the other side. His fingertips grazed the mottled flesh; then he met her eyes, his expression hardening to a mask. "I hurt you."

Before she could respond, he hurtled out of the bed. He shut himself in the bathroom, and she detected the sound of water, the rustle of clothes. Clearly, he was planning to escape.

Determined not to let that happen, she wrapped her fuzzy robe around herself, taking a seat on the mattress. A second thought had her scurrying to the kitchen, and then she was back on the bed, hands folded in her lap as she prepared to drag the truth out of him.

The bathroom door popped open and he came into the room, pausing when he saw her expectant pose.

"You're going to tell me what that was about," she said.

His expression still unreadable, he shook his head. "No." He slid his hands in his pockets as his gaze roamed the room. "Have you seen my keys?"

Lifting one hand, she let them dangle.

He zeroed in on their merry jangle, then strode toward her.

Skye shoved them deep in the patch pocket of her robe. "Tell me what happened first. I'll give them to you after."

His expression darkened as he halted a few feet away from her. "Don't play games."

"I'm serious."

Shaking his head, he started forward again. Skye instinctively shrank back, and he stopped, pushing the heels of his hands into his eyes. "Shit!" he said. "Now I'm scaring you. Give me the keys and let me get the hell out of here."

Skye straightened her spine. "Not until you talk to me."

"You don't know what you're asking for," he said,

the stony mask falling from his face. Temper vibrated his body and throbbed in the air. "You'll wish you never knew."

It made her belly jump, but she didn't let that or his menacing stare move her. Crossing her arms over her chest, she pinned him with her gaze. "Tell me anyhow."

And when he did, Skye realized she'd never have to worry about sleeping alone.

Because she'd probably never sleep again.

January 20
Dear Gage,
After a week of low skies and drizzle, we're enjoy-ing a string of halcyon days—you know the kind, when we hope they're not televising a golf tourna-ment from Pebble Beach or a surf competition in San Diego. When that happens, and the forecast is 77 and sunny on the SoCal sand...well, you can hear the stakes pulling up all over the rest of coun-try and we brace for more freeway traffic.

The ocean is winter-green and white, its sur-face choppy, the waves throwing themselves on the shore like temperamental teenagers taking to their beds. But warmth radiates from the golden sand, and the jade plants are flowering, the scent from their pink, star-shaped flowers sweet and allur-ing. My mother used to tell my sister and me it was the perfume of the fairies, lingering in the air after their nights of mischief and magic.
Best, Skye

Skye:
Please send more word warmth! Our high yes-

terday was 2 degrees Celsius (that's 35 to those Fahrenheit-inclined). After reading your letter, I shivered my way to the bazaar and found a shemagh (desert scarf) in the cove colors of sun and skye (sic). I told the shopkeeper it's because I'm from California and he wanted to know which of the L.A. Lakers live next door to me. I didn't have the heart to tell him I can't claim actual neighbors because I haven't had a permanent address in years. When I think of home, however, my mind increasingly turns to Crescent Cove. Perhaps the fairies' magic at work?
Gage

Fuming at Skye's stubbornness, Gage stalked about the room. The nightmare was still clanking inside his skull like a tossed salad of nuts and bolts, bruising his synapses and scrambling his mental processes. He should come up with a cover story, blame some innocuous trigger like indigestion or allergies, but his head felt heavy, making it too clumsy to concoct believable untruths.

And then there was Skye herself. Thoughts of her had been the only dependable illumination for two terrifying weeks in the darkness. Her letters the good-luck charms that had gotten him through. When she looked at him the way she was and when he thought of how she'd trusted so much of herself to him, he couldn't lie to her.

Still, it made him angry as hell, because he'd never intended to tell anyone. "I was kidnapped," he stated baldly. Because what was the sugarcoat?

Her sharp intake of breath was a second delayed—as if her mind needed a moment to catch up—but it sounded loud and shocked in the quiet, shadowed room. "H-how?"

"I wrote you about that new contact I'd made, remember?"

She swallowed. "Yes."

"He was supposed to take me to a new Taliban training camp in the border region." Jahandar had been too smiley, too obsequious, Gage thought now. Except that wasn't true. The young man had seemed sincere, and the money he wanted to act as guide was within the norms of what Gage had given to others.

"But instead?"

"Every time you get a new opportunity, you've got to make a decision," he told her. "You weigh what you know, what could go wrong, what you hope to accomplish."

"You take a gamble with your life."

"No." His temper was rising again, making his voice harsh. "Well, yes. But it's not a death wish like you're implying."

She raised a brow.

"Somebody's got to get the information, Skye." He dropped into an upholstered chair positioned in the corner of the room. "I'm good at what I do. I'm good at seeing things in a way that clarifies what's going on out there."

"And you thrive on the danger."

She didn't get it, he thought, shaking his head. "If I consider myself in actual, impending peril, I don't take the chance. Yes, I'm aware I could get hit by a stray bullet or have the bad luck of running over an IED, but that's different than thinking I'm an actual target."

Gage felt his hands tightened into fists. "That day I was set up," he said. "Instead of taking me to the Taliban, Jahandar drove to the site of his family's lucrative business. A ransom farm."

She flinched.

"It's exactly what it sounds like. The family specialized in kidnapping wealthy businessmen, mostly, but they were willing to branch out to journalists, too. Anyone who they suspected had family in America from whom they could extort cash."

"Were you…were you held at an actual farm?" Skye asked.

His sharp laugh tore at his throat on its way out. "I was put in a hole in the ground."

She went still. "I think you better give me the details before the ones I make up are worse than reality."

"Reality likely isn't much better." But he explained that after being driven to Nowheresville, he'd expected to be met and vetted by the Taliban leader. Instead, he'd been confronted by three young men with Kalashnikov assault rifles. Adrenaline had flooded Gage's system, though he'd tried to keep calm as they ordered him away from the car and up a dirt track. There, they'd slid away a piece of plywood the size of a manhole cover.

"That was home, sweet home," he told Skye now. "They didn't bother trying to coax me into the shaft, they just picked me up and dropped me down, about eight feet. One of my new friends followed me in, shooing me forward into a tunnel by prodding me with the nuzzle of a pistol."

Shoving his hand through his hair, he tried to forget the smell of the earth, the tannic and ash taste of it on his tongue. "Then we got to a square-sized 'chamber,' that was six feet long, three feet wide, four feet high and braced with pieces of half-rotted wood. Inside was a dirty blanket, a dirtier pillow and a single lightbulb hooked up by wires to a corroded car battery.

"Once I was shown my new digs, my captor backed

out and put another piece of wood over the opening that led to the shaft. I tried moving it, of course, but it wouldn't budge."

Skye stared at him. "How did you breathe?"

"There was a pipe that poked up to the surface. Oh, and I had a waste bucket, a watering can filled with rust-flavored H-two-O, and a backpack stuffed with boxes of mango juice and packaged cheese cracker sandwiches."

All the temper was drained out of him now, leaving only the dark, oily stain of the memories.

"You were there for how long?"

"I was in that hole for two weeks."

Skye shuddered. "How did you manage?"

"You..." He hesitated, sliding his palms down the denim of his jeans. "You got me through."

"Me?" Her eyes went round.

"Your letters. I happened to have them with me." She didn't need to know he'd carried the thin packet whenever he left the place he rented in Kabul—he was that afraid they might get lost if someone robbed his rooms while he was out. "I'd read them, imagining you and the cove. Almost better than TV."

She tried to put on a smile, but it quickly failed. "You didn't always have light, though."

His fingers tightened on his knees. "How...?"

One of her shoulders lifted. "When you were dreaming, you were demanding it."

Begging, probably, Gage thought, feeling heat crawl over his neck. For a guy used to action, to movement, independence, autonomy, when the bulb sputtered out he'd believed he was being smothered. If he couldn't see himself, there *was* no self. If he couldn't read Skye's letters—even though after a few days he could whisper aloud each word by heart—then there was no sunlight or ocean or Crescent Cove where he might someday return.

He tried on his own smile. "Let me just say I have a new appreciation for fresh car batteries."

Frowning, Skye eyed him as she drew the edges of her robe more tightly around her. It was the color of a duckling and looked just as soft. "How did you get free?"

"I have a colleague, an Afghani photojournalist. They asked for a cell phone number and I gave his. We have an…agreement of sorts. To make a two-week-long story short, he has a contact in the national police. They ultimately arrested the patriarch of my kidnapping crime family. Then a deal was struck—he was freed upon the release of the farm's current hostages."

Skye blinked. Dawn was delivering its gray-fingered light into the room, mingling with the glow from the lamp. It created an odd visual field around her, obscuring the edges of her body. Squeezing his knees, Gage stayed where he was, ignoring a sudden and urgent craving to touch her, to make sure she was solid and real.

"You're going back to that place, aren't you?" she asked. "You're going back to see if that family is at it again."

His jaw dropped.

"I overheard you discussing your next assignment with Rex one afternoon," she said. "And I can't believe you'd walk into the lion's den like that."

He frowned at her. "Look, they are no more lions than I'm a lamb. And from what I've learned, that particular group has scattered."

"Then why—"

His temper took hold of his tongue again. "Because I have to. Because I have to go back and photograph those holes in the ground. Those empty holes in the ground, to prove that I didn't leave anything of myself behind."

She opened her mouth, but he pointed a finger at her before a word came out. "You of all people should understand that, Skye," he said. "You should get that I can't allow anyone to keep a piece of me."

The room was light enough now that he could see the flush on her face. "I…" She subsided. "But…" She subsided again, then sent him a truculent glance from under lowered brows.

Point made. He relaxed back on the chair cushions. Crisis passed.

Then she opened her mouth again. "How come Griffin doesn't know about this?"

Gage froze. "I…"

"Why wasn't he the one you had the kidnappers contact? Or why didn't your Afghani colleague call your twin? Isn't the protocol to leave information on where you're going and when you're expected back and what to do if you don't return?"

The nuts and bolts were jumping around again in his mental hopper. He pushed the heel of his hand against his forehead, trying to keep them still. "I couldn't… I don't…"

"Oh, my God," Skye said, sounding shocked. Her hand crept toward her throat. "You ignore the protocol."

Once again, he couldn't lie. "I do," he agreed, sighing. "You know what happened when Charlie was taken. You know the position that put Mara in. So I'm protecting Griffin, my folks, all of them. I don't want my family to ever blame themselves like she does now."

Skye was staring at him. "So…so it's acceptable to you that you'll go off and they won't be alerted that you're in danger and need help? Gage, you could die and they might never know it."

"Skye—"

"I…" She swallowed, but her voice remained tight. "*I* might never know it."

His chest took each word like a blow. "Honey," he said softly, aching from his heart outward. "That's not something to think about."

Her voice rose. "Of course it's something to think about."

"Skye." Gage got to his feet, approaching with the single idea of offering comfort. To both of them.

She scrambled back on the mattress, her face pale. "Stay away from me."

He halted, staring at her. "What?"

"I want you to go." Her palms went up, warding him off.

"Skye," he chided, holding out his arms. "Come here, baby."

"Don't 'come here, baby,' me." She leaped off the bed.

"Just take it easy," he suggested.

With a furious sound, she turned, drew his keys out of her pocket and threw them at him.

"Shit!" Only a last-minute knee tuck saved him from a blow of sharp metal to precious jewels. "What's gotten into you?"

Instead of an answer, she sent him a fulminating look, then slammed into the bathroom. He heard the click of locks on both sets of doors.

The whole house seemed to pulse with her temper. Well, he was mad, too, Goddamn it. Hadn't he tried to protect her, protect everyone from this? "I told you," he yelled through the door. "I said you'd wish you never knew."

She yelled back, "I don't want to know you."

Seething, he shot eye daggers through the wood. He had the distinct sense she was doing the same from the other side. Damn it. *Goddamn it!* Where the hell had sweet, shy, reserved Skye Alexander gone?

Feeling put upon and more than a little put out that the siren of the cove was suddenly showing her true—cruel—colors, Gage stalked out of her place. Maybe Beach House No. 9 would have the magic to let him forget any of this had ever happened.

CHAPTER SEVENTEEN

TEAGUE DIDN'T KNOW WHAT to do with himself now that he'd lost his best friend. Work was there, of course, but when he wasn't at the station, he felt rootless. He'd inherited a small, craftsman-style house built in the 1930s from his paternal grandparents. The garage had been converted into a woodshop of sorts, and he'd put his grandfather's tools to good use from the day he'd moved in.

Teague was handy.

Efficient, too, because after a year of occupancy, the paint was tight inside and out, the woodwork refinished, the kitchen and baths updated. The yards, front and back, were also well tended. Lawns had been mowed, shrubbery trimmed, even the birdbath was clean and held fresh water.

That left him with nothing to do but brood.

There's all your big talk about wanting kids, wanting a family, but then you go and fall for someone who's already taken...because it means you risk nothing.

On the second morning of life without Polly, he was driven to seek company. Not until he knocked on a familiar door did he realize he'd chosen to visit the only man he knew more miserable than himself.

Without a word, Gary White pushed open the screen door.

"Dad," Teague acknowledged, then followed his silent and stiff-spined father into the kitchen.

The newspaper was open on the table, and a thick, utilitarian mug sat beside it, filled with black coffee. The older man poured a second one for his son, and Teague took it, even though he knew the caffeinated stuff his father made was caustic. "Thanks," he said, cupping his palms around the heated white ceramic as he leaned against the countertop.

Gary returned to his chair and continued perusing the sports section of the paper.

Teague ran his gaze around the room that hadn't changed since the day his mother had walked out when he was fifteen years old. The curtains over the sink had been a jaunty yellow when his mother had run them up on her sewing machine, but they'd gone grayish now, and hung with the limpness of surrender flags.

An old rotary phone, installed on the wall beside the refrigerator, still had a sticker with lines printed on it for emergency numbers. In his mother's handwriting there was the listing for the pediatrician's office, the poison control center, her parents' home phone—that hadn't been relevant in the decade since their deaths.

"Whatcha been doing to keep busy, Dad?" Teague ventured. His father had retired from the fire department with a full pension. Still in good health, he could have sought a second career or traveled or taken up square dancing.

His father turned the page of his paper. "I'm in the middle of replacing the valves and floats in all the toilets."

The house had two and a half baths. The man would probably stretch out the task for the entire week. Teague sipped at the terrible coffee and wondered why the hell he'd hied himself here.

"Did you look at that brochure I left the last time I visited?" It was for an Alaskan fishing excursion company. Teague had suggested the two of them might take a week and do one together.

Getting out of town sounded even more attractive now. "Silver salmon and rainbow trout in September and October." They might be a little late on booking, but hell, he was willing to pay a premium price for the vacation. Arranging time off work was less of a problem. Firefighters were always willing to switch shifts.

And God knew his dad never had anything pressing on his schedule.

He cast a glance at the older man. "I'm serious. If you had a computer, right now we could—"

"I don't need a computer."

Teague sighed. His father didn't need or want anything that hadn't been in this house fifteen years ago— except the one person who'd packed her bags and walked away from it.

Janet White had never explained to Teague why she'd left her marriage. About abandoning him—well, that had come with the justification that a son belonged with his father. Truthfully, nothing much had changed upon her absence. He and his father had learned to do laundry and put together meals, but the silence around the dinner table had been the same.

His father had forever been of the mind that what happened on the job stayed on the job. Naturally taciturn, he hadn't sought other topics of conversation that might engage his wife and son. Teague had moved outward, seeking friends and activities to fill the void, but he supposed his mother could only crave the companionship her emotionally unavailable husband was powerless to provide.

Teague swigged down more of the dark brew, his gaze resting on his father. There were threads of silver in his hair, but he'd lost none of the brawn in his shoulders and arms. His belly was as flat as ever. At fifty-seven, he could pass for years younger.

"You know, Dad, you look pretty good for an old geezer." He said it with a smile, hoping to tease one out of his father. "Have you thought about sending out some feelers to friends or looking into a dating service? Bet you could find a lady to share your golden years."

Gary White's brown eyes shot up to his, their shocked expression telling everything the man wouldn't—he was still hung up on his ex-wife.

Shit. "Never mind," Teague muttered. "Let's start with salmon. What do you say to a week away next month?"

His father immediately shook his head. "I could never be gone that long."

"Why?"

"You never know if…" The older man made a vague gesture.

Exasperated, Teague set his coffee on the counter. "Dad, she's never coming home," he said, and heard the echo of other, similar-sounding words. *"Teague, you're never going to have her."*

His father's gaze dropped back to the baseball box scores. "That's private," he mumbled.

As everything was private, Teague thought, his jaw hardening. Work, worry, stress, feelings. It had become a habit in this house. A habit of the two men in this kitchen.

Everything uncomfortable, everything honest, every raw, stripped-to-the bone emotion put up on a high shelf. Out of reach. Unattainable, like the women he and his father had set their sights on.

"Because it means you risk nothing."

Jesus.

What's wrong with me? Teague thought, now as frustrated with himself as with his dad. *Why the fuck did I come here?*

Because you're in danger of becoming just like the man at the table, his common sense answered. *A stunted, closed-off human being.*

That truth was only darker and more bitter than the coffee he dashed into the sink before striding out of the house and into the too-bright sunshine. It struck the top of his head like a smite from God.

Only one person, one relationship, Teague realized, could save him. And getting her back would mean reaching high and then laying everything he had at her feet.

BEHIND THE WHEEL OF HIS truck, traveling the narrow road that ran along the bluffs above Crescent Cove, Teague finally found Polly. Seated on a fat-tired, single-speed cruiser bicycle, she pedaled along the crumbling edge of asphalt, as yet unaware of the vehicle tracking her progress.

Her hair gleamed bright in the sunlight. He frowned a little, thinking she should be wearing a helmet. One was available; it sat in the wire basket mounted above the rear tire. There was a sheaf of daisies resting there, too, white-and-yellow heads nodding with each bump in the road.

She'd probably run the roses he'd brought her through the garbage disposal.

The thought made him grind his back teeth for a moment, but then he forced his jaw to relax. The situation was dicey enough without getting overwrought. He and Polly needed to have a quiet, rational conversation.

They could manage that, he was sure of it. Before everything started going wonky this month, they'd always been of an easygoing, like-minded temperament.

Taking a deep breath, he goosed the gas. The truck eased forward, and he kept it at a slow pace. When he came abreast of her, he rolled down the passenger window.

She glanced over; then her eyes went wide. The bike's front tire wobbled.

"Watch out!" he cautioned. To the right of the road, the earth fell away to brush-covered hillside and she was dangerously close to going over it. He braked, watching her wrangle the handlebars.

The bicycle straightened out. Polly continued pedaling. Riding faster away from him.

Frowning, he gave a little more gas. "Hey!" he called through the open window as he caught up to her again. "I've been looking for you. I thought we could talk."

"You thought wrong. I told you to stay away." Then she lifted her cute fanny off the bicycle seat and started pumping, moving with surprising speed.

A burst of irritation heated his blood. His fingers tightened on the steering wheel, even as he told himself to chill. *Calm down. Keep your cool. We're going to have a quiet, rational conversation.*

Surely two people who had been friends as long as they could manage that.

Keeping hold of his patience, he pushed down on the gas pedal again. She was really moving now, the muscles in her slim legs flexing below a pair of blue jean cutoffs. Their golden length distracted him a little, and he didn't realize that the road had narrowed. As he approached her again, his side-view mirror came too close to her shoulder, and he jerked the wheel to avoid it brushing her.

The truck jolted left, her startled blue gaze followed suit and in that moment when her attention wandered from the road, she dropped off it.

Between one blink and the next, Polly had disappeared.

Teague's heart slammed into his tonsils. He was out of the truck before his brain even engaged. "Polly!" he yelled, panicking. *"Polly!"*

At the edge of the road, he looked down, scanning the dirt and scrubby chaparral bushes. At the sight of a scrap of bright color, he launched himself in its direction, sliding on the silty orange dirt. It was a running shoe.

Polly's *shoe.*

He squeezed it between his fingers, mimicking the painful clutch of his heart. *God, oh, God.* "Polly!"

A dozen feet to his left, something started rustling in a dense-leaved, dusty-green shrub. Either it was a maddened animal or his woman was alive.

"Are you hurt?" he yelled, scrambling and slipping across the uneven terrain.

A blond head poked out between two prickly branches. "I'm pissed," said the wild-haired, angry-eyed creature glaring his way. *"What* were you thinking?"

Relief tasted like cool water to his parched throat. She was alive, thank God. Alive and unhurt enough to hiss and spit. "Is anything broken?" he asked.

She ignored the hand he held out and managed to step free of the chaparral. Other than a few scratches on her legs and arms, she looked okay.

But the thin red lines spiked his temper. "Where's your helmet, damn it?"

Pausing in brushing the dust off her backside, she glanced over at him. "With the bike, about six feet farther down the hill."

He pretended he wasn't seeing red. His point was to woo her, after all. "I mean, why aren't you wearing it?"

"I didn't know I was going to encounter the trucker from hell. Now go down there and get Skye's bicycle, would you? If it's damaged, it's all your fault."

Muttering under his breath, Teague handed over her missing shoe, then slipped and slid around more bushes until he came across a metal frame and fat tires. All looked intact, with the exception of the bunch of daisies, their stems now mangled. With vicious satisfaction, he threw them farther down the hill, then shouldered the bike and trudged back toward the road.

Polly was standing beside his truck. The instant he set the bike down, she tried to wrest it from his grasp. He held on. "What are you doing?"

"I'm getting on my way," she said, still tugging.

Without another word, he swung it from her hands, lifting it over her head to set it in the bed of his truck. Then, letting his temper get the better of him, he crossed his arms over his chest and stared down at her with *Take that* in his gaze.

She stared back, her blue eyes glinting fire like the sunlight catching in the Pacific Ocean over her shoulder. A breeze blew across them, ruffling their hair, but doing nothing to cool the mood that shimmered in the air.

Another tense moment passed, and then she turned smartly on the heel of the shoe that he'd found in the dirt—that goddamn shoe, it still had the power to turn his pulse erratic—and took off down the road. Stunned that she'd walk away from him, he watched her in silence a moment, then leaped forward to grab her by the elbow.

She whirled around, glaring again. "What's gotten into you?"

"I…I…" Teague tried to slow the swirling tangle of feelings that were spinning, Tasmanian Devil–style, in his gut. He reminded himself of the relaxed conversation he wanted. He recalled she'd been his best friend for years. They'd always been levelheaded, even-keeled companions.

But then he thought of her hot tears, her confession— *"I've loved you for years"*—her command for him to go away and leave her alone. And words just burst from his mouth.

"I'm fucking furious with you," he said.

Yelled maybe, because they both staggered back. Teague struggled to restrain his revving heartbeat and gain control again. God, he'd never been this mad at a woman in his life. He charmed; he didn't shout.

For a moment, he reconsidered what he was doing. The desperate man he'd become in the past few days without Polly wasn't a comfortable fit. His skin and bones didn't seem big enough to hold all that he was feeling inside. All that he was feeling for her.

But if he succumbed to the habits of a lifetime, by diminishing those feelings or by putting them at a distance, then he'd turn into his father. Drying up, one long, lonely day at a time. Never getting what he truly wanted. Who he wanted, despite the risk.

He gave himself another moment to level out his breathing, then met her gaze, willing himself to sound sane. "You accuse me of not seeing you when that's just a crock, Polly. You didn't *let* me see."

"I—"

"No." He pointed a finger at her pretty, cheerleader nose. "It's my turn to tell some truths. I might have my high shelf, but you, you have your impervious, perky shell and your glued-to-the-soul secrets."

Her mouth opened.

"Don't even start complaining about the perky. I happen to adore the perky in you. But God, couldn't you at least drop a hint or two before blindsiding a guy with the truth?"

Her arms lifted, fell again to her sides. "I threw my dress on the ground! You don't call standing naked in front of you a hint?"

She had a point. And the fact was, he knew why she'd taken so long to be truthful with him, one of the consequences of being such close friends. A little of his anger evaporated. Men, starting with her father, had taken advantage of her. His gender hadn't given her much reason to trust, and that she'd allowed herself feelings for him— even confessed them—was probably the biggest compliment Teague had ever been paid in his life.

"Oh, Polly," he said, reaching for her.

She stepped back, her eyes wary.

Oh, Polly. "I love you," he said softly, his chest aching like hell. "I know I'm an idiot for taking so long to acknowledge it, but I'm in love with you. I suspect it's been that way for a long time."

If he'd expected her to fall into his arms—but he didn't; he knew her that well. When she took another step back, he sighed. His temper was still on edge, but he couldn't be angry in the face of those big, scared blue eyes that fixed on his face with patent disbelief. "You don't believe me," he said.

"Of course I don't." She tapped her forefinger against her chest. "Unattainable. *Now* you care about me."

"I—" His breath sighed out. Damn. He should have seen that coming. It was just that what he felt for Polly, his best-friend-who-was-a-girl, who was no longer his best friend but was something so much bigger, was not at all like the stupid crushes he'd had on Tess or on Amethyst Lake or the Belgian exchange student. This was so much more...vital.

Urgent.

Risky.

His father had loved his mother, and yet she'd still packed her bags. But his father hadn't been willing to share his life or his heart. Teague was going to have to do both.

"C'mon, Pol," he said, opening the passenger door. "Get in."

"Why?"

He squeezed the chrome door handle as if it were her neck. "I want to show you something." When she didn't move, he decided throwing her bodily into the seat wasn't his greatest idea. So he gave her another chance. "Please, Gator. For old times' sake."

The suspicious look on her face didn't waver, causing his ire to rise once again. Damn, he wasn't used to this... this passion. She'd always mattered so much to him, but now...now *they* mattered infinitely more. He hoped like hell he could convince her of his love before he killed her out of frustration.

POLLY FELT BATTERED all over, inside and out, as Teague drove northward. It was mostly silent between them, though every once in a while she saw his grip go white-knuckled on the steering wheel. Then he'd mutter, "You should give me the benefit of the doubt" or "At least you could credit me with the ability to take my head out of my ass."

She just had to stay strong for a while longer, she consoled herself. He'd drop this harebrained notion of his—love! now, after all this time?—soon. They wouldn't be friends like before; that relationship had been buried between the sheets of her bed, but they'd both be in a place to move on.

Except he'd moved into her workplace, she realized, trailing him from the parking lot of her elementary school to the classroom she'd occupy in just a few days. He hesitated outside the locked door. "Do you have your keys?" he asked. "Or I could track down Ted."

She glanced up at him. "Ted? You know our janitor?"

Teague ran a hand through his hair. "We're recent acquaintances. He let me in yesterday and this morning."

"You've been in my room?" Polly dug into the pocket of her cutoffs. "Ted opened the door for a stranger?"

"Don't blame him. I can be pretty persuasive," he admitted. "And the firefighter thing is sort of like a free pass."

"Don't I know it?" Polly grumbled. She inserted the key in the lock and then pulled open the heavy metal door, latching it on the doorstop set in the outside wall. The scent of new paint and raw wood reached her nose.

"What—?" She made to step inside.

Teague caught her arm. She winced and he instantly turned it up, inspecting the scrape he'd brushed with his thumb. "Oh, sweetheart," he said, so sympathetic she wanted to weep. "I should have looked you over before now. Let's find your first-aid kit and I'll take care of everywhere you hurt."

"No," she said, pulling away. He couldn't reach the place she was really wounded.

"Pol—"

She stepped across the threshold. "Tell me why we're…" Her voice trailed off as her gaze fell upon the structure built into one corner of her room.

"I planned for it to be done before I showed it to you," he said. "But wuss that I am, I missed you too much to wait that long."

Surrounding the room's bookcases was a floor-to-ceiling edifice made of plywood. "A castle?" On the outside, someone had inked in the suggestion of bricks on the turret and vines climbing the walls.

"The artwork is thanks to my buddy Vin at the station. It's just a suggestion for now. He'll come back and do the details after I get the thing finished and painted."

Her imagination could picture it. A whimsical and appealing palace for the kindergarten princes and princesses, knights and warrior maidens who would pass through her door for years to come. "They won't be able to resist reading time."

"That's the plan," Teague said.

Her heart was swelling in her chest, no longer tucked into itself for protection. Still, there was pain. "It's the kind of thing a…a friend would do," she murmured.

"It's the kind of thing a person who loves you would do," Teague corrected.

"No," she whispered, feeling the sting of tears.

"Yes." Teague pulled her around, then lifted her chin so her watery gaze met his. "I might have been saying the wrong words to you, Polly, but I've been doing the right things all this time."

"What do you mean?"

He slipped his free hand into his back pocket and pulled out a printed receipt. "Construction materials. Check the date. I ordered them the day you mentioned wanting a reading nook in your new classroom."

She had to take his word for it, because the tears made the numbers waver. "I don't understand."

"It was a way of showing you how I feel—and it showed me how I feel, too. I've always enjoyed doing things for you. Bringing you muffins. Finding your keys. I've always enjoyed spending time with you, too." He ran a hand over the back of her hair. "For over four years, *you* have been in the woman in my life, because *you* are the woman I love."

"But…but…"

"I know what you're going to say. Yes, it took me long enough to figure out. But we both had some trust issues to overcome."

His mother. Her father.

Teague stared into her eyes. "But we did overcome them, didn't we, sweetheart? I've never let anyone get closer to me than you."

Polly's face went hot as she thought of him coming inside her, skin to skin, the ultimate, physical trust. But to give him a chance at her heart…?

His voice softened, and his gaze turned tender. "You've trusted me so often and for so long. Please, take another leap of faith. Believe me when I say I'll never give up on us."

A shiver worked its way down her back. "It's so risky."

"You're the one who pointed that out to me," Teague said. "But I'm taking a real chance now, aren't I?"

When she looked away again, he brought her face back toward his. "I love you, Gator. I love you so very much."

She sniffed. "Are you…are you sure it's not because I'm the unattainable one now?"

"Of course I'm sure." He laughed, sexy and low. "Because that's exactly how I'll disprove your theory." Then he bent his head and took her mouth, kissing her with heat and passion and masculine intent. There was nothing friendly about it, and she melted against him. "See?" he said against her lips. "You're perfectly attainable. Not to mention mine."

And because she'd once read that best friends made the best lovers—and now knew that to be true—Polly pulled him as close as she'd always dreamed she could. "And you're mine right back."

CHAPTER EIGHTEEN

SKYE WAS SITTING BEHIND the desk in the property management office, sifting through mail, when she heard a cheerful knock on the jamb of the open door. Gage? For a moment her heart shifted in her chest, but then it returned to its regular place. The way things had been left between them didn't warrant anything "cheerful." The ensuing twenty-four hours of mutual silence only cemented that fact.

Glancing up, she saw it was Polly hesitating on the tiny porch. "Busy?" the other woman asked, holding up a pair of to-go cups.

"Nothing that can't wait," Skye said, and managed to smile as her friend handed over one of the coffees.

Frowning, Polly dropped into the visitor chair on the other side of the desk. "What's the matter? You don't look happy."

"Of course I'm happy," Skye countered. "It's summer, you brought me a free beverage and…" Her words faded away, but her inner voice kept talking…*reckless Gage is going back to danger—and doing it in the most dangerous manner possible.*

That was why she'd decided to put him out of her mind.

She sipped at the hot drink. "Perfect latte."

Polly shrugged. "From your favorite barista at Captain Crow's. He sends his best."

"Mmm." Skye sat back in her chair, her gaze running over her friend. "You look energized."

"Yes. Well." Polly shifted on her seat. "I have a confession to make."

"You're going out with Maureen's brother again."

"Who?" The other woman's face went blank.

"Your teacher friend. Her cute brother. That blind date?"

"Oh." Polly shook her head. "I'd completely forgotten about him."

Skye set down her cup to play with the envelopes she'd yet to open. "I can't say I'm sad to hear that. While he sounded nice, I got the impression there weren't any sparks."

Sparks. The word made her think of Gage and that final, fiery argument. After he'd slammed out of the house, the smoke of their last exchange had lingered in the air.

Didn't I say you wouldn't want to know!

I don't want to know you!

"Skye, what's wrong?" Polly's voice interrupted the memory.

"Nothing," Skye said. Using her letter opener, she slit the manila envelope on top of the pile. "Nothing at all." She was forgetting about Gage.

"So, I came to say…" Polly's head bent over her cup.

Frowning, Skye stared at her friend, sensing something amiss. "How was your bike ride this morning?"

"I'm afraid I crashed your bicycle." Polly grimaced, her face going red.

"Are you all right?"

"Yes. I... Yes. Fabulous, actually." She glanced up, her expression sheepish. "Teague ran me off the road."

"What?"

"But he was very sweet about it...well, no, he actually was very angry, though—"

"Teague *angry?*" Even when he claimed to be heart-broken over Tess, he'd never shown a surfeit of emotion. Skye wasn't sure the easygoing man had it in him.

"There might have even been a whiff of rage," Polly confessed. "Then he became very, very determined."

"Determined to do...what?"

A smile broke over her friend's face, lighting her eyes, lighting the whole room. She put her coffee on the desk, then fluttered her left hand. "Determined to get me to say I'll marry him."

A diamond winked on Polly's finger. Skye stared at it before lifting her gaze to meet her friend's bright eyes. "Pol, this is great! He finally came to his senses?"

She nodded. "He built me a castle." Then Always Private Polly burst into tears.

Of course tissues and hugs happened next, and Skye got the whole story from "friends with benefits" to the visit to a jeweler. She had to scold, however. "You didn't tell me anything about going to bed with Teague."

"You've been too busy doing the same with Gage."

"Oh," Skye said, returning to her seat without bothering to explain there'd been a change in circumstances. She wasn't thinking about him anymore, she reminded herself, sliding a sheet from the envelope she'd opened.

"I still haven't gotten to my confession," Polly said, her voice going quiet.

Skye looked up. "What could be bigger than getting

engaged to the man you were convinced you could never have?"

"I'm moving in with him. With Teague. This is official notice that I'll be leaving the cove."

Shadows invaded the corners of the room. Had a cloud passed over the sun? "O-of course," Skye managed to say, casting a wary glance over her shoulder. "I'm so happy for you both."

Polly bit her bottom lip. "Thank you…and I'm sorry. I realize I'm breaking our friends-before-men pledge."

"Oh." Skye tried to laugh. "I didn't take that seriously, no worries. I'm just thrilled you worked things out with Teague." She hoped her voice didn't sound as hollow as her stomach felt, and she dropped her gaze to camouflage her sudden dread.

Come fall, she'd be alone.

"Skye…"

She pretended to study the piece of correspondence in her hand. "Hey, look at this," she said. "It's an early copy of the Crescent Cove article being published in Sunday's paper." Thrusting it toward her friend, she jumped from her chair.

In the doorway, she inhaled great gulps of sunny, salt-laden air. "Tell me I don't come off sounding like an idiot."

She'd done so many idiotic things lately. Going to bed with Gage, not just once, but many times, letting him into her—

No, she had put him out of her mind.

"It's a great article, Skye," Polly said after a few moments. "Hits all the right notes. The devoted romance of your great-great-grandparents, the mystery of the jeweled collar. I predict you'll be getting bookings for next summer as soon as it comes out."

"Fabulous," she replied, without enthusiasm.

Polly got to her feet and came to stand in the doorway, as well. "What are you looking at?"

Nothing. Skye was staring, unseeing, down the beach, trying to erase memories and fears from her mind.

"Uh-oh," Polly said. "Someone's climbing the bluff, despite those new signs you posted."

Frowning, Skye narrowed her eyes. From here, the figure was of indeterminate size and had no distinguishing features, but it was definitely a person scrambling up the unstable side face. There was another route, leading directly to the top of the bluff, that most people used to enjoy the view. Those taking the alternative track were likely intent on cliff-jumping, not sightseeing.

"Hell," she muttered, digging for her keys. She pushed Polly out the door and locked the office behind them. "I'm going to put a stop to this once and for all."

"Once and for all" might be an impossible order, but that didn't prevent her from stomping down the beach. It was time to get control of something in her world.

She didn't spare a glance for Beach House No. 9, breezing right past it and starting up the side-winding trail better suited for goats. It stopped at several different outcroppings that intrepid visitors used as launching pads for their leaps into the sea below. Sharp rocks gathered at the base of the bluff, and while there weren't a lot of them, a careless move could cause real harm.

There was no sign of the figure she'd seen before, but the person could very well be tucked against the cliff-face at a higher elevation or around the other side, out of her view. She was certain no one had jumped yet.

Fingers curled around the fibrous branch of sagebrush for stability, she sidled around a rock toward the next flat position, one of the lower and more popular jumping points. As she planted both feet on the shelf of rock, a strong breeze buffeted her, and she wobbled. A lean arm caught at her waist and pulled her into the shelter of hard, muscled warmth.

Another gust of wind tore at her startled cry.

"Relax, honey," Gage said in her ear. "It's me."

She struggled against his hold, but it only tightened. Turning her head, she glared at him. "Let go."

"There's not a lot of room," he said.

She answered with an elbow in his belly. His arm loosened as he *oofed,* and she sidestepped away from him. There was enough space for both of them on the ledge, and it had a protruding overhang that gave it the feel of a shallow cave. Refusing to look at him again, she directed her gaze out across the water. It stretched before them like liquid silk, rippling in colors that ranged from silver to blue to green. "I thought you told Rex cliff-jumping was stupid kid stuff."

"You really *were* eavesdropping."

"I admitted to it," she said, defensive. "Now it's your turn to confess. You came up here to jump, didn't you?"

"What's the big deal? I'm nostalgic, okay?"

"You're…you're something," she shot back as the breeze blew her hair across her eyes. Gathering the long strands in her fist, she held them away so she could face him down.

"You shouldn't be up here. Didn't you see my warning signs?"

"Oh, baby," Gage said, in his best Prince of Hell imitation, "surely you realize I've been ignoring all those ever since I came to the cove."

Heat prickled across her skin now, as she remembered—*no,* she was pushing him out of her mind, kicking him out of her thoughts. "Just shut up," she grumbled, and this time he did, subsiding into silence.

She stood without speaking, too, unsure of her next move. If she left, he'd probably follow through on his intention to leap into the water. Worse, he'd think she was running away from him.

Setting her jaw, she stood her ground and leaned against the warm rock at her back. The ocean's wet rush filled her ears, the breeze blew cool against skin her temper had made hot. She found herself closing her eyes as the moment turned oddly peaceful despite the discord between them.

Gage was the first to break the quiet as he began singing in a low croon. "'Beautiful dreamer, queen of my song…'"

Her heart lurched in her chest. She pressed tighter to the rock, her eyes still shut, frozen as if under a sudden spell. Those were lyrics to Stephen Foster's classic "Beautiful Dreamer." In a fit of whimsy, she'd written them to him in a letter, relating how her mother had sung the song for her and her sister, claiming it was the anthem of the merfolk of the cove.

"'List while I woo thee with soft melody; Gone are the cares of life's busy throng.'"

Skye felt him move, and the light on the other side of her eyelids dimmed; the wind no longer stroked her body. He surrounded her, protecting her from the breeze, her face delicately caged by his hands. Then it was he who stroked her, his thumbs caressing her cheekbones.

"'Beautiful dreamer, awake unto me,'" he murmured in that soft, musical murmur.

And Skye obeyed, opening her eyes to take him in, his attention focused on her face. He was so impossibly handsome, a thousand times more beautiful than in the fantasies she'd woven when they were only paper acquaintances.

He smiled at her now, then sang the final line a second time. "'Beautiful dreamer, awake unto me.'"

That's what she'd done, she thought, struck by the sudden truth. She'd been slumbering, her whole self in hiding, until Gage had arrived at the cove and shaken her from sleep.

She stared into his eyes, knowing that all the warning signs in the world could not offset the essential attraction of some things. As risk takers were drawn to the bluff, Skye had no protection against Gage's cell-deep allure.

I'm in love with him, she thought, unsurprised, and already half resigned to it. *I've fallen in love with him.*

"Skye," he whispered, and she read the words on his lips. "You're my very own mermaid."

Then he bent his head, and the kiss was tender and slow and she floated away on the sweetness and the possibilities. When they came up for air, her fingers were curled in the soft cotton of his shirt. She gazed up at him, bemused, and maybe more than a little be-spelled.

"There's something I need to ask you," he said.

"Mmm?" The wind caught at his hair, lifting the back of it into a rooster tail. She smiled at how boyish it made him look—so like her long-ago summer friend.

"You won't tell Griffin or anyone about my little… uh, event, right?" He kissed her nose, her right eyebrow and then her left.

"What?"

His lips feathered across her brow. "God, I've missed you. Let's not fight ever again."

"What?" she repeated, her fingers tightening into fists.

"Missed you." He drew his mouth along the edge of her cheekbone. "Let's not fight."

"No. The other," she said, pulling away from his distracting kisses.

He still wore a half smile as he caressed her face again with his thumbs. "I'm just saying the family knowing about the…the…"

"Kidnapping."

"Could ruin the we're-about-to-have-a-wedding mood."

She looked at him, temper beginning to rekindle. "Oh, I can see that it would. Not to mention the truth about the way you handle yourself when you're on assignment. I'll bet that would worry the whole lot of them just as you're about to embark again."

He looked relieved. "I knew you'd understand. Thank you, baby." His lips bent toward hers.

She held him off, her palms pressed to his chest, both disappointment and fury now roaring through her. He was Satan, all right. The Prince of Hell. Or maybe just a plain old dog.

Because now she recognized what all the crooning, the kissing, the *sweethearts* and the *babys* were about. Her cooperation. He wanted her complicit in the dangerous decisions he made for himself.

His mermaid? Ha. His stooge was more like it.

Scalding tears pricked the corners of her eyes, but she blinked them back. She wouldn't let him see them! Her pride deserved better.

His brows drew together, as if he was beginning to sense her mood. "Skye…"

Before he could guess, before the tears had a chance to spill, she had to act.

And so she did, without malice aforethought…or not much anyway. Giving a mighty shove to his shoulders, she sent him stumbling back. It only took a second to push him over the bluff.

Without even waiting to hear the resulting splash, she scampered down the trail toward home, not the least bit satisfied, only unhappily aware that while her vengeful action might have saved face—it had done nothing to expel him from her head.

Or her heart.

SKYE DECIDED ON A NIGHT of wallowing in lonesome self-pity after her encounter with Gage on the bluff…and her acknowledgment of her feelings for him. Her hand had hovered over her phone, coming a hairbreadth away from calling her sister for a couple of woe-is-me hours. Meg had loved and lost once upon a time.

But now her sister was in a blissful new marriage, and not only did Skye not want to be the dark cloud in her sister's sunshine, but she just wasn't in the mood to witness—even via telephone—someone else's happy pairing-up.

Yes, Skye thought with a grimace. *Woe* is *me.*

It wasn't even six o'clock, but she'd pulled the drapes and flipped on the TV when the cowbell she'd hung on her front knob started clanging. Bolting from her couch, she approached the entryway. "Yes?" she called through the door, wary.

The bell's clapper began another racket, joined by

louder knocking. "Open up," a familiar female voice called. "Long John Silver and Peg Leg Polly are itching to come in."

Frowning, Skye put the cowbell aside, then unlocked and inched open the door. All she could see was her best friend in one of her kindergarten costumes—a black felt pirate hat with luxurious red feather—and a man standing behind her. "Uh, isn't it too early for Halloween, Peg Leg?"

Polly-Peg wouldn't be deterred. She pushed on the door, forcing Skye to step back. Then she marched in, a troop of people behind her. Well, Teague, Jane and Griffin, who was helping elderly Rex Monroe with a hand under his elbow.

They brought the smell of fried chicken with them.

"We're having a treasure-hunting party," Polly said, practically dancing into the kitchen. She was flying high on fiancée fumes, Skye figured.

Teague grinned as he carried in beer in one hand and a pair of wine bottles in another. "Isn't she something?" he asked Skye, pausing to buss her on the top of her head. "That's the woman I'm marrying."

His happiness was adorable enough to make her cry. Refusing to give in to tears, though, Skye pasted on a smile and watched Griffin escort Rex to a comfortable chair. "I appreciate the intrusion—"

"She's calling it an intrusion," Griffin called toward the kitchen. "Jane, I told you and Polly we should have called her first."

Heat crawled up Skye's cheeks. "I meant, uh, interruption."

"She meant interruption," Polly repeated, bearing a glass of white wine that she passed to Skye. "And it doesn't matter what she thinks now, she'll be thanking us later."

"If I knew what this was about, I might thank you sooner," Skye put in, but she was ignored as the kindergarten teacher directed the action. Soon the guys had carried a long picnic table from the side yard to the front so they could enjoy the sunset. Then paper goods, the buckets of food and the drinks were all paraded outside again and placed on the table. They gathered around it, Rex given a place of honor at the head, to share the feast.

Skye's self-pity didn't abate, though she laughed when it appeared appropriate and tried to smile the rest of the time.

A body slid onto the bench beside her. "Don't let that smile drop," the man she'd tossed into the ocean that afternoon murmured against her ear.

"I wouldn't dream of it." She slid Gage a glance, steeling herself not to react to his delicious spicy scent. He didn't look any worse for his impromptu dunking. Was that what had held him up? He was probably late to the party because he'd had to shampoo the salt water out of his hair, and she didn't feel the least bit guilty about that. "What would I have to frown about?"

Except for the fact that you made me love you while all along making clear you were leaving me.

"Here's the deal." He was still murmuring. "They all pronounced dire consequences if we slept together, and I, for one, don't want to give them the satisfaction of being right."

Her smile's wattage went into the mega range. "Of course. Especially when they *are* wrong. Nothing dire, nothing consequential."

"Except for my half a lung of seawater," he muttered.

Again, not a single pang of contrition. "That's what happens when you do stupid, childish things."

"Or consort with childish women."

"What are you two whispering about?" Rex demanded from his end of the table.

"I thought Gage might explain exactly what treasure you hope to find," Skye said, raising her voice.

"The jeweled collar, of course," Polly answered. "When I read the newspaper article today, it got me thinking. If it's never been found, not in a safe-deposit box, not among any family effects, it must be somewhere in the house itself."

"I don't know…" Rumors of the famous piece of jewelry had been more interesting to the public than to Skye's relatives. None of them, in her memory, had actually believed it might still exist. Maybe Edith had thrown it into the ocean, as she'd once considered. Maybe Max had dismantled the piece and sold it off, stone by stone.

"Well, it'll be exciting to look anyway," Polly said. Beneath her ridiculous pirate hat, her gaze settled on Skye's face. "I think you could use some fun."

Best friends often saw way too much. Or maybe it was the kindergarten teacher in her who could sense tantrums and crying jags in the offing. "Sure," Skye said, suppressing her sigh and pinning on another carefree smile. "Sounds great."

Gage spoke up from beside her. "I call her underwear drawer."

"Ha-ha." Skye slid him a lethal look. "If you guys are serious, it's not going to be hidden in the furniture. The older pieces went with my parents to Provence."

"So we'll check walls and built-ins, then," Teague said.

Skye faked another smile. "There's a plan."

After the food was consumed and cleaned up, they really went at it, her friends. Tapping, knocking, running fingers over rough plaster walls and cupboard seams. All their banter and enthusiasm brought Skye's mood to a new low, as she realized that if—when—she left the cove, she'd be leaving them, too.

It seemed a given, though, that she'd end up traveling to France to be near her parents, or San Francisco, where Meg was living. Staying in the area would only make abandoning her heritage that much more difficult. *Goodbye, Edith, goodbye, Max,* she thought, trying out the words. She'd be walking out on all they'd first dreamed of and then established at the cove, as well as the efforts of the generations that came after.

There'd be no one left here to remember her own family or the tribe of never-never land kids that had made it back this summer: Tess, Griffin, Teague and Gage.

As the treasure seekers finally called it quits two hours later, Skye couldn't help following her former lover with her gaze. He'd done his share of good-natured searching, but now he was helping Rex out of the chair from where he'd played a supervisory role. "I'll take him back to his place," he told his twin. His eyes flicked toward Skye, then darted away. "Night, all."

There was an echoing chorus before the rest exited, as well. Polly was the last to cross the threshold. "We didn't find the collar," she said.

"Did you really expect to?" Skye asked.

"I expected to cheer you up."

Skye smiled. "I'm cheered."

Polly snorted from beneath her pirate hat. "You can do better than that," she said, then headed next door, where the love of her life waited.

Skye watched until her best friend's jaunty feather disappeared. Then she spent an hour returning the house to its former order as Polly's words echoed over and over in her ears. *You can do better than that.*

Maybe she could, she thought. Maybe instead of standing here mired in self-pity, she should do something proactive, like walking down the beach to No. 9 to give arrogant and annoying Gage Lowell a piece of her mind. Before she had a chance for second thoughts, she was jogging down the moonlit sand.

She'd start by telling him he was crazy for going back to that ransom farm, perhaps putting himself in harm's way. He could be recaptured. Or even killed in retaliation for getting the police involved.

You of all people should understand that, Skye. You should get that I can't allow anyone to keep a piece of me.

Fine. Instead, she'd point out how wrong he was to ignore the customary foreign correspondent protocol.

Except that he did so in order to protect his family from difficult, torturous decision-making. Mara's face, weary with pain and racked with guilt, floated in Skye's mind's eye. *Some days I have a hard time forgiving myself.*

Still, she didn't hesitate to mount the steps leading from the beach to the deck. At the top, she paused, taking a minute to steady her heartbeat and smooth out her breath. Automatic landscape lights washed along the boards, a pale glow that illuminated the patio furniture: umbrella table and chairs, two single chaises and double-wide lounger.

Eyes closed, Gage lay stretched on the latter's cushions, a blanket over his legs and bunched at his hips. *Beautiful dreamer.*

Her mouth went dry as she stared at his face, studying the lean planes and the curves of spiky lashes. His hair was rumpled over his brow and she walked forward, her fingers itching to push it off his forehead.

She gazed down at him. His relaxed hands were linked over his belly, and his chest rose and fell in a slow rhythm. He was asleep, and she knew that didn't come easy to him.

But she had something to get off her chest. She should shake him awake, stare straight into his amazing, laser-blue eyes and tell him that leaving her wouldn't be right. Perhaps she'd even tell him why.

But he would end up leaving anyway, she thought, resignation a heavy weight on her shoulders. Because that's who he was, who he'd always been: an adventurer, a risk taker. He'd been clear on that from the very beginning. He lived for the adrenaline rush, and only one thing would prevent him from seeking out the next thrill.

If you love somebody enough, you won't chance putting them through that.

If he was going back, it was because he didn't love anybody enough to stop him.

Including her.

CHAPTER NINETEEN

DREAMS HAD COME TO GAGE in the dark, hellish pit where he'd been held captive for two weeks. That was no surprise; it was the fact that he'd fallen asleep in the first place that had amazed him. You'd think when you suspected your life was being measured in minutes, you'd want to stay awake for each and every one of them.

But the mind was a powerful instrument, and while his body had been imprisoned eight thousand miles away, in his dreams he'd traveled to California. The cove had looked much as he'd remembered, the beach houses, the blue sky, the scarlet and salmon bougainvillea winding up the scaled trunks of palm trees. Skye had been there, too, but not skipping on the sand or splashing in the shallows as she had done when she was small. Instead, she'd grown into a lovely mermaid, and he'd seen her from a distance, flipping her tail and tumbling in the water with the grace of a seal.

In his dreams, he'd smiled at her playful antics and longed to reach her. But despite how far out he swam, how long he stayed in the water, he never managed to get close enough to touch. Each and every time, the tide would eventually catch him up and drag him back to shore, leaving him sprawled on the sand.

Now, like then, his limbs felt heavy, his eyes reluctant to open. The end of those prisoner dreams meant remembering he was still underground. Who wouldn't put off that ugly jolt of reality as long as possible?

But something compelled him to lift his lids. Twinkling stars. A pale half-moon, glowing. Relief washed through him and he felt almost drunk on the fresh air.

A movement caught his eye. He rolled his head, and there was Skye, out of her tail and standing on two human legs.

Another high-octane shot of relief poured through his bloodstream. He held out his hand, found her wrist, pulled her nearer. "You're here," he said, his voice still hoarse and sluggish with sleep. "Where you're supposed to be."

"Is that right?" She sounded doubtful.

He frowned, and then recent events caught up with him. "You're still mad at me."

Hesitating, she looked down, hiding the mysterious depths of her eyes. "Oh, Gage. I'm so conflicted about… about what we're doing. Whether I should be with you right now."

Without letting go of her, he scooted on the cushions, and drew her down, so she sat beside his still-reclining body. "What if I told you I had a method to clarify your thinking?"

"What if I told you I'm sure you think you do, arrogant man?"

He laughed. "I'm not such a bad guy."

"No." She shook her head. "That's one of the problems. You're not a bad guy at all."

"C'mere, then," he said, "and let me tell you about how we resolve your concerns." Picking up the edge of the blanket covering his bottom half, he held it open in invitation. He didn't dare let his satisfaction show as she slid in beside him.

They lay side by side, staring up at the sky. "So…" she said, after a few moments of silence, "I'm waiting."

"Impatient girl."

"We don't have forever."

He turned his head to study her profile, the curl of her lashes, the straight edge of her nose, the full curves of her mouth. "That's where you're wrong. If we frame this moment just right, it will remain how we want it until the very end of time."

She glanced over. "Is that so?"

He moved closer, then slipped an arm beneath her so her head rested on his shoulder. Lifting both hands, he shaped his fingers into a box. "Let me give you a perfect picture."

Her body stilled.

"Now close one eye," he advised, and adjusted his hands so they matched up with her line of sight. "What do you see?"

"The half-moon, a star."

"Blink once." When she did, he smiled. "You just took a photo of them."

Her gaze slid to him, skeptical.

"Really. Close your eyes." He let his hands drop. "What do you see?"

"Half a moon," she whispered slowly. "A star."

"There. Captured forever."

Her small sigh still sounded a bit forlorn.

He didn't let it deter him. To the marrow of his bones, he knew they were supposed to be together—tonight, and for the remaining nights he had at the cove. Sliding his arm from beneath her, he sat up. Once more he made a frame with his hands, and looked at her through them. "There," he said. "Your pretty face, always mine."

She stuck her tongue out at him, and he pretended to take a photo of that, too, before swooping down to steal a kiss. Her taste lingered on his mouth, and he knew he'd possess that forever, too.

Then he straightened again, and used the edge of his thumb to dry the moisture from her lips. "Take it from an experienced photo editor. There's an easy way to eliminate those conflicts and doubts that are bothering you."

"I'm listening."

He once more boxed his fingers, then moved them this way and that, capturing her eyes, her ear, her mouth, her chin. "Crop out what's too loud, pare away anything that clashes with the image you see in your head, strip off the extraneous. Then what you have is pure. The truth."

"And what's the truth?" Skye asked.

His hands cupped her cherished, now so-familiar face. "That we're here, right now, together. That this moment, these moments at the cove are ours to enjoy. They belong to us."

The next kiss was longer. She tasted like sweet surrender, and Gage felt a surge of heated satisfaction. He came down over her, a primitive part of him insisting he prevent her escape. Her legs parted, a willing cradle for his sex.

Caution urged him to go slow and gentle. There was tension in her, not from her body but from her busy brain. So he took a deep breath and tried slowing the primal beat of his heart. *Take a picture,* he reminded himself.

Her drowsy eyes.

Her swollen mouth.

The contrast of his big, tanned hands on the delicate

buttons of her white blouse. Her bra was stretchy lace, and he drew the cups beneath her breasts, letting the material plump the soft flesh, glowing in the moonlight. The tips hardened under his gaze and he thumbed them, hearing her soft pants in response, feeling her shift beneath his hips.

Still unhurried, he drew away her shirt, letting it drift to the deck. Then he dipped his head to her nipples, drawing them into his mouth, sucking on them with thirsty, yet slow intent. She whimpered, and her legs drew up to clasp his hips. He pressed into the juncture of her thighs, the ridge of his cock aching to join with her there.

"Gage," she whispered, her fingers sifting through his hair as he continued to lick and gently bite at her breasts. "Take me inside."

"No," he said, drawing his mouth up her neck. "Let's make our forever right here, under the moon I framed for you."

She shuddered as he reached her ear. "Someone will see."

"Only me. And I want to look at you bathed in starlight."

Her mouth opened, but he stole the argument from her, kissing her until she was helpless to speak, her hands sliding from his shoulders to land on the cushions beside her hips, boneless.

His to do with as he pleased.

Yet her acquiescence suddenly wasn't soothing. It honed a desperate edge on his need for her as his pulse ratcheted higher and his heart pounded like tribal drums in his chest. Afraid she'd glimpse the hotheaded animal that was his lust, he reared back, turning her body beneath him so her belly lay against the cushions.

His hands fumbled with her bra fastening and he had to wrench it free. He flung it away, breathing hard as he stared down at the smooth valley of her spine. With shaking fingers, he drew her hair off her neck, baring her to him from her vulnerable nape to the precious dip at the small of her back.

Lifting her head, she glanced at him over her shoulder, her eyes slumberous. Without resistance.

The sight only further fed his desire.

Gage's hot mouth dropped to her flesh, cooling in the open air. He ran his tongue across the wings of her shoulder blades, then traced the delicate ladder of her vertebrae, feeling her tremble beneath his ministrations.

Reaching the back waistband of her jeans, he paused, sitting up to get control of his ragged breathing.

"Gage," she said, wiggling beneath him.

Her movement panicked him. He couldn't lose her now! Dipping low again, he ran his whiskered cheeks over her skin, moving upward, along the inward bend of her waist to the resilient curve where her neck met her shoulder. Driven by an impulse he couldn't explain, he bit her there, gently holding her in place as his hands reached around for the fastenings of her jeans.

Her voice was music in his ears, a siren's song of pleasured moans and heated whimpers. He moved his mouth to her cheek as he pushed away denim and a silky scrap of panties, whispering her praises. "You smell so good. Your body is so beautiful." His hand slid up her sleek inner thigh. "Oh, baby, you're so wet."

She choked out a sound as her arousal flooded his hand, and he could feel her flesh heat in a blush. "Don't be embarrassed. You don't know what it means to me, that I can do this to you."

"I want you, Gage." Her voice was hoarse.

"I know." He had two fingers inside her now, where she was smooth and giving, but tight enough to make him sweat. "I want you, too."

His other palm stroked the round curve of her bottom, and she lifted into the caress, canting her hips and half rising on her knees. The moonlight revealed the glazed petals of her sex and he closed his eyes. It was too good. God, it was so good.

It had never been like this for him before. He liked women. He liked sex. Hell, he loved sex, but this was a different plane of sex, this was sex-to-the-nth sex.

Adrenaline was pumping into his bloodstream, as if bullets were flying or bombs were going off, or like that time he'd been mugged in Cairo.

Only he was suddenly worried about losing more than his passport and *piastres* now. Maybe he should back away. Make an excuse, climb into his car and speed from the cove. Head for what now seemed like the relative safety of a war zone.

But then she tightened on his fingers, moaned with sweet urgency, and he was lost—a slave to her needs. Her muscles were clenching on him now, and he was shaking all over, his fingers fumbling with his zipper.

His cock sprang free, the wet tip caressing her flank. They both groaned, and it was enough to jar him into re-membering protection. Cursing, sweating, he found his wallet, searched for the condom packet with one hand, the other still moving in and out of her twitching body.

"Gage," she pleaded. "Hurry."

"I know, I know," he muttered, then bit into foil. Finally, covered, he came over her back, shoving up his shirt so that he could feel her bare flesh against his chest. She moved, her hips tilting, her sweet bottom lifting to him.

He pulled his fingers free, and she cried out in disappointment.

"It's okay, baby," he said against her neck, tasting the salt of her sweat. "Almost there." Then he fitted the swollen head of him to her heated wetness and pushed inside, her body giving way to his penetration in slow, delicious degrees.

When he was all the way in, he used his knees to widen hers, and took another decadent inch. She moaned again, low and hoarse, and he brushed her hair from her face. "Okay?" he asked, caressing her face.

Instead of answering, she turned her head, caught at his thumb and sucked it into her mouth. *Shit.* He froze as chills broke out across his skin and his cock seemed to expand. Shaking with the effort to remain still, he let her get accustomed to his possession.

And then he had to move, he *had* to, as unstoppable as the waves on the beach. In time to their rhythm, he retreated and advanced, their bodies as tight as puzzle pieces. The image bothered him a moment—what would happen to his edges when they weren't bound by hers?— but then the pleasure was just too mind-blowing. She responded like a dream. Impaled on his cock, covered by his much bigger body, she didn't have much room to move, but her very pliancy turned him on. Open to him, trusting, she accepted his thrusts, and as he sped them up, he felt her rise into them as best she could, her growing tension testament to her nearing orgasm.

He let his palm stroke over her hip to her belly. The muscles there quivered as he passed, and then he felt her soft hair, her wet flesh opened around him, her knot of nerves, primed for his touch. She jerked as he circled there, but he didn't let up, rubbing, swirling, even as he thrust with more deliberation, withdrawing to the tip, driving to the root.

Climax was imminent. His balls were drawn tight, oxygen trapped in his chest. He gave her little clit a gentle pinch and she jolted, bit his thumb, and then it was on her, her hips rolling, her inner muscles clenching, releasing, clenching, pulling him with her into the sweet, dark deep.

He would never look at death by drowning the same way again.

GAGE DIDN'T KNOW MUCH about wedding rehearsal dinners, but the one at Captain Crow's for the next-day nuptials struck him as particularly relaxed. Maybe because the "rehearsing" earlier had been kept to a minimum. Beyond being told where he'd stand and not to forget the ring, his responsibilities had centered on helping his mother and father ferry boxes of decorations from their rental car. A party planner was taking care of most of the details, including handling the catering issues, but his mom had a crafty DIY streak and she wanted to be the one to embellish the deck where the ceremony would take place.

His parents had been staying at a hotel since flying in from Hawaii four days before, but tonight they'd sleep in the master bedroom at No. 9 in order to get an early start on the process.

Gage would stay with Skye—if she'd let him. He slid a glance at her now, sitting across the table, and watched her fuss with the napkin in her lap as they waited for the plethora of appetizers that had been ordered. It was his intent to keep a close eye on her for the duration of his stay at the cove. As the days ticked by, she'd become increasingly on edge, as jumpy as she'd been when he first arrived.

That unsettled him, too, an uncomfortable reminder that the mystery of the home invasion hadn't been solved. Before he left the country, he'd speak to both Teague and Griffin. They'd look out for her.

Though it wouldn't be the same as his doing so. The thought made him twitch, and at his involuntary movement, Skye looked over. Their gazes met and he twitched again, the jolt of sexual awareness impossible to tamp down. Her sleeveless, V-necked dress was an amazing two-piece thing, a formfitting aqua sheath topped by a filmy second layer in the same color that acted like a filter over a camera lens. The lightweight fabric moved over her body like water, and the image was reinforced by the small starfish clip she wore, holding back the dark mass of her hair from a deep side part.

Both brought to mind his mermaid dreams, disquieting him further as he remembered his unrequited yearning. In every one, he never managed to reach her before the tide returned him to shore.

Well, he'd touch her now, he decided. A kiss, a caress, just a breath of her fresh perfume would calm the jagged edges of his mood.

Half rising from his chair, he saw her eyes widen as she guessed his intent. With a subtle shake of her head, she sent him a pointed message: *Not here. Not now.*

Frustrated, he settled back in his seat, delivering his own unspoken memo by folding his arms across his chest. Stubborn woman. He'd barely managed to get her to the table. She'd been present at the rehearsal as the cove's property manager, on hand to answer questions or help with details, but when it was finished she'd tried slinking away, claiming she had no place at the celebratory meal.

His parents had overheard her remark and squashed the objection. They'd been delighted to renew their acquaintance with the grown-up version of the little girl they'd remembered. Perhaps they'd picked up on her link with Gage—Griff claimed they lit the air between them like flying embers from a bonfire—but they hadn't given a sign.

Servers arrived then, bearing plates of sashimi, coconut shrimp, fried calamari and hummus with pita. A waitress had mixed drinks on a tray, and the guy who was usually behind the bar followed, a wine bottle in each hand, topping off glasses of red and white. He lingered behind Skye, and Gage narrowed his eyes as she turned around to exchange a few words with him.

Something tickled the back of his neck and he glanced right, at his mother, seated beside him. She was leaning over, whispering in her husband's ear. Noting Gage's attention, she straightened in her chair and threw him an innocent smile.

"What was that about?" he asked. "You know gossip is bad for the soul."

"Gossip is speculation," his mother pronounced as she lifted her martini. She was a Tess prototype, with dark, unsilvered hair and ageless cheekbones. "Facts are a balm to the heart."

He sent her a suspicious look. "Exactly what 'facts' are balming your heart?"

"I'd love to see all three of my children settled," she said.

Gage groaned. There were facts, and then there were false hopes. "Look, Mom—"

"A toast!" his dad's voice boomed down the table.

Since there'd already been several when the first round of drinks had arrived, each focused on wishing the bride and groom good health and long happiness, they were all practiced in raising their glasses. "To my second son…" Alec Lowell said, this time directing his focus on Gage.

Hell. He swallowed his second groan. Following on the heels of his mother's whisper, this didn't bode well.

His father lifted his glass higher. "Wishing him much success and a safe return to those who love him."

Across the table, Skye jumped as if she'd been jabbed with a bamboo skewer. Gage noticed, but everyone else proceeded as normal, hear-hearing and then tipping back their beverages.

Gage took a healthy gulp of his own, while assessing the damage of that "safe return" on his siren of the cove. He didn't *think* she'd spill his secrets, but there was her steadily rising stress level to take into account. And that stress wasn't only because he was leaving in three days. Polly was on the move, as well. Skye's best friend had already transferred most of her things from the little beachside dollhouse to Teague's larger home in the suburbs.

The ping of fork on glass drew the table's attention to Tess, sitting at the opposite end from Gage, between both of Jane's brothers. They didn't appear to be chatty types, but his sister took her matron-of-honor duties seriously and had been coaxing conversation from them. Most everyone had given up on getting much out of Griffin's future father-in-law.

Tess tapped her fork again, then stood up, her gaze directed at Gage.

Crap, he thought. Since she'd already aimed words

of wisdom at both Jane and his twin, he could guess her next target.

"To Gage," she said. "Who will promise right now, in front of witnesses, not to go incommunicado again!"

The sound of shattering glass punctuated her line. All heads turned from Tess to focus on Skye, who was standing, her chair pushed back, shards of her broken goblet at her feet.

Gage didn't think. Perhaps he jumped over the table. All he knew was that he was beside the siren, his hands on her shoulders as he looked her over from head to toes bared by strappy sandals. "Don't move," he ordered. "Are you hurt? Did you get cut?"

"No." She flushed. "I'm embarrassed."

Beneath his hands, she trembled, and he could feel her ready to bolt. "You're okay," he said, then nudged his brother, who had the chair beside hers. "Griff, switch with me."

Already a busboy was there with a broom and dustbin.

In moments, Gage had taken Skye's seat—in case there were errant glass slivers—she was in his twin's, and Griffin was across the table. An awkward quiet lingered, however. He tried thinking of some comment to ignite new conversation, but hell, he wasn't the wordsmith.

His gaze shot to Griffin's.

His twin instantly cleared his throat. "Uh…" He threw a look toward his bride. "Jane? Weren't you telling me something interesting about, uh…?"

It wasn't panic, exactly, that clutched at Gage's gut, but even with inches between them he could feel Skye's mounting strain. She was keeping his secrets—the kidnapping, the way he did his job, the dangerous aspect of his next assignment—and each passing moment made it harder for her to remain quiet about them.

He stared at his brother. *Come on.*

"The article!" Griffin said, triumphant. Smiling, he looked around the table. "There's an article coming out in tomorrow's paper about the cove. It details the love story of the founders, and the mystery of a missing priceless piece of jewelry."

The dude with the wine bottles was back, carrying a new glass for Skye. Gage watched as he placed it near her hand and filled it with the white she preferred. Then he stepped back, yet still hovered, taking his wine-replenishment duties seriously.

The table conversation—thank God—had been successfully manipulated by his brother. Jane chimed in, too, and together they related the history of Crescent Cove to her family, as well as the rumors about the jeweled necklace known as the Collar. The information appeared to intrigue the Pearson clan. Jane's father and brothers, all scientists, tossed around hypotheses as everyone enjoyed the appetizers.

Skye explained that the Collar had never shown up in a bank or in a memento box. No mention of it had been made in any last wills and testaments. The only record was the old rumors and the letter written by Edith Essex in which she claimed it was safely put away where she and her husband wouldn't have to think about it or look at it again.

Edith and Max's former house was the natural presumed repository, of course, but Skye explained it had never shown up there—not in the past eighty-five years, not during the search they'd just conducted days before.

"However," Corbett Pearson—Jane's father—said,

forefingers tapping his chin, "it could be that a later renovation changed the lines of the original house, concealing
old nooks and crannies. Are there architectural records?"

"Well, yes," Skye said. "In the property management
office. I actually do have plans for many—maybe all—
of the cottages."

Tess scooted forward in her chair. "Oh, fun! We should
get them, look them over. What if we found the Collar
tonight?"

"I think there's enough excitement on the agenda as it
is," Gage said. Beneath the table, he found Skye's hand,
squeezed.

But she was slipping her fingers from his, and on her
feet in the next breath. "There's no harm in me looking
through my files," she said, moving toward the exit. "It
won't take long—I'll be back before dinner is served."

Gage started to get up. "I'll come—"

"Of course you won't leave your family," she said,
shaking her head. "You only have a short while with
them left." In a blink, she was nothing but a flutter of
color going out the exit.

He stared after her, wincing as the little barb of her
last line sank into his skin. It didn't make him feel any
better to understand exactly why she'd grabbed at the opportunity to run off. She needed to escape the pressure
cooker of the situation for a short while.

Or a long while.

Perhaps it only seemed that way to him, but when he
started drumming his fingers on the tabletop, his twin
sent him a sharp look. "I'd think she'd be back by now,"
he said to Gage. "You're just going to sit there?"

"She needs some breathing room," he confessed, murmuring to his twin under the general conversation at the table. "The situation has her a little…wound up."

His brother shook his head, expression disapproving. "I told you—"

"You don't know anything about it." His hot rejoinder didn't alleviate the guilt simmering in his belly. Yeah, Griffin wasn't aware of all that was bothering Skye, but the blame for that did sit squarely at Gage's door.

Still, he believed it was the right way to handle things.

But it was wrong to leave Skye alone for so long, he decided. Hadn't he promised himself he'd keep an eye on her? What if something had happened—

He was out of his chair before completing the thought. Then he leaped down the steps to the beach and ran toward the property management office, a quarter-mile dash that he made in record time. What if she needed him and he arrived too late?

Shit. She should at least be able to count on him now, while he still lived at the cove.

The office door was propped open and the room brightly lit when he sprinted over the threshold. *There. There she is,* he thought, relieved. She stood at her desk, yellowed papers strewn in front of her, a handful of old black-and-white photographs scattered on top of them.

"Skye?"

She glanced up, barely noting his presence before she redirected her gaze to the plans and photos. It was as if Gage were a stranger to her.

At best a former friend, already half-forgotten.

With souvenirs of the past surrounding the siren of the cove, Gage caught a glimpse of his future.

CHAPTER TWENTY

A FEW DAYS AGO, THE MERE act of looking at Gage had begun to cause Skye pain, each glance setting off an ache that pulsed beneath her breastbone, not unlike a second heart. But this beat didn't cause blood to travel through her veins, instead offering only a cold taste of the loneliness to come. So she kept her head down now, and turned over one of the photos on the desk, rechecking the dates written in an old-fashioned hand, probably Edith's. Maybe Max's.

Gage's footsteps were nearly silent on the hardwood floor, but she sensed him coming closer, walking warily as if she were a cornered animal.

He should know; he'd put her in that corner.

Being around his family while privy to things they were unaware of made her miserable. Of course, just knowing what she knew made her miserable.

Still, though it was nice to take a breather away from the rehearsal dinner, she'd planned to go back.

Because despite her growing low mood, she'd given up on distance. Instead, she continued to hold Gage's hand when she could, kiss his mouth when possible, share his bed every night. With the sand running out of their hourglass, what other choice was there? She could deny herself his company sooner, of course, but what was the point of that, when either way the days without him stretched endlessly ahead, like the vast Pacific on its infinite journey toward the horizon?

"What did you find?" he asked, coming around the desk to look over her shoulder.

"I'm not sure."

The fingers of one big hand stroked through her hair while the other flipped the photo back to its image side. "Edith and Max?"

She nodded.

"On the deck of Beach House No. 9," he said.

Nodding again, she studied the pictured pair. Max, debonair in white slacks and shirt, his dark hair slicked back. Edith, in a lightweight flowered dress, was half turned to gaze into her husband's face, her hand resting over his heart. Her devotion to him was palpable.

"I think they lived there for a while, probably to get away from the sounds of hammers and saws." Skye tapped on the set of plans, the paper yellowed and brittle. "About the time they got out of the movie business, they added a couple of rooms to their home. My home. The one where we've never found the Collar."

His hand stilled, midstroke. "What are you saying?"

She glanced at him over her shoulder, then quickly looked away. *So handsome. So dear to me.* "If I match the date on the renovation plans to the date on the back of this photo to the date on the letter Edith wrote to Max…"

His fingers tangled in her hair, tugged. "Are you saying she may have hidden the Collar at No. 9?"

"Maybe. It seems a possibility, though whether it might still be there…" She shrugged.

He turned her then, stepping close so that she could count each of his sharp black lashes and the silver striations in his turquoise eyes. The back of his knuckles caressed her cheek. "Be honest about something else, will you?"

"What?" she whispered, his tender touch tightening her throat. His body, tall, strong and aligned with hers, made her feel small and safe at the same time. A harbor. His warmth enveloped her, his exotic scent stirring up everything female inside her. She wanted to press herself to his bare skin, rub her face along his tanned throat, nip a path down his chest. Trembling in sudden need, she dropped her forehead to his shoulder, the single point of contact enough to almost settle her jittering pulse.

"Do you want to go home now? Skip the rest of the party? I can make your excuses."

She glanced up, surprised he was offering her an out after insisting she attend. "What makes you ask that?"

"I'll feel like a shit if the transitory nature of…of this thing between us is making you unhappy."

His intent gaze turned her heart over. "I thought you said we had forever if we framed it right."

A wry smile played at one corner of his mouth. "You know I would have said anything right then. I was dying to get into your pants."

The admission startled a laugh from her. "You're horrible!"

"I am." He nodded.

What was he saying? "Are you…would *you* rather we stop things here?"

"Hell, no! You know how selfish I am. If I have my way, I'll be breathing you in until the very last second. But, baby…" His fingers gently combed through her hair and then he kissed her forehead, her nose, her mouth. "Talk to me. Tell me the truth."

Three words gathered on the tip of her tongue. They'd

be so easy to release. They wanted out, like wild birds caged in an aviary. Terrified she'd say them, she swallowed hard. "The truth is…" They welled up again, clogging her throat like tears. She swallowed them back once more, then spoke in a rush. "The truth is, everything's okay and we should get back to the party."

She didn't breathe easy until he nodded, took her arm and led her in the direction of Captain Crow's. She'd thought she wanted to take a break from the family event, but now she figured being around his relatives was the best way to keep her from a dangerous confession.

THE INSTANT GAGE SHEPHERDED Skye back to the long table at the restaurant, Tess insisted on a full report. While a train of servers began delivering steaming plates of steak and seafood, Skye reported on what she'd found. Gage's sister was all for turning the meal into takeout and heading down the beach for a full frontal assault on No. 9's mysteries, but it was their mother who put her foot down.

"We're having a nice, leisurely meal tonight, then a lovely sunset wedding tomorrow. A search will come after both of those occur—*if* that's what Skye chooses to do."

Tess acquiesced to their mother's wishes with better grace than Gage expected. "All right," she said, with only the slightest of grumbles. "But, Skye, if—*when*—you do decide to rummage around No. 9, can I help?"

Skye smiled at her wheedling tone. "Um—"

"I'll blend a batch of my special mojitos and we'll make a girls' night of it."

"Well, if mojitos are involved…" Skye said. "Of course."

Gage frowned down at her as people around them

picked up their knives and forks. "Have you ever had her special mojitos?"

"No."

"She has a very liberal hand with the rum." At her inquiring look, he further elaborated. "They'll knock you on your ass. After one of Tess's mojito parties, there have been verified reports of inhibition shortfalls, not to mention memory loss—which is why she never serves her special concoction in mixed company."

"Inhibition shortfalls? Memory loss?" Skye gave him a guileless smile. "Sounds good to me."

Frown deepening, Gage picked up his own utensils and contemplated his dinner. He'd ordered steak, just like his first meal at the cove. A fat, foil-jacketed baked potato sat beside it, topped with a cloud of sour cream and a scattering of chives. Steamed to their brightest summer colors, baby carrots, string beans and yellow squash were drizzled with a sauce that gave off a faint lemon fragrance.

Given that the number of stateside meals he had left was dwindling, he should have fallen on the meal like a hungry wolf.

Weirdly, though, he'd lost his appetite.

His knife cut into his meat and he put a piece in his mouth, but didn't taste it as he chewed. His mind was on the future: girls' nights and mojito parties. The idea of Tess keeping Skye company should please him, but the siren's pleasure at the idea of memory loss curdled the food going into his belly.

She wanted to forget about him.

As for the inhibition shortfalls? He figured she might have some concerns about her physical response to the next man who interested her. And there would be one, he knew that. Because when Gage left the cove, unless she wanted to be alone for the rest of her life, she'd be looking for new male companionship.

He didn't like thinking about her and new male companionship.

Pushing his food around his plate, he sent Skye a sidelong glance. She didn't look any more enamored with her red snapper than he was with his sirloin. As if she sensed his regard, she glanced up, looking at him through those big, deep-in-the-cove-green eyes of hers.

Pain pierced his chest. For a second he thought, heart attack, but it was beating just fine, he was breathing just fine. Something inside him was clenching like a fist, though, pounding on his ribs, shouting for his attention.

How can you leave her? What if something happens to her again? How can you go without knowing she'll be safe?

It was the fucking dream, he thought, that was messing with his head. It had always bugged him that in it he couldn't reach her; that although he struggled forward, the tide always tossed him back to shore. But now…now he saw the other side of it. In the dream, Skye was at the whim of the water, too. And it controlled her, sweeping her up in its force, causing her to drift farther and farther away, out of the cove.

To the dangerous waters of the open sea. All alone.

As if she could read his mind, Skye shivered, then rubbed at her bare arms with her palms.

He had to clear his throat to speak. "Are you all right?"

"I'm cold." She glanced at her nearly untouched meal. "I think I'll dash out and get a sweater from my place."

"Let me do it," he offered. He needed air, space, a

fresh breeze to blow that damn dream from his mind and this nauseating anxiety from his belly.

"You're sure?"

He was already holding out his hand for her keys. Then he slipped away from the table, his fingertips skimming her shoulder but not touching as he passed. The walk did him good. His breath came easier. When he reached her house, the scent of her on the sweater he grabbed from a hook by the door didn't send him into that cardiac-arrest level agony again.

Still, he lingered on the beach in front of her place for a few minutes, stalling his return to Captain Crow's. Christ, he thought, rubbing his palm over his chest, which still held a residual ache. He really didn't want a replay of that pain.

What he needed was some detachment. Why the hell was he finding that so hard? His line of work required it, but now when he could use a little cushion of emotional separation, it eluded him.

Fucking nautical knots. All of them were at work it seemed, the Bowline on a Bight, the Icicle Hitch, the Rat-Tail Stopper, each woven into one elaborate tangle of Big Trouble. He rubbed his chest again, then held out his hand, staring at the empty palm.

That was it! There was the source of his problem. He'd been walking around for weeks, his hands empty of his cameras. Since making those images of Skye, he'd left the devices untouched, packed away in their cases. What had he been thinking? Hadn't he told Rex how important they were?

"It's like armor...it's a layer between me and what I see."

No. 9 was only another mile down the beach. Gage

jogged the distance, anxious to have the solid heft of a camera's body between his fingers. Then he could adjust the focal length between himself and the world around him. No matter how close the subject, he could change the focus to make it appear farther away.

As he approached the house from the beachside, he slowed. Puzzled, he noted the elf-sized door that led to the crawl space beneath the raised deck was open. And stranger yet, the automatic landscape lights that usually lit the perimeter of the house hadn't come on, though it was full dark.

The caterers? The wedding planner? That must be it. Someone had arrived with equipment necessary for the next day's event. Strolling closer, he placed his hand on the elf door. "Hello?" he called out, bending to peer inside.

A blow to the back of his head staggered him. He lurched around, still gripping the door to stay upright. Two figures wavered in his line of sight. One in a ski mask, another in a baseball cap and bandanna.

Gage blinked, nothing making sense. He put a hand to his throbbing head and saw Bandanna lift a heavy flashlight. Its light blinded Gage and before he could think or move, its metal body slammed against his temple. His legs crumpled and he fell to his knees on the sand.

A voice sounded from far, far away. "Put him under there."

Under? No, hell, no. Gage worked to marshal his thoughts and control his body. He felt hands on him and he pushed them away and kicked out with his legs. He wasn't going under anywhere. *No more under!*

But his limbs refused to cooperate. Inside his head he was screaming around the fracturing pain, yet he still found himself being rolled and pushed toward that dark space beneath the deck. Eyes half-open, he heard the men grunt and curse as they struggled to maneuver his dead-weight and he was grimly happy it was hard on them. One of the bastards, the one in the ski mask, was breathing harder than the other, and with an oath, he stripped off the disguise.

As they shoved Gage into the black hole in front of him, rolling him once again, he tried holding on to the image of the man's face. He knew him, he thought, consciousness dimming. It was the guy from behind the bar at Captain Crow's, the one who'd been filling the wine-glasses...

He tried swimming up from the depths of unconsciousness. He despised the smothering dark, the cloying taste of it in his mouth and the weight of it against his chest. This time it would smother him, and the thought was so wearying that he let the blackness descend, welcoming—

No!

He had to rally. Two men. One in a ski mask, one in a ball cap and bandanna. Where had he heard...

Skye's attackers. The men who'd invaded her home.

Needed to tell her. Protect her. Stop them from ever having the chance to hurt her again.

Gage realized he was facedown on the sand. As he tried crawling forward, he got some in his mouth and he choked on it. *No matter. Move. Get out of the fucking dark.*

But then it descended again.

SKYE WAS DETERMINED not to spoil the celebratory mood at the rehearsal dinner, and though she didn't much feel like eating, she enjoyed the happiness circling the table. Griffin's smugness over his upcoming marriage was both amusing and endearing. He wore a boyish look-what-I've-got expression whenever he glanced Jane's way. As for his bride-to-be, she glowed. And there was the sassiest glint in her eye when she caught Griffin looking.

"Chili-dog," she chided him, shaking her head back and forth.

He laughed. "You know what I'm thinking, honey-pie?"

"I know what you're thinking *about*."

He'd only laughed harder as Jane's face went pink.

It made Skye long for such familiar, assured intimacy. The ache urged her up from the table. She murmured an excuse about a visit to the ladies' room, but instead she wandered about the restaurant, half listening to the complaints of the regular bartender, Tom, who wanted to know where his backup had disappeared to.

It made her wonder the same about Gage.

Another shiver worked its way across her skin and she rubbed briskly at the gooseflesh on her arms. She'd meet him and get her sweater, she decided, descending the steps to the beach.

Of course it wasn't any warmer outside, but instead of retreating, she walked briskly forward, or as briskly as she could in her strappy sandals. When one ankle wobbled, she paused to remove her shoes, then resumed her walk, the sand cool and silky beneath her bare feet.

It surprised her not to glimpse Gage's figure striding in her direction. The beach was deserted, though lamps burned in most cottage windows. Fewer of the spotlights designed to focus on the incoming waves were on, giving a checkerboard effect to the surf line. They created a more varied play of shadows on the sand, too, so Skye supposed she was just having trouble making him out.

But then she reached her house and there was still no sign of him.

Frowning, she checked the front door. Locked.

Feet planted on her porch, she glanced in the direction of Captain Crow's. Had they somehow missed each other? Not on the sand, but perhaps he'd taken the track behind the beach houses that would bring him to the restaurant's parking lot and front entrance.

Though taking that longer route didn't make any sense.

Dropping her sandals, she hopped off her porch and strolled to the middle of the beach outside her house, standing almost at the exact center of the cove. Still no sign of a male figure between where she was and Captain Crow's. Turning her head, she perused the sand in the direction of the southern bluff. Nobody visible in that direction, either, though there were plenty of shadows and dunes that could camouflage a man.

Who had no reason to be hiding, of course.

Still baffled, she continued staring down the beach. Would he have gone to No. 9 for some reason? It was the logical answer, of course, and she decided to head that way herself, some instinct urging her forward.

She moved quickly again, aware of the goose bumps on her arms and legs. As summer ended, the days remained warm, but that changed once the sun went down. The expected overnight low was a nippy fifty-nine degrees.

As she approached No. 9, she noted the landscape lights weren't on. That fact didn't alarm her, because she and Gage's mother, Dana, had discussed turning them off the next day. The wedding was timed for sunset, and there were going to be candles everywhere, protected from the wind by hurricane glass. The low-glow lights might detract from the mood, and so she'd shown the older woman the location of the switch.

The looming shape of the nearby bluff added to the darkness and explained why she stumbled near the steps to the deck. Muttering a curse, she bent down to pick up the shoe that had nearly taken her down. Uneasiness wiggled up her spine.

It was Gage's shoe, a distressed leather loafer that he'd been wearing with slacks and an open-collar dress shirt. Narrowing her eyes, she inspected the sand around her, in search of its mate. It wasn't in plain sight, and a second nervous niggle wormed up her back.

Still holding the shoe, she walked to the bottom of the steps. "Gage?" she called. Her voice came out thready and dry. She swallowed, then put her free hand on the handrail. The wood was cool and stickily damp beneath her palm as was the surface of the treads as she ascended. "Gage?" she called again, reaching the deck.

Her gaze roamed the space. Everything appeared as they'd left it that afternoon. The patio furniture had been removed to the garage and there were stacks of white folding chairs ready to be put in place for the ceremony. Then she noticed that the interior of the house was dark, too. Pitch-dark.

"Oh, damn," she muttered. The electricity must be out.

Wasn't that always the way? The garbage disposal dying on Thanksgiving, the toilet overflowing on Easter. She started to turn back to the beach, already thinking of the file of emergency repair contractors in the property management office. But then she looked down at the shoe in her hand.

Where was Gage?

Probably trying to locate the electric panel, she thought. Aware it was on the outside north wall, she began to cross the deck, then halted when she saw a flashlight beam roam the living room. "Gage!" she called out. "If you're looking for…"

Her words petered out. It wasn't Gage's figure stepping from the living room onto the deck. It was a different man.

In a ball cap and bandanna.

She screamed as adrenaline flooded her system, fueling her instant reaction: flight.

But her bare soles slipped on the damp surface of the painted-wood deck and instead of racing back to the beach, she found herself on her butt. The jolt of the fall barely registered before she was up on her feet once more.

"Well, well, well," the man said. "I promised we'd see each other again."

His voice paralyzed her. A flash of memory layered over the present and she was naked again, made immobile by the bungee cords he'd used to tie her to the chair. His stale-sweat smell was in her nose, and she could feel the scrape of a knife blade tracing her belly. *We're going to have so much fun.*

"Stay right there," he said now, approaching her slowly. "And nobody else will get hurt."

Nobody else. Who was hurt? Gage? "You stay away from me, you son of a bitch," Skye said, backing toward the steps. "Where's Gage? What did you do with Gage?"

Another man emerged from the sliding glass doors, this one in a ski mask. "Oh, shit," he said, upon seeing Skye.

She didn't stop her backward movement. "Tell me where Gage is, right this minute."

"Go get her," the man in the bandanna said to his partner, gesturing with his flashlight. "If you cooperate, sweet thing, we'll tell you what we did with your friend."

"Oh, shit," the second man said again.

"'Oh, shit,' is not going to get us those jewels you promised me, cuz."

The man in the ball cap's voice hardened. "And it's not going to get me my consolation prize, either. Now grab the girl."

Ski Mask moved and Skye knew she must also. Ready to fly down the steps, she whirled. She had one foot in the air when a hand clamped on her arm, yanking her back.

She screamed again.

CHAPTER TWENTY-ONE

GAGE HEARD NOISE IN THE distance, voices. One of his captors, he thought, coming to check on him. Jahandar or a brother of his showed up every couple of days, with a new container of water and to exchange his slops bucket. Yeah, first-class service at this joint.

He wasn't going to bother waking up for the visit. Reasoning with the fucking wankers had gotten him nowhere and he wasn't up to small talk. He'd taken a course in hostile environment training a few years back. In regards to kidnapping, the instructor had informed the students that you bettered your chance of survival if the people holding you prisoner saw you as a fellow human. A few months later, one of the other class members, a reporter friend of Gage's, had been mistaken for a spy and held for twelve hours by a tribal warlord. Remembering the hostage lecture, he'd gone weepy, showing off his wedding ring, wailing about his kids. Trying so hard to be human.

Come to find out, that tribe found tears shameful, and a sure sign of guilt. His buddy was lucky he wasn't shot on the spot.

So Gage hadn't attempted any waterworks. Instead, he'd chatted about his childhood in California. He'd made up a devoted girlfriend and called her Skye. But when Jahandar's younger brother had pressed for salacious details about Gage's American lady, he'd regretted bringing his pen pal's name into the ugliness of his captivity.

So he wasn't going to even open his eyes.

He wasn't sure he could anyhow, because his head was pounding like a bitch and there seemed to be some sort of crust gluing his eyelashes together. God, he just got filthier by the day, and the beckoning sleep was at least one way to escape it.

But the throbbing in his head wouldn't let him rest. Despite himself, he roused a little. Maybe he should try to talk to the assholes again. Maybe get a fresh car battery. His lightbulb had been working okay—

No, no, it wasn't working, he thought, panic setting in as he registered the darkness behind his closed eyelids. *Fuck. Fuck!*

He rolled to his back, hands patting his chest, desperate to hear the crackle of paper—the packet of letters that he stashed next to his heart. They weren't there. *Fuck!*

Sitting up, he felt the earth around him. It was hard-packed, orangish stuff—

But this wasn't hard-packed. This was soft. This was... sand.

Recent events came to him in a rush. Crescent Cove. Wedding. Skye. Dinner. His decision to go to No. 9.

A flashlight to the head.

A scream.

He'd screamed? No. *Shit.* That scream was in real time. A real, feminine scream.

Gage jackknifed up, and the drums in his head redoubled their beat. Ignoring them, he swiped at his eyes, rubbing his sleeve against them. Then he blinked, blinked again and saw...

Nothing.

Like the hole at the ransom farm, he was in pitch-darkness. Smothering.

Helpless.

Another scream.

Skye.

The helplessness burned off in a fire that left only rage behind. Someone was hurting her—those two men, he remembered, who had terrorized her before. On hands and knees, he moved about the dark space, seeking a way out. But the deck's concrete footings made the area into a maze and he was clammy with sweat by the time he realized he'd probably crawled away from the exit instead of toward it. *Calm down,* he ordered himself. *Use your head.*

He took in a long breath, let it out, then tried honing his senses. He couldn't see, but he could hear. Orienting his body so that the sound of the surf was ahead of him, he turned right, recalling the location of that small door.

He bumped his head on one cement pier, his knee on a second, but then he found the outer wall. Sweeping along it with his hands, he discovered the door handle and gave it a mighty shove.

Cool, damp air blew across his face. He blinked, the moonlight almost bright to him now, and crawled out. Then he pushed to his feet, and stumbled toward the stairs leading to the deck. "Skye!" he yelled, letting her know he was coming. That she wasn't alone. "Where are you?"

"Gage!"

"Here, honey. Here!" He slogged as quickly as he could through the soft sand in the direction of her voice. "Are you all right?"

As he made his way to the bottom step, he saw her at the top. She leaped, and he jumped back to avoid a collision. She rolled but came back up and as he reached for her, she whirled around to face the deck again.

A man, in ball cap and bandanna, was scrambling down the steps.

"Stay away from us!" Skye shrieked at the intruder. Her shoulder blades hit Gage's chest and he tripped backward, barely staying on his feet.

Bandanna didn't heed her warning, and that's when she cranked back her arm, something clutched in her hand. She threw it with all her might at the man coming toward them.

He howled, his hands going to his nose. Then he growled, another animalistic noise, and staggered forward, hands outstretched.

Skye was still between Gage and her attacker, her arms wide, as if to protect him. His brave mermaid.

Curling his hands about her waist, he plucked her aside and slammed his fist into Bandanna's oncoming jaw. The guy grunted, but kept on his feet, his fingers closing over Gage's shirt.

Remembering another lesson from hostile environment school, Gage jerked up a bent leg, sending a vicious knee into the other man's balls, nothing held back. The man dropped. Forget the Queensberry rules, his instructor had said. When you can, fight like a woman.

Breathing hard, Gage stood over the moaning assailant. With his right foot—the only one with a shoe, he realized now—he nudged the brim of the guy's hat, revealing a shaved head. Then he leaned down to yank the bandanna away from his face.

Blood poured from the guy's nose.

Gage glanced back at Skye. She was staring at the

man, her face pale in the moonlight. "You know him?" he asked.

"Not his name, but…but he's one of the pair who invaded my house." She stepped closer, and he felt her hand clutch at the back of his shirt. "He's—" she pointed to the top of the stairs "—the other."

It was the bartender from Captain Crow's, the guy who'd removed the ski mask before shoving Gage below the deck. "You stay out of the way," he told Skye.

With Bandanna harmless for the moment, Gage grimly started for the second assailant, his fingers already curling into fists. "I'm coming for you."

"Don't bother," the man said, holding up his cell phone. "I already called the police."

THE BRIDE AND MATRON of honor were getting wedding-ready at No. 9, while Gage and Griffin had been assigned to Rex Monroe's. They each had a whiskey in hand and were sitting on the porch, waiting for the signal from their mother. Gage felt remarkably content, and was determined to hold on to that feeling with everything he had.

It had taken him and his brother little time to dress. They both wore linen slacks and pin-tucked Mexican wedding shirts. Since the bride was going shoeless, so were they. "If a guy's got to get married, this is the way to do it," Gage remarked. "No monkey suits."

"Yeah," Griffin said. "And thank God we talked the women out of dressing us exactly alike. That would have been like first grade."

Gage slid his brother a sidelong look. They both wore turquoise-blue shirts, one a slight shade lighter than the other. "Hey, I have an idea. We could pull the ol' twin switcheroo. See if Jane notices I'm not the real groom."

"Not a chance she wouldn't notice, not even for a second," Griffin said. "You forget your stitches?"

"Oh, yeah." Gage put his hand to his hairline and touched the bandage. "Thanks to those assholes I'm going to look battered in your wedding photos."

"Jane likes that. She says it will help us all remember the night before even better."

Gage didn't think he'd ever forget. Not his panic, not his fear for Skye, not the sight of her placing herself between him and the bad guys. "She broke that guy's nose with my shoe," he murmured. "You shoulda seen it, Griff."

"I saw what you looked like. Blood all over your face and soaked into your shirt. No wonder she thought she had to save you from further harm."

"Head wounds bleed like a bitch. My skull still aches, too, but I bet our friend Bandanna will be talking to his lawyer in falsetto for a few more days." There was satisfaction in that. Thanks to Ski Mask—Steve—they knew the whole story now. Yes, he and his cousin had been the duo who invaded Skye's home months back. A film lit major, Steve had fixated on rumors of the Collar. His cousin had fixated on the money they could make upon finding it. So they'd searched Skye's place.

"My cousin Doug is not a good person," Steve had said, not meeting Gage's gaze and conveniently forgetting his own larceny as they waited for the police to arrive. "I'm sorry for what happened to her."

"You should have reported him to the cops the first time," Gage had answered, barely suppressing the urge to strangle the moron. "And why'd you call him back tonight for another search?"

"I heard your party talking during dinner—how the

Collar might be at No. 9. I thought there was a narrow window of opportunity—and Doug was nearby and available."

Because Doug was an unemployed petty criminal who appeared to be on his way to bigger, nastier things. But with Steve's confession, the police hoped they could put the brutish thug away for some time.

With the cove mysteries solved—Steve had also been the man in the ski mask who'd ransacked the Sunrise Studios archives the month before, again looking for the Collar or information leading to acquiring it—Skye was once more secure in her special corner of the world.

On a relaxed sigh, Gage stretched out his legs, crossing them at the ankle. There was probably forty minutes until sunset, and the sky was just beginning to take on tangerine and scarlet tones.

He leaned over to tap his glass against his twin's. "A monkey that amuses me is better than a deer astray."

Griffin raised a brow. "I guess I'll drink to that, whatever the hell it means."

It meant life was good at this moment, Gage thought. There was the beautiful cove now cleared of crime. The imminent nuptials, which would join together his brother and the woman he adored. "Do you need me to give you any wedding night advice?" he teased Griffin. "Shall we have the Talk?"

His brother knocked back the remainder of his whiskey. "Yeah. There's a talk we need to have. Something I need to tell you."

Frowning, Gage turned his head. "What?"

"You're a fucking idiot!"

"Huh? What—"

"Cut the bullshit," Griffin said, his eyes going hard.

"I know all about your little adventure, your next assignment, the stupid way you've been going about your business."

Shit. "Skye shouldn't have—"

"Skye didn't." A speculative look entered his brother's gaze. "I'm surprised you told her."

"She's impossible to lie to," Gage muttered, looking down at his feet.

"Maybe you'll think about why that's the case, *after* I kick your ass."

Gage took in a breath. "How'd you find out?"

"You're not the only one with friends on the other side of the world. I put out feelers. It took a while for the intel to reach me, but it did."

"Don't tell Mom and Dad," Gage said quickly, feeling as if he were ten again and hiding a bad test paper. "Or Tess, either."

"Only if you promise to start being responsible about—"

"I have been responsible! This way no one but me is accountable."

"Yeah, I get that's what you tell yourself. Don't forget I know well how your mind works. But it's no good, Gage. Think about it, think about if it had been me no one could find, me who just disappeared off the face of the earth without a trace."

The whiskey sloshed in Gage's belly like stormy seas. "It's not the same."

"It's *exactly* the same."

"All right. Fine. But think about Charlie."

"Mara had a tough decision to make, I agree, and I also agree that the outcome was damn rough. But in your scenario, she'd never have had a chance to help him and maybe never even know what became of him. Is that any better?"

"I hate when you lecture," Gage said.

"You hate when I'm right." Griffin looked over. "So...I need a wedding present."

"I went in with Tess and David on something already. I hope it's lace doilies or some ugly chip and dip bowl."

His brother ignored that. "You put me on your list. I'm the contact name. I'm the decision-maker, if it comes to any decisions needing to be made."

Gage closed his eyes. "You're totally fucking up my day."

"You'll make mine if you agree," his brother said. "I need this from you."

"Shit. You've never played fair."

"It's the elder brother thing."

"By eleven stinking minutes!"

Griffin shrugged. "Eleven minutes is eleven minutes." Then he hesitated. "Trust me to do right by you."

"Of course I trust you." Gage knew he sounded surly. "It's just...I'm going to be all right. I'm not going to get into any more tight places."

"Yes, you are. You're planning to go straight back to that ransom farm. I'm worried that it's stress that's driving you there."

"It's not. It's..." God, he wasn't the word guy. "Griff, you've got to trust me, too."

A long moment passed; then his brother nodded. "Okay. You're right, and I do." His cell phone rang, and he pulled it out to check the screen, a smile breaking over his face and dispatching the tension between them.

"Showtime?" Gage asked.

"Showtime," Griffin confirmed.

They stood as one, then looked at each other. "Are you going to get sappy again?" Gage asked.

"Briefly."

The man hug was hard…and heartfelt. "I'm happy for you, Griff."

His twin pushed away and slapped his hands together. "Let's go get me a wife."

Gage could only smile at his brother's enthusiasm, feeling his own mood rise again. "Let's."

As his brother made to move off, Gage caught his arm. Griffin turned, eyebrows rising.

"About…"

"About Skye?"

"Yeah." This was when the twin thing came in handy. It made articulation often unnecessary.

"Jane and I will look out for her."

"I'm still going to be writing her letters," Gage promised. "I'm not walking out of her life."

Griffin smiled. "There's not a doubt in my mind."

GAGE DIDN'T HAVE ANY doubts about his brother's future marital happiness, either. The wedding ceremony went off without a hitch. The sunset arrived as predicted by the weather service, and the group of seventy guests were in place as the music began. Jane looked beautiful in a shoulder-baring white dress, its hem skimming the sand aisle that her techie father and brothers had mapped out and then executed with the help of no fewer than three laptops running five separate programs.

They looked pretty happy about the outcome. Gage noticed the pleased smiles on their faces as they sat in the front row. Jane walked alone down the aisle, choosing to give herself to her groom. Her gaze never wavered from his face.

Rex married them. The old reporter had gotten himself some sort of lifetime pass as a wedding officiant. He did a fine job, his voice strong, his comments a combination of the traditional and personal. Best of all, they were brief.

The bride and groom had written their own vows. Gage was going to have to check out the video to listen to them a second time. He'd been distracted, his gaze lingering on Skye, who was standing near the glass door leading into the house. His siren of the cove, the self-appointed "fixer" for any last-minute problems.

She didn't look as if she'd been fighting bad guys the night before. She was in green again, an early morning ocean shade. Her hair streamed over her shoulders in rippling waves and he remembered filling his hands with the stuff last night, once they'd finally made it to her bed.

He'd been so relieved to have her there, against him, and that euphoric feeling had yet to abate, even after the tense exchange he'd had with his brother on Rex's porch. The deal he'd struck with Griffin grated on him a little, but he hoped it would amount to nothing. As he'd said, he wasn't planning on getting into any more tight places.

Then it was time for the ring, so he had to pay attention again. From there, the ceremony wrapped up quickly. They kissed, the audience clapped and then the steel drum band set up on the beach began to play.

The chairs were whisked away, small tables set out where people could imbibe food and drink and it was time to enjoy the rest of the evening.

He sought out Skye. She was standing with Vance and Layla, both of them giving off love fumes. "It was lovely," Layla said on a sigh, her big brown eyes looking dreamy.

Vance slanted a glance at her. "You want a beach wedding now?"

"Nope, I haven't changed my mind. Ours is going to be on the grounds of the avocado ranch. Skye, what do you think? Should I go up on the aisle on horseback?"

Vance groaned. "Say no, Skye. And tell Layla to stop listening to my mother. God knows what that woman has in mind for us."

Before Skye had a chance to engage in the discussion, Gage coaxed her away from the couple. "They're playing our song," he said. And they were. It was "The White Sandy Beach of Hawai'i." With her in his arms, he experienced another euphoric wave, lifting him up. He kept riding it high, all night long.

Finally the place was clearing out. The guests were gone. Bride and groom took off for their secret honeymoon destination. Since Gage would be eight thousand miles away by the time they returned, Griffin gave him a speaking look as he left.

"Yeah, yeah," he'd assured his twin with a slap on the back, then kissed his new sister-in-law.

He said his farewells to his parents, too, since he wouldn't see them again before his plane left in a couple of days. His mom took it better than he had expected, but she had the prospect of two weeks at Tess and David's to look forward to. Grandkids apparently went a long way to making up for absent sons.

Finally it was just him and Skye, standing in the driveway of No. 9, seeing them off. He smiled, looking forward to alone time with her. The siren of the cove, all to himself.

"It's been great seeing you!" she called, waving as his parents' car turned in the driveway. "Good—"

Gage grabbed her, out of patience. He lifted her off her feet.

Her mouth curved as she gazed into his face. "...bye," she finished.

And that's when he dropped off the wave. Crashed with bone-crunching force. Because, he realized, the next time she said that word, she'd be saying it to him.

SKYE MADE A VOW TO REMAIN firmly fused in each moment. It didn't matter how many of them were left, she assured herself. It only mattered that she enjoyed each one she had with Gage. No tears, no regrets, nothing but smiles.

Still, despite the promise to herself, she was miserable the day after the wedding, and even more miserable the day after that.

But hiding it well, she thought. She was still keeping it together, though Gage's plane was scheduled to leave late the following night.

This morning they'd packed a lunch and gone for a hike, visiting places that had been their childhood haunts. On a knoll above the cove, they sat down to rest. Side by side, they gazed out over the ocean.

"Another perfect day," he murmured.

"The weather's spectacular," she agreed.

"The ocean temps are peaking." He rummaged for a bottle of water in the backpack they'd brought.

"It's that time of year."

At the same moment, they glanced at each other. Gage grimaced. "We're talking like strangers."

In a few months, that's what they'd be, Skye thought. He claimed they'd resume their correspondence; she didn't think she wanted a long-distance pen affair with the man she loved.

When she didn't answer, he lay back on the sunbaked grass and threw his forearm over his eyes. "This summer hasn't been all bad, has it?"

"No." She pasted on a smile, even though he couldn't see her. "This summer's been great."

He lifted his arm, cast her a baleful look. "Your enthusiasm could use a little work."

"Your brother's wedding *was* great. And we caught the bad guys."

"Both true." He sat up again. "Are you going to be all right now, being here at the cove?"

"Yes." That was absolutely true. "The monsters in the corners are gone."

"What about the necklace? Are you going to let Tessie ply you with mojitos and attempt another treasure hunt?"

"I don't know. It was Edith's, after all, and she wanted to keep it hidden. Maybe it's better that we never find it."

He took a swig of water, his gaze back on the ocean. "This morning I got around to reading the article from Sunday's paper."

"You did?" Polly had been right; it had already sparked a flurry of interest. Skye had let the phone messages go to voice mail, but she'd taken a quick peek at her email. Reservation requests were steady.

"I didn't realize Max had given up the movie business for her." When she didn't comment, he glanced her way. "I missed out on that detail. I guess I supposed it was the advent of the talkies that meant the end of Sunrise Studios."

Skye clambered to her feet, not wanting to get into stories of men who gave up their work for the women they loved. "Shall we keep going?" she asked, brushing at the dust on her shorts. "We planned to stop by the tide pools before turning back."

They were both tired and a little sunburned by the time they made it to No. 9. Neither of them was doing very good with the smiles.

After they'd showered and put together a quick dinner, Gage surprised her by pulling out one of his cameras. He held it a little awkwardly, looking it over as if he wasn't sure how it worked anymore.

Taking pity on him, Skye leaned close and touched her fingertip to the shutter release. "See, you press the big black button right here, and then it saves the image in the viewfinder."

He sent her a look. "Very funny."

"I just thought you might have forgotten."

"I didn't forget." Then he left the living room, presumably putting it away again. When he came back a few minutes later, he sat on the opposite end of the couch, a heavy, awkward silence occupying the cushion between them.

Skye shivered, glancing toward him in the near-dark room.

"Cold?"

"No."

On the coffee table in front of the couch was the Sunday paper, the Lifestyles section on top. Above the fold was a panoramic photo of the cove. Gage nudged it with his foot. "Edith Essex died young."

"Virulent case of pneumonia. Left Max with two babies to bring up on his own."

"He never married again?"

"No."

"Did he—"

"Can we talk about something else?" Skye demanded. Discussing what Max had willingly sacrificed to make his wife happy seemed an awkward subject to hash out now.

"I just wanted to know if there's any record of his thoughts. How he felt about giving up his life's work—"

"We don't know, okay? We just don't know."

"All right, all right," Gage said. "I didn't mean to rile you up. As a matter of fact…"

Suspicious, she looked over at him. "As a matter of fact, what?"

"I thought you should know I made a deal with Griffin. He found out about the kidnapping and made me promise to…to change my ways. When I go out I'll be leaving notes behind, setting up backup plans, making sure I'm covered if something goes wrong."

Skye stared at him, feeling as if half the weight on her soul had been lifted. "I can't tell you enough…" Her breath released in a shaky sigh. "I'm so glad to hear that."

He smiled at her, then reached out a hand. "Then how come you're still sitting way over there?"

They met each other halfway. The kiss tasted like desperation and impending grief, but Skye's desire rose despite that. As the night fell, they continued kissing, one eager melding of mouths flowing into another. She thought Gage might object to the growing darkness— there was always some small source of light while they slept—but he didn't say a word. Instead he became more demanding, his tongue thrusting into her mouth, his hands firm on her breasts, the heel of his palm insistent between her thighs.

While still fully dressed, she felt herself peaking, and

jolted away from him, wanting more intimacy. Wanting skin to skin. Standing up, she tugged on his hands. "This way," she whispered. "I want you on the bed."

She took over then, ushering him down the hall and then undressing him in the shadowy bedroom. Again, she was surprised that he didn't insist on some source of light. Later, she figured he'd used it as a cover. There were things he didn't want her to see just yet.

With gentle hands, she pushed him naked onto the sheets. Her clothes went next and when she joined him on the mattress, he pulled her close. She reveled for a moment in the heat of him, in the hard length of his masculine muscles against hers as they dove into another voluptuous kiss. But it was going all too fast again, the pressure of his hard thigh at the juncture of hers taking her too quickly toward climax.

Despite his groan of protest, she backed out of his arms. But then she knelt next to his heavily breathing, splayed body and began to touch him with her fingertips, her palms, her lips, the flat of her tongue. Gage's next groan was louder, and one of his hands fell heavy onto the back of her head. His fingers flexed in her hair as she licked his nipples and tested the resilience of his biceps with the edge of her teeth, and swirled a wet pattern toward his navel.

Her tongue found the hot, plum-shaped head of his erection, and she lapped there, too. His breathing was loud in the room, a fractured sound of need, and she felt excitement fizz in her bloodstream.

She did this to him. She did this to the man she loved.

Cupping the cool weights between his legs, she continued to explore the silky steel of him, sliding her tongue along its length, then sucking him into the hot cavern of her mouth. The sound he made in response caused her nipples to contract to aching points, and she pressed them against his sleek side, rubbing there while she continued to slide him in and out between her lips.

She glanced up, even in the gloom able to detect the hard set of his jaw, the flare of his nostrils, the avid glitter in his eyes. He gathered her hair in his fist, pulling it away from her face, and she took him deeper, knowing that he loved seeing her pleasure him this way.

On another upstroke, she swirled her tongue around his head, and then he broke. On a curse, he pulled out of her mouth and dove for a condom. She was flat on her back next, and he was over her, pushing her thighs wide, penetrating her wetness in a thick, heavy slide.

Her legs lifted, crossing over his hips to draw him closer, and he started a heavy, lunging rhythm of advance and retreat. Her hips lifted into each stroke and she gasped as he toyed with her sensitive nipples. When his mouth found her neck, kissing, sucking, marking, she let her head fall back, reveling in the sweet and stinging possession.

Then he lifted his head, his gaze glittering down at her, while his body continued to plunge and retreat, plunge and retreat. "Do you have something you want to ask me, Skye?" he said, his voice heavy and rough.

Ask him? Ask him what?

"You can," he said. "Like Edith asked Max."

Like Edith asked Max to give up making movies. Like Edith asked Max to give up his career. Her heart redoubled its already frantic tempo. Ask him…she could ask Gage to stay.

She wrapped her arms around his neck and pulled him to her, kissing him with a wild, almost frantic abandon. Thoughts raced through her head, and goose bumps broke across her skin.

She could ask him to stay.

But…but it wouldn't be right.

"No," she said against his mouth, and hot tears trickled from the corners of her eyes. "No, I won't ask you anything."

He lifted his head. "You won't?"

Another tear slid along her temple. "Never."

His body slowed then, his hips moving in deliberate, incendiary pitches. His tongue licked at her tears. And when the orgasm finally broke over her, it completely shattered her heart.

But still, there remained pieces of it left to splinter, she discovered. That happened a little later, after he'd come back with a warm washcloth used to soothe her face and body. Next he tucked her into the bed, pulling the sheets and blanket to her chin. Only then did he turn on a lamp. Only then did he crush whatever was left beating in her chest.

He was dressed. His bags were packed. There were just two, a duffel and a backpack.

Skye sat up, feeling the color drain from her face.

"It wasn't going to be any better tomorrow," he said, sitting on the edge of the mattress. His palm cupped her cheek. "We're both wretched. So I moved up my flight."

She continued staring at him.

"I'm going now. It will be better this way."

"I…" Her voice deserted her. "You…"

He smiled a little, rubbed his thumb over a fresh tear. "Yeah." Then he placed a last kiss on her forehead, and was gone.

STUNNED, SKYE LAY BACK on the bed. Overwrought with emotion, she stared at the bedroom walls and tried absorbing what had happened. He'd gone. She'd let him go.

If she'd begged him to stay, would he be beside her right now?

Yes. He wouldn't have made the offer unless he'd been willing to follow through with it. But that wasn't how she wanted to have him.

Gathering his pillow into her arms, she closed her eyes and listened to the waves sliding onto the sand, just as they had in Edith's time, and just as they had when Edith was gone. Just as they had when Gage spent part of a summer with her, and just as they would now that he was gone.

Skye slept.

At first light, she awoke. Her body felt heavy as she dressed, then made her way into the kitchen. She brewed coffee, because that's what people did in the morning. A steaming mug in hand, she walked out onto the deck and took a seat at the table, staring out to sea.

The dark heads of a pair of seals popped up from the surf. They gamboled in the waves, enjoying their morning swim. People supposed they were the source of the mermaid and merman legends. In the right light—say the gray of early morning—someone could mistake their sleek figures for those of a water-dwelling race. Skye found herself smiling at their antics.

Smiling!

But why not? She let her gaze follow the crescent shape of the beach. This was her place, her legacy, and she was still here, wasn't she? Still in her magical, wonderful corner of the world. Gage had helped her recapture her sense of security and her ability to appreciate her beautiful surroundings.

Closing her eyes, she filled her chest with the salt-laden air. Maybe the merfolk in the cove could find a way to rebuild her heart.

Her name floated past her on the breeze. She smiled again, bemused by the power of her imagination. Gage was thousands of miles away by now, so that couldn't be his voice.

"Skye!"

She jolted, her eyes going wide. That...that sounded so like him. Standing, she heard footsteps on the stairs leading from the beach. The top of a familiar head came into view.

Her mouth went dry. "Gage?"

Reaching the deck, he dropped his bags, then held his arms wide.

In one magnificent rush, she leaped onto him, causing him to stagger back. He laughed, his arms closing tight around her as her legs clasped his waist. "Hey, baby," he said, pressing his face against her neck. "Miss me?"

Her fingers twined in his hair and she pulled on his head to lift his gaze to hers. "Did your flight get canceled?"

"Something better than that. My life plan got canceled."

"I...I don't understand."

"I know." He hitched her up, then carried her to the double-wide lounger, where he sat with her in his lap. His mouth found hers, and she fell headlong into the kiss—that he cut short. "Let me tell you something first."

"All right," she said, suddenly wary again.

"During the drive to the airport, questions kept running through my head. First and foremost, why I'd been avoiding taking pictures. Hell, I couldn't even make myself take a final photo of you last night."

"I thought maybe it was because of my sunburned nose."

"Brat," he said, then kissed it. "The answer was actually pretty simple. I'd always used the camera lens as a buffer between me and my subjects. I didn't want any buffer from you. Not last night. Not ever."

Skye's heart was pounding in her chest. The merfolk must be fast workers, she thought, dizzy with the new rush of blood zinging through her veins.

"I love you, Skye," Gage said. "I'm so in love with you."

Her body started to tremble. "You know, you know I—"

"I know." His grin was easy, and very pleased. "No doubt I'll insist you say it a hell of a lot, too, but let me finish telling you why I didn't make that plane."

She clasped her hands together.

"When I learned about Griff's PTSD, I did a little research. Scientists have named another condition that happens to people who experience an impactful life event—PTG, post-traumatic growth. It leaves a person with a new outlook on life and relationships. A man may discover that he wants to spend more time with family instead of his career. Maybe he sees himself putting down roots—still taking photographs, mind you—but from a home base and with a woman beside him who can fill his heart, not just his zest for adventure."

Skye frowned. "That woman might not like the idea of being the one who curtails his zest."

He smiled at her. "She's going to provide plenty of zest, don't you worry."

At her doubtful expression, he laughed.

"Trust me, honey," he said, then, sobering, he gathered her even closer. "While I was driving, I kept remembering Charlie, something he told me. Just a few weeks before his kidnapping, he was walking through Kabul and a bullet pierced a wall right by his head. Pure good luck that it didn't kill him outright. And he wondered if that wasn't a sign from the universe. He thought about going home to Mara and Anthony, right then and there."

Skye frowned. "So your sign from the universe was the kidnapping?"

"My sign from the universe was you. At first your letters, and then your smile, and then your love. It made no sense not to heed it…not to be with you, the person who makes me happy. So…here I am."

"So…here you are." She smiled, her heart whole and clamoring for its turn to talk. "Do I get to say I love you now?"

"Sure, I—" His gaze suddenly shifted over her shoulder, and he blinked. "Jesus," he murmured. "Skye, there's… there's merpeople out there."

Seals. "But of course," she replied, without even bothering to look. "They're here to welcome you home."

EPILOGUE

SKYE STOOD AT THE RAILING on the deck of Beach House No. 9, her hand shading her eyes as she gazed up the sand. No fog shrouded the cove this afternoon; instead the sun was beaming down in warm welcome for the Memorial Day weekend visitors. Her shoulder muscles ached a little, but she didn't mind, because the hard work of preparing for another Crescent Cove summer was now completed.

Their group of friends had even managed to make time for a simultaneous week-long visit, with the exception of Addy and her husband, Baxter, who were living in France. For the rest of them, those who considered themselves the happy recipients of No. 9's magic, it was going to be seven days of horseshoes on the beach and barbecues on the deck. There was talk of making some after-dark visits to Captain Crow's for a little dancing.

That was, if they could talk Tess and David's teenage boys into babysitting. Their daughter Rebecca would want to go along to the bar with the other adults.

The passel of kids she was expecting came into view and Skye smiled, remembering her days as part of a Neverland tribe just like this one. It only made the memory sweeter to know that a good number of those jostling each other as they made their way along the beach were the progeny of her own childhood posse. Jane and Griffin's two children, dark-haired R.J.—Rex Joseph—and dainty Amaryllis led the way. Skye's sister's daughter with her husband, Caleb, was named Starr just like her mother had once been, and she had her arms slung around Tina and Karen, the offspring of Polly and Teague White, who had fallen in love here at the cove a decade before.

Ten years had indeed elapsed since that fateful summer, and it would seem like the time had passed in the blink of an eye unless you took into account the growing families. Vance and Layla Smith had managed to produce three kids in those years, though only the oldest two—boys—were part of the group heading for No. 9. Baby Katherine was napping with her mother inside the house.

Straggling behind the rest of the kids were a pair of scamps. Hard to believe Max and Neal were six already, Skye thought, but Gage claimed they'd lost two years in a sleepless delirium of diapers and spit-up. As if sensing her regard, Max looked up, saw her on the deck, and gave her the exuberant wave of a sailor sighting land. Then Neal did the same, and she grinned, her heart swelling with intense, almost painful love. Her little men.

She put her hand over her belly and wondered if she'd be introducing a daughter to this paradise next. Tonight, when she was snuggled in bed with her husband at their house just up the beach, she'd give him the news of the pregnancy and see if he had a prediction.

I bet it's a girl, she thought, rubbing her palm over her navel. *Edith.*

Her sons were waving at her again and in response, she threw up her arm. It hit solid metal.

And she woke up.

Blinking, Skye struggled to orient herself. She wasn't standing on No. 9's deck. She was stretched out on one of its loungers, under the shade of a patio umbrella. Her dream gesture had caused her hand to encounter its center pole. Sitting up, she rubbed at her tender knuckles. What a dream! It had felt so real, even though ten years had not passed since the Summer of Love—as she and Gage had come to talk of it—at Beach House No. 9.

It was only the end of September, and just a few weeks since her pen pal who was also the man she loved had entered her life. She'd come here this afternoon to shut up the house for the season since Gage had moved in with her. After doing all the necessary chores, she'd taken a break on the lounger and then apparently taken a nap.

Smiling, she got to her feet. She and Gage had stayed up too late the night before, practicing for that baby-making that her dream portended. Max and Neal and Edith? Wow.

She gathered the lounge cushions in her arms, intending to stow them in the storage area beneath the deck. Using her foot, she shoved the lounger's metal frame against the side of the house and heard an ominous crack.

"Darn," she muttered, dropping the cushions to survey the damage. The metal teeth that propped up the chair's back had caught one of the siding shingles at the base of the house and half ripped it away. After moving the metal frame, she hunkered down and fiddled with the broken piece. It came off in her hand and with another curse she went belly-down on the deck to see if she could retrieve the rest from beneath its overlapping partner.

What she saw instead was a small, shadowy niche that had a canvas drawstring bag stuffed inside.

"What are you doing?"

Skye started, then turned her head toward her fiancé, who was striding across the deck. "I think I'm playing pirate and this is the hidden treasure." Refusing to think about spiders and snakes, she reached in the shallow nook and pulled out the fabric sack. It was heavy in her hand.

She rolled over and sat up as Gage settled on the painted wooden surface beside her. Her pulse fluttered as she looked at him. "Could it be…?"

"Only one way to find out, honey." He leaned close to kiss her temple. "What are you waiting for?"

"I don't know." Her fingers tightened on the dirty, yellowed material and she forced them to loosen. "You do it," she said, holding the package toward him.

He held up both hands. "Not me."

She hesitated another moment, then with a little growl, attacked the strings. There was another sack inside the first, this one made of oilcloth. Inside that was a velvet pouch.

From the soft, silk-lined material, Skye drew out a magnificent necklace made up of four parallel lines of precious stones, graduating from the size of her thumbnail to the size of a pea. "The Collar," she breathed, and held it with two hands, the jeweled rows flowing like water over her palms.

Gage let out a long whistle. "I'm no gem expert, but I would guess those are rubies, sapphires, emeralds, and amethysts."

"They say Nicky Aston adored Edith," Skye said slowly, dazzled by the way the sun set the colors blazing. "She thought his avowed feelings were more publicity stunt than sincerity, but you have to wonder…"

They studied it in silence for several long moments, the only sound that of the ocean breathing in and breathing out. "What are you going to do with it?" Gage finally asked.

"Good question. I don't know…" But then she thought

she did. She looked over her shoulder, through the glass that led into Beach House No. 9. The bungalow had brought several lives together this summer, and probably other times, as well. Her mother had always claimed so, anyway.

Without its magic, would she be sitting here with the love of her life?

"You might think I'm crazy," she warned Gage.

"As long as you're still crazy about me," he said, smiling, "I'm happy."

She stretched over to kiss his mouth, fierce and hot. "That's a foregone conclusion." Then, with only the slightest twinge of regret, she bundled the magnificent piece into its protective layers and returned it to the hidey-hole, carefully positioning the half-broken shingle over it. Tomorrow she'd come back for a more secure repair.

Gage's eyebrows were raised when she turned to face him. "You're leaving it then?" he asked.

"At least for now." Because as woo-woo as it might sound, she sensed its placement could be part of Crescent Cove's mystique—perhaps the very source of the enchantment that Beach House No. 9 held. To her mind, the necklace symbolized a yearning heart, the kind of heart that had found its mate here this summer—and hopefully for many more seasons to come.

Gage got to his feet, pulling her up with him. "What now?"

She smiled, thrilling again that this beautiful man was hers. "Let's go for a walk to the tide pools. I want to tell you about my dream."

And how she felt certain that it was sure to come true.

* * * * *

USA TODAY Bestselling Author

VICTORIA DAHL

This good girl's going bad...

Merry Kade has always been the good girl. The best friend. The one who patiently waits for the guy to notice her. Well, no more. Merry has just scored her dream job, and it's time for her life to change. As the new curator of a museum in Wyoming, she'll supervise some—okay, a lot of—restoration work. Luckily she's found the perfect contractor for the job.

Shane Harcourt can't believe that someone wants to turn a beat-up ghost town into a museum attraction. After all, the last thing he needs is the site of his dream ranch turning into a tourist trap. He'll work on the project, if only to hasten its failure... until the beautiful, quirky woman in charge starts to change his mind.

For the first time ever, Merry has a gorgeous stud hot on her heels. But can she trust this strong, silent man, even if he is a force of nature in bed? When Shane's ulterior motives come out, he'll need to prove to Merry that a love like theirs may be too hot to handle, but it's impossible to resist.

Available wherever books are sold!

Be sure to connect with us at:

Harlequin.com/Newsletters

Facebook.com/HarlequinBooks

Twitter.com/HarlequinBooks

HARLEQUIN® HQN™
www.Harlequin.com

PHVD746

REQUEST YOUR FREE BOOKS!

2 FREE NOVELS
FROM THE ROMANCE COLLECTION
PLUS 2 FREE GIFTS!

YES! Please send me 2 FREE novels from the Romance Collection and my 2 FREE gifts (gifts are worth about $10). After receiving them, if I don't wish to receive any more books, I can return the shipping statement marked "cancel." If I don't cancel, I will receive 4 brand-new novels every month and be billed just $5.99 per book in the U.S. or $6.49 per book in Canada. That's a savings of at least 25% off the cover price. It's quite a bargain! Shipping and handling is just 50¢ per book in the U.S. and 75¢ per book in Canada.* I understand that accepting the 2 free books and gifts places me under no obligation to buy anything. I can always return a shipment and cancel at any time. Even if I never buy another book, the two free books and gifts are mine to keep forever.

194/394 MDN FVU7

Name	(PLEASE PRINT)	
Address		Apt. #
City	State/Prov.	Zip/Postal Code

Signature (if under 18, a parent or guardian must sign)

Mail to the Harlequin® Reader Service:
IN U.S.A.: P.O. Box 1867, Buffalo, NY 14240-1867
IN CANADA: P.O. Box 609, Fort Erie, Ontario L2A 5X3

Want to try two free books from another line?
Call 1-800-873-8635 or visit www.ReaderService.com.

* Terms and prices subject to change without notice. Prices do not include applicable taxes. Sales tax applicable in N.Y. Canadian residents will be charged applicable taxes. Offer not valid in Quebec. This offer is limited to one order per household. Not valid for current subscribers to the Romance Collection or the Romance/Suspense Collection. All orders subject to credit approval. Credit or debit balances in a customer's account(s) may be offset by any other outstanding balance owed by or to the customer. Please allow 4 to 6 weeks for delivery. Offer available while quantities last.

Your Privacy—The Harlequin® Reader Service is committed to protecting your privacy. Our Privacy Policy is available online at www.ReaderService.com or upon request from the Harlequin Reader Service.

We make a portion of our mailing list available to reputable third parties that offer products we believe may interest you. If you prefer that we not exchange your name with third parties, or if you wish to clarify or modify your communication preferences, please visit us at www.ReaderService.com/consumerschoice or write to us at Harlequin Reader Service Preference Service, P.O. Box 9062, Buffalo, NY 14269. Include your complete name and address.

SASKIA WALKER

Once ignited, a witch's carnal curiosity knows no bounds

On the run from her powerful benefactor, whose unscrupulous interest in her magic has forced her to flee, Margaret Taskill has never needed a hero more. In order to gain passage from England to her homeland in Dundee, she plans to win over a rugged Scottish sea captain with the only currency she has: her virginity.

Maisie submits to Captain Roderick Cameron's raw sexuality in search of protection, but as their initial attraction grows into obsessive desire, devastating powers are unleashed within her. But the journey threatens to take a dangerous turn, forcing Maisie to keep close the secret truth about what she is, and keep the superstitious crew—unhappy at having a woman on board—at bay.

With Maisie's wealthy sponsor giving chase, Roderick must stay one step ahead of the British navy before her seductive magic causes a full-scale mutiny. He may believe he has full command of his ship, but he's about to get much more than he bargained for.

Available wherever books are sold!

Be sure to connect with us at:

Harlequin.com/Newsletters
Facebook.com/HarlequinBooks
Twitter.com/HarlequinBooks

HARLEQUIN® HQN™
www.Harlequin.com

PHSW744

CHRISTIE RIDGWAY

77740 BEACH HOUSE NO. 9   ___ $7.99 U.S. ___ $9.99 CAN.
77745 BUNGALOW NIGHTS   ___ $7.99 U.S. ___ $9.99 CAN.

(limited quantities available)

TOTAL AMOUNT	$ _____
POSTAGE & HANDLING	$ _____
($1.00 FOR 1 BOOK, 50¢ for each additional)	
APPLICABLE TAXES*	$ _____
TOTAL PAYABLE	$ _____

(check or money order—please do not send cash)

To order, complete this form and send it, along with a check or money order for the total above, payable to Harlequin HQN, to: **In the U.S.:** 3010 Walden Avenue, P.O. Box 9077, Buffalo, NY 14269-9077; **In Canada:** P.O. Box 636, Fort Erie, Ontario, L2A 5X3.

Name: _____
Address: _____ City: _____
State/Prov.: _____ Zip/Postal Code: _____
Account Number (if applicable): _____

075 CSAS

*New York residents remit applicable sales taxes.
*Canadian residents remit applicable GST and provincial taxes.

HARLEQUIN® HQN™
www.Harlequin.com

PHCR0313BL